Dreaming in French

Leesteffy Jenkins

Upland Publishing
Cambridge, Massachusetts

ISBN: 9780989347624

Cover design by Kit Foster of kitfosterdesign.com

Dedication

To my grandfather, Francis William DeMuth – may you rest in peace.

We know through epigenetics, that trauma is passed on through genes and even continues, some say, up to seven generations. This is not fiction. It's fact.

One

Even as a child she was prone to knowing things others did not. Or rather, she knew things others would know later, but she knew them as they happened or often before. When she was young, a murder, a lie, an accident—but as she got older she gained access to more private moments: the morbid thoughts of a friend, her husband's treachery, her lover masturbating to a picture of her six thousand miles away. Images of these events slipped into her mind without warning, settling there with clarity. It was a talent she recognized early—not as a talent, but as something to hide.

Even from herself.

Two

It is the Fourth of July, and a miasma of heat hangs over the city. Birds perch low on wide-stretched rows of telephone wire, stock-still: eavesdroppers. Even in the house, Lena's skin is cloaked with a thin sheen of sweat. Where do the dead go when they . . .? She stops this thought even as it is forming. She doesn't let thoughts of death intrude anymore, not since her mother died when she was twelve. She wills them away. It doesn't matter, she tells herself, holding her mind blank and still, until the thoughts of death recede. Only then does she turn to her friend, Isaiah.

"It's hot here. How can you stand it? " Isaiah says, fanning himself with a National Geographic magazine. He arrived in DC two days ago for a volunteer stint with his congressman to research a screenplay he's writing. "It's much cooler in LA. Come back home—I miss you," he says, winding his arm around her waist.

On Lena's mantel is a picture of her and Isaiah taken twenty-two years ago when they were ten, barely a year after Isaiah had moved from New Orleans to Los Angeles with his mother and father. Dark-haired Isaiah with his Créole skin is lanky in his orange swim trunks, and Lena, petite with long fair hair and pale skin, wears a dark blue swimmer's tank. They couldn't have looked more different—yet somehow there was something the same about them.

"You never did tell me how you got this gig with Congressman Rod—I hope you haven't slept with him—he's gross."

Isaiah arches his eyebrow. "Be nice. Your grandmother made the connection for me, actually. And I have better personal taste in men than C-Rod." He grimaces. "Hey, by the way, what time is Gran arriving?"

Lena shrugs. "She had to delay a few days. Aunt Clarissa, or one of the twins, or someone needed her for something, so she changed her flight."

"She's your grandmother—it would be nice if you could remember the details."

Lena frowns. "Don't be mean. With that side of the family it's always something, so I tune out. I think one of the twins needed a babysitter because their nanny had to fly back to the Dominican Republic for a funeral. Hey, did you hear that Tommy and Mark have another kid on the way?

He nods. "Same birth mother—she's great. I had dinner with them last week. I wonder if the second kid will be as gorgeous as Isabella—such a cutie."

Lena smirks at him.

"What?" he asks.

"Nothing, it's just that you keep better tabs on my family then I do, and sometimes I think . . . Hey, let's go, they're here," she says, interrupting herself, her highly developed sixth sense at work.

Isaiah looks out the window. "I don't see a car."

They've been waiting for Lena's neighbors, Anita and John, to pick them up to take them to a boat party on the Potomac River. "Come on," Lena says again. "Grab your stuff. It'll be cooler at the river."

She locks the door just as Anita's car appears noiselessly around the bend in her road and comes to a stop in front of her gate.

At the car, Isaiah ducks in, but some shift of the air or change in the light, or some internal prompting makes Lena stop and look back. The windows of her house are dark, and in her mind the house looks empty—like everyone has died and gone away. Death and the Fourth of July have always been intertwined, in Lena's mind, at least, ever since that Fourth of July when she was twelve and had foreseen how and when her mother would die. She and Isaiah had just come home from a cookout at the beach with their school friends. Lena ran up the stairs and found her mother at her dressing table brushing her brown curly hair. She wore a blue silk mini and matching stilettos. When Lena asked her where she was going, her mother gave her a look that Lena knew meant she'd crossed an invisible but clear line. "Come help me with my dress," her mother said. Lena hopped from the bed to her mother's chair to zip her dress. Her mother's hair was caught, and while Lena carefully removed the hair from the zipper, she thought, as she had so many times before, about how beautiful her mother was. And how she herself, in comparison, was an ugly duckling. She lifted her eyes to the mirror to see her mother's beautiful face, but instead saw her mother being knifed in the throat and then falling into a swimming pool, where she floated face down in a circle of blood. Lena reached toward the mirror to touch her mother's neck, to stop the blood she saw spurt, but of course, when it happened that night at the party, Lena wasn't there.

She wanted to shout Mama, don't go! but she said nothing because she knew her mother would get angry, and she also feared that the words, once spoken, would mean that what she saw was real—that her mother would die.

Lena throws off the eerie sensation that death is near, and walks to the car. She climbs into the back seat with Isaiah.

"You okay?" Isaiah asks.

Lena nods.

"You look like you've seen a ghost."

Pursing her lips, Lena shakes her head ever so slightly as if to say, not now. Over the years, Lena had worked hard to convince herself that the things she sees are not real. It is like a trick of light the way she can forget instantaneously what a moment ago felt true. This effort of hers started after her grandfather died in a car crash (only six months after her mother's death) and she woke screaming just as he was blinded by the headlights of an oncoming car. She saw the accident as though she were there in the car with him. Or did she?

She stretches forward to give Anita a kiss on both her checks. "You look nice," Lena says. The kisses were to please Anita, who liked to be a little European.

"What about me?" John asks, offering his cheek.

Lena pinches it. "You're British, don't be cheeky."

"Ya, but the bitch you kissed is American."

"John!" Lena and Isaiah scold in unison, though Anita seems to ignore his outburst. She holds up her hand for Lena and Isaiah to see. "Did you notice the nails? Midnight blue—the color of the season." She smiles. "I wanted to be patriotic." She rests her hand on the back of her shoulder against her red and white striped shirt. "For the Fourth."

Lena shivers.

"Is the car too cold?" Anita asks, looking into the rearview mirror. Lena wears a short cotton shift, and Isaiah wears a shirt that matches Lena's dress. They've mysteriously color-coordinated since they were kids.

Lena shakes her head.

Isaiah looks questioningly at Lena, as though he has read something dark in Lena's expression and knows that Lena is making an effort to be sociable and peppy. When Lena shrugs, Isaiah squeezes her hand. Tell me later, he mouths.

Lena's road is narrow; there is only enough room for the passage of Anita's black Beetle and cars parked on one side of the street. The Victorian row houses are linked porch to porch, their upper bay windows protruding in a line. Only the roofs—turret, cap, flat top—and the adornments along the street—flowers, fence, grass, a stone wall—mark a difference.

Lena expects Anita to turn right at the end of their street, to slope down and around the curved base of the hill past the old mansions of Mount Pleasant and into Rock Creek Park, but instead, Anita inches through the stop sign and heads straight down into the belly of the city. The circuitous route, she says, is so they can pick up Nick, a friend of John's from the World Bank. "Nick's an economist specializing in Latin America. John, stop." Anita slaps John's hand away from the radio dial. "I don't think you know him. He's another Brit."

Isaiah snorts. "What is it with you two and your Brits? Sorry John," he says, punching John in a friendly way on the shoulder. "I thought we won the Revolution, and yet, you guys seem to be everywhere."

Anita laughs in falsetto. Lena taps her on the shoulder. "Don't encourage him. He's working on lines for his screenplay, and if we aren't honest about how bad they are he'll embarrass himself with the final product."

Chagrined, Anita looks briefly over her shoulder at Lena. "Any news from the cold outback of Svalbard? How's Daniel and the filming?"

At the mention of her husband, Lena is momentarily lost in the lilt of his voice. She had talked with him for nearly an hour last night before his coins ran out—she hadn't heard from him in nearly two weeks. He had finally called when he came back to town to get more food supplies. Her husband was both scared and exhilarated about being so close to the bears. "From his description it sounds gorgeous. The long daylight, the cubs at the doors of dens, the drama of icebergs breaking and floating away. But he also has to ski from place to place with his film camera and pack on his back, so that's hard."

"Can't he hire someone to carry his gear?" John turns to ask.

Lena tells him that they want candid shots so they're hoofing it on their own with skis. She turns toward Isaiah. "It seems like he's been gone forever."

Isaiah squeezes her hand. "He'll be back before you know it."

Lena sighs. "I know. At least you're here with me for four weeks."

"It's nice to have you here," Anita says, glancing back at Isaiah. "We hardly ever get to see you—you always seem to come when we are out of town."

Lena leans forward between the bucket seats. John is fidgeting again with the radio. "Are we picking up just your one friend, John? Tell me his name again."

"Only Nick. His girlfriend is in Asia on business."

Nick. The name reverberates through Lena like something old, like a shout called down a tunnel, like the image in Lena's mind of a wine bottle spinning round and round on an ancient stone floor in a house that she has long forgotten existed.

♠♠♠

Nick's living room is stark, almost empty, in hues of beige and tan with blips of color from what look like two Warhol paintings and a giant triangular vase filled with dark blue delphiniums. Nick wears pressed tan chinos and a crisp white t-shirt, his dark cropped hair still wet.

For a moment, the five of them crowd around the front door, removing their shoes and making introductions. Nick's brown eyes come to rest on Lena. Though she can't describe to herself why, something about Nick reminds her of Isaiah and of her childhood—and for a moment, she is caught in something she can't describe even to herself. Without meaning to, she looks more closely at Nick. He is neither handsome nor her type—she likes outdoorsy men, not men with desk jobs at The World Bank.

Isaiah clears his throat, nudging Lena in the small of her back. Lena looks down at her fingers in Nick's hand. She doesn't remember holding out her hand to shake; she has no idea how long her hand has been in his. Blushing, she moves past Nick as he ushers them further into the living room.

"Have a seat," Nick says, turning on two tall floor lamps. "Let me get you some drinks."

When Nick comes back into the room with wine and beer, Lena notices he is stocky and pale in that pasty British way—too pale to be handsome—but his brown eyes are bright, and there is something pleasing to her about his suppressed smile.

She pulls her eyes away from his face. "Wow! Interesting paintings," she says, pointing to the two pictures she saw when she walked in the door. Turning back, she watches the slight flush of Nick's cheeks and touch of shyness that creeps into his face.

"Do you like them?" he asks, putting down the drinks.

She gets up and steps closer to the paintings, staring for a moment at the blue imagistic faces of a man and a woman. The faces look distorted, almost in pain.

"They aren't Warhol's," he says, coming up behind her. "It's a Czech artist. He's titled these Flatfish."

She glances at him. "That's a strange name for those pictures."

"It's a Greek term from Plato's Symposium. It refers to our lost half."

Lena steps back laughing. "I wonder which half I've lost." For the barest moment, Lena's image of herself slips and she glimpses a part of herself she has completely forgotten about.

"They look like they're in pain."

Nick faces her. "I like the half images of the man in the woman and the woman in the man. They are in shadow. You have to look closely to see it."

She moves nearer to the painting. "Ah, it's in the face."

"That's it," he says, stepping so close behind her that his shoulder brushes her back. "What you see as pain in him is really the shadow of her and vice versa."

"You two are getting way too philosophical for me," Anita says, grabbing Lena's arm and pulling her back toward the couch.

Nick smiles and walks back to his seat. John and Isaiah are talking about English politics.

Lena watches Nick hold the stem of his wine glass. His long nimble fingers seem to contradict his husky frame. A curl of hair, dry now, falls over his forehead. She has the urge to brush his hair back out of his face—an urge filled with such tenderness, it startles her.

She draws her slender bare feet up cross-legged under her thighs to warm them. Air conditioning makes the house cold.

"Here, let me rub them." Isaiah reaches over to pull her feet into his lap.

Nick leaves the room, returning with a pair of socks, which he starts to hand to Isaiah, but then he changes his mind mid-reach and gives them to Lena. Their eyes catch and hold. In her mind a picture unfolds: Nick in a hospital room, a nurse at his bedside. The nurse moves aside and Lena bends forward to touch Nick's powdery-pale cheek, to check if the smell of the hospital, which clings to the nurse's skin, has changed his scent. Tiny particles of his skin imprint her fingers. She closes her eyes, rubs her finger across her lip, just under her nose, to marry that tiny part of him to her. . . And then the image is gone. She is back in Nick's living room with his eyes still locked on hers, his hand still holding the socks.

Whoa. What the—? Lena takes the socks, embarrassed by what she's just seen. She looks quickly at Isaiah and then at Anita and John. Isaiah looks puzzled, but Anita and John don't seem to notice that anything is amiss. Nick watches her intently.

Lena closes her eyes, trying to conjure her husband's face. When she opens them, she looks at the socks. They are vibrant blue with swirls that look vaguely like red hearts.

She fingers the socks, feeling strange.

The brown murky water of the Potomac rolls gently under Lena's feet as she, Isaiah, and Anita walk along the grey wooden dock. She knows that Nick and John can't find the boat; in the twilight, they've lost their way—she knows this in the way she has of knowing without knowing that she knows.

Usually she fights to maintain the distance between her odd perceptions and hard facts, but the boats and slips are unorganized, a giant beehive of activity, and her exchanges with Nick—the peculiar way he's made her feel—all of it torques her mind from its normally entrenched position. She feels like a rabbit disappearing down a hole.

"Nick!" she shouts through cupped hands. He and John have stridden thirty feet ahead. "Turn left!" She firmly points in the direction she knows they need to go, even though she's never been to this boat before.

John and Nick turn in the direction she points and eventually stop in front of a forty-foot catamaran. "Howdy there," John calls out to a man with a ruddy bearded face and a white captain's hat.

"Here we are," Anita says when the three of them arrive. She steps onto the ramp and pulls the handsome Isaiah up beside her. Lena steps up behind the two of them. She can hear loud voices and the laughter of other guests already on the boat. Before Lena can get her bearings, the captain's burly arms reach out to swing her over the railing and onto the deck. A beer bottle presses into her arm. Nick slides down behind her, having jumped the rail himself. He reaches out a hand to steady her.

The captain welcomes them, his voice swelling, the nearly empty beer bottle still in his hand. He points to the cabin with its stacks of covered dishes and ice overflowing in buckets, the brown-necked bottles like stumps in snow.

The ice makes Lena think of Daniel filming in the Arctic. She wonders what he's doing. Usually they traveled together—it's a promise they made when they married. But the Arctic was a long trip, the locale not easily accessible, and the soundman on his crew was an incurable and excessive smoker (something Lena could not tolerate). For once, he suggested she stay behind. For days, Lena fiercely objected, though in her heart she knew he was right—his soundman was a chauvinist, perhaps even a misogynist, as well as a bore, and surely the soundman and Lena would fight the whole trip, making it more difficult for her husband to get the footage he wanted.

At the railing, Lena looks out at the night sky.

In the distance, bright lights dot the growing darkness, metal decks shine like foil. Below, in the blackness of the Potomac River, a small indistinct blob twirls and turns. Something about the movement of the water reminds her of the television shows of her youth—the swirling patterns that were used to make a transition from reality into fantasy or a dream. As a child living in California with her mother, Lena had a recurring dream of a town made up of rolling hills, green meadows, prodigious houses that were imbued—with what? In the dream, she wandered up and down blue hills, her feet not really feet because she floated. The air was thicker, more buoyant, and the light always tinged with oranges and pinks.

Her mind is murky when she thinks of that dream—it feels almost like a gap in her life rather than a dream. But why a gap? She wasn't spirited away, and can account for all her time since she was born, can't she? Of course she can—as a child she always lived with her mother and grandparents in Hermosa Beach, her deadbeat father having run away before she was born. This is what her mother told her. But the dream always made Lena feel both special and afraid. She knew the details in each room of one particular house as though she lived there herself. But where were the people who lived in that house? That's what she can't decipher—no matter how hard she tries.

"Lena, come get dinner," Anita calls from the other side of the deck. Reluctantly, Lena lets go of the rail and her thoughts, and turns back to the party. Isaiah chats with a male friend of Anita's from Capitol Hill. Lena smiles. Isaiah is between boyfriends, and Lena wonders whether he'll meet someone on this visit. Maybe he'll even fall in love and move to DC. She misses Isaiah and the easy camaraderie they share when together. She loves her husband, but it's just not the same.

"Lena." Anita waves her over. She sits with two of her coworkers from IBM. The women are tan and blonde, with similar bobbed haircuts. Their hands move animatedly as they talk about gossip, office politics, and people they know. Behind them, their husbands or lovers are huddled talking sports—everyone at ease because they are coupled, because in some way they are all the same. When Lena was a child, before she met Isaiah, she often had the sense of being a bit odd and of having a secret she couldn't tell—a secret so secret that even as a child she'd forgotten what the secret was. That feeling creeps upon her again on the boat. Her throat constricts; she feels like she's swallowed an orange.

"I'm coming," she shouts, pushing back from the rail. "Yum. Looks good," she says to Anita when, a few minutes later, they dish out food and pour wine. Lena chit-chats for a while with the others, but then when they go sit in a group, she slips into the cockpit of the boat, where she can be alone to take in the gentle gurgle of the current against the hull and the smell of summer on the river. She's tipsy from her red wine, the hushed silence, the open air, the memory of something she can't get a grip on. Fourth of July fireworks boom and crackle. While colored lights explode overhead, she sits huddled watching a rainbow of colors float down to dark water. The faint smell of sulfur hangs in the air.

After the grand finale, Nick stoops down next to Lena. "Can I sit here?" he asks, even as he steps down and squeezes into the small two-seat bench in the cockpit.

She moves over as much as she can to give him more room.

"It's a beautiful night," he says.

She nods, disturbed by his pleasant musky smell, and not wanting to speak of the colored lights that still float in her mind.

"Anita says you're a big reader."

Lena laughs. "That's probably an understatement. I've been accused of having a reading addiction."

"Nice. I like to read too. I don't think there is such a thing as a reading addiction—books are good for the mind and soul—if you believe in such a thing."

She smiles at him.

They sit nestled together on beige plastic cushions, almost but not quite touching. Her body gathers heat from his closeness; her breath glances off his shoulder, misting back into her face as tiny particles that prickle her skin.

Lena closes her eyes and sinks farther down into the cushions. The softness of the night air and the rhythm of lapping water lull her.

"Do you remember the first time you saw fireworks?" Nick asks quietly.

She opens her eyes. His body blocks her sight of the deck, creating an intimacy that shuts the others out. Words rush into her mind from somewhere dark; she fishes them out. "When I was a kid, I—" she says, expelling her breath.

"Yes?" He bends toward her. His face is so close she can see the sheen of his white teeth, smell the sweetness of wine on his breath. "I thought . . ." She imagines his mouth forming an entrance for her to step into, and then feels déjà vu.

Startled, she pulls back; her head turns to watch the moonlit water gently roll.

Nick leans toward her again.

Something inside her whispers He's too close! but she's caught up in a dream, a somnambulist heading back to her long forgotten past. A picture unfolds in her mind: Under her knees she feels the coolness of polished slab. Out an ancient-looking window, blue hills rise into a lapis sky. The window is like the frame around an impressionist's painting, the painting so lovely her heart aches. She is filled with the sense of something inviting, warm, jewel-like, a mystery that . . . And then the picture is gone, the shutters snap shut, she's back in the boat with Nick, fear clutching a little at her stomach.

Somehow she knows what she's seeing is not the future, but rather the past. She wants to tell him how it hurts when she can no longer remember (whatever it is she can't remember) and how absurd it is that she can sometimes see the future when something from her past is somehow invisible—but her throat is locked shut, stretched taut with pain. Her eyes move to the North Star—it seems to glint against her cheek, while the midnight sky dips down to cloak them in its softness, wrap them deep into the dark folds of the night. Her lips part. She wants to tell him something, to spit out what it is that she can't quiet grasp, but somehow she knows that neither she nor he understands the deep current that runs between them.

He smiles.

Her hand flutters up to touch the sleeve of his white shirt.

He shivers.

A mirror image of heat rises in her.

Three

Two days later, Lena's Gran arrives at National Airport for a weeklong visit. She comes with her gray toy poodle, Fifi, and greets Lena with the briefest kiss on her cheek. Isaiah, not standing for her formality, wraps his arms around her and smooches her cheek with a loud wet kiss. She laughs, and to Lena's eyes, seems to relax in Isaiah's embrace. Gran hunts in her bag and hands Isaiah a box of See's chocolates. Though she pretends not to notice, Lena is a little hurt there is nothing in Gran's bag for her. Not for the first time, Lena wonders why Gran always seems a little on guard with her, as though she has something to hide. Lena wonders briefly if the root of the problem doesn't go back to her own fatherless state. Her tall, slender, elegant grandmother, while gracefully liberal, has always frowned at the concept of divorce, wondering why people don't somehow just work it out.

With her red shoes and bag and black and white poka-dotted dress, her grandmother looks younger than her years—only the tiny lines around her eyes and the tired look on her face would tell a keen observer that she is in fact, much older than she appears. Lena wonders how it is that she failed to acquire her mother and grandmother's elegance—in her mind, she has never fully grown out of her skinny awkward teenage years.

Isaiah interrupts her thoughts. "Okay, Girlfriend. Why the frown? Gran is here, you should be happy." He hands Lena Fifi's leash.

Lena smiles. "Don't be a dolt. I am happy," she says, bending down to pet the dog.

"Moi? Dolt?

Lena looks up at him from her crouched position.

"Don't act innocent. Anyone can see you are vying for the favored position with Gran."

"Lena," her grandmother says, acting shocked. "You better than anyone know that I don't have favorites. And why be unkind to Isaiah?"

Behind Gran's back Isaiah makes a childish face at Lena. She mentally rolls her eyes, but stands and lays a hand on Gran's arm. "It's a childhood joke between Isaiah and me. We don't mean anything by our insults and torments."

Gran hands Isaiah her carry-on bag. "I would think that after all these years you two could act a little more adult with each other. You are best friends."

Isaiah snickers silently so that only Lena can see. She hides her irritation from Gran, wondering how it is that Isaiah somehow always manages to manouver her into the worst possible light with Gran. It's so unfair.

She links her arm with Isaiah. "We love each other, don't worry. I promise I am very charming with him when you aren't around. You just happen to always catch me in my bad moments. Isn't that true?" she says, discretely pinching Isaiah.

Isaiah smiles broadly. "Absolutely." He holds up Lena's hand for Gran to see. "No ring yet, but I have asked her a hundred times and I will continue to ask her a hundred more until she agrees."

Gran frowns. "Isaiah," she says a little sharply.

Sheepishly he grins at her.

"I don't think that's funny. Obviously, if Lena wasn't already married and you weren't otherwise inclined, I'd welcome you into our family—you are like a grandson to me already—but it's not amusing of you to make fun of marriage. Your turn, so-to-speak, will come."

Isaiah looks hurt. "I'm not making fun. I'd marry Lena if she wasn't already married—irrespective of my sexual orientation."

Gran stops in the middle of the terminal floor. "Now just stop it, both of you. It's been a long flight and I'm tired. You both are acting like you are still twelve. Honestly, sometimes I wonder whether I shouldn't have separated you two when you were young."

Lena feels hurt that somehow in Gran's mind, she, too, has misbehaved. That's how it always was when she was young. When she misbehaved, she got in trouble. When Isaiah misbehaved, she and Isaiah got in trouble. It always made her feel like she was the unwanted step-sister in the family.

Determined to be adult about things she pushes these thoughts from her mind and tells Gran about Daniel's trip to the Arctic and the footage he's shot. Always interested in her grandson-in-law's career, Gran asks many questions and they talk about the filming—and Daniel's upcoming projects—all the way to the house. As they are getting out of the car, Gran offers to make a few calls if it would help, but Lena, as always, demurs, saying that Daniel is doing fine all on his own, and that he prefers to stand on his own two feet, so to speak.

Lena can tell that her Gran approves of this response. While she is always happy to help her children and grandchildren, she takes pride in their self-sufficiency.

During the week that Gran is in D.C., she and Lena go shopping and Gran buys her and Daniel two down reading pillows and some silver candle sticks for their mantel. Afterwards, they stop for tea and crumpets at the Four Seasons hotel in Georgetown. Each night Gran takes Lena and Isaiah out to dinner or they all cook an elaborate meal. The three of them see a play at the Kennedy Center and stay up late playing cards. With all the activities, the week passes quickly.

When it is time for Gran to leave, Lena alone takes her to the airport. Isaiah has a previously scheduled work engagement that Gran insists he not cancel. Lena waves to Gran as she disappears through her gate, and then walks back through the nearly empty terminal thinking about the activities of the week, wondering where the time had gone, and at the same time, feeling a little nostalgic that she has again missed an opportunity to initiate a conversation that will somehow draw them closer in an adult way.

She stops suddenly in front of an Aunt Annie's pretzel

stand in the terminal. What had they talked about? She can't remember what they said to each other all week.

Or whether they said anything real at all.

Four

A few weeks after the Fourth of July, Nick calls Lena at work. "Would you like to meet for lunch sometime?" he asks. "I have a book you might like to read."

With Gran's visit and the distraction that brought, Lena had suppressed any thoughts of Nick and is surprised he went to the trouble to track her down and call. But now she smiles. Outside her office window, the sun is obscured behind the haze and heat shimmering above gray-pallored buildings. In the distance, barely visible over the office buildings, the Statue of Freedom (woman, bird, or mythical creature?) perches indistinct atop the gold Capitol dome. She reasons that surely he must know that she is faithful. Then she chides herself for even thinking he might be attracted, reassuring herself that he is just being friendly to a fellow book lover. "Sure—how about tomorrow? I have no lunch plans." They agree to meet at Union Station. "I'll bring a book, too," she says, "for an even exchange."

The next day, Nick circles the white marbled hall of Union Station watching for Lena. The round, high-vaulted ceiling of the station catches and compresses sound as it bounds up from the floor, like the slap of a ball in a catcher's mitt.

He jumps when her hand rests lightly on his back.

"Sorry I'm late. I got hung up with some biologists from Ecuador," Lena says, stepping back. "Have you asked for a table?" Her short black dress shows off her bare legs.

"I haven't asked yet," he says, watching the goose bumps on her forearms. "I was waiting for you. Here, take my coat." He lays his hand on the small of her back as a waiter takes them to their seats.

After they order, Nick places a book on the table—*A Suitable Boy*, by Vikram Seth. He is curious if she'll think the main character, Lata Mehra, chose right: a partner based on compatibility. Compatibility is something he's settled for with his girlfriend, Hildy, and though for the most part their arrangement has worked, he feels twinges of regret. "You haven't read it yet, have you?" he asks.

She shakes her head; her eyes lock with his.

For a fleeting instant, something unsaid opens between them. His insides twang. But in the next instant, the feeling is gone—so fleeting, he wonders if he's imagined the exchange.

Their food comes quickly. While she eats her tofu burger and mesclun salad, and he pan-roasted sweetbreads with morels, they talk about the book he's brought her to read and then move on to Isaiah's visit and the chicaneries of Capitol Hill. When they are almost finished with their food, he points to her books.

He is surprised Lena seems embarrassed by her own choice of books. Diane Ackerman's *The Moon by Whale Light* is a logical choice given her marine biologist background, but she tries to hide her second book, *The Soul of Sex*, by Thomas Moore.

"It's not about sex, I swear," Lena says blushing.

Nick takes the book from Lena's reluctant hands, flips it to the back cover and then opens the book to a random page.

charming to look at,
with eyes as soft as honey,
and a face that Love has lighted
with his own beauty

"It's by Sappho," he says. "Don't be embarrassed. The book looks interesting. And I can see that it's not about sex." He grins. "I once wanted to be a poet—I studied poetry at university, before I realized I had to be more practical."

She tilts her head quizzically. "Practical?"

He laughs. "Most English poets were. . . are either paupers or from the upper class. I was not the latter and didn't want to end up the former, so I switched to economics."

"Sad for the world—we need more poets, fewer

economists," she teases, smiling at him. The wine they've ordered, her smile, the strange way she has of stretching him open makes everything more tangible, sharp-edged, as though his senses have become more deeply rooted in his body. He is lost in color—her green eyes, red lips, the way the neckline of her black dress falls just below the delicate bones of her clavicle.

"Does your girlfriend read a lot as well?" she asks.

He looks down. "She doesn't like to read," he mumbles. "Occasionally I harass her, but then I give up. Is Daniel coming home this weekend?"

Lena pauses, her fork in midair over a shared slice of chocolate cake. "Yes . . . and then he, Isaiah, and I are going to our farm in Vermont." She sighs. "It's Daniel's project. Not my style of house—it's too modern for me. I prefer something really old, something that holds memories, sounds I can almost hear when I walk through the rooms. Like ghosts." She smiles. "Isaiah is looking forward to it—he's already getting tired of Capitol Hill, and I think the level of repression of gay men here is a little depressing for him."

"Are there many gay men on Capitol Hill?"

Lena laughs. "You're joking, right?"

Nick shrugs. "I think it would be hard to be a gay man on Capitol Hill."

"It's not hard to be gay, but it's hard to be out and gay. And you? Will you and Hildy go away for August?" Her tongue darts out to clear the crumbs from her lips.

They chat like this for a few more minutes—she tells him she's working on a project to get observers aboard tuna fishing vessels in the Pacific. "That's why I was meeting with the Ecuadorians," she says. "The problem is that it's a really dangerous job—these guys come back with cigarette burns on their bodies, and sometimes they never come back, weights on their feet and all that."

He shudders, unable for a moment to respond. His mind goes back to his own childhood in Coventry. Almost every morning of Nick's childhood, he was beaten by his grandfather. He learned never to flinch when his grandfather lashed his shoulders and buttocks—as he liked to do to wake Nick up, or when he reached under Nick's foot and pressed the tip of his hot fag into the tender hollow of Nick's sole.

Lena places her hand on his arm. "Nick, you okay?"

He looks up into her concerned face, mentally shaking the cobwebs from his mind. "Yes, why?"

"For a moment, you had a strange look on your face. You looked sad, or scared, or . . . lost," she says, her voice trailing off.

"Sorry, my mind was somewhere else for a moment. I'm fine. Really, fine." He straightens in his chair.

When their conversation winds down, they agree to complete their "reading assignments" before they meet again for lunch the Tuesday after Labor Day. "A book club of two," he says, grinning.

"Yes, and maybe after this you'll share your poems with me. I'd love to read them." She smiles. "Never give up a dream."

He laughs. "Perhaps the world is a better place without my poetry."

She shakes her head, then lifts his book in the air, judging its weight. "Daniel will kill me for taking such a big book to our Vermont house—he hates that I'm an obsessive reader because he thinks it takes time from him, particularly if we are on vacation. But I'll risk the wrath of Daniel and sneak it into my bag."

He laughs again, but then his thoughts sober him. It's just lunch and an exchange of books; she's going off with her husband for three weeks. There is nothing real between them, he tells himself sternly, though he does think it a bit strange that her husband doesn't like her to read, and maybe she really is interested in his poetry, rather than just being nice.

She rises. "Thanks for the use of your coat."

When he steps to her side to take the coat from her shoulders, he notices the pearl earring in her ear, the delicate curve of her jaw, the soft lay of her hair—he catches a strand between his fingers and then lets it fall away. He knows instinctually there is something unusual about this woman and the ineffable sense of . . . ease, happiness, connection, wholeness—he can't put his finger on the exact word that describes how she makes him feel.

She turns to face him, a confused look on her face.

"Your hair was caught," he says.

"I. . . the word Père just floated across my mind," she stammers. "For a moment, it was like I could remember . . . it was familiar—I could almost see . . ."

He reaches out to touch her bare arm.

She looks away. "Nick, I better go."

He opens his mouth to speak, to stop her, to ask what's wrong, but before he can say anything she is gone.

Later that night Lena wonders Who is *Père*? Why "father" in French?—she's been obsessing about this all afternoon. She gets up off her living room couch and goes to the kitchen to get a glass of wine. She wishes Isaiah were here to talk with, but Isaiah worked late and then had a date, and had no time to talk.

Lena opens the fridge and stares inside. Just as she reaches for the bottle of Chardonnay, she remembers something about her lunch with Nick. The waiter had just brought their meal—they were drinking red wine and laughing about something (she can't remember what)—when a thought or memory, or perhaps it was a dream she'd had, played out in her mind: A soft light cast into a room. A gold-colored duvet floated up and over a bed, draped itself on a divan. A few feet away, a fire crackled and warmed the linen's threads. A white china plate with delicate pink flowers rimming its edge and a matching cup and oval tea pot stood on a small cloth-covered table. A pair of men's black lace-up boots lay before the fire.

At lunch, she'd been so focused on Nick and their conversation that she hadn't paid attention—but now, it seems that both the memory and the word Père had been hanging between them, hovering over her, so invisible, so out of the ordinary, perhaps so unwanted, that she couldn't see it.

Why? As far as she remembers, she had never known her father; he had left her mother before Lena was born. The way her mother, Rita, told it, her father never wanted a child. "I dodged a nasty bullet," Rita said. After college, Rita shunned the office job her lawyer father found for her and worked instead as an extra for Goldwyn Studios. When, in 1962, Rita's agent told her he could possibly get her a lead part in a film directed by Éric Rohmer, she flew immediately to Paris, telling her father (Lena's grandfather) that her college degree in French wasn't a waste after all. Rita met Lena's father in Paris. According to her mother, the affair was tumultuous and brief. It ended in a pregnancy, a quick in-and-out marriage (for the sake of propriety) and the end of Rita's big chance in Paris. "Your father hated children," Rita said. "That's why you never met him—he wanted to forget you were his child."

Thinking back to her lunch with Nick, Lena wonders why her mother never seemed bitter about the affair, or her father. She knew that she herself would be bitter if someone like Nick got her pregnant and dumped her. But when asked, Rita always said, "I never really wanted to marry him." As a child, Lena learned not to ask too many questions about her mother's past. When she did, Rita would look vacant, while her Gran's jaw would tense.

Not for the first time, Lena wonders What's missing from my mother's story? What part of the script did she cut out to suit her own purposes? It would be just like Rita to rewrite things to give herself a starring role.

5. France 1963

An ever-lightening gray ebbed into her room through the tiny window. The sky slowly pinked. Lena was already awake when the church bells rang. Chickens cackled, a rooster crowed, dogs bayed with the bells. These were moments in Lena's life that were caught, stilled, like a snapshot. She knew these sounds; she heard them every morning while she lay in her crib waiting for her father—her Père—or while she played with the plush pastel animals that hung down from above. The mobile was a present from her American grandparents. The soft figures emitted sounds that made her laugh. But only when Père made them move.

Out her window, the dog Silence sat on his haunches, one leg scratching his ear. Silence was helping her learn to stand. When he sat next to her, she'd take fistfuls of his brown matted hair, and then, when he stood up, he'd pull her up too. And sometimes over. Père, if he noticed, came running. He'd swing her into the air before she cried; sometimes he'd make her laugh and cry all at once.

"*Ma chère*?" Her father peeked around the door.

She turned to look at him. She smiled. He was all bright and golden, or maybe it was the way the light shone in through the door.

"*Ma petite puce*." He picked her up. Her fat dumpling legs kicked inside her pink bunting. She was too old for a bunting, but she was small for her age and her bedroom was cold. For over three hundred years, her father's family had lived in the house. When it was cold outside, only the front room with its large stone fireplace, and the kitchen with its cook stove, stayed warm in the night.

"*Ma petite puce*," he said again, swinging her high in the air to make her laugh. From that height, he brought her to his chest and cradled her tight. They walked from her room into the warmth of the kitchen. He kissed her head, then laid her down on a table to unwrap her bedclothes.

She kicked her arms and her legs, freed from the warmth of her bunting. She looked into her father's face.

She laughed.

She was happy.

She was only one when she learned to walk. From then on, she and Père would walk each day in the blue hills that surrounded their grey stone house while their dog, Silence, chased rabbits through the trees. When it was misty and cold, Père took her pink-mittened hand in his or held her by the hood of her coat—like a leash—in case she fell. Or sometimes he'd swing her up onto his shoulders. From that height she could see the village below—the way the stone houses pressed close together even as they scaled the blue hills.

When Père stopped to pick some *maquis* and white heather, she'd whine to get down. "En bas!" She wanted to pick some too.

Side by side they squatted to examine the plants. Some were in full bloom, others still closed. A giant bee buzzed by.

Silence dropped a stick on her foot. He wanted to play, but in his excitement and with his large bulky body, he bumped her over.

Enraged, she began to scream and then kick at the dog from her seated position.

The dog yelped.

Père picked her up to quiet her. "Ma petite puce, we do not kick our animals."

She flayed her arms and kicked her legs.

"Lena, what is wrong? Such a temper in one so young." He tapped her on the nose. It was cold. "Perhaps it is too cold outside for you today. Your père needed the walk to clear his head." He picked her up and buried her in his leather jacket. "We will make you some hot chocolate when we get home."

He reached under her red coat to tickle her tummy.

She giggled.

"Ah, that's my sweet. Now you have a lovely smile."

With her thumb in her mouth she looked up at him.

His bearded face was ruddy from the cold and his green eyes were bright. She reached up to touch his black hair, and then kneaded a few strands between her fingers while she sucked her thumb.

"My sweet puce likes to be my baby again," Père said, smiling at her.

She shook her head.

"Shall we walk?"

She nodded.

"What is the word?"

"*Oui.*"

"*Nous promenons?*"

"*Oui*, Papa."

They descended the hill, taking the short cut down through brown scrabble and rock. The path was one the goats often took, and she could smell their presence. She looked around, but she couldn't see them, though in the distance, she heard their bells. "*Les moutons*," she said.

"So many words! Soon you will be writing plays or poetry like me." Père squeezed her hand. "But never an actress like your mother."

"Maman?"

"No, Maman is not home; she is away."

"*Père Maman Père Maman Père Maman. . .*"

"*Ma petite*, a different song," her father said. "How about this? *Alouette, gentille alouette, alouette, je te plumerais.*"

When they reached the house, he bent down to take off her coat. It was hot in the kitchen. "*Alouette, gentille alouette, alouette, je te plumerais*," he sang to her.

She clapped her hands and squinched her face into a half laugh, half smile showing two front teeth.

He squeezed her tight. "Ma petite, you are so precious I couldn't live without you."

"Papa," she whispered in his ear.

Six

As the summer slides by and the sun slips lower in the sky, as the last of the weed flowers—the Black-eyed Susan and Echinacea—come into bloom, as the heat holds the day but dips down to coolness at night, Lena starts to detect Nick's thoughts and physical movements. Images of him slide into her mind so unexpectedly and with such vividness that even Lena is surprised. It is the end of August, and the three of them, Daniel, Lena, and Isaiah, are at their farmhouse in Vermont. For the last hour, they've been planting bulbs, which Isaiah declares is like planting a little bit of heaven. In Créoleville, as he calls Louisiana, "it's too gawd-dang hot to grow bulbs. L.A. too. You know," he says, turning to Lena, "we had a deprived childhood. No flowers."

"You're as bad as my mother, believing in the silly characters you pretend to be. You ain't got no southern accent, and what do you call Gran's enormous garden?"

"Wow, that accent was pretty good, maybe you should become an actress," Isaiah teases. "Allium would be a nice name for a girl," he says, hefting the baseball-sized bulb into the air before lowering it into the ground. He mutters something Lena can't hear.

Lena stands, trying to brush hair out of her eyes but managing only to transfer dirt to her face. "If it weren't for the fact that your skin is too much the color of Coca-Cola to be Rita's kid, I'd swear she was your mother."

"Don't you go being mean to me, girl. Yore butt will get a lickin."

"Um, the accent doesn't work for D.C.—I'd lose it for the screenplay if I were you. And we want our child to have a traditional name in keeping with her ethnicity. It's not like we will be able to hide she is adopted." She tamps down the earth over the bulb she's just planted, then leans toward Isaiah. "What are you muttering about?" she asks softly, so Daniel can't hear. Daniel doesn't always understand why Lena and Isaiah have stayed so close over the years, perhaps because he's always been just the tiniest bit jealous of their close relationship—almost like twins more than friends. Also, Daniel never knew Lena when she was younger, when visions and crazy antics were more a part of her everyday life, so he doesn't understand that Isaiah is a reflection of some underground part of Lena. Truth be told, Isaiah anchors Lena to her past.

"A fertility prayer. I'm asking the Goddess to grant you a new life."

Lena laughs. "I don't need a new life, I just need—" She stops mid-sentence, feeling pensive. In her mind she sees Nick dodge a car that barrels around a blind corner just as Nick crosses a highway on his way to the beach. She wonders briefly what beach he is at. Her visions are strange in terms of what she sees, but also, in terms of what is missing. She doesn't know who he is with or where exactly he is—only snippets of moments like this near accident.

"You okay?" Isaiah asks, touching Lena's hand.

Lena stares at Isaiah, not seeing him; she's still holding on to the image of Nick. "Wow, that was close."

"What did you see?" Isaiah demands, gripping Lena's arm.

"Shh." Lena quickly glances at Daniel.

Isaiah gives her a quizzical look. "Lordy, it's not as if he doesn't know."

"He doesn't know everything, and besides I've told him it's something I outgrew."

"Lena."

"Don't lecture me."

"What did you see? Something about the baby?"

Lena shakes her head. As close as they are, she hasn't been able to tell Isaiah about her visions of Nick. Or how, since they've been in Vermont, she's been remembering things from her childhood that she'd forgotten, or never knew she knew.

She doesn't know why she is hiding these things from him, only that something is making her mute.

"Remember that boy from when I was young?" she asks Isaiah.

"The one you thought you would marry? The boy from the meadow? The one who, from your description, I wanted to meet and marry too?"

"He wasn't from a meadow, it's just that in my mind I would often see us running down a path lined with daffodils." She laughs. "Like the ones we're planting here. We'd run from that path into a meadow full of fruit trees in bloom. The air was lighter, softer somehow, and the buildings were golden, a shade of raw sienna." Lena is lost for a moment in her own reverie, remembering how that place and that boy sometimes seemed more real to her than her own life in Los Angeles. And how, as a child, she assumed that when she grew older she'd meet him in person. But she never did. Instead, as she grew older, she learned to ignore his voice in her head. Secret friends were for children, weren't they?

Isaiah interrupts her thoughts. "What does he have to do with you now?" He grabs Lena's arm and shakes her a little. "What is it that you see?"

Lena turns away from Isaiah. "I'm not sure." She can't bring herself to confide just how much she's been tuning in to Nick.

Isaiah steps in front of her, his broad chest and slender hips blocking her way. If it wasn't Isaiah, she would have been annoyed at the aggressiveness of his pose. "What do you mean you aren't sure? Is it a person, plant, or thing?" he asks. "It's something—I can tell from the look on your face."

Shrugging, Lena drops down to the ground, to the hole she's dug for a bulb. "I keep thinking of Nick at odd moments. Must be the book he gave me to read."

Lena glances up at Isaiah. She can tell from the look on his face that Isaiah doesn't believe her. To ward off further questions, Lena puts down her bulb digger and saunters over to Daniel.

The dirt where he has been digging is richly brown and wormy, full of the compost they'd double dug last year. Daniel had worked hard to convert the soil from clay to a growable medium. Lena knew he hoped to move to the farm permanently, as soon as he could convince her to leave her job on Capitol Hill. She loved the farm, but she just wasn't ready to live in such an isolated place full-time.

"It will be lovely," she says, playing lightly with Daniel's hair. "You've done a great job. I love how this bed swoops out into the grass and then bends back to the barn. The effect is really pleasing."

He stands and kisses his wife. "I'm glad you like it. I want you to be happy here."

She stiffens slightly. They've had talks about when they would move, but each time Daniel presses for a timeline, Lena always says she's not ready to decide.

"I'm going in to start dinner."

He looks the sky and then at his watch. "This early?"

She shrugs. "Why not, we're on vacation. Besides, I thought I'd make something special."

"Are you sure you aren't going in to read that monster book you brought? And burn our dinner in the process?"

Lena frowns. Why is it that he always complains about her reading? She'd think he'd be happy to have a well-read wife. "I might read a little. . . we're on vacation."

"Exactly, which means you should be spending time with me and Isaiah, instead of being anti-social."

"Reading isn't anti-social."

He sits back on his heels. "It is when you're on vacation with people you don't get to spend much quality time with."

"We spend quality time in D.C. "

"Isaiah doesn't live in D.C."

Since when has he become so fond of her spending time with Isaiah, she wants to ask, but she bites her tongue. She knows she can never win this discussion. Sooner or later, he will circle back to her dysfunctional upbringing and the fact that her mother died when she was young and she had no father. And in his most uncharitable moments, the fact that her best friend is a down-and-out actor and a gay man. In her mind, Lena can hear him haranguing about the parental defects of her mother. He didn't even know her mother, and yet, in some not-so-subtle way, Daniel always seems jealous of Lena's connection to her own dead mother. As though her thoughts of Rita somehow take her attention away from him.

She leans over to kiss him. "I promise, more cooking than reading, and no burning. Isaiah will probably come inside with me, which means I'll get very little reading done."

Just as she pivots to go into the house, she sees Nick again. He sits in a beach chair staring out to sea, wishing she were there with him. For a moment, she feels his nostalgia so strongly it hurts. I miss him, she realizes, even while, at the same time, she chides herself for being absurd. It's your imagination—you don't even know him. Slowly she walks toward the house, past Isaiah without saying a word, as though she doesn't see Isaiah or has forgotten he is there. She almost trips over a pitchfork, but somehow navigates around it and the little red wagon Daniel has been using to distribute bulbs around the yard. Lost in thought, Lena floats into the house carrying with her the image of Nick, while the world around her loses its edge and disappears.

A few days after Labor Day, Nick calls Lena at work to ask when they might meet. She is happy to hear his voice—his odd unplaceable accent that is the result, he says, of growing up in Coventry and then trying to hide his Midlands working-class background while at Oxford. "I never made it out nor made it in," he told her during one of their numerous talks. His voice was deep, and it pleased Lena in a way that made her uncomfortable. She was too happy to hear from him. What is wrong with me, she wonders, annoyed at herself while at the same time she is lit up. I'm acting like a kid. Yet she can't help but laugh and entertain him with stories of Vermont. She tells him how she'd overturned their dingy when she, Isaiah, and Daniel had gone for a picnic on Lake Champlain, and though their food and towels had fallen out, the book he'd lent her had miraculously stayed put and dry in the crevice she'd stuck it in for safe keeping.

"Sounds like fate," he says, laughing.

She doesn't tell him how bullshit mad Daniel was when he saw that the book was the only thing that didn't fall into the water. She had negotiated the book when they planned a lazy day of boating, eating, reading, and hanging out on the shore.

"When can we meet?" he asks when she comes to a lull in her storytelling. "For our bookclub," he adds, when she hesitates.

"I have meetings all week," she tells him. "And then Daniel's brother will be here the week after." The truth was that Daniel's brother was only in town for a day, but Lena couldn't bring herself to have lunch with Nick, not when she was feeling so happy. "Can I call you next week when I have a better sense of my schedule?"

"Sure, of course."

Lena's heart races a little at the disappointment she hears in his voice.

"I promise, I'll call," she says. "I want to do another exchange. I liked this book and I want to talk about why and hear what you thought about it, and why you thought I'd like it. " They chatted a little more before they hung up.

But as the week passed and then the next, as the weather turned unseasonably cold and the air blustery, Lena avoided calling Nick. Her energy lagged, and when she wasn't working, she stayed home, curled up with Daniel to watch a movie or read a book. It wasn't that she forgot about Nick or her promise to call him; rather, it was that she wanted to call him more than she should. Every time she turned a corner, she wondered if she'd see him. Afraid of all this wondering, she couldn't call him at all, and instead sunk deeper down into a quiet place inside herself.

Tamped down like this, images ranged inside her like the sun and clouds playing hide and seek, disappearing before she could grasp them firmly in her mind. A smell—maquis? Heather? Does heather smell?—would alight in some deep part of her brain, making her feel like she knew something. . .what had she forgotten? When she couldn't gain a hold on what she was seeing, she began to wonder if she was simply going crazy, maybe schizophrenic. Some part of her knew that this fear was absurd, yet the thought of going crazy was almost more calming than her attraction to Nick.

She struggled through her days on Capitol Hill, in a meeting with a senator, at a press conference, hashing out a position paper with colleagues, trying to catch what lingered under the surface and eluded her grasp.

At night, at home with Daniel, she worked hard to pay attention and not space out about Nick. Daniel was thrilled with the footage he shot in the Arctic, but he wondered if it was enough and whether the budget would allow him to return.

"It seems like you have far more than you need," Lena says one night in early October as Daniel wrestles with his script on polar bears. "Look, each of these elements is covered by footage." She taps the computer screen to make her point. "Here, you might expand on the Arctic fox, but look at all the footage you have on those critters." She points to his shot list on the desk. "I'd say you are A-okay."

He puts his arm around her waist as she stands next to him. "I wish you could have been there," he says. "I don't like having these kinds of life changing experiences without you."

She kisses the top of his head. "Without me there you were more focused. You've shot gorgeous footage and are producing a brilliant—I'd say award-winning—film. That means more to me than being there. I was with you in spirit." She smiles at him.

He gets up and takes her in his arms. "I like it when you travel with me. I don't like leaving you at home."

"Don't you trust me?" she teases, looking beyond his eyes at the photos of seals and walrus he's hung on the walls. She moves from his arms to straighten a picture, her gaze falling on the book Nick gave her laying on the shelf. She tenses. Suddenly Nick is in her mind—so real she can almost feel his breath—like a time warp, he and she are here, in a space of their own. She knows without any doubt that he is thinking of her. The image of him in her mind is so clear that for a moment, he feels almost more present than her husband.

Daniel reaches past her for Nick's book. "You haven't given this back to him? Didn't you finish it in Vermont?"

She shrugs, turning back to the computer, the image of Nick broken. "I haven't seen him."

"Why not? I thought you two were going to exchange another book."

She laughs. "You want me to ask him for another gargantuan book?"

Daniel frowns. "He shouldn't have given you such a big book when he knew we were going on vacation."

"Readers don't think about size, unless they are traveling themselves. Let's go make dinner," she says, turning toward the door. As she steps over the door jam, suddenly she sees Nick in his Porsche banking around a steep incline, his tires skittering sideways on gravel. She stops abruptly, inhaling sharply.

Daniel puts his hand around her waist to steady himself. He had been right behind her when she stopped. "Whoa! What's the sudden holdup?" He presses so close to her she feels his arousal.

She disentangles herself from his arms, smiling back at him. "Just trying to remember what we have in the fridge for dinner." She hates when she lies like this, but she can't help herself. She can't explain to Daniel what she can't explain to herself. While her visions aren't anything new, they feel different: almost like a tidal wave gathering in the distance, pressing upon her like untouched grief.

Seven

It is a Friday in late October, an evening that is neither hot nor cold, but somehow perfect—like a memory caught in one's mind.

"Friday's a strange day to get married, don't you think?" Daniel asks, tightening his belt.

Lena wonders for a moment about the biological and social impulses that cause people to couple even without real love—like her own parents, who never lived together, but got married anyway so that Lena wouldn't be a bastard child.

She glances at her husband and feels grateful that she is luckier than her mother.

Daniel lifts his foot to a stool to polish his black shoes with a cloth. "Is Anita going to wear white, even though she and John have been living together for five years?"

Lena sits down at her dressing table and opens her jewelry box. "What do you expect—a brilliant hand-painted kimono? Or an embossed red silk sari? Or maybe a black cotton robe embellished with silver coins like that Bedouin woman we saw in the recent National Geographic last week."

He laughs.

She stands and faces her husband. "It's Anita and John we're talking about. She'll probably have on a white organza cloud with a long train."

He rolls his eyes. "I'm glad we eloped."

She smiles at him. "It was thoughtful of you to agree to photograph their wedding. Now help me." She hands him her pearl earring.

On a chair next to the door is the wedding present, wrapped in gilded paper and tied with a bronze bow. She got them an antique cut-glass bowl with a diamond pattern. She wanted something more rounded, less cleanly contoured, but

Anita would like the more traditional diamond shape. In the store, Lena imagined her own face staring out from the bowl, as from a looking glass, and the sound of tinkling crystal rang in her head. For Lena, the autumn has been full of contrast: a brilliant blue fall sky with air that felt like that of summer, and she a mosaic that included some other self from some other life. Since meeting Nick, her senses have swept open at odd moments, capturing something distant but palpable. When that happens, a simple thing like the sweet tinkle of crystal can echo in her mind and form a pattern or vague pictures that she can't quite grasp.

"Remind me again why we're doing this?" Daniel's voice sounds far away.

She shrugs, coming back to herself. "Maybe Anita has doubts and needs her friends to be there to make sure she marries him. Who knows?"

Daniel snorts. "That's an understatement. John has never been nice to her. By the way, can you check on Isaiah? I don't want to be late."

When they arrive at the old mahogany-pewed church, Lena trails behind Daniel, carrying his flash and extra gear, clinging to the wrap that covers her slinky purple velvet dress as she follows him down the corridor toward the dais. Nick sits a few pews from the front, scanning the crowd. When he sees her, he rises and happily waves. She smiles and nods, decorous, her hands full of velvet and camera gear.

"He seems happy to see you," Daniel says, raising an eyebrow.

She shrugs, acting more nonchalant than she feels. Anita's mother walks down the aisle. Lena follows Daniel up the three stone altar steps to photograph her.

"This is good," he says. He kneels for the shot, taking his time. The altar is lit like a stage, and Lena feels bare standing there, in plain view in her slinky dress. The stone walls and high ceilings of the church diffract the sound, so the nave feels hushed. A pillar shadows Nick, though she can see him smile. She smiles back, then looks away, reaching down to place her hand tenderly on Daniel's wavy hair.

Later, at the reception at the Cosmo Club, after the champagne and toast, the kisses and well-wishes, everyone dances. The room is a swirl of suits and silks and bright taffeta. After taking pictures of the newly married and the guests dancing, Daniel takes a turn, circling Lena round and round the dance floor, cradling her tight.

"You are the most beautiful woman here," he whispers.

She smiles up at him. "Shh. The bride is always the most beautiful." She leans her head against his chest. He makes her more aware of her bone and sinew—that she is in a body, in the here and now. With Daniel, the Lena who breaches physical boundaries is never conjured up.

The music stops.

Daniel gently kisses her on the lips.

While he goes to fetch drinks, Lena wanders over to Nick. "Did I tell you Daniel almost killed me when he found your book in my bag?" she asks.

He steps back, startled.

She wants to ask him to dance (it seems she has danced with everyone else), but suddenly the smells (his cognac, tobacco, sweat, her own jasmine perfume) make her dizzy. She thinks back to the morning—to the images and silvery crystalline sound she heard while she and Daniel dressed. Then, like now, she's like a sleeper who wakens and wants to step back into a particular dream in order to capture something she can't quite remember.

She grabs his arm. "No really, don't worry. It wasn't like that." She tells him of their drive to Vermont, the flat tire, the car full of dogs and a screeching cat, and how Daniel, in his irritation over the flat tire, accused her and Isaiah of weighing down the car with too much stuff. She's embellishing the story on purpose to make him laugh, to compare his laugh with the crystalline sound from the morning that still flits through her mind.

But then Daniel is beside her again. He's handing her a glass of red wine. He smiles shyly in that way he has of letting her know how beautiful he thinks she is. She can't tell how much time has passed while she's been talking to Nick.

Suddenly, she's even unsure of what she's been saying; she was telling Nick a story, wasn't she? But now with Daniel beside her, Nick seems to be standing too close, watching her too intently. Daniel laughs as though she's just said something funny. Nick smiles too.

Slowly the room, the band, the people dancing, come back into a clearer focus.

Nothing is wrong, Lena tells herself sternly, moving a step or two away from Nick. She turns to her husband and places her hand on his arm. "Have you met Nick?"

Daniel turns to Nick and smiles. "This is my husband, Daniel," Lena says, as Daniel lightly drapes his arm around her waist. While the two men talk, an impeccably dressed, diminutive woman comes up to Nick. "Ah, Hildy, let me introduce you," he says.

Startled, Lena wonders why she didn't see Hildy in the church—she wasn't sitting with Nick, so Lena assumed he came alone.

After being introduced, Hildy turns to Daniel. "Anita tells me you are a famous photographer. Are weddings your normal business?"

"Actually, I make films. I'm doing this as a favor—a wedding present."

She smiles. "How kind." She turns to Nick. "You left their gift on the kitchen table. I brought it and put it over there." She points to a table laden with brightly colored packages. "We bought them a Tiffany cachepot," she says, turning back to Daniel and Lena. "I don't garden, but Nick says Anita likes plants."

"It's nice to finally meet you," Lena says. "I didn't see you in the church."

"She wasn't there," Nick says.

"My sister and her husband are hosting a dinner tonight for the senator from Maryland—I was helping her get ready. In fact," Hildy looks at her watch, "I need to get back soon. Tell me about your films," she says turning back to Daniel.

Lena half listens to Hildy and the men chat. It's not until Daniel nods to Nick, then Hildy, and firmly takes hold of her elbow to steer her toward a different huddle of people that the words she's been hearing over and over become clearer, sharper: Alouette gentille alouette, alouette, je te plumerais . . . Puzzled, she wonders where she's heard this song before.

All evening, Lena and Nick circle back to each other—a quick chat over hors d'oeuvres as she finishes the Vermont story, a smile exchanged at the bar—no impropriety that anyone would notice, and yet Daniel suddenly materializes beside her, every time she and Nick meet.

As the night wears on, Daniel steps up his drinking until finally he sits slumped in a dim corner of the bar. Lena lingers near him, aware of his drinking even while she talks to other guests and watches Nick out of the corner of her eye. She feels responsible for Daniel's drunkenness, though she doesn't know why. He rarely drinks hard liquor, and now he's looking rather morose. When Lena asks him what's wrong, he shakes his head and just sits there, brooding. She squeezes his shoulder and then turns back to the crowd, searching for Isaiah. She sees him leaning against the bar talking to a man she knows from Capitol Hill. Catching Isaiah's eye, Lena makes a cutting motion across her throat warning her friend, not this one. Over the years, Isaiah has had a propensity to choose men who lash out at him for bringing them out of the closet, as he calls it. "It's not like I'm hitting on a straight man," he would say when Lena would shake her head and ask, haven't you learned yet? Isaiah felt these men were essentially gay. Lena disagreed, arguing that some men—and women—just like to experiment, without making the life choice of being gay. For him being gay is not a life choice—it's a fact. It was a running topic of discussion between them. She knew Isaiah wanted to find a life partner and settle down like her cousin Tommy and his partner Mark. "So why do you keep picking men who are unavailable?" she'd ask.

As Lena watches Anita and John mingle with their guests, she wonders why marriage has such an allure—particularly to those who have never been married. To her, the institution of marriage seems vaguely like a dollhouse: hers had come with furniture, and around it she'd placed the blue sky, the brown earth, the oversized tree, the stick figures she drew as a child. She remembers reading in National Geographic that the Wodabee of Niger court their cousins for marriage, and if two cousins desire the same girl, the girl chooses the one she wishes, but the other is welcomed into the home and invited to share the marriage bed if consent is given by the bride. Maybe that's more sensible, she thinks, as she hovers under Daniel's shoulder, trying to hoist him up. By now, the band has finished for the night and the lights are on.

"Is he okay?" Isaiah asks, looking worried. He knew it was not like Daniel to drink so much. "Want help?"

A few feet behind Isaiah is the man he was talking to at the bar, obviously waiting for him. "No, you go on."

When Isaiah leaves, Nick appears at her side and takes Daniel's other arm. "Steady there," he says to Daniel, leading him toward the door. "Watch it, there's a step."

Lena wants to shout, No Daniel, let's do this ourselves, don't let Nick get between us, but it is too late. Both Nick and Daniel have crossed the threshold, moved through the door.

Outside, the three of them huddle together for a moment. The midnight sky is velvety despite the city lights.

Jupiter winks at her.

Daniel stumbles, but Nick keeps a firm hand on his elbow.

"Taxi?" Nick asks.

Lena shakes her head. "We'll walk."

"Don't be absurd, it's too cold and he's had too much to drink."

Lena tells Nick that she and Daniel had come in the bride's limousine, and with all the camera gear, she hadn't brought her purse and Daniel had forgotten his wallet.

Nick hands her a twenty-dollar bill and then moves a few steps away.

Lena takes Daniel's hand, squeezes it tight, moves closer to him.

A taxi pulls up. Nick steps forward to open the door.

Daniel sways. He drops her hand to clutch his cameras, and climbs into the cab.

Nick turns and walks away.

Lena steps one leg into the taxi then hesitates, looks up at Jupiter, then turns to watch Nick receding back before ducking into the cab.

Eight

A week after the wedding, the autumn sun emerges from a bank of clouds and blankets Lena with a sense of happiness. She has just cut across Dupont Circle on her way to Georgetown. Though she planned to run errands downtown, her legs, having a mind of their own, carry her toward Nick's house.

When she arrives, even before she knocks, before she has time to think or change her mind, Nick materializes at the door. He has a red bandana on his head and blue paint on his cheek.

"Oh," she says, surprised. "Did you see me through the window coming up the walk?"

"No, I just. . . I don't know why I opened the door."

"Am I interrupting?" she asks, embarrassed now. "I was around the corner. . . "

"I'm glad you're here," he says, stepping back to invite her in, while she makes up reasons why she can't stay.

Still hesitating on the threshold, she holds out a twenty-dollar bill. "Thanks for lending us money for the cab, " she says.

"Don't be silly." He pushes the money away, grabs her by the wrist and pulls her inside. "How about lunch?" he asks, tugging on her coat.

"What about your painting?"

"Wedgewood blue, do you like it? We're still in the process of decorating—it's taken longer than I'd hoped. I think Hildy thought if she stalled long enough, I'd hire an interior designer." He grimaces. "She's traveling and I'm trying to get the painting done before she comes home and changes her mind about the color. Lunch?" he asks again, but he's already headed toward the basement stairs.

The basement kitchen, narrow and small, has been squeezed into a dark corner against a lacquered red wall. Lena is surprised the kitchen is so small given the large size of the house.

Nick rummages in the refrigerator.

Lena stands by a black metal chair. "Does Hildy usually do the cooking? Or do you like to cook as well?"

He raises an eyebrow. "She'd like a cook."

"A cook?" Lena exclaims. "Sounds fancy." Though her grandparents had money, Lena grew up helping her Gran cook and clean their modest 1920s California-style bungalow.

He grins. "That's my reaction exactly." He rummages through the fridge while she settles into an uncomfortable ultra-modern black swivel chair. "I don't have much to offer, just a fresh bagel and canned lentil soup. Is that okay?"

She nods.

They talk while he prepares the meal. She tells him about the book she's reading—"Not my normal kind of book, but I'm enjoying it."

He asks if he can borrow it when she's done and tells her about the movie he went to see the night before. They chat like this, keeping the conversation light and impersonal, when out of nowhere, he says, "I have a reception at the British Embassy in an hour . . . would you come with me?"

Lena twists her wedding band round and round. "I can't," she says looking down. She hesitates before adding, "Are you and Hildy getting married soon?"

He looks at her quizzically while she explains that she and Daniel are in the process of adopting a baby from India.

"Why are you adopting? Why not one of your own?"

She shrugs. "I'm thirty-four and we want two kids so we decided to adopt one while I try to get pregnant. We don't care if they are close in age," Lena says. "In fact, we prefer it that way. You and Hildy must have made decisions about marriage and children yourselves by now."

Nick turns back to the stove. Orange and blue flames lick at the black-bottomed pot. The smell of canned soup fills the air. He reaches into the cabinet for a ceramic bowl. "She calls motherhood male oppression. She'd like a Weimaraner puppy."

Lena laughs.

"But she does expect me to marry her. In her culture, women don't sleep with men they aren't married to. And besides, her father is my boss of sorts," he says, sipping a spoonful of soup to see if it's hot enough.

"Of sorts?"

"He's the chief economist and a senior VP of the division he works in. He's not my direct boss—he's higher up than that, but he could eliminate my chances for promotion if he wanted to."

While Nick ladles soup, Lena glances at her watch.

"You're not in a hurry, are you? I thought we could eat lunch out on the deck." He stacks the bowls of soup and bagels on a tray and carries it upstairs, turning on the stereo as he heads to the deck. A sultry Latin voice fills the air. He glances at her with a sheepish grin.

From the deck they can see out over the street. An old woman in a blue dress pushes her cart out her front gate; her orange cat follows a pace or two behind. Unruly red roses creep up her yellow house.

"The light is sharp-edged today," he says, looking up at the sky. Then he nods toward the old woman walking down the street. "I should ask her if she needs help trimming the climbers back."

"Her roses are lovely."

He looks down at his hands.

They eat in silence.

"When can we meet for lunch and book exchange?" Lena says finally, her hands folded primly in her lap.

Nick leans over a planter that hangs on his deck. "Smell this," he says, his nose close to the fall Clematis. She bends down to smell. The flower smells faintly like vanilla, but Nick smells musky. She knows that if she turns her head, his lips would brush hers. Instead, she slowly sits down.

"I'm leaving for Costa Rica in a week," he says.

She glances at him. "Daniel and I are leaving for

Malaysia and Singapore in a few weeks and we won't get back until just before Christmas."

"So long?" Nick stacks the empty dishes.

"The trip is part vacation, part work." Lena rises, grabbing a few empty glasses and hurries into the kitchen.

"Why the hurry?" Nick asks catching up to her.

She looks at her watch. "You said you have an engagement at the embassy."

"I'll drive you home."

"That's silly. The embassy is closer to here than my house."

He shrugs. "I want to take you home," he says, with a look that she cannot decipher.

She blushes and looks away.

"I hate it when people can't be honest about how they feel," Nick says.

An image begins to crack open in her mind, but she forces it away, holding her mind very still—a trick she taught herself when she was young. "I've got to go," she says finally. " I guess this is goodbye for a while." She picks up her coat and purse.

"Lena." He bends to kiss her good-bye.

She moves quickly, circumventing him by stepping sideways toward the door. "Bye," she says softly, shutting the door firmly behind her.

Later that night, light and shadow shift across Lena's bedroom, like shadow puppets playing. The French lace curtains flutter in the breeze. The moon, round and nearly full, frames a single piece of furniture—an amber-colored rocker swaying almost imperceptibly on a hand-hooked rug the shade of the sea. Pressed back into the darkened room is the bed, where Lena lies awake next to Daniel.

Daniel's breathing is reedy and rhythmic. The sound makes Lena melancholy. Her husband's eyes flutter in his sleep; she moves closer to the warmth of his body. A lock of his auburn hair rests on her pillow; she touches its soft curl.

Her mind turns to Nick and his agitation at the table and to the heat she felt as he reached over to kiss her goodbye.

Slowly, she pushes back the covers and emerges out of bed, tucking the cornflower comforter around Daniel so he doesn't feel her absence.

Downstairs, she is bodiless, the phone strange in her hand, like an object from a dream. The Tuscan-colored tiles of the kitchen floor are cold under her feet. She traces the grout with her toe. She wants to shake loose her thoughts, to crawl back to the warmth of her marriage bed, but then Nick answers and her voice is caught, her fingers tremble against the receiver. Yes, I can meet you for lunch Monday, he is saying, as though she's asked him a question. They are making plans, firm plans to meet at his house, six blocks from his workplace, a short interlude in their tight schedules. She offers to bring sandwiches from the deli by her office. She rests her forehead against the stainless steel refrigerator, traces her finger along its smooth surface, watches the outline of her face grow clearer the farther away she moves. Twelve-thirty it is. I'll see you then. His voice echoes in her ears.

She's like a walking stick, elongated and wingless; with one hand she clenches a sandwich bag, with the other she knocks. Lena's become twig-like so that a predatory bird won't carry her away—so she can expose the secret side of her existence when she's ready.

Nick ushers her in.

"I brought sandwiches," she says, holding the brown bag in the air.

His fingers brush hers as she hands him the bag. She bends to remove her red leather shoes. A bare window reflects Nick standing behind her: they sway like willows.

And then his reflection is gone.

Behind her, she hears a soft thunk as he places the sandwiches on the coffee table in the living room.

She stands and pushes her hair behind one ear.

Back again, he touches her arm. "Do you want a drink?"

"Water is fine." While he goes to the kitchen, she wanders to the living room, wafts like a cloud in an empty sky. For her, things have disappeared—there is no beige couch, no glass tables, no blue silk delphiniums in an oversized triangular vase. She sits down. Then some formless thought of Daniel, the to-be-adopted baby, Vermont, their dinner plans make her remember herself and jump up. She bends to grab her red leather satchel.

"Here's your water," Nick says as she straightens. He eyes her satchel as he holds out the glass.

She lets the satchel sink back to the floor.

They sit side by side, she perched on the edge of the couch, he lounging back. She rummages in the paper bag and brings out two sandwiches, laughing awkwardly as she tries to figure out which is vegetable and which is turkey. She hands him his and they eat silently.

"Were you angry the other day?" she asks finally, crumpling the white parchment paper from her sandwich.

His eyes narrow. "No. Why?"

She shrugs.

"Not angry—frustrated maybe."

Their hands accidentally touch as they both lean forward to toss the crumpled wrappers from their sandwiches on the coffee table.

She pulls back as though stung.

He does too.

Then, in fluidly synchronized movement, they both lean forward until their lips gently meet, their tongues slowly explore, their bodies meld creating an aura around them that Lena would have actually seen had her eyes been open.

"This isn't right," she says, pulling back, gasping a little. But then his lips are against hers again—time passes, she doesn't know how long, all she knows is that she's intoxicated by a sense of joy, and the feeling of his kiss.

"I've been here before—in this moment," he says when they stop kissing.

"Yes," she murmurs.

They raise their hands to shoulder height and press finger tip to finger tip.

"Can you take tomorrow afternoon off?" he asks, his head bent close to hers.

"Yes," she whispers, her eyes closed.

The next day the clear blue sky stretches all the way down to the road as the Porsche streaks ahead, full throttle.

Nick laughs.

Lena too. Her orange scarf balloons out the sunroof. "Take me up, Chitty-Chitty Bang Bang," she yells, as they bank and dip their way down the long steep road that leads to Great Falls Park. Signs warn that the rapids below can be dangerous.

They park and walk down a dirt footpath. Above them orange and reds have only begun to nip at the trees. The soft autumn sun casts shadows at their feet. "An eagle," Nick says, pointing skyward. "Over there. Out over the falls."

Lena tugs him toward a large smooth rock surrounded by a half arc of gray boulders.

He unfolds a small blanket. Its rust color is pleasing against the mottled stone. She stretches her long legs, crosses her ankles. He pulls her closer until they lie together, he on his back, she to his side while he closes his eyes wanting to define to himself the difference he feels in this moment.

"Nick?" She touches his cheek.

"Hmm?" He opens his eyes.

"Do you think each person only ever has one great love in their life? You said you were married before. I mean, perhaps Hildy is the love of your life?"

He laughs, leaning up on his elbow. "Hildy is definitely not the love of my life. And with my ex-wife, it was her artsy intellectual family that enthralled me the most. I'm not sure I've ever had a great love, as you put it. And you?"

She shrugs. "I suppose I have. I mean, I'm married." She looks at him, embarrassed that she's said something so idiotic.

Nick pulls Lena close. "With my ex-wife, the obsessive need to be close to someone grew stronger in her, while it diminished in me. Sometimes it felt like she wanted to step right into my skin." Suddenly, Nick remembers a dream from his childhood. When he was young, he often dreamed about one particular girl—the girl was so familiar it was as if Nick knew her: sometimes he even wondered if the girl was him somehow. But in this particular dream, he'd slid down the girl's incredibly long brown hair into a field of flowers (hundreds of blossoms) where they ran hand in hand laughing, her hair flying behind. When they stopped, nearly out of breath, he looked into her eyes and said, I'll find you.

Now, he hears Lena's voice. "Finding the one who is meant for you is hard," she says. "But being close doesn't always mean obsessing over someone. Although, I suppose it can make one feel wide open and vulnerable."

He strokes her shoulder, wondering about his dream, wondering why he is remembering it now. "I think I would feel a tad too vulnerable to love someone so much I felt they were part of me, almost as if they were me." He watches the rapids. "Hildy and I have fun but we don't have deep emotional conversations—that's what attracted me to her in the first place."

She frowns. "But we have deep conversations."

He takes her hand. "With you I feel, well, warmth I suppose. Which both confuses me and gives me hope."

"Hope?"

He tells her hope that he can live more fully. His finger gently traces the features of her face. Aroused, he holds back, feeling that anything more is impossible for her. It's something he doesn't need to put into words; it's something he simply knows.

9. France 1965

The white Citroën passed Lena and her father at a bend in the road as they headed home from Comeirol, a *hameau* of five houses below the village. In the late July air, dead with heat, Lena's father carted his half-asleep daughter up the hill on his back. They had just finished a *fête* of lunch and *gâteau* at a neighbor's house for Lena's third birthday, and Pére was surprised when the white Citroën—more pristine than other cars in the village—passed them by. And though the road extended seven kilometers down the hill, all the way to the bottom where St-Laurent-le-Minier sat tucked along the Hérault River, hardly anyone used the road anymore because a newer one had been built on the other side of the hill.

The car stopped abruptly and then rolled backward on the tarmac, its tires making tiny popping sounds on the rocks and bits of broken blacktop. When the car reached Père, the driver, an attractive young woman, leaned over the passenger seat. "Want a ride?" she asked through the open window, smiling at the sleeping Lena. Her French, though good, was clearly foreign. English, Père guessed, mostly because there were very few other types of Anglos who came to this area. In fact, the English weren't even that common. Mostly they visited Provence and Aix-en-provence, having not yet discovered the Languadoc-Roussillon.

Père shrugged his shoulders. "It isn't that far," he said. "We are just going to the center of the village. But thank you."

"I'm going there myself—to see Christian Bertram. Do you know him?"

Père nodded. "He's our neighbor."

Lena began to whine. She kicked her feet and then, perhaps in her sleepiness forgetting she was on her father's back, slammed her head against his.

"*Aïe! Mon dieu*!" Père took Lena, crying now, from his back and stood her up next to him.

The woman got out of the car and approached them. "Oh! Sweet thing," she said, touching Lena's cheek. Lena shrank behind her father's leg.

"She's hot and tired. Today is her birthday, and she had too much gâteau," he said, picking her up.

"Please let me drive you to the village. I'm going there myself." The young woman opened the passenger door. "She's too hot for you to continue walking up this hill. Come on now." She gently pushed Père and the crying Lena toward the car. "Look," she said, lifting her tennis shoe. "It's so hot my foot is sticking to the pavement."

For some reason, this made Lena laugh. As they got into the car, the woman continued to say funny things in French and make faces so Lena would laugh. Soon Lena was laughing as hard as she had been crying a few minutes before.

"My name is Vivian," the woman said, as she downshifted up the hill. "But my friends call me Vivi."

"This is Lena," Pére said, kissing the top of Lena's head.

Lena shrieked and giggled and twisted back to push her father's face away. "I a big girl," she announced to Vivi.

"I can see that." Vivi smiled.

"And I am Jean-Paul. It is kind of you to give us a ride."

Lena had settled back against her father and stared at Vivi intently.

"Papa," Lena said, turning to her father. "*J'aime*." She turned to Vivi and reached out her hand. "*Vivi est mon ami*."

Vivi smiled, "I'm delighted to be your friend." She met Jean-Paul's gaze above the head of his daughter.

"Are you English?"

"American."

"Ah," he said. Then, in English, he said, "Please excuse my daughter. Her mother is not often home and I have noticed she craves female attention."

"I love children." Vivi turned to Lena and said, in

French, "What special things did you do on your very special day, Lena?"

Lena told her about the picnic and the *gâteau* and the neighbor's big black dog that barked when they tried to play ball. "*Chien méchant*," Lena said firmly.

"Only one bad dog?"

Lena nodded.

Vivi turned to Jean-Paul. "Is she afraid of dogs?"

"Au contraire." He smiled. We have a big hairy dog that she loves as much as she loves me.

As if on cue, the dog Silence came bounding over to the car just as they arrived at the place in the center of the village. Silence stood on his hind legs, put his giant hairy paws on the car door and stuck his head through the window.

"Oh my." Vivi laughed.

"*Le ba*!" Jean-Paul and Lena shouted in unison, both waving their arms at the happy dog. Silence backed down, his tail wagging fast, and bounded over to Jean-Paul's side of the car, where he started barking. Jean-Paul apologized and turned to Vivi. "The beast has no manners."

"He's happy to see you." She got out of the car. "What's his name?"

"*Silence*."

"Funny name."

"Until Lena was born, he never barked. Now he only barks when we come home or when he knows it's time for our walk."

She called the dog over to her. He came and leaned into her, happy to be petted. "He seems so sweet."

"He's very gentle with Lena."

Lena came up and flopped her head over Silence's back. "J'aime."

Jean-Paul looks sheepish. "She loves everything today. It's her favorite word."

"And why not? She's three. The world is perfect."

He grabbed Lena and held her up toward the sky. "Is that so, *mon amour*?"

"*Oui*, papa!" she giggled. He brought her back close to him and cradled her against his chest.

"Thank you for the ride. You were right—it was too hot for the little one to be trudging up the hill with me." They were stopped in front of a three-story stone house that was perched on the edge of the precipice, seven kilometers up the hill, and looked like it rose from the mountain. Stone-walled flower beds circled the facade. Roses in various shades of pink and mauve climbed the walls, and scampered over the red tile roof. In front of the house were two large medieval-looking doors with medieval-looking knockers set into a stone wall with rusted hinges. The cobble stones in front of the doors were swept clean and polished from wear.

Vivi breathed in sharply. "This is your house?"

Jean-Paul nodded.

"It's like a fairy tale. You are very lucky."

Jean-Paul laughed. "Unfortunately the house is ancient. Medieval even. We tell visitors our village is like a history book. My house, like most of the houses in our village, was built around the time of the first printing press, the Wars of Religion between the Catholics and Huguenots—or Protestants as you Americans call them—and the Reformation, the period when England split from the Catholic church. See the black cross up there over the door?" He pointed to the terrace on the second level of the house. "The family living in the house at the time would have painted the cross so the King's army would know that Catholics lived there and would leave the house and its inhabitants unharmed."

Vivi stepped closer to the sienna-colored walls and caressed the stone. "Impressive. How old is the house?"

Jean-Paul shrugged. "We don't know for sure. The original title was lost during the French Revolution. But we estimate five hundred years old."

Beyond the house, blue hills towered skyward. Just below, the new road cut a windy swath through the chestnut trees, while far below, the village of St Laurent-le-Minier lay nestled along the blue snake of the Hérault.

"The wisteria must be fantastic when in bloom," Vivi

said, staring up at the tree that twisted and turned around the archways of the house. "Good thing your house is stone. In the south of the United States, where I'm from, wisteria is known to yank a porch from its anchoring."

"This old thing has been here forever. But yes, it's beautiful in the spring. Like living inside of a giant purple flower. See how it creeps inside all the windows? I have to cut it back every year."

Lena, tired of all this talk, climbed out of her father's arms and went over to Vivi and took her hand. "Please come in," she said in a prim, but babyish voice. She was so perfectly parroting someone older and more old-fashioned, that Jean-Paul and Vivi started laughing and then couldn't stop.

"Ahahaha," Lena joined in, though it was clear she wasn't quite sure what she was laughing at. But her Père was happy and so was her new friend, and so she was happy too. "Please come in," she said again, amid new laughter.

"Yes, please do," Jean-Paul said. "I'm so rude, you must be thirsty after your long drive—that is, I assume you drove from elsewhere."

"Actually, I'm staying in Montpellier—I've been studying there." As she talked, she stepped back to her car, reached into the back seat and pulled out a neatly wrapped package. "But one of my friends from home, in Georgia, asked me to give these photos to Christian Bertram. Do you know where he lives?"

Jean-Paul pointed to a decrepit-looking house with a blue door.

Vivi looked down at the child, who had taken her hand again, possessively, as if she were never going to let Vivi go. "Shall we go visit Mr. Bertram?" Vivi asked. She looked up at Jean-Paul. "Do you mind if I take her?"

"Not at all. She's a well-behaved child and welcome in all the houses of the village." Jean-Paul turned toward his door, but then, as if deciding something, turned back. "Lena and I would be very pleased if you could join us for dinner—that is, if you don't have to get back to Montpellier right away."

"But that's such a bother for you."

"No bother, I like to cook."

"We cook. You eat," Lena says stamping her foot.

Vivi laughed. "If you both insist."

"Please," Jean-Paul said. "We'd like you to stay."

Later that evening, lingering over dinner, the three of them sat around a wrought-iron table on the upper terrace of the house. In the French style, they had prepared a leisurely meal of several courses—to celebrate Lena's birthday, as they said. Though the sun was still high in the sky, the terrace was shaded by a huge plane tree that grew in the place, as well as by wisteria that grew over the old stone arbor that was perhaps once meant for grapes. In the distance, lining the hills, were row upon row of grapes growing in home-style vineyards, the ripened fruit now almost ready for picking.

"Who owns the vineyards?" Vivi asked.

"Many families in the village."

"Does each family process its own grapes?"

"No, there is a cooperative in Le Vigan—the other side of the hill—that everyone takes them to."

"Ah, I think I saw a caves cooperative in Ganges on my way here."

Jean-Paul smiled at her accent—not quite perfect, but almost so. "Yes, that's an option too."

Lena, who had been getting sleepy even before they brought out dessert and cheese, became heavy in Vivi's lap. She had first wanted to hold Vivi's hand, then later, when they finished their meal, she crawled into Vivi's lap. When Jean-Paul saw what Lena was up to, he told her to get down, reaching for his daughter, but Vivi had waived him off, saying she felt honored that Lena wanted to cuddle with her. At first, Jean-Paul looked uncomfortable, but then soon relaxed.

"It is past her bedtime," Jean-Paul said, leaning over to pick up his sleeping child.

But as he lifted her out of Vivi's lap, Lena woke up and clung to Vivi's neck. "No, papa," she said, whining.

He tugged a little harder but Lena kept her hold on

Vivi, until Vivi stood with the child still in her arms. "Let me carry her to bed."

Jean-Paul started to object, but at once saw that he was no match for these two stubborn females. "As you wish," he said, moving the chair out of the way so Vivi could navigate freely with Lena in her arms. She followed him through the living room and kitchen, up the back stairs to Lena's room, and then gently laid her on the small bed. When Vivi went to stand up, Lena refused to let go.

"Lena, stop," her father said sharply.

Lena, in her tired state, started to cry. "Vivi read," Lena sobbed, her fists balled up to her eyes. She kicked her feet in frustration and sheer child-like exhaustion. She'd had a long day with first the birthday party and now Vivi's company. It was far more stimulation than she was used to in her solitary life with Pére.

"Sweet girl," Vivi said soothingly, sitting down next to Lena on the bed and stroking her head.

"Vivi here," Lena said, pointing to her pillow.

"I usually lie down with her and read," Pére said, sorting through the books on the shelf.

"Let me," Vivi said, lying down next to Lena while Jean-Paul approached them with a book in his hand.

When Pére turned to leave, Lena cried out, "Papa!" and gave him a look that made both Pére and Vivi laugh. Lena laughed too, scooching over to make room for Pére on the tiny bed. Together the three of them read through the book, until finally Lena fell asleep.

"Is it safe to get up?" Vivi whispered, lying on her side.

"She sleeps soundly once she's down for the night," Pére said, carefully sitting up and moving from the bed. He came over to the other side to help Vivi up. His hand lingered on hers for a few beats longer than necessary.

Blushing, she turned away. "She's a beautiful child," Vivi said over her shoulder as she descended the narrow stone stairs leading back to the kitchen. "And so smart."

"I try to tell her mother that," Jean-Paul said, following her back into the kitchen and reaching into the cupboard for another bottle of wine.

"No more for me," Vivi said, holding up her hands. "I won't make it down the hill."

"The hill is very dangerous at night, if you don't know it well. Just last week a tourist's car went over the edge." Jean-Paul stood staring at Vivi, with a look on his face that said he was struggling with something. "You should stay the night," he said finally.

"I'll be fine."

"It's not safe," he said again, stepping closer to her and brushing away a hair that lay matted on her cheek. "Thank you for being so kind to my daughter."

She reached up to touch his face. "And her mother?" she asked.

Jean-Paul turned away. "She's rarely here." He hesitated, and then turned back to her. "She's American, like you. An actress in Paris at the moment."

Vivi nodded as though she understood, but Jean-Paul wondered what it was that she could possibly understand—even he didn't understand Rita or the force that pulled them together. "Would I know her?" Vivi asked.

Jean-Paul shook his head. "She's still waiting for her big break."

Vivi stepped closer to him. "And you? What are you waiting for?"

Brown eyes met brown eyes looking beyond their mere faces into some unseen but mutally understood territory. "I think sometimes the only reason two people come together is to have a particular child," Jean-Paul said finally.

"Lena?"

He nodded. "Her mother and I have nothing in common. She insisted we get married so she could stay in France."

"Do you think that's why she got pregnant?"

He shrugged. "With Rita, one never knows. She is, to say the least, complicated." He grabbed the bottle of wine and headed back toward the terrace. "It is settled that you must stay the night," he said over his shoulder. When Vivi said that she didn't want to keep him from his room, he said, "It's okay. You can have my bed." He pointed to the day bed next to the fireplace. "I often sleep there."

On the terrace stairs he turned back and stepped down to take her hand. "It's settled," he said looking deeply into her eyes.

Unseen by them, Lena had come silently down the back stairs, half-asleep but wanting some water. She was just about to call out for her Père when she saw them and stopped, hearing her father say, It's settled. Her Père and Vivi were standing so close that Lena could see the heat rise off of them. To her, it looked like there was a blue halo surrounding them, or like they were standing in a circle of light.

"I suppose it is," she heard Vivi say just as her father reached down and kissed Vivi on the lips. She watched her father take Vivi's hand as he and Vivi climbed the stairs to the terrace. Lena went upstairs and got into bed, forgetting about her need for water.

Ten

Morning sounds filter into her consciousness—the neighbor calling to her dog, the thud of the paperboy lobbing the Post, the stream of cars heading toward the Capitol in the still-dark morning—until she can no longer pretend she is asleep. She opens her eyes and looks at the clock. It's early still. She curls back under the covers.

She'd been dreaming about a bird, a small delicate wren-sized creature with a pale yellow head, cream body, and white rings around its eyes. In her dream, the bird was perched on a thin whip of budding cherry with white flowers, half formed, popping from their ruby husks. As she lies there, trying to identify the type of bird, or trace her memory to determine why the picture feels so familiar, something stirs in her that she can't quite grab hold of. In the dream, the landscape was grayed out and fuzzy so that the bird and the flower buds came into sharp focus and somehow made her happy, and excited—about what she doesn't know.

Lena rolls over to find her husband's side of the bed empty. For a moment she is puzzled. Then she remembers: Daniel is away on a one-week shoot down South. She kicks off the covers, grabs her robe, and heads downstairs to the kitchen to make tea.

Outside her kitchen window, a thin layer of frost blankets her garden. While she watches, the sun hits the yard, crystallizing the plants and leaving her with a warm feeling inside, not unlike she felt waking from her dream. She thinks of Nick. He called her yesterday morning while he was waiting for his plane to Costa Rica. They had talked for nearly an hour.

With her teacup in hand, Lena mounts the stairs heading to her office. She feels Nick's presence—not separate from herself like a ghost, but almost as if she is him. She hears his thoughts play out in her mind as her own thoughts do—his so tangibly that she knows he is both startled and confused by how he pines for her. Lena doesn't stop to wonder why she knows what she knows—her divining is so seamless it's like she's sitting in Nick's head. "Nick," she says, feeling the weight of his emotion rise up and almost overwhelm him. She reaches out to touch him but her hand falls through space—he's not there.

She sits at her computer to send Nick a letter. She's following a thread, a thin blade of light—something she sees, though not with her eyes. Though she doesn't know it, she wants to tether Nick to her so he himself feels more secure and doesn't disappear. Lena knows she frightens people sometimes. She doesn't know how or why or what she does exactly, but she knows that the light that binds her to some people grows darker until they've disappeared.

Nicks letters help. As the days pass, she floats from letter to letter, from intuition to intuition, as though the rest of her life is grayed out, like her dream of the bird. If asked, she couldn't say to whom she talked or what it was she did each day, though she knew with clarity the rhythm of Nick's movements and thoughts.

Dear L

I had hoped to write you yesterday, but the bank holiday put a spanner in my plans. I didn't realize the chemist would be closed (they sell stamps and envelopes here) or that there would be such a queue to get out of the city. (The chemist is on a road heading west toward the beach.)The traffic here is stunning for such a sleepy city.

I wondered if perhaps I should wait to write until I heard from you again, but then I thought about how you suggested I turn my hand to writing, just for fun. A letter is not a poem, and I hope you will forgive my rusty pen. To my ears, I perhaps sound like a cheeky state school lad(!) though I am trying to remember what I know of the English language from my years at Oxford. I'm afraid letter writing is very different than economist reports.

Yesterday was hot and humid and as I sat at a café near the block of flats where I am staying I couldn't help but wonder was last week all a dream? I ask this not because I really doubt we spent a lot of time together last week but because it does seem, at least in my memory, to have been fantastical. Wonderful, of course, but also having elements of fantasy.

I cannot think it would have been possible to construct a better dream, which may be the best guarantee that it was indeed real. Our connection (as you would call it) was not only intensely enjoyable, it was so effortless. Perhaps that's why I have moments when I'm not sure what to make of what's happened, or how to sort through my feelings about us. I have a strong sense that really good things have to be worked at. Only dreams are effortless.

I do so want to be able to make more memories with you. It is such a frustration that the coming months are already programmed leaving us so little time. N

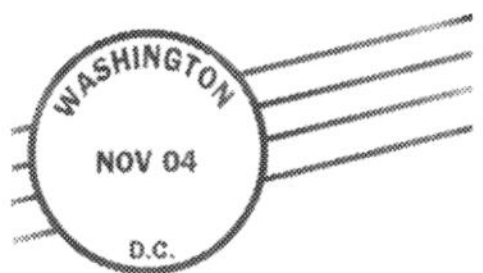

Dear Nick,

Daniel is back from his trip South and I must make this quick as we have dinner plans. It seems to me that the best things in life should come effortlessly—and that's why I'm so confused. You've slipped inside me and taken up residence so easily it's as if I've always known you. I've asked myself, how can that be when I'm committed to someone else in marriage? But there you are—inside me. Logic doesn't displace you. I say this not to give you hope, but to be honest with you and myself about our inexplicable connection.

We will find time to meet when you get back and before Daniel and I leave for Malaysia. I promise.

I must go. Daniel has just come home, I hear him downstairs. L

Dear L

The cats were at the dustbins again all night keeping me awake. As I may have told you, there are no hotels in this area, so I've paid to board at the flat of an elderly woman who rents rooms to students on a weekly basis. I am supposed to be studying at a desk the woman has given me in the lounge, but I am drowsy so instead I am lying here on my bed thinking of you.

In my mind, I circle back to this memory: I'm lying on a rock looking up at the simple colour of your hair, the clear blue sky, and the complex colour of your eyes. You are lying at my side but pressed close against me. The river rushes by, only inches away, and its noise drowns out everything except our voices. In a wholly carefree way, we are becoming closer. We are warm together.

Autumn is my favourite time of the year. The air is clearer, the light softer, the colours sharper, the smells crisper, without the fetid heat of summer.

You are a very beautiful woman and I feel at ease lying next to you, doing no more than talking. Although I do have sexual fantasies about you, I also dream about just spending the night with you, lying naked in each other's arms, gently falling asleep with your breast in my hand. Awakening with your leg over mine, your arm across my chest. Perhaps one day? N

In the midst of her correspondence with Nick, Lena gets a letter from Gran.

Dear Lena,

As you may have been told, Tommy and Mark are expecting another child. I am delighted. They are using Marisa again, and both mother and child seem to be in excellent health. I am happy to report that Tommy is again the sperm donor (in case you had felt it improper to ask.) As you may know, they had talked about "taking turns, " but your Aunt Clarissa and I convinced them that it would be better for the children to be full blood siblings. While I trust Marisa, a child's bond to a mother is particularly strong and it would be a shame if Marisa were the only blood link between the children. It would make them a party of three, so to speak, and I counseled the boys that that would be an undue risk to take. They accused me of sounding like grandfather, or at least like a lawyer!

I am telling you now, way in advance, that I am having a baby shower for them, and I would like you to attend. Mark has an enormous family, and I would like Tommy to feel that he has the support of his family as well. Though you do not come home to visit often, Tommy adores you and I know he'd like it if you and Daniel would be there. And so would I. I assume you are still on the board of that environmental organization and are planning on attending the annual meeting again this year. If so, I will plan it for the weekend of the annual meeting, so you will have no excuse not to come.

I hope you are well. Give Daniel my love. And please do keep me informed about the progress of your adoption.

Lovingly,
Gran

Dear L

I found a single impossibly long brown hair on my dressing gown before I left. I will not speculate how it got there given that you never saw me in my knickers or dressing gown (!) but perhaps it escaped from my jumper. I know you will say it appeared as if by magic—somehow teleported from you to me. If only it were that easy to have the scent of your hair on my pillow!

In any event, I curled it up and brought it with me. Tonight I ran it across my chest and thought of you. I wrapped it around my erection and wished I had more of you. Your hand, your mouth, your insides, wrapped around me instead. I hope one day this is true. N

Dear Gran,

Let me check the dates and get back with you. Of course I'd want to be there if I can. You make it sound as if I am purposefully avoiding family obligations—not true, I'm just busy. Please remember it is easier for the twins because they live in Los Angeles, and so can find moments to visit that I cannot living so far away. And we have to balance our visits to LA with visits to Daniel's family in England. And then there is our Vermont house and all the travel we both do for work. Honestly, I'm not avoiding coming home. I love you, and the twins, and even Aunt Clarissa! (Though I dare say she doesn't love me!) Isaiah tells me he still avoids her—that Tommy says she hasn't yet forgiven us for our wild youth.

Big hug,
Lena

Dear L

I have been in Costa Rica a fortnight now, which for me means I must start looking forward to the future rather than back at our short (but exceptional) past.

This morning at breakfast I could feel the landlady, an elderly woman, staring at my back wondering why a man as old as me would be a lodger in her home for these several weeks. She serves me up courgettes and tomatoes with eggs and toast, while I see her giving her college-aged lodgers corn flakes. Perhaps she feels that corn flakes aren't dignified enough for someone my age, or perhaps she simply thinks what she feeds me is English. I haven't had the heart to make her wiser about English fare. In any event, I too have to pause and wonder why am I here?

But enough of this darkness—what I want to say is how much I am looking forward to seeing you, however brief. I feel that we will know what we are constructing together when we meet again. And yes I know you will say you have other commitments, but nonetheless, I want to see you, even if this means only catching brief moments of time together for the rest of our lives. Lena, I cannot imagine my life without you in it—whatever that may mean.

I will call you again later today if I can find a phone box without an hour's line. I know it is silly to tell you I will call when the call will happen before this letter arrives, but I want you to know how much I look forward to speaking with you.

I am yours, N

Almost the moment Nick puts his last letter in the mailbox, Lena smiles to herself. For her, it's like the bright blue sky has broken open and some secret existence awaits her on the other side, where everything—her house, the office, the city, trees, grass, plants, animals, people, even the sidewalk pavement with its colored bits of trash to the beat of a secret incandescent heat. Even now, she has the urge to lay her ear down in the silvery-green grass and feel the circular shape of

Earth's gravitational pull, tugging her down and into her beautiful glorious body. Somehow, Nick makes her feel this way.

While she waits for Nick's call, she doodles pictures of an old stone house on a scrap of paper wondering if she should tell Nick about her dream. Since he's left, she's been joining him some nights in sleep, at a point in their joint dreams. It's a phenomena that doesn't startle her, though she can't explain it to herself, or even how she knows that they are having the same dream. When she told him the details of his dream two days ago he freaked. "You scare me, Lena," he said. "How is it possible that you know my dreams?" What she couldn't explain to him is that they are her dreams, too—she was afraid he would freak more if she did. Truth be told, she doesn't understand either— that's why she keeps this part of herself locked away in a secret place of its own. But with Nick in her life, Lena's propensity to know things—to be a trespasser into another's intimate domain, has gained a momentum that surprises even her.

Lena lays aside her doodling sketch. The sun through the window warms her face. If she closes her eyes, and stretches her—what? (she tries to name what part of her she uses) she can almost hear Nick's husky voice. Her hand reaches for the phone on her desk just as it rings.

"Hello, you," she says.

"How do you do that?" Nick asks.

She laughs. "How are you?"

"It's raining."

She swivels to look out the window (her eyes avoid the silver-framed photo of her and Daniel hanging on the wall). "But you're in the country of consummate sun. Are you drenched?"

"I'm a little wet, but I want to talk."

They talk for over an hour—about San Jose, his Spanish classes, her work, books they are reading, the meaning of life. His words make her happy, and in this happy state she convinces herself it's okay to be talking to Nick from her home while Daniel is out.

But then Nick's mood changes. "Lena, it seems impossible that we'll have, what, two hours, to spend together in person in the next two months?" he says bitterly.

Startled by the vehemence in his voice, she tries to distract him from his mood by telling him a story, but in the midst of her efforts, suddenly she wonders why is he spending three weeks of precious vacation time alone in Costa Rica studying Spanish, when from what he says he's already nearly fluent? "Nick, do you and Hildy have anything in common?" The question leaps off her tongue before she can stop it.

"Only eating," he replies solemnly.

She laughs, knowing that he must be exaggerating, if only slightly.

He clears his throat. "I'm serious. She wants to know what I've eaten, down to the last detail—it's always her first question."

"I don't believe you—you're pulling my leg."

"I promise you, I'm not."

"She asks you what you had for dinner? That's the first thing she says when you're away traveling?" Lena is dumbfounded. "Not I miss you? Or I lust after you? Nothing like that?"

He laughs. "I told you before, we don't have that kind of relationship. We do have things we like to do together, like running and hiking, and we both like good food and traveling, and we both pay attention to the world economy—but we aren't emotionally engaged, as you would put it. "

It's hard for Lena to imagine Nick with the woman he describes.

"Lena?"

"I don't want to know what you had for breakfast," she says, teasing him.

"Someone is waiting to use this phone." His voice is soft, caressing—she can tell he doesn't want to get off the phone. "I think he's circled the block several times already and he seems to be getting angry. Perhaps I should get off." Nick hesitates. "I miss you," he says. And then as though afraid of her reply, he quickly adds, "I'll call again soon. Bye."

"I miss you too," she whispers, though she's not sure he heard her before he hung up.

She lays down the phone and sits quietly for a long time while images run through her mind—the softness of Nick's face as they lay close on the warm ledge, the light in his eyes as they talked at the wedding reception, the way he wildly waved to her from the pew. The images canter into words under her fingertips as she types Nick a brief letter. But then another image gallops up from some distant point, becomes bigger, more distinct, until it takes up all the space in her mind. She closes her eyes. Against the blackness of her lids an image appears of a large ewe in the bed of a black pick-up truck. The sun, its round belly almost resting on the horizon, engorges the sky, while concentric circles of heat beat down on the animal. The animal is breathing quickly, groaning quietly, as it lays with its head on the wheel-well. Resting or dying? A woman reaches out to stroke the animal's head. The woman looks up right at Lena. Lena struggles to see the woman's face, but then jumps, her heart pounding, when Daniel lays his hand on her shoulder.

"What are you doing?" he asks.

She looks at her computer screen, afraid for a moment that the letter she wrote Nick is still there. Though the screen is blank (thank god for screen savers), she is unable to shift the sick feeling from the pit of her stomach. "Nothing. I was. . .just thinking."

"I'm going to walk the dogs—want to come?"

She wonders briefly why she hasn't told Daniel about the visions she's been having. But she knows why. Somehow the visions seem too tied to Nick—not that they are about him, but he seems to trigger them somehow. "I'll pass, if you don't mind." She stands and stretches. "But I'll help you leash."

"You work too hard," Daniel says.

Lena stiffens at his words.

"What's wrong?" Daniel asks, softly kissing her forehead.

"Nothing. I'm just tired, and maybe a little uptight." She smiles at him. "Nothing you've done, so don't worry."

"You should come on the walk," he says, a little more persistently this time. She knows the look on his face and what's coming. "To spend time with me."

"We spend quality time every day. I'll cook tonight. And afterwards. . ." she smiles.

He takes her hand and they walk down the stairs together.

From the living room window, Lena watches Daniel and the dogs lope out the front yard. She hears the gate slam and then the crack of a bat and yelling. The kids next door are in the cul-de-sac playing ball. Daniel calls out to a neighbor.

Lena steps into the vestibule and places her palm against the cool glass of the front door. Her sneakers, side by side, are pointed toward the door, ready for her feet. Instinctively she reaches down, touched the laces, but then stops.

Her head turns. A flicker of light inside the house catches her attention; the last rays of the sun are sweeping over the skylight in their hallway.

She pivots and climbs the stairs.

In her room, she reaches for her journal nestled amongst the books on her nightstand. Her fingers trace the flowers on her duvet: red, orange and yellow tulips, and a lattice of Provence blue. She writes about plants dancing to a secret beat. She writes about a big sun in a pinking sky. She writes about a green queen and another domain. She writes what she can't express in words. She writes about Nick.

Eleven

Time is a jester, a magician with his bag of tricks—time extends and compresses, inverts and reverts plays with nature—an Autumn sun scales a summer sky and time bends back in memory to the past, or races forward to a time when the summer's gone.

Twelve

Yellow sun, blue sky, and water first brought Daniel into Lena's life. They met in the Amazon when she went for a three-month stint to do field research on the Balinas Rojas, the nearly extinct pink river dolphin. Daniel was in the Amazon filming the pink river dolphin for the BBC.

It was equatorial summer, and a thick wetness hung in the air. Lena's first impression stepping out of the airport terminal was of a riotous green. Vines curled around the steel girders of the airport terminal as though bent on reclaiming what man had made.

Outside of the terminal, a van was waiting curbside to take her to the home of a local scientist, an expert on the pink river dolphin. Lena had been corresponding with this scientist for two years hoping she could help save this nearly extinct species.

As the van left the small town of Leticia and drove deeper into the Colombian jungle, Lena briefly wondered what she or anyone could do to save a species. Flocks of red and blue Macaw and brightly colored Amazonian parrots canopied trees. All around her the forest was literally teeming with flora, fauna, and insects. She was surprised to realize that in its own way, Nature is as aggressive as man, maybe even more so. How long would it take, she wondered, for these vines to take over the road? Or even the van? She shuddered, looking over her shoulder. The road behind them was empty. The vast jungle felt omnipresent—an otherworldly presence that could transport her at its will to some other place that she couldn't even begin to imagine. Caught in this reverie, she could almost imagine ancient civilizations disappearing under the vast green dome of the jungle.

When the van finally arrived at the scientist's hacienda

almost two hours later, Lena had to shake herself out of her strange mood. Large iron gates opened to admit her into a large, though sparse, courtyard. Lena jumped when the gates clanged shut.

Looking up, she spied a small huddle of pale-faced people already gathered in a room at the top of the outdoor stairs. As she climbed the stairs, she caught the scientist's eye and smiled at him.

He excused himself quickly, and met her outside, kissing her on both cheeks. "Mi amor, how delightful to meet you in person finally. You are even more beautiful than your pictures." Lena blushed. With his arm still around her, she was on the verge of telling him about her trip when he interrupted, speaking now in a hushed Spanish. He told her that a BBC film crew had come to film the dolphins and that she might help if she had time—to watch the crew to make sure they didn't harass the dolphins or disturb them too much. "Can you do this for me? I don't trust them."

Lena glanced over the scientist's shoulder at the group in the room. "Of course. I'll make sure they don't get too close."

"Good. I will tell them that you are here to do research and that I promised you the use of the boat as well. And since I only have one boat to spare, you'll all have to go out together. I doubt they'll object," he added, his smile dimpling.

Lena followed the scientist back into the room where he introduced her to the crew.

"As I was saying," he remarked when they had all seated themselves again in the large sparsely furnished room, "in the Amazon, the pink dolphin is revered, though rarely seen. The dolphin's habitat has been destroyed, mainly by fishermen, but also by the construction on the river. They are desperate to avoid human contact and have of late become aggressive, and bite."

To Lena's right a man in a black t-shirt and jeans sat slightly apart from the group, staring quizzically at the scientist's photographs. His face, though stubbled, was delicate and sharply defined.

"I'm not sure you can do it," the scientist said to the man. "But it's your money—or I should say, the BBC's. They, these dolphins are very hard to film. I've been working with them for nearly fifteen years, and even I only have a few good pictures," the scientist said.

The man in the black t-shirt bent forward, his elbows on his knees. His dark wavy hair fell forward over his forehead, but he didn't bother to brush it back. The eyes of Lena's future husband were focused; they seemed to absorb the light of the photograph—the pink and orange sherbet swirl of sky, the gray river.

For five weeks Lena and the crew lived in a small hut on stilts in the murky water of the Great River. No electricity, no running water, baths in the river each day. Daybreak brought the scents of honey and dew, eerie whistles, weeping. In the shallows of the river, giant trees bent their hairy arms to scoop the sunlight. Within the first week swarms of mosquitoes ate the tender skin of the British crew, making them sick—not sick enough to make them stay in the hut, but sick enough that they weren't much help on the boat. Lena remained unharmed. Each day she sat in the boat's tiny dinghy hoping for another peek at the pink river dolphin. Lulled by repetitious swaying of the river and the sun beating on her back, her eyes glued to the surface line of the water (pink dolphins barely breach and were hard to see), the otherworldly feeling of the river sank into her. The pink river dolphin was considered to be a deity by the local Ticuna Indians, and she hoped that somehow she could help preserve its existence.[1] Despite the sick crew, Daniel pushed on, doing the best he could. Gradually, the crew became sicker, and Lena took on the duties of assistant to the cameraman, helping out in whatever roles the others could barely manage or no longer do. Daniel clung to her in an odd way. In the boat she stayed close to him, supporting his back in the choppy water, giving him the steady hand he needed to film the murky shapes of the

[1] The *Balinas Rojas* and the *Baji* dolphin in China are the only fresh water dolphins in the world. The *Baji* are now believed to be extinct.

pink dolphin below. Each evening, with mud-streaked limbs, she jumped into the river to take the rope Daniel threw from the boat as he maneuvered to shore. Together they carried gear from boat to hut, silent but at ease with each other. The rest of the crew barely managed to crawl inside the hut.

Daniel was shy; he barely spoke, even to the crew, though he seemed more sweet than stern. He had the ability to meld into the background and wait until nature resumed its course, unaware of his presence. He wove his way through the animal world, his camera capturing crystalline moments of life. Under a green canopy of heat and moisture, battling to save something that perhaps couldn't be saved, Lena fell in love with Daniel. She loved him, as she later told Isaiah, because of his heart, his shyness, and because he needed her to love him. She believed that if he needed her he would never leave her.

When they married six months later, Lena paused only once in her steps toward the altar—only when the words remember me flashed through her mind. Ignoring them, she took her about-to-be-husband's hand and smiled at him. When they kissed after their vows, she felt a surge of security—something she hadn't felt in a long time. With Daniel, she thought she'd finally found the mooring she'd lost when her mother died.

Lena and Daniel had been married only a year when Daniel persuaded her to go on a trip to a small island off Tasmania to film black tiger snakes for National Geographic. "I don't want to be without you for the two months I'll be gone," he said.

On the day before Christmas, in Australia's summer, their small bi-plane touched down just past dawn and taxied toward a yellow sun that rose in a sky so large it met the sea and swallowed the earth.

A cold southern wind blew off the ocean, and she felt chilled despite the summer sun. Daniel put his arm around her shoulders and hugged her close. Their gear sat in a pile beside them as the small plane taxied off toward the sun.

"I thought you said it was a paradise of white sandy

beaches and sun," she said, shivering as she looked around at the brown soil, which was full of thistle and a thick weed she couldn't name.

He shrugged. "I lied so you would come."

She was stunned, but said nothing—she was still in the honeymoon stage of her marriage.

For two months they lived on the deserted island—helping each other survive the difficult terrain. Birds burrowed under the surface of the dusty soil, creating nests where bird and snake, predator and prey, lived together. Daniel had come to film the interaction between the island's black tiger snake and the mutton birds on which they fed. The black tiger snake, passive, big, and poisonous—the third most poisonous snake in the world—fed only one month a year on mutton bird chicks.

The birds, raven-like in appearance, flew down from the Aleutian Islands in the far north to breed and feed their young.

For the first few weeks Lena felt afraid—it seemed that every few steps either she or Daniel or sometimes both would break through the thin layer of soil that covered each burrow. As they worked from dawn until dusk carting their gear across the delicate terrain, she worried constantly about the snake's venom. And the chicks—fat, fluffy balls of fur—who would squeak when her foot broke through their nest.

But as the days wore on, she gradually gained courage at Daniel's urging to step more confidently, to better judge the solidity of the ground under her feet. She helped camel Daniel's gear from dusty burrow to water's edge while he shot reel after reel of film.

One morning they used canned lights to capture the birds as they flew out over the ocean at daybreak to hunt for their young. Lena was lying on her belly, holding the canned-lights and waiting for Daniel to give her the signal.

"Hurry," she pleaded, trying not to think of the snakes in the burrows beneath her.

"Now!" Daniel shouted, just as the sun broke the horizon. Thousands of birds gracefully rose into the air.

Lena watched in awe, holding the lights steady. And then, horrified, she watched as the birds suddenly turned and rushed back at her. They landed on her head, hit her back and even knocked the lights from her hands as they landed on the ground around her.

"Turn the lights off!" Daniel was screaming, but she couldn't find them among the mass of birds that flocked around her—nothing but feathers, wings, beaks, scaly legs and dander that flew into her eyes, nose and mouth. She inched forward on her belly through feathers and down until her fingers touched metal and she could push the off switch. Someone was still screaming and she realized it was her. She couldn't stop.

Daniel waded through the birds and finally reached her. He cradled her in his arms, shushing her. "It's okay. Did they hurt you?" When she was finally able to calm herself, she shook her head. "They thought you were the sun," he said. "I didn't realize that would happen." The birds were calm; they sat staring at her, as though waiting for her cue. For some reason, this made her burst out crying again—she felt foolish and scared and for some reason, at fault.

"Did I hurt any of them?" She asked sitting up.

"Don't worry about them," Daniel said rocking her until she calmed down. "I will never let anything hurt you. Never."

She stared at her husband, wondering how she had been so lucky to find a man like him.

13. France 1965

The man next door was renovating his barn into a house. Every winter morning when it wasn't raining, at sunrise he was at it with a power drill and sledge hammer. The barn, like all the buildings in the village, had walls of stone two meters thick.

From her bed Lena could hear her Père yell at the man. Always the same. "Damn you! My daughter needs her sleep! Wait 'til a civilized hour!" That was her signal to crawl out of bed.

When she entered the kitchen in her pink pajamas, her Père had the wooden shutters thrown open and was leaning out the window. The neighbor, Christian, was standing below, yelling back exchanging insults. She wasn't afraid; she knew her Père was having fun in that way adults do. He took an old tomato and threw it at the man's barn. Then he took yesterday's *mâche* and showered it down on the man's head. The green leaves looked quite pretty falling through the winter morning sun.

"*Bâtard*!" Her father slammed the shutters shut. Beneath his frown was a tiny smile. "Today I was trying to finish a love scene, a romantic interlude, when that imbecile started his drilling and ruined the mood. May pigs shit on his head every day!"

"Papa," she said, taking his hand.

"*Ma petite puce*. Did that nasty man wake you?"

She shook her head. She was always happy to hear him yelling when she got up. If instead she got up in silence, in the quiet of the morning before the church bells rang, before the man started hammering, and if she went to the front room where Père had his desk and his daybed, a fire already started, he would frown or, worse, not notice her. She'd stand quietly for a very long time before he'd look up. She didn't like it when he was lost in a world that excluded her, talking to himself, one pencil in his mouth, another used to scribble on the page.

"*As-tu faim?*

She nodded.

"Lena, where are your words this morning? That man has taken all the words from this house!" He banged a pot on the stove. The match he was using to light the pilot burned out. He struck another. And then another. "Get dressed," he finally bellowed. "We'll go to the café for breakfast."

"*Papa, je t'adore*," she said, taking his hand. Even at this early age she'd learned how to sooth her father.

He looked down at her tangled brown hair. "Ah, my petite. Your poor Père has a temper. Come here." He pulled her onto his lap. "Vivianne is coming today for an early Christmas celebration. Isn't that a nice surprise?"

She nodded, her thumb in her mouth.

"Père wanted to surprise her with his new play. But that imbecile next door has been banging all week and Père hasn't been able to write. The animals will have calves with three heads this year from all that banging. Just wait until spring and he has to bring a deformed goat down from the hills, he will see!"

"Sophie?"

He kissed the top of her head. "Non, ma petite, Sophie is dead. Remember Père told you? In October? She was looking for some lost goats when she slipped and fell. Her son, Christian, takes care of the mouton now."

"Sophie était là-bas," she said, pointing to the barn.

"Yes, Sophie is there—her spirit, at least, is always with her moutons."

"*Maman était ici hier soir*." She pointed to a chair in the corner of the room.

"No, my sweet, Maman wasn't here last night, she hasn't been home in over four months—since summer."

She shook her head and walked to the chair. "*Ici,*" she said again, more insistent this time.

"No Lina, *Maman n' était pas ici hier soir.*" He took her hand and led her back to the table.

"Maman will come soon, maybe for Christmas, but this weekend Vivianne will visit. On Sunday as usual." He sat down beside her. "I will make you breakfast and then we will wash your hair and make you *très jolie* for Vivianne, *oui*?"

She nodded.

"How about your yellow dress and blue sweater—the one with the lambs that Sophie knitted you last year? *C'est très jolie.*"

"*Oui*, papa." She picked up the bread and sausage her father placed before her. Vivianne was nice and had brought her a doll last time, but it was Maman she wanted. Maman she loved better than anyone else—except of course, her dear Père.

But Maman did come; she surprised Père with a weekend visit. All Saturday, Lena watched Père pace in the front room back and forth, back and forth. Maman laughed, complained she was bored, and sometimes shouted back at Père. Père had been shouting about Lena to her Maman, and this scared her.

She was drawn to her mother, but also a little afraid. Maman was so beautiful—her hair like the gold of her bracelets. Her blue dress seemed so delicate compared to the village women in their baggy cotton shifts. And she smelled so good. Like Parisian parfum her mother said. But there was Père, redfaced and yelling again. To Lena it seemed that he wanted maman to go away and leave Lena behind—which she did each time anyway.

In fact, her father was asking her mother for a divorce and custody of his daughter. Her mother flatly refused.

"You didn't even want her!" Père said.

"Don't be silly," her mother said. "Women say that all the time—it was the jitters from the thought of childbirth."

"You're never here. You didn't even come home for her birthday."

Maman shrugged. “She’s too young to know about things like birthdays. She’s my daughter and I won’t give her up.”

“I will sue you for adultery.”

She studied her nails. “You will lose your daughter. They will never take her from me.” She looked up. “And if you try, I will take her to America to live with my parents.”

“Is it money you want? I will sell the house.”

“Don’t be absurd, where would you and Lena live?”

“I’ll rent out Christian’s barn, he’s making it into a house.”

“Jean-Paul. She’s my daughter and I will see her when I want and for as long as I choose. I like it the way it is. I have a home to come to when I need a break from location. And, I can come and go as I please.”

“You’re an evil woman.”

“But I gave you a perfect child.”

“She will hate you one day.”

Her Maman laughed. “Come here, baby girl,” she said to Lena.

Lena crawled out from under the kitchen table. Her mother took her in her arms and lifted her up. “Oof, you’re getting to be a big girl. Do you hate your Maman?” she asked, peering into Lena’s face.

Lena shook her head.

“Give Maman a kiss.”

Lena kissed her.

“You see, she is my child. She even kisses on cue,” Maman said, laughing. Lena laughed too. “You will be an actress yet, my sweet girl.”

“Over my dead body,” Père said.

“Don’t tempt me.” She stood up and took Lena’s hand. “Shall we go for a walk?”

Lena nodded.

“Your Père is in a foul mood. Let’s walk down to the bakers for fresh bread while père prepares us lunch. Kiss kiss,” she said to Père, kissing the air before she slammed the door behind her.

That was yesterday. Maman and Père had fought again last night—Lena could hear them from her bed. And then this morning her Maman left right after the church bells rang. She walked out the door, with her red suitcase in hand without saying goodbye. In her pajamas, Lena ran out the door shouting Maman!

Her Maman turned and scooped her up in her arms. Tears ran down her maman's cheeks.

"Poor Maman," Lena said.

"It's okay, baby girl, I'll be back soon. You be a good girl for Père. Maybe Maman will take you to Paris soon where she is filming. Would you like that?"

She nodded. "Maman, don't leave," she said.

"I have to, baby girl, but I'll be back soon. I promise."

And then it seemed that in no time Vivianne was there. Vivianne with her dark hair scooped into a bun and plain yellow cotton dress that smelled more of onions than parfum. It wasn't that Lena didn't like Vivianne, it was that Vivianne, as nice as she was, wasn't her mother. And at that moment, didn't seem like second best.

Perhaps that's why Lena kicked her hard in the shin shortly after she arrived. Vivianne had been leaning into the car getting the groceries she always brought, when Lena walked out of the house and right up to the car, and bam! She kicked her so hard the bunch of flowers Vivianne held in her hand fell against the door of her white Citroën. Vivianne was stunned, but not as stunned as Lena when Père spanked her.

"Say you're sorry," he said, holding Lena by the forearm.

She twisted and turned, yelped once and held her breath.

"Lena."

She squeezed her eyes shut and tried to squirm out of Père's grasp by sitting on the ground.

"Her mother was here this weekend and left this morning."

"Rita was here? You never said."

"I didn't know until just before. She called me from the train station."

"And?"

"I love you, Vivianne. I always have."

"She said no."

He shook his head. Lena was lying on the ground. "I can't have custody if I divorce her. She'll take her to America to her parents if I insist."

"Lena," Père said, bending down. "*Ma petite puce*, will you please give Vivianne a kiss and say you're sorry?"

Lena stared at him stonily.

"*Mon dieu*, she is her mother's daughter."

"Don't be silly, Jean-Paul, she's only three." Vivianne bent down until she was face to face with Lena. "I know you didn't mean to hurt me. Will you help me bring the flowers in?"

Lena stared at her. She wanted to give in, but she didn't want to lose her sense of her mother so shortly after she'd left. Vivianne had come to visit every week for as long as Lena could remember. Every Sunday Lena waited by the window and ran outside as soon as she spied the white Citroën pulling up the lane. But today her beloved Maman had been here, and it seemed to Lena that her mother left because Vivianne came.

Père bent down. "Why did you kick Vivianne?" he asked.

Lena shook her head.

"Lena?"

But Lena couldn't answer.

She was Père's girl. His companion. She loved him—but she was only three.

Fourteen

The dust on the streets of San Jose blows up into Nick's face, leaving him feeling dirty all over. It is siesta time, and the shutters of all the houses are drawn tight. He turns down a narrow alley that is silent except for the clip-clap of his shoes. He's headed for school, the cinder block building where he's studying Spanish (a three-week accelerated program) in the back streets of San Jose. Why am I here? he wonders, kicking a can. Did he really need to become more proficient in Spanish? Or is it that he needed to plan a vacation and this was the best he could do? A tinge of fear creeps into his belly. Why is it his choices are never quite right? He's always left with this feeling of—

He kicks a flattened juice carton and watches it skitter over the cobblestones, coming to rest against two abandoned hubcaps. He came to Costa Rica for reasons that just two months ago seemed reasonable. Was it a colleague at the World Bank who suggested that his Spanish was a little too formal? It seemed a good idea when he made the plans; he and Hildy rarely traveled together—unless, of course, she joined him in one of the more upscale locales he frequented for Bank business. She preferred, he knew, the swank of a five-star hotel to the ancient character of a history-ladened place. And so he usually traveled on his own, frequently to England to see his sister, but even that he couldn't do all the time.

When he planned the trip to Costa Rica he didn't mind the idea of traveling alone for vacation; in the back of his mind he knew there was always home, a distant point on the spectrum to go back to. Now he realizes that home is no different from Costa Rica and the other locales he has frequented by himself. In some way that he can't quite articulate, his time away and his time at home are both quiet—

they've flattened into a straight line.

He swings open the metal door of the school and steps into the empty, dark hallway. Odd they don't lock up, he thinks while he props the door with a rock to allow sunlight into the hallway. When he flips the light switch, nothing happens. The neighborhood must be having a power outage again. Cautiously, he makes his way to his classroom.

He'd been cautious when he first started dating Hildy, not wanting to get embroiled in the same kind of emotional conundrum he'd experienced when married, but Hildy's tendency to stay on the surface of most topics helped him relax more than he had at any time since he was young. Compared to Hildy, Nick felt he wasn't the emotional pygmy he had come to view himself as during his years with his ex-wife. In fact, up to now, he's quite enjoyed staying distant from the emotional chaos of that other kind of relationship—where couples get enmeshed and dependent on each other. He always thought he could return to the emotional fray if, and when, he wanted. Now he's not so sure.

Is Lena back yet? he wonders, glancing down at his wristwatch (it's too dim to see the dial). Her assistant said she was out for the morning but would likely be back before noon.

He finds his classroom and grabs the book he forgot (a book of Spanish poems he had thrown on the floor beneath his seat) and hurries back down the empty corridor. A very clear picture of Lena sitting in her office fills his mind. Chills creep up his spine. The picture is so clear, so full-bodied, it's like she's sitting right in front of Nick—like he can reach out and touch her, almost smell her, even. How does she do that? he wonders—enters him as though she is part of him.

With a loud bang, the door he propped open slams shut, startling him. Jumpy now, he heads back down the hallway toward the door. The silence in the hall is creepy, and the corridor suddenly seems longer than he remembers. For one irrational moment, he panics, thinking he won't find his way back out into the sunshine. He knows this thought is irrational, and he quickens his steps, half running. Tiny beads of sweat trickle down his temples as he looks for the door. The dust has settled as grit in his mouth. Bloody hell, where's the fucking door? He must have passed it.

He retraces his steps, groping the wall in the dark, but he can't find the door. He stops to collect himself and think. Something that isn't quite sound but more like Lena's presence captures his attention. Nick? He strains to hear. Lena? He looks down the hall and sees a strip of light, almost like under a curtain on a stage. He strides toward that light, and suddenly, bam—he pushes so hard on the metal bar of the door that it slams open, shaking the cinder block wall.

In the sunlight, Nick looks around expecting to see Lena, but no one is there. Embarrassed, he closes the door and leans on it, wiping his brow. The wind probably slammed it shut. Or an alley cat creeping by. He starts to shake a bit and then tells himself don't be daft, it was just a dark hallway and your imagination. But the odd feeling persists. He gropes in his mind for the image of Lena that felt so compelling just minutes ago, but he can't conjure her. He is alone with his thoughts and the fear that took hold, shook him up, and propelled him out the door.

Three days later, Nick arrives back in D.C. , disembarking into a chilly, nearly empty terminal. The air is so cold he shivers in his thin red windbreaker. In Costa Rica it was so hot, the air was vacuumed dry after rain.

He quickens his step, wondering whether he's missed something crucial with Lena by being away. Why hadn't he simply changed his plans once he met Lena? And what of Daniel? Can I do to some man what I wouldn't want done to myself? The thought lingers until he dismisses it, telling himself that surely Lena is living a lie. Certainly, what's between them is unique enough to show her that.

Nick stops near a bank of payphones to dial Lena's cell.

When she answers, his voice falters. For once, she sounds surprised to hear from him.

"I'm at the airport . . . I just got in. I want to see you."

"Me too," she whispers.

"When?"

"Nick, Daniel's home. I . . . we have plans tonight and tomorrow."

His throat aches in an odd way, making it difficult to speak. "I leave for Venezuela on Monday. Can you meet me for lunch before my flight?"

"But Nick, it's already Saturday evening. Why even come home?"

"It's complicated to fly within Latin America and I wanted to see you." His voice sounds calm to his ears. "Can I see you on Monday for lunch before I leave?"

"Can we have breakfast too?" she teases.

He smiles to himself and tells her about his meetings on Monday. They make plans to meet in front of his office at eleven o'clock.

"You'll recognize me by the flower I'll wear in my hair . . . just over my left ear . . . a lavender rose."

He laughs. "Lena, it's only been three weeks. . . but yes, *mi amor*, I do miss you. "

The weekend passes like an endless day from Lena's childhood when she would wait and wait for something to happen. She tries to focus on the dinner party she and Daniel go to on Saturday night, the movie they watch on Sunday, the chores they do together, but her mind keeps wandering. She feels guilty and not guilty at the same time. At dinner on Sunday (they are sharing a pizza), Daniel catches her staring into space. Her mind keeps circling back to the excitement she feels, and yet, when she tries to pinpoint the exact thing that makes her feel this way, there is nothing. Just a brief meeting with Nick. Yet she feels like a kid who is about to return to a favorite place. "You okay?" Daniel asks her. She nods and takes such a big bite of pizza that the cheese slops, making a mess of her face. She wipes her mouth and tries to contain herself for Daniel's sake.

When Monday arrives, her nerves are set on edge. Perhaps that's why she gets to the lobby of the office building where Nick works, a little late. She's just about to ask the attendant if he's seen Nick, when Nick calls her name.

She turns. For a moment, she just stares. Then, with a suppressed smile, she points at his Glen-Plaid blazer. She's wearing one, too.

"I'm not surprised," he says, grinning openly. "One beast with two backs."

He takes her hand, heedless of who might see them, and leads her out the building and down the street to Café Atlantico, a popular Brazilian restaurant.

They are led to a table near a large window.

"Will you have a caipirinha?" he asks after they are seated.

She nods. "So why did you come home?"

"Honestly?"

"Yes."

"To see you."

Light beams from her face.

"I want time to be together," Nick says. He studies her face, the way she becomes more beautiful when she's with him. For a moment he wonders, how would I describe the look on her face? Surprised, he realizes it's joy. He takes her fingers and squeezes them tight.

She opens her mouth to speak, but says nothing.

"What?" he asks.

She shakes her head, smiling. Her face draws close to his. Her eyes are shining, her chin tilted upwards, her lips curved with fullness. "How long will you be gone?" she asks, finally.

"A week." He turns his head, surveys the restaurant, and then looks back at her. "We're being watched," he says, nodding sideways.

She looks up to see an older couple at the next table watching them with a knowing smile on their face. Two waiters stand at the bar staring in their direction with a look on their faces that says they, too, wished they were in love. In this moment, it seems to Lena that she and Nick and the onlookers are all part of an endless continuum.

Lena and Nick talk about his trip to Venezuela, her upcoming trip to Malaysia and Singapore, events at their respective offices, people they know, books they've read. They are drawing out their lunch, trying to slow down time in order to linger together as long as they can.

"Lena," he says gently when she's finished her story about work. "It's time."

"Time?" She looks puzzled.

"I've got to catch my plane."

"Oh, sorry, I forgot." She gives him a smile so tender his heart leaps out of his chest. He is about to say something that reflects back what he sees when the lamp over their table flickers, leaving them for a moment in shadow. When the light returns, the look on her face is replaced by something more guarded, making him wonder briefly if he imagined something more.

He kisses her knuckles. "You're beautiful," is all he says.

After lunch, Lena goes home rather than back to the office. She enters the house and calls Daniel's name. The dogs rush at her in greeting, but she hears no reply—only the tick tock of their grandfather clock. She bends down to pat her dogs, a half-suppressed smile still on her face.

Slowly, she climbs the stairs, her jacket trailing behind along the banister.

In her room, she flops on the bed and pulls a pillow to her chest. She raises one foot straight up in the air, pointing her toes at the ceiling. She is so lost in her thoughts she doesn't hear Daniel come into the room.

He grabs her toes. "What's up with you?" he asks, looming over her.

Startled, she kicks at his hand. "Nothing, I just got sick of being in the office." She sits up and brushes the hair out of her face.

"What's for dinner?" he asks.

"What are you cooking?"

He studies her without answering.

She looks away.

"Why are you home early?" he asks, but she demurs. "Come downstairs and help cook," she says, jumping off the bed.

With his back to her, he searches through his dresser drawers.

"Daniel?

"In a minute."

Frowning, she goes downstairs.

In the kitchen, she chops tomatoes, her knife rapping loudly against the cutting board. "What are you doing?" she yells from the kitchen door.

From their bedroom his voice sounds muffled. "Nothing," he says.

She hovers in the doorway, her heart ricocheting in her chest. For some reason she thinks of her journal. "Come and help with dinner." Her voice sounds too high-pitched.

A few minutes later he enters the kitchen, pilfering a black olive from the wooden cutting board. She asks what took him so long and hands him a paring knife. He lays the knife back on the counter and asks what's for dinner and whether she is excited about their trip. Their conversation circles around like this until finally he says, casually, "Did you see Nick today?"

Startled, she looks up at him and then away. It is she who usually knows what he is doing, not vice versa. "We had lunch."

"You never mentioned it."

"He just got back from Costa Rica. He called and asked if I could have lunch."

"He called you at the office?"

"No, he called my cell."

"Seems odd."

She turns back to chopping the vegetables for the pizza. "Odd?"

"You could have invited me, unless of course, he called you at the last minute."

Frowning, she turns to look at him. "You don't like to read and you've never shown any interest in our discussions about books before."

He pops another olive in his mouth and turns to the fridge for a beer. "Is that all you talk about? Books?"

She brushes the pizza crust with olive oil. "Of course not. But that's the basis of our friendship. Why are you asking so many questions?"

Daniel sits down on a bar stool. "When's your next book club meeting?"

"He left today for Venezuela. He won't be back until we've left for Asia."

"Does Hildy know you had lunch?"

She turns her back to him. "We had a brief lunch at Café Atlantico. Please set the table. And stop questioning me like this."

Behind her he is silent. She turns to look at him.

His eyes are moist.

She lays down her butcher knife and wipes her hand on her apron. "Look," she says, "I'm sorry. I'm on edge—maybe it's the trip. I have too much to do before we leave."

He pulls away from her.

"Wait."

He pauses in the kitchen doorway.

She wraps her arms around his slim waist, lays her head on his chest. "I love you. You're my husband. There is nothing for you to worry about. I promise."

Fifteen

Over the next few days, the clock speeds up—winds around so fast that too soon she and Daniel are heading toward Malaysia, on a plane, a flash of light in a translucent sky while Nick is only a speck on some distant horizon.

Lena and Daniel arrive in Penang, the Chinese capital of Malaysia, just before dawn in mid-November. They are there for two weeks of vacation before they travel to Singapore where Lena has work meetings. Even before they deplane, the heat punctuates the cabin, making Lena gasp. What will it be like when the sun finally rises? Normally she sleeps during long flights, but she was restless the whole trip, and now is tired.

She stands, crouching over so not to hit her head on the overhead compartment. Though the plane has just landed, the aisle is already packed with tired people pushing toward the door. She steps her way into the line. Behind her, a woman in a black veil is holding an infant, with two small whiny children clinging to her robes. Lena watches as the woman tries to maneuver a too-large bag from under the seat. "Daniel, help her," Lena says, taking their green carry-on bag from his hand. Daniel says something to the woman and then hoists her maroon bag on his shoulder. The woman also hands him two small dark blue flight bags stuffed so full of magazines, toys, and airline blankets that neither could be zipped.

"I guess she thinks I'm the porter," Daniel mumbles out of the side of his mouth.

Lena gently pushes him forward warning him to be quiet.

In the terminal, a sea of dark veils, white shirts, and brown faces act as a barricade to the deplaning passengers. People are waving and shouting, some stand on tiptoe looking for their friends or family, some hold placards with names, looking for clients. The smell of too many bodies, food, trash, and tropical moisture permeates the air, making Lena feel sick. The sun, barely a slit on the horizon when the plane skidded to its stop, has moved up and over the sky at an astonishing speed.

Lena feels rubbery, like she'd been turned upside down; the floor rushes up to her face. Dust flies into her face, not from a breeze but from some invisible place, while the heat punctuates the air, making it hard to breathe.

She squats down.

"You okay?" Daniel asks, kneeling beside her.

"Yes, I just feel . . . strange. Like the floor is going to slap me in the face."

"That's jet leg."

She smiles sheepishly. "I must be getting old. With all the travel I've done, I've never felt this before. It's horrid."

He helps her up. "You've been lucky. But then, we know you're not normal." He grins at her.

She glances at him appreciatively. I hope I don't lose him. Her adrenaline rushes at this sudden thought. No, she thinks firmly. It's just a thought, nothing real.

Daniel leads her protectively out of the terminal and into a waiting taxi.

The days pass while Lena and Daniel tour the city on foot. It doesn't take Lena long to realize that the heat, dust, and sun are small things compared to the construction sounds that rock the city. *Kaboom. Kabang*. Morning, noon, and night giant wrecking balls thud against beautiful wooden Chinese-style buildings, taking down the old in the name of progress. In three days, Lena has counted more than a hundred wrecking balls. She wonders where the money comes from for the heavy equipment. In the rubble and dust, a mirage emerges splattered across giant billboards: a new generation of skyscrapers, glassed exclamation points. A hunger for modernity has outdistanced the once-polished teak boards of the old temples and the four- and five-family homes that had existed for generations. To Lena, there is something sorrowful in the city's movement skywards. "We could almost be in any Midwestern city," she says to Daniel. He shrugs; he doesn't seem to mind. But as the days pass, the demolished spaces leave her feeling empty inside, like a wide-open vista that has no perspective because of the vast distance.

Lena can't admit to herself that it's more than the city that causes her sadness. She hasn't spoken to Nick since that day at Café Atlantico, even though he's left her messages on her work voicemail. She's been determined to build a bridge back to her husband. And yet with Daniel by her side, the empty spaces of the demolished buildings occupy her mind, making her silent inside and out.

Almost a week into their trip, to escape the heat, she and Daniel step into a small store selling silk scarves, wooden elephant marionettes, and other trinkets. They poke among the wares—she buys a pink silk scarf. When they can no longer linger, they exit the air-conditioned space, the bell on the door jingling as they enter the dusty, noisy hub of downtown Penang.

With barely a word between them (who can talk in all this heat and noise?), they walk several miles until finally they stop at the intricate gates of a Buddhist temple. A few tourists loiter, taking photographs and talking loudly. Two red Fu dogs stand guarding black gates. "I think this is the one we're looking for," Daniel says, pointing to a passage in their guide book.

The noonday sun slants against the bright white temple walls, creating a glare in the courtyard. Lena spies a small sanctuary tucked back beyond the gates in a corner among the green shade of ancient twisted trees.

She slips through the gate, crosses the courtyard, and enters the darkened space of the sanctuary, taking off her tennis shoes at the door. They are alone in the space, so she crouches down on an orange-colored cushion to pray. Hundreds of small manila-colored candles fill the space. Lena stretches out her hand to touch—what? She doesn't know—the image is vaporous.

Beside her Daniel kneels with closed eyes. With her own eyes closed, Lena suddenly knows that his mind is topsy-turvy, that he feels the import of something strong pressing against him, as it does her. She is about to reach across the distance between them, to squeeze his hand and whisper It's okay, when her thoughts ricochet. A scene she can't place presses against her throat until it binds with a familiar kind of pain. A pair of black women's pumps lay before the fire. A woman is singing softly. The woman calls out a name. Lena looks down at the soft balled fist of a child—her fist. The child crawls toward a table, toward a sliver of light between the tablecloth and the floor. The floor is cold beneath her knees. She turns her face to the breath of a giant brown dog. He pads past her and toward the table. Just as she reaches the table, light from the fire falls across her. The woman picks her up, swings her into the air. There you are. I've been looking for you, the woman says. The dog pads up beside her; he licks the woman's hand.

For a long while, Lena remains bowed down trying to make sense of this vision, and the fear that it stirs in the pit of her stomach. Finally, she stands and lays the pink scarf she'd bought that day at the feet of what she hopes is a beneficent god. She exits the shrine without looking at Daniel.

Outside, the heat beats down; the noonday sun nearly blinds her. Before she can reach for her sunglasses, she is retching violently in the dusty soil by the temple gates.

"You okay?" Daniel asks, having exited the temple right after her.

She nods. "It's the heat." She still hasn't told him of the strange images that keep haunting her, nor of the fear they evoke—mostly because they somehow still feel tied to Nick.

He rubs her neck. "There's a bench by those trees." He leads her to the shade.

She wipes her mouth on his white handkerchief, gulps water from the bottle in her leather bag. "I'm okay." Her voice sounds croaked.

She sees fright in Daniel's face and knows that

somehow the wordless fear that has crept into her, now eats at him too. I've done this to us both.

Daniel flags a taxi, keeping a firm hold on her hand.

Silently, they ride across town.

Two days later, Lena is lying on their hotel bed reading a book. She looks at her watch and stretches her limbs, then places the book on the bedside table. The hotel is elegant in a rustic way. Bamboo curtains bar the sun, mottled azure walls create an underwater effect, beige terracotta tiles cool her feet. She and Daniel have always wanted to visit Malaysia to experience the culture before it was ruined by the rampant industrialization taking hold of the world in the guise of free trade. But now that she is here, now that she's counted seven McDonald's restaurants in a two hour walk through Penang, seen temples turned into money machines, and witnessed the birth of a whole city of skyscrapers, the allure has given way. She picks at the warp and weave of the bamboo rug. She declined to go with Daniel to photograph the full moon over Penang, having had another one of her episodes, as she is now referring to her visions to herself. The thing that bothers her the most is that the images that play out in her mind, feel so real, yet she has no memory of the place or the people.

When she stands up, her weight feels disproportionate, like gravity has let go. She steps to her computer and re-reads an email she received from Nick this morning.

From:	Nicolas Block
Date:	January 16
To:	Lena Holloman

Dear L

It is a cold, windy, wet day here in D.C. Sitting before the fire, visions of you flicker across my mind. I had hoped to have more time to myself this long weekend, thinking about us and where we are going, but somehow time slipped away. My thoughts of you excite me. I miss you. I wanted to spend the day before the fire dreaming of you, your arms intertwined around my chest, your legs thrown over mine, me pulling you close. But alas, Hildy committed us to lunch with friends and then her mother is here, so there hasn't been much time to be alone.

The fear you expressed in your voice message yesterday is misplaced. There is nothing wrong here. Everything is normal, except that I miss you more than I thought I would. Tomorrow is Monday and we will finally speak again. I will be in a meeting in the morning until eleven, but I hope to speak with you soon thereafter.

I am yours, N

Shortly after she and Daniel returned from their excursion to the temple two days ago, Lena had called Nick. Though it was nighttime in Penang, in D.C. it was the Saturday morning after Thanksgiving, so she knew he wouldn't be in, but she wanted to express out loud the fear she's felt ever since her arrival in Penang.

Hildy knew.

But according to Nick, apparently not. And in any event, what is there to know? Lena reasons to herself.

She reaches for a pen and paper lying on the white rattan desk. Be back soon, L—She props the note next to the phone, hoping Daniel will see it if he returns while she is gone.

In the lobby, the bellhop points to a bank of phones tucked in a corner behind a painted silk screen.

She dials Nick's number. The clock ticks slowly. The phone against her ear sounds like a conch in her hand, like the sea, when as a child in Los Angeles, she lay in the wet sand waiting for the waves to wash over her.

Nick answers. "Sorry it took me so long to answer. One of the idiots in my office was on the other line from Brazil," he says.

"How are you?" Lena asks.

"Not so good," he says right away. "Hildy found out about us."

"What do you mean, found out about us?"

Nick tells her that a friend of Hildy's saw them together at Café Atlantico. "Hildy put two and two together, and yesterday, she finally confronted me."

Lena's face warms. "We haven't done anything wrong. . . well, hardly anything."

"I know. But for Hildy, two and two equals five. "

Lena hears his words from far away. On the wall next to the phones is a relief sculpture of Medusa, her hair piled on her head like a nest of snakes.

"She told me I was not to see you again or she would leave me."

Lena is silent, lost in her muddled thoughts.

"Lena?"

She's thinking about what it felt like when she lost her mother, and then her grandfather—the pain that lived in her chest for a number of years, and also the feeling of somehow being at fault.

"Can we talk, please?"

She wiggles her toes, wondering what it would feel like to have fins instead of feet. "What's there to talk about?" she says, coming back to herself.

"I don't think I can keep my promise to her," he says softly.

"What about her father? Your job?"

"That's not important—I can always get another job."

Suddenly, she feels buoyant again, like when she's propelled to the surface having held her breath too long under water. She glances at the red Persian rug, the bright yellow and green orchids perched in an oversized glass vase on a nearby table. "What if she leaves you?"

"I'll have to live with my decision. Lena, we haven't accumulated enough memories yet—I can't let you go."

Two women dressed in vivid blue hijabs and matching suits chat quietly a few feet away from Lena. The hotel manager, short, overfed, and formal, smiles as he rocks on his feet.

In her mind, she sees a fire burning in a stone fireplace,

a man standing next to an old black cook stove, a big brown dog.

"It's been too hard already, Lena. I can't lose you."

16. France 1965

The wind beat down on the tile roof of their house like a base drum. Though it was nearly midnight, Lena woke to the sound. Her Père heard her crying in an intermittent break in the sound.

"Vivi," Lena said when Père picked her up.

"It's just the wind, baby girl," Père said cradling her tight. "Vivi will be here this weekend as usual."

"Jamais. Vivi ne reviendra jamais ici, Père."

"Silly girl, of course Vivi will come here again. This is her home too. You must have had a nightmare sweet girl." He pointed out the window. "Look, it's snowing."

She turned her head to look.

"See the white flakes falling in the light of the street lamp?"

She nodded.

"You've never seen snow. Maybe in the morning there will be enough to play."

"Jamais," she said crying louder.

"Ma petite puce, it was just a nightmare. Vivi is okay. Shall we call her on the phone?"

Lena nodded again, still crying. She had once talked to her mother on the phone and the event had fascinated her.

When Père got Vivianne on the line he told her about Lena's nightmare and that she wouldn't stop crying. "See I told you—she loves you."

Père put Lena on the phone.

"I'm okay, sweet baby girl. Vivi's okay."

"No, Vivi! No!" Lena said, almost shrieking.

"Lena. Lena. It's okay. I'm here. Vivi's here. Shall I come see you now? Right now?"

Lena nodded, grasping the phone.

"Baby girl, let me speak to Père, okay?"

Lena nodded and put down the phone.

"Jean-Paul?"

"It was just a nightmare," he said when he picked up the phone.

"I told her I'd come."

"Yes, I told her we'd see you on the weekend."

"No. I told her now, I'll come tonight."

"Vivi, don't be silly, you're in Monaco. The trains have stopped running for the night."

"I'll borrow a car and be there by morning. I can drive it in seven hours."

"Don't be absurd. The roads are dark and windy and the weather is terrible. It was just a nightmare. She'll be okay."

"The weather here isn't bad. And I want to be there, Jean-Paul. I want to be there for her."

"She knows you love her."

"No, it's not that."

"What is it then?"

"Sometimes she just knows. Haven't you noticed?"

"Noticed what? Vivi, you aren't making sense. Vivi—"

"No Jean-Paul, you are the one who isn't making sense. Sometimes you don't see what's right before your eyes."

"I've told you, Rita—"

"This isn't about you or me or Rita. It's about Lena."

"Vivianne—"

"Quit arguing. I'm coming." And with that, she hung up the phone.

Seventeen

No sooner do Lena and Daniel return home from Asia than Lena begins to have nightmares that she can't explain, even to herself. The nightmares make her scream in her sleep but as soon as she awakens she can't remember the dream—only the feeling of dread.

Daniel sits next to her rubbing her back. Her t-shirt, wet from fright, clings to her back. "Wow, let's get this off of you," he says, yanking at her shirt. "You don't want to get chilled."

Lena looks at him wide-eyed, and then curls into his chest. "Give me a moment," she says.

He takes her chin and lifts it. "Can you talk to me?"

She shakes her head, and avoids his eyes.

"What is it?" he asks again, as he has the last two mornings. "This is the third time you've had a nightmare like this. What have you seen?"

But Lena can't tell him. Truth be told, she doesn't know herself what she is dreaming about. All she can remember is that the dream is about Nick. And that each time she dreams this dream she wakes, screaming, No! I can't go through that again!

Perhaps the dreams are why she's avoided meeting Nick, though he called her the day she and Daniel got back and asked when he could see her. She tells herself she's been too busy at work to engage him in more than a cursory way. Or perhaps her hesitancy is due to her loyalty to Daniel. Or because she's had a jittery stomach ever since Penang, when she discovered—no knew even before Nick told her—that Hildy had found out.

Lena has had moments these past five days where she feels like she's falling apart—but she keeps these feelings at bay, so that on the outside she appears like the normal busy Lena.

"Busy day today?" Daniel asks.

"Not too," she says, stripping off her wet clothes and heading toward the shower. "But," she says, turning back to Daniel, just as he says, "Well, then."

She stops him mid-sentence. "I can't."

"Lena—"

"I can't have lunch with you." She knows he hates it when she reads his mind and finishes his sentences, but this morning she is too blown out by her nightmare to care.

"Don't tell me you don't have time. Bloody hell, we were just in Asia for five weeks, and shod it if you worked your ass off at meetings for three of those weeks, not to mention all the prep work you did during our vacation. Bloody bastards. It's Christmas—what about shopping?"

"Shopping?" she asks.

"They don't know that you finished your Christmas shopping six months ago, tell them you need time off for that."

Lena laughs. "Actually, my colleagues probably do know. They certainly know I buy things when I travel." She turns back toward the bathroom. "And our presents closet is infamous," she says as she closes the door.

"You know what I mean," Daniel says, opening the door and entering the quickly steaming bathroom.

"You're sweet to offer, but I can't today," she says, shutting the shower door. "Maybe tomorrow, or better yet Friday."

Daniel frowns. "I have meetings on Friday."

"Well it's not like I don't see you every day," she says from the shower. "We are married, you know."

"Ha, ha, funny. Lena, we don't spend—"

"Daniel, don't start this morning, please. We have dinner tonight with your crowd from Nat Geo, and we have plans with Anita and John tomorrow night. Friday night we can stay home and watch a movie if you want. Or go shopping," she says, shutting off the water.

She opens the shower door. "Now, I've got to get ready. Will you feed the dogs?"

When Daniel leaves the bathroom, Lena sits for a long moment on the edge of the tub with her head in her hands. She hasn't told Daniel she is meeting Nick today for lunch. Why not? This question circles around in her head, but no answer comes. It's not that she wants to be deceptive—rather, she doesn't know how to broach the subject without conflict. Daniel gets pissed when she has a social engagement with anyone when he's not included—at least that's what she tells herself. I have the right, she thinks, getting up off the tub. But she knows even as she thinks this that she's missed the mark. Something is making her have nightmares. Something is propelling her toward Nick. What if the two things are the same?

The Metro hurls though a dark tunnel, shunting side-to-side at each bend in the track, jostling passengers who are lost in thought and distant from one another. Lena is crammed in a seat next to a burly man who takes up more than his fair share of space. She glances at her reflection in the mirrored window of the train. Her hat is askew. She pulls her cap further down on her head and sits up taller in her seat.

When the train comes to a stop at Metro Center, Lena stands to leave but her exit is blocked by muffled torsos and coated arms. Pushing through a tired crowd disinclined to move, she finally makes it off the train just as the doors close.

On the station platform she looks around for Nick but he is nowhere in sight. The cavernous beige walls of the Metro station both condense and magnify the cacophony of rush hour. When they spoke yesterday, Nick asked Lena to accompany him to National Airport. "It's not much, but it's something, and I want to see you," he said. "I'll be in Ottawa for two days of meetings."

She agreed because he sounded so hopeful, because she felt guilty about avoiding him, and because, honestly, she wants to see him—she's just afraid.

On tiptoe, Lena cranes her neck to see over the crowd. Finally, she spies Nick across the platform. He's been leaning against a column watching her search for him, a mischievous smile on his face. She waves and pushes through the crowd.

When she approaches, his repressed grin turns into a full smile. "You look beautiful," he says.

She laughs. "You're looking dapper yourself." (Her mind registers his pleasing scent.) "But why didn't you wave or say yoo-hoo or something so I knew where you were?"

"I'm British," he says. "And I wanted to capture the picture of you standing on the platform looking for me."

"Capture? Why?"

"For something to hold onto in the future," he says, sounding wistful.

She laughs. "You make it sound like I'm going to die soon or something."

Nick looks at her with a solemn, almost pained expression she can't decipher. "Shall we make our way to the next train?" he asks, looping his arm through hers.

She places her hand on the nubby wool of his coat, and lets him tug her along.

In the crowded train they stand close together, delighting in the sensation of body pressed to body. Her new hat, a soft, black wool felt pulled down around her face, French style, brushes against his skin. She feels coy in her hat, nestled up close to him. His striped wool scarf dangles over her arm. She's light-hearted, effervescent, like bubbles blown through a child's pink plastic wand. She knows they both want this moment of rhythm with the train to go on and on.

At National Airport they depart. Chill wind bites their faces, vaporizes their breath as they mount the stairs to the terminal. Once inside, they both unbutton their coats and unwind their scarves. Normally the gray peeling walls of the terminal would depress Lena, but today the old terminal seems to catch and radiate warmth as she and Nick move down the hall.

At the check-in counter, Nick learns his flight has been delayed an hour or more. Lena steps back from the counter hardly disguising her delight. They decide to look for a quiet corner to occupy, but when they round a bank of pay phones, Nick stops. He takes out his cell. "I forgot, I need to make a call—do you mind?"

She shakes her head and then reaches into the pocket of her green overcoat and pulls out a small black camera as he talks to his colleague. Click, click, click, she captures him perfectly: the corners of his eyes tilting upward as he swats away the camera; the deep stillness and sense of hope that envelop his face, its hard contours softened; the smile that lifts the corners of his mouth, laughter rumbling from deep within him as he holds the phone, trying to concentrate but watching her instead. She looks through the lens into Nick's chocolate brown eyes and sees flecks of light not normally present. He hides much from the world.

Outside a storm rages, but inside they are warm. She takes more photos, oblivious to where she is. People push past, angry at the storm, at events, perhaps even at God for closing other airports and delaying departures, yet the world outside the terminal does not penetrate Lena's lens.

When Nick hangs up he reaches out to enfold her, but she backs away laughing. "Lena, you made me forget what I was saying."

Over the loudspeaker a metallic voice announces another delay in Nick's flight. Shadows cross his face, but when she tilts her head to look into his eyes a grin spreads across his mouth. "You're more beautiful when you're with me," he says hesitantly, smoothing the hair back from her face.

She waits, watching him.

He shrugs and looks away, then turns back. His eyes look innocent, almost wondrous. "I mean, you're always beautiful, but when you're with me, after a few minutes you begin to glow."

"It's joy." she says, kissing his fingers.

They float silently along the stained blue-carpeted floors, past psychedelic walls and tattered plastic seats, until they reach Anton's Café. Neither Nick nor Lena are hungry,

but they sit down anyway because the café is tucked

away from the hub of the terminal.

Nick plays with her fingers while the waitress takes their order. "You know what I think?" he says when the waitress leaves their table. "You and me, both of us—we're thinking of each other as lifelong partners." He looks down at the table as his words wind to an end.

She sits utterly still listening to his words reverberate through her mind.

Nick takes her fingers. "One day soon we may have to take each other's hand and jump," he murmurs.

"I can't," she whispers, pulling back from Nick's touch. "I can't leave him. I'm afraid of what will happen if I do."

"Lena," he says in a serious tone. "You may have to."

She looks away, lost for a moment in a sense of foreboding that rises inside her. And then a memory: A lone black boot lies on its side, laces loose. A little blue pill, half crushed, peeks out from under the heel. A small balled fist—a child's hand, reaches toward a stilled leg.

And then the image is gone. Lena is back at the airport sitting with Nick. She glances at her watch. "It's getting late. I'd better go. Daniel will be worried." She turns to grab her hat and scarf from the back of her chair.

"I'll talk to you soon?" he asks.

She nods.

"Lena," he says when she makes a move to rise. "We don't need to make this complicated."

She stares at him.

"You just need to tell me what you want."

She buttons her coat. "I don't know, Nick. But I have to go."

Eighteen

Imagine a Lego construction: pieces connected forward or backward, upward, outward, sideways—all at once. A new beginning with each turn, even if only a flourish, an embellishment of the longitude or latitude, that snap snap of pieces being put together. Often in the making there is no perspective. Only in looking back after the work is done can the shape be seen.

Nineteen

Lena sits in her office haloed in light from the lamp on her desk. Everything but what is before her—white paper, black pen, the report from the Inter-Tropical Tuna Commission—is grayed out like the backdrop on a stage. In her own busy way she is happy—she likes it when her focused attention makes the larger world disappear.

From somewhere under the papers on her desk her phone rings. She pushes aside the pile to answer it.

"You're back," Isaiah says.

"Hey there! Yes, almost a week now." Lena tells him about their time in Penang, the resort they stayed in along the Malaysian coast, their final stay in Singapore for business. "We were in the most amazing monsoon at the resort," she says. "Even Daniel was scared." Lena describes how the sea water rose up and spilled over the fake sand brought in for the tourists, how the spray sounded like gunshots against their door, how the sea sucked out towels and tables and chairs, even the stucco from the walls. "The stairs were so submerged we couldn't even leave our room to get food." And without stopping to let Isaiah ask questions, Lena goes on to describe how in Singapore, they endured fake snow, ninety-degree weather, twelve-foot-high Santas, gnome-looking elves in front of each hotel, and Sinatra crooning Christmas carols over every PA. "And the country isn't even Christian!"

Isaiah waits, not even trying to interrupt.

Lena continues talking anxiously for a few more minutes and then stops. What's wrong with me? It's just Isaiah. She knows Isaiah wants to ask her about Nick, but she's not yet ready to share. For some reason, Nick seems more a part of her inner world of crazy dreams and broken visions than someone to talk about out loud. But then Lena chuckles to herself.

Isaiah abhors secrets. When they were children and banished from a room, Isaiah would drag Lena outside and climb on Lena's shoulders to peek through windows, and Lena would think why bother? I already know what's there.

"Are you there?" Isaiah says finally, interrupting her thoughts.

Lena shuffles the report on her desk into a neat stack. "Of course."

"And?"

Lena sighs. Then tells Isaiah about her conversation with Nick in Penang.

"Do you think he'll leave her?" Isaiah asks.

"I don't know. They have a strange relationship. Seems more like a business arrangement, but then I haven't seen them together much."

"When I saw them at the wedding, I got the feeling he was playing it safe—like Hildy was an easy reach for him. But of course he's going to play it safe—he's an economist."

"What does that mean?"

"Just what I said. The more interesting question is why are you so attracted? It's not the sex, is it?"

For a moment, Lena is stunned. It never occurred to her that Isaiah would assume they were having a real affair. "We haven't had sex . . .I am committed to Daniel."

"Of course! I wasn't presuming . . . and you don't have to explain. I know you. It's just that—" Isaiah pauses.

"What's wrong?" Lena can sense Isaiah's sudden dark mood.

"Why do men always fall in love with you?" Isaiah blurts, sounding pained.

"Ouch, you're supposed to be my best friend."

"I didn't mean it that way. I meant, why don't they fall for me?"

Lena sighs. "You can't compare the men in my world to those in yours—it's totally different. Straight men look for safety and someone to give them a fam—okay, don't say it, I know I just said something totally stupid. I'm sorry."

"No worries, I'm used to the ignorance of smug

heteros."

"Ouch. Don't be such a bastard. I know that was stupid of me to say and I'm sorry. What I meant to say is you like a challenge. I like nice guys—even if they finish last. Don't be mad."

"Of course I'm not mad. But it's good to remind you of how homogenizing and stuffy D.C. is. What are you and Daniel doing for Christmas?"

Lena tells him of the feast she plans to cook and of Daniel's plans to visit friends in Georgia the day after Christmas.

"Without you?"

"I asked him to go. I can't remember the last time I was alone."

"Daniel was in the Arctic in the summer."

Lena looks down at her gold wedding band. She had forgotten about the Arctic. "I had a terrible nightmare a couple nights ago."

"About what?"

"I don't remember the dream. But I screamed so loud I woke myself up. And Daniel too."

"You screamed out loud? But you can't remember the dream itself?"

"Nope. But Daniel could hardly calm me down."

There is a rap at Lena's office door.

"There's someone at my door. I'll call you later—we can more talk then."

Later that night when the street outside is quiet Lena lays on the couch reading a book, her foot moving to the tempo of Lorena McKennitt. An orange-scented candle burns brightly on the glass-topped coffee table. The dogs lie sleeping, tails thumping, feet bicycling in their dreams.

Lena looks up from her book as Daniel descends the stairs with her journal in his hand.

For a moment she is puzzled. Why does he have my journal? Then she sits up.

He walks down slowly, pausing deliberately before the end of the stairs. "What did you say to Nick before we left for Asia that's so private I'd be hurt if I read it?"

She throws off her red mohair blanket. "Why are you reading my journal? It's mine!"

Standing above her, he hesitates, one leg resting against the bottom banister. "I'm your husband. I think I have a right to know what kind of emails you write to other men. How long has this been going on?"

For a moment, Lena doesn't know what to say. But then a thought—he has no right—intrudes upon her mind. She leaps over the arm of the couch, up the stairs and grabs his arm. "It's private. Don't ever read it again," she says, her mouth compressed in anger.

He holds the journal in the air—just out of her reach, and asks what's going on between her and Nick.

"Nothing!" Lena says a little too loudly. Startled from sleep, the dogs bark wildly. "We're friends. That's all."

He points at the ink scrawled across the page.

"Daniel, I—" She yanks at his arm.

For a moment, he holds the book away, but then relents.

She runs up the stairs, the book in her hands.

He follows more slowly. When he enters their room, he closes the door softly behind him as if not to disturb her, as though he knows there is something invisible pushing them apart.

She glances at him and then beyond him into space.

He pauses next to the bed. "I want to discuss this," he says softly.

She turns from him. "Apologize first for reading my journal," she says stubbornly.

He sits down on the edge of the bed, but then almost falls over as though someone has shaken him loose. "Look, I want to know: Are you having an affair?"

"No, of course not," she says, still mad.

"What is it, then?"

She stares at Daniel unable to answer. How can she tell

him what she doesn't understand herself? How she is drawn to Nick, but. . . But what? She doesn't know. Can you love more than one man at a time?

"Lena?"

She closes her eyes.

His hand rests on her thigh. "I want you to promise not to speak to him again—or see him alone. Do you want to adopt this baby? I thought that's what you've wanted."

Tears form in her eyes. She wants to tell Daniel Don't worry, it'll be okay. To lay out a picture of them as grandparents on the porch of their country house with generations of family around them, but the words won't come. She wants to say it's just some crazy kink inside me—I'll straighten it out. Instead she stares at the pile of dirty clothes next to his dresser. "I need some time, and a little space," she says in a small voice, squeezing his hand. "I think I'm just feeling stressed from our trip to Asia. We were gone too long." She winces, realizing too late that he might think that comment related to Nick.

Daniel sits as though frozen.

She knows she's gone too far, but she can't help it. She hunches over, her elbows on her knees. Ever since he came back from the Arctic, she chafed at his need for her presence. Whenever she tries to maneuver for space, even dinner with a girlfriend or a long conversation with Isaiah, who's not easy to talk to given the three-hour time difference, he grumbles.

She squeezes her eyes shut. It's not her husband's fault that ever since she met Nick she's felt almost disconnected from her marriage. In fact, disconnected from almost everything around her. As though her dreams and strange visions are more real than her life.

She looks at Daniel out of the corner of her eye.

He is sitting slumped over, staring straight ahead. Tears drip down his cheeks.

She reaches her arm around his waist, lays her head on his shoulder. "I'm going to take a bath," she says finally.

While the bath water runs she leans against the wall closing her eyes. She sinks down the wall to her haunches. The smell of the bath oil reminds her of her mother—but not Rita as she knew her, rather a dream-like Rita that Lena can't place. Suddenly she has an image of her mother in a golden yellow dress taking about parfum. Funny, Rita never spoke with a French accent—as far as Lena could tell, her mother disdained anything French. Lena knew her mother had remained bitter about getting pregnant in Paris and missing out on her big chance for success. Despite this thought, Lena knew her mother loved her. She wasn't perfect, but she was all I had. Not for the first time, Lena wishes she had known her father. Certainly he would have been proud of her accomplishments, wouldn't he? Regardless of what Rita said. She knew her mother was prone to exaggerate.

Gathering herself up from the floor, Lena climbs into the tub and sinks down, submerging herself until in her underwater world, she hears the echo of her own heartbeat and feels the ripples of her body's movement. She lays suspended underwater as though in a dream, wishing to erase the evening, wanting only to stay in this moment.

She lies like this for a long time—until the water grows cold.

Then, she pushes herself up and out, water churning behind her in the gap where her body had been.

Slowly she dries herself off, delaying the moment she must face Daniel.

Finally, she tiptoes into their bedroom. Daniel is lying with his eyes closed as though he is asleep.

She carefully lifts the comforter and crawls under the sheets, smelling of jasmine.

Daniel turns to her, fully awake. He wraps his arm tightly around her, nuzzles her neck. "Lena?" he whispers softly, pushing against her so gently it seems he thinks she'll break.

She takes his hand and kisses it. Then turns to him. She sees wanting in his eyes—something more than just her physical touch. She closes her eyes, wills herself to respond in kind to her husband's yearning. She moves closer to him though she knows she feels dry and brittle. She's too disturbed by a ghost to feel the warm buoyancy of her marriage bed.

Twenty

Two days later, Anita pokes her head into Lena's office just as Lena is hanging up with Isaiah.

"Want to have lunch?" Anita asks.

Lena is surprised to see Anita—they've barely talked since Anita's wedding. I am he as you are he as you are me and we are all together—Lena doesn't know why this line from John Lennon is suddenly in her mind. Lena points to her crumpled brown bag. "I ate already."

Anita presses into the office and places her Coach purse on Lena's desk. "I hope you don't mind, but Daniel came to my office for coffee this morning."

Lena stiffens. She turns to her credenza, her cheeks crimson.

"I know I'm interfering, but when Daniel told me—"

"Anita, it's not—"

Anita rests her folded hands in her lap. "Maybe it's just . . . bad genes."

"Excuse me?" Lena says, turning back to Anita in shock.

"Daniel told me about your mother dying that way." Anita shudders. "No, don't say anything." She raises her hand.

Lena's guilt and surprise turns to rage at Daniel for sharing this intimate detail of her life with Anita.

"Lena, you can't . . . think of all you'll lose. The investment."

"Investment?"

"Your marriage, your house, your vacation home in Vermont—it's everything you've ever wanted."

Lena closes her eyes. For a moment she is back in a world where the sky is cerulean and the air thicker, imbued with something she can't put into words. Down a long dark corridor she hears a man's voice, sees a sliver of light.

Anita calls her name, and Lena's eyes snap open. She pushes back her chair. "I appreciate your concern for Daniel and me, but it's really not what you think. It's just a little crisis, that's all. We'll get through it."

Anita looks down at her polished nails. "My parents have been married forty years. My mom said it's for the investment that we get through the crises that occur in all marriages. The investment is what's important. You have a good life with Daniel. You travel, you have a wonderful home." She leans forward. "How could you do better?"

"You're right," Lena says standing. "I do have a good life and I don't need to be reminded of that. Daniel and I have a solid marriage." She grabs her wool scarf and coat from the chair where she dumped it. "I have a meeting to go to," she says, picking up her briefcase. "Let me walk you out."

But instead of a meeting, Lena goes to meet Nick. They agreed to meet at Arlington Center for a matinee movie, a Metro stop that wasn't close, but also not too far away. When she arrives at the station, she ascends the long escalator to street level. A sharp wind grabs Lena's velvet scarf.

"I was wondering if you'd come," Nick says as she looms up and steps off the moving stairs. He kisses her gently. "I bought the tickets." He waves them in the air. "Let's go across the street and get you something warm." Snow packs the ground though the sky is bright.

At Starbucks, they stand in line for coffee then grab seats tucked away in a corner of the cafe. She wriggles out of her red coat, balancing her coffee cup in one hand.

"Let me help you."

"I'm okay." She slides the hot cup onto the marble topped table and drapes her coat over her chair.

She folds her hands and rests them on the tabletop. Nick sips his coffee. They stare at each other. "I'm glad—" they both begin.

"Sorry, you first," she says.

He reaches across the table and takes her fingers, squeezing them. "Are you okay?"

She nods. She had told him on the phone about Daniel reading her journal and the spat they had.

"What do you think he'll do?"

She shrugs. "You don't have to be worried. He's not that kind of man.

"Lena, stop," he says. "Don't make this harder on yourself. It's not your fault."

"Whose is it then?"

He stares at her but doesn't answer.

Just then a picture of her mother flits across Lena's mind. The memory is so vivid that for a moment, Nick and Starbucks disappear. Her mother, dressed in an elegant blue dress with gold bangles around her wrists, is screaming at someone Lena can't see, though she senses it is a man. Unconsciously, she leans forward on the table struggling to bring more of the picture into view. Her mother is standing before a fireplace in an old-fashioned kitchen—a movie set maybe? Where am I? She takes a deep breath and forces her mind to stay steady on the picture. She looks around the room trying to find herself, to determine the vantage point from which she's viewing this scene. . . a pair of men's black boots lay by the fire next to a big shaggy paw, on the floor a shattered porcelain plate. . .

"Lena?" Nick places his hand on her arm. "You okay?"

She looks up at Nick, but for a moment doesn't see him; instead she's looking at the face of the man she'd been struggling to see. But before her mind can latch onto his features, he disappears. She closes her eyes trying to recapture his face, but it's too late, he's gone.

"What is it?" Nick asks, more insistently.

She opens her eyes and stares at him while her mind adjusts back to Starbucks. She shakes her head. "I'm sorry," she says. "It's nothing. . . I just had a thought."

"A thought? Must have been a scary one from the look on your face." He takes her hands and holds them. "You okay?"

"I'm fine." She removes her hands from his and picks up her coffee cup. "It's nothing, really."

He leans in and kisses her briefly on the lips. "You sure?"

"Yes," she says firmly, the memory having faded now.

Nick smiles. "I'm glad you're here. I've missed you. And I'm excited about the movie. I hope you like it."

She asks about the movie (she hasn't seen the trailers) and he tells her the plot line, but says he doesn't want to tell her too much. They talk for a while about other things, catching up on books and friends and everyday events, lingering a few minutes too long over their coffees.

When they finally realize the time, they scramble across the street and have to sneak into a darkened theater. Nick points to two seats in a back corner. "Let's sit here," he says, helping her off with her coat. "Is this alright?"

"Yes," she whispers, as she follows him into the row.

In the darkened room, Nick draws her close. She fidgets for a moment, but then relaxes against him. After a few minutes, she slips her hand inside his shirt and discovers the soft hair that grows just below his navel.

Then he is kissing her, and she, him back. They are light bodies, growing ever more incandescent by the moment. Leg crosses thigh, arms encircling, until like Vishnu, they become almost a single body of heat in the darkened room.

But it is he who stops them. Without speaking, he pushes down on his sex rearranging himself inside his unzipped trousers. She knows what he is thinking and that they share the same thought: neither wants their first physical encounter to be in a darkened movie theater, like teenagers.

He takes her hand and kisses her fingers, one by one.

Tenderness envelops her face. They stare at each other for a long moment in the darkened space and then finally, turn back to the movie, where they are drawn into the story of the English Patient as it unfolds on the screen.

When Count Almasy loses Katherine, Lena looks over at Nick and sees a tear creep down his cheek. Gently, she wipes it away.

Long past when the movie ends, they sit immobile, watching the credits roll by.

"He was a fool to have lost her," she says fiercely, when the lights go on. They are the only ones left in the theater.

"He couldn't help it," Nick says quietly. "Sometimes memory is all the heart can manage."

"I don't understand—what does that mean?"

"Lena, I love you," Nick says, moving a piece of hair from her face.

She stares at him, not knowing what to say.

"But as I've told you, a deep relationship is hard for me. I'm afraid love will steal away my calmness."

"Nick, I—"

He leans over and kisses her to still her response.

"I want your spirit, your laughter, the softness of your body," he whispers, his finger on her lips. "How do you know me so well?"

Tears form in her eyes.

He gently sucks her index finger, arousing them both. "I yearned for you so much the other day at the airport. Our brief time together was not enough for me. I wanted more. And the more I wanted, the more miserable I felt."

He pulls her tightly to his side. You appear in my mind at odd times," he says. "I can hear your voice in my head. This frightens me. At those moments, no matter how hard I try to stay centered in my life, I can't. Everything falls away. I reach for the phone to call you and then stop myself, asking, is this any way to live? I want our connection," he smiles at her, "to use your word. But I'm afraid of what it will mean to my life."

"Nick," she whispers, crying now, "this is how it will always be. The happiness and the sadness. I want you in my life, but . . . we're adopting a baby. Daniel is being torn apart." She moves closer to him. "Please hold me."

He kisses her gently on the lips, smoothing her hair from her forehead. "If only we could have met ten years ago, it could've been different."

She pulls back, surprised. "What do you mean?" she asks.

"I want you, but can I recreate myself now? Be more like Daniel—move to the country, ride horses, run around the world adopting babies? Bring out those old wants? Lena, I'm not sure I want to or can change."

A teenage boy enters the room to sweep popcorn and littered cups off the theater floor.

Embarrassed but still crying, Lena stands and pulls on her coat, telling Nick she's not asking him to change. "Besides, " she says, as he finishes putting on his own coat and turns back to her, "you can't change just for me."

"Why not?"

She stares at him. Something ancient and old tells her it doesn't work that way—except in fiction or the movies. It is something she knows, but can't find words to express.

Twenty-one

Christmas came and went, measured mostly by the postman who marked the days by the weight he carried, and the shopkeepers who stood bored by their tills during the after-Christmas sales. The trees noted the season by the light frock of snow that covered their bare bodies, though it was gone before their branches could freeze. The season wound out like a visitor on the run to somewhere else.

Lena didn't mind. She had enough of Christmas in the hot tropics; and for her, time was not time at all but rather a sensory impression. More and more she dips down into a different world of vivid color: dappled light kisses blue hills, steepled roofs of red and terracota tile, moss and stucco walls and stone paths in hues that lack a name. And a man's voice, always a man's voice pressed back into shadow. For Lena, it is peculiar being in that place but still knowing that her everyday reality exists too. Somehow Lena straddles both worlds at once. And when she does return to the present, to the office, to the city block where she lives, no time seems to have passed at all. The experience is pleasing, if not a little disconcerting; it moves her a distance not measured in miles, and without her knowing it, it moves her away from the people she knows.

Gran had asked her to come home for Christmas—as she has every year since Lena moved to the East Coast and then got married. It was a ritual between them: Gran would mail her a beautiful cream card embossed with a bit of holly or some other tasteful botanical design, and invite Lena home for the holidays. Lena would wait a week or two, enough time for it to seem that she was considering the invitation, and then call Gran and decline. Her reasons were always good—good enough for Gran to invite her home the next year. Lena couldn't explain to Daniel, or even to herself, why she declined to go home at Christmas. Part of it was that Lena felt Gran's sadness—as though Lena reminded Gran of Rita's death. But it was also that she never really felt loved by Gran—not like Gran had loved Rita. She had adored that girl, as her Aunt Clarrisa would say. And now she doted on Aunt Clarrisa's twins, Tommy and Johnny—and even seemed to prefer Isaiah over her. Of course, Lena knew she was being sensitive, but still she never went home. Even when she was single, she stayed away.

Now, the day before New Year's, Lena is cooking in her kitchen while she waits for Nick. Daniel has gone to visit friends for the week in Georgia. One half of her is concentrated on food, anticipating the pleasure of Nick's visit, while the other half is miles away imagining Daniel walking along a Georgian beach. She's like a spider spinning thread, bridging space.

When Nick knocks at her kitchen door it takes her a moment to gather all the parts of herself back into her body.

She lays her wooden spoon on the edge of the orange enamel pot, wipes her hands on her apron, and opens the door.

Nick encircles her in his arms. "Happy New Year's eve," he murmurs against her lips.

She steps back to let him pass. "Was there anyone in the office this morning?"

He shrugs. "One or two."

"Lunch is ready. We're gonna have a picnic!" She points toward the red Persian rug in the living room. She's laid a white tablecloth and utensils in front of the fire.

They sit cross-legged on the floor. "You look magnificent, Lena." He tilts her chin to look eye to eye. For a moment, they say nothing. The beat of their hearts tells a story of love that is delicate, fearful, yet made up of bold hues. Like the Persian rug under them—tribal, with small emblematic symbols, vivid colors, a unique shape, snug between her fireplace and couch.

He kisses the top of her head. "Why didn't Daniel come back today?"

She looks away. "He wanted to stay a few more days."

Nick takes her hand in his. "Did he say why?"

She pulls out of his grasp. "He's having a good time. And maybe he's trying to give me the space I asked for." Daniel was supposed to come back today, but he extended his trip. He didn't say why and she didn't ask. She wanted him to come home, but she didn't push him to return. Her feelings simply bounced around inside the hollowness she'd felt for the past two days. She touches her stomach. When Daniel called there had been pain so deep in her stomach it felt as though it was not inside her body.

"You okay?" Nick asks.

She nods. "I was yesterday. It was strange—I was fine, then suddenly I couldn't stop throwing up."

He touches her stomach. "Are you better?"

Is she better? The question echoes in her mind full of static, like a long-distance call. She reaches across the States to find Daniel, but all she finds is blank space.

"Lena?"

"Yes, I'm okay," she says.

She lets herself be drawn into the circle of Nick's heat. They kiss, they touch, they sink down to the floor, though even now they don't have sex: not yet, not while she's still with Daniel.

The next morning, Nick shuffles down the stairs just before dawn hoping not to wake Hildy. The last few stairs twist down and around so suddenly that Nick almost stumbles. He rights himself, a bitter taste in his mouth. He's like a Lego construction: pieces connected forward and backward, upward, outward—snap snap all at once. Nick stayed out until half past two, drinking more than his share of cognac, while Hildy and her friends conversed about the bond market and how best to make money. He laughed, made small talk, embellished himself to fit in—but some part of him, the him he is inside his heart—stayed with Lena.

Nick dumps a single portion of dark granules into the coffee pot, then listens to the mechanical rise of heat hit water.

He lay in bed wanting to talk to Lena—his hand on the phone even as Hildy's dead weight snored beside him—but he resisted his desire and lay restlessly waiting for time to pass until he couldn't stand it anymore and came down to the kitchen. His mind goes back to the dinner last night. They had gone to the Prime Rib and been sat in an area of the restaurant that was cold. Hildy didn't seem to mind; she simply pulled her fur-lined sweater more closely around her thin frame. Their friends—two couples from Hildy's office—didn't seem fussed about the cold either: the men sat with their arms around the backs of their wives chairs, their hands gently brushing their wives shoulders. Each wife sat with her body curled toward her husband, occasionally touching his hand or arm or giving him an intimate smile. Only Nick seemed to notice the cold. He and Hildy sat a foot apart and barely looked at each other all night. Hildy was clearly more focused on the talk of the Asian bond market than she was on Nick. Though the distance between them never bothered Nick before, now he realizes it does.

He picks up the phone to call Lena, taking his coffee to his study.

"Where are you?" she asks, not sounding at all groggy at this early hour.

He fingers the metal tabs on his leather chair wondering how long she's been up. He tells her about a dream he had last night.

Usually she will interpret his dreams for him, but this morning she tells him she is puzzled by his call, puzzled that he doesn't seem afraid Hildy will come down and catch him in an intimate moment on the phone.

He laughs carelessly. "Are you mad at me?" he asks.

When she doesn't answer, he bends to place his cup on the floor. From this perspective the sun seems higher on the horizon. As he rights himself, he wonders, has she been crying?

"Did you understand what I was asking as you were leaving yesterday?"

"I'm not sure. Refresh me."

"Yesterday it seemed you were saying that you've been

trying to please Hildy so she won't question whether you are with me, and as a result, your relationship has become smoother."

Nick hesitates. "Yes, I suppose that's what I was saying."

"Why would you do that? It seems like an act."

Nick watches the sun bend behind the trees across the street until it disappears. He's confused by Lena's reaction, unsure of his place in this space between them. He stands and paces the room. The black and maroon kilim is scratchy under his bare feet. He draws his blue striped bathrobe more tightly around him, glancing up toward the darkened stairs. He is wary of his impulses, the emotional synapses that tend to rise more frequently with Lena around. He wants to give in to her and his feelings, to soften and bend, but often he's not sure how.

Nick pauses in front of a mullioned window in his study. Outside, two red squirrels run toward and away from each other, leaping from limb to limb on the barren tree. "Shouldn't I try to remain focused on my life with Hildy? Isn't that what you're doing with Daniel?"

"But Nick, I'm married to Daniel! You've said you don't even love Hildy."

He bows his head, rubs his temples. "I think I see more risks than you do."

"You don't see more risk than me," she snaps. You focus on the potential loss—in your case, a relationship that doesn't even give you much pleasure. Oh yeah, and I forgot, your job."

"Lena, I'm not saying—"

"Daniel and I have a good relationship. We love each other. We're adopting a child, moving to the country—all the things I've always wanted."

He wishes that he were with her, that he could place his hand on her heart and feel the pounding of her blood. He knows this is an irrational thought, but he can't help himself.

"And then there is you," she whispers. "I can't help but

feel what we have is special and unique and adds to my life in a way that nothing else does."

Nick surveys his study. The room feels static, everything lined up in its place. For a brief moment, he wonders how he's gotten into this scrape with Lena on New Year's morning. "The difference," he says, choosing his words carefully, "is that you like being emotional. I don't."

"How can you say that? And I don't agree that you don't like being emotional. You are emotional with me."

"Aw, but that's the risk. And not one I take lightly. On the one hand there is you, and to be honest, no words describe how I feel. On the other hand, I can't help but wonder if it might be possible to suppress emotions until one simply stops remembering how one once felt. "

"But why would you want to?" Lena asks.

He sits back down in his brown leather chair. "I don't know, Lena. It's a question that nags at the back of my mind."

"You don't want to remember how you feel about me?"

Nick knows he's missing something important, but he doesn't know what. If he were with her he'd take Lena in his arms so she could help him re-construct what he's lost; he feels her capacity every time he's with her. And that's the rub: with her he feels more than he's grown accustomed to feeling. "It's the way I was raised, Lena."

"I don't understand what you are trying to tell me."

"It's just that— "

"If you want to talk about risk, think of my risk. Daniel specifically asked me not to see you or speak with you again. By talking to you or seeing you I'm risking that he'll get fed up and leave me."

Nick closes his eyes, rubs his temples. When he was one, his father left his mother—told her he was going on a business trip but never came back. Although Nick never spoke to his father again after that, somehow Nick always knew his father. For instance, he knew that every afternoon after he was born, his father went down to the sea-lock, a spur that stretches away from the high peaks of Lochalsh (where Nick was born), to collect the black pebbles that came up from the sea. From the shore, Nick watched his father throw pebbles higher and higher until they sank into sky and disappeared. Nick doesn't know how he acquired this memory (if it is a memory); maybe someone in town told him when he was young. Certainly, not his mother. After his father left, his mother burned all the pictures, so the only thing left of father was their front stoop. It was made of slate from the local quarry where he worked, a wedding present from husband to wife. Nick once killed a bird against that stoop, watched the red blood seep into the slate's spidery purple veins causing a permanent stain. When Nick thinks of his mother as she was when he was young, she's always hunched over a pot, her deflated body a silhouette against their black coal-fired stove.

Suddenly he realizes that Lena is talking to him and she's getting madder and madder. He listens for a moment to catch the thread of what he's missed.

". . . the more I think about it, the angrier I get that you would perceive that you have more risk than me. And what if there is risk? So what? What do you think I'm doing, Nick? I'm taking risk."

"Lena, that's not my point."

But in a flash point of anger, her mind has extrapolated further and further out—so far out, he can't even follow her train of thought. All he wanted this morning was to hear Lena's voice and tell her how much he loved her. How did he get her so bloody mad? "Think about it," he hears her say. "How does change occur except by courage to follow one's inner compass? If such courage didn't exist, we'd still be living on a flat earth!"

"Lena?"

"What!?"

"I love you."

22. France 1965

The Christmas trees were delivered to town in a truck three days before Christmas. They were meant for the shopkeepers—four-foot-high trees flocked in white to stand out in front of all of the shops, but Lena and Père got one too, as their house was on the *place.* Though the *Mairie* said that the trees were to be decorated with red velvet ribbons, Lena and Pére decorated theirs with gaudy gold garland and silver-colored balls, both of which seemed to overwhelm the small tree. Plus, at Lena's insistence, they dragged the tree inside the house instead of leaving it outside on the ancient place for all to see.

No doubt the neighbor, Christian, would grumble to Jean-Paul and perhaps even start a fight on Christmas Eve after he had imbibed too much *pastis,* or perhaps champagne if he was given a bottle for Christmas from his son and daughter-in-law. In past years, the feuds Christian pursued with the villagers had known no respect for Christmas or Easter or even a funeral or birth of a child. Christian was bound to cause trouble, to argue and fight, because that was his role in the small village. Lena loved Christian—she'd walk through the village with him slowly because of his limp and his cane (due to an accident with a grenade in the war), and when he became acrimonious with the other villagers, she would march over to him and take his rough hairy hand in hers, tugging at him to come play. The two of them—he with his bent back and gray hair and she, a petite blonde doll, had their favorite games: tossing cards into an old hat, building a house of cards, or, if the weather was nice, playing with the *boule* balls in the field across from the *Mairie*. She was his friend and seemingly took it upon herself to distract him from his cross and ornery ways.

Mostly Père smiled when he saw Lena soundlessly at work soothing the ranting Christian, but sometimes he worried that she was becoming too mature, taking too much on her young shoulders. He knew he himself depended upon her in a way that was undoubtedly inappropriate for a grown man; it was not good to lean on a three-year-old child, however smart and mature she may be.

Père lifted Lena so she could place the last bauble on the top branch of the tree. Vivi was due to arrive that night, and though he knew it was perhaps kinder to wait for her to decorate the tree, Père wanted this moment with Lena to himself. "Shall we go and pick out Vivi's Christmas present today?" Pére asked when they were done, feeling a tad guilty.

Lena clapped her hands and stamped her feet in glee. He knew she loved to buy presents and that to her young mind, the small store in Le Vigan had a vast assortment of gifts to chose from. "*Maman aussi*," she said in a tone that would not accept an argument from her father.

Jean-Paul sat down on the brown divan and pulled Lena into his lap. "Maman won't be here for Christmas—remember I told you? She's going to visit her Mama and Papa—your Grand-mère and Grand-père—in the U.S. Your Grand-père is sick and Maman needs to be with him. But Vivi is coming tonight—shall we surprise her with a special dinner?"

Lena looked pensive. Jean-Paul could tell she was processing the information about her mother, wondering what it all meant. And he could tell also the exact moment she finally alighted on the fact that her beloved Vivi would be arriving that evening. "*Oui, papa. Vivi aime le poisson.*" Lena leapt up and tugged at her father's hand.

"Fish it will be. We will go to Le Vigan to buy Vivi a present and to get fish for dinner tonight—does that sound good?"

Lena nodded, grabbed her blue wool coat, which was hanging on the back of the kitchen chair, and marched to the front door, looking more like a miniature adult than a child of three.

Later that night, the three of them were sitting in the salon in front of the fire having supper. Only one lamp was lit, and the fire threw shadows on the white-washed plaster walls. Vivi found a small antique wooden table tucked back in a corner under an eave, and placed it before the divan for them to eat on.

"*J'aime*," Lena said when Vivi asked her if she liked eating before the fire.

"Me too," Vivi said. She told them that when she was growing up, the children—she and her two brothers—were never allowed to eat in the living room, where the fireplace was. "My mother was from New York and believed children should be taught proper etiquette. Now, when my brother's kids come to visit, she lets them eat on trays in the living room while they watch television."

Lena and Jean-Paul were amazed at the idea of eating supper while watching television, both because meal times were sacrosanct—a time you spent with family—and because they didn't own a television. Hardly anyone in the village did. Television was considered a luxury item and taxed heavily by the government. And besides, reception up on the hill was not very good.

Jean-Paul's initial amazement over eating while watching television turned to confusion. "I thought Georgia was warm, no? Is my geography wrong?"

Vivi laughed. "Georgia is in the south and it is too warm for a fireplace, for the most part. Mother insisted that my father have a fireplace constructed when they built their house—she grew up in New York City and believed that every proper house had a fireplace."

"And your mother, did she like living in Georgia?"

Lena, finished with her supper, pushed her plate—white porcelain with pink flowers rimming its edge—further back on the small table and climbed into Vivi's lap.

"Lena," Jean-Paul scolded. "Vivi isn't finished with her meal." He moved to pluck her from Vivi's lap.

"She's fine." Vivi said, reaching her arm around Lena's small frame. She continued to eat, resting her chin on Lena's soft hair.

"Mother was never really happy in Georgia," Vivi continued. "We lived in Atlanta when I was a toddler, but then daddy wanted a bigger house in the country. He'd been born on a plantation, and though he wasn't a farmer like my granddad, he wanted the land."

The adults lingered over chevre cheese and wine and talked more about Vivi's youth in Georgia, what it meant to be a farmer in America—Vivi blushing when she had to confess that her grandfather wasn't the dirty fingernails type of farmer—more of a gentleman farmer, with lots of help, growing cotton and such. And her mother was from an old Bostonian family, though her mother had mostly grown up in New York City.

Perhaps a little bored, Lena climbed out of Vivi's lap and ran over to the Christmas tree, where she played for a bit with the white flocking.

Vivi looked at the tree and then back at Jean-Paul. "Why always the flocking? It never snows here at Christmas does it?"

"The mayor saw the white Christmas tree in Paris a few years back, and I suppose he thinks it's sophisticated."

Vivi wrinkled her nose. "It's tacky," she mouthed, "but I can tell Lena likes it, doesn't she?"

"Les moutons," Lena interjected suddenly, frowning. A puzzled look crossed her face. A few minutes later the sound of the flock's bells could be heard getting louder as they grew nearer.

"Isn't it late for Christian to be coming off the hills with the sheep?" Vivi asked. Just then the church bells started clanging, signaling that it was eight o'clock.

"Maybe I should check to make sure Christian is okay," Jean-Paul said, standing up. Two years before, Christian's aged mother went out one night to recover a few stray sheep after a neighbor stopped by to report that they were in her yard munching on her herbs. When Christian's mother arrived, the sheep were gone. It was only seven in the evening when she made her way out of the village and further back into the hills to recover the sheep, but that winter had been unseasonably cold and wet. Still, the old woman knew the hills well—she had been born in the village and tended sheep all her life, so the two villagers who caught sight of her as she trudged up the path thought nothing of her leaving, despite the inclement weather.

When she didn't return within the hour, Christian, who'd been in Montpellier picking up supplies, went out to look for her. After two hours of searching the village and the frost-covered hillside, he came back wet and chilled, but without his mother. At his request, the *Monsieur l'Abbé*, who luckily was in the village that night for his monthly rotation between three parishes, rang the church bells continuously—signaling an emergency—and all of the men of the village, and many of the women too, poured into the place.

They found her in the wee hours of the morning, in the pre-dawn light, near a dead sheep. The small sheep looked like it had fallen from the crest of the hill and broken its leg, perhaps slipping on a piece of icy rock. Christian's mother was further down the hill, wedged between some maquis and covered with mud, as though she had slid down. She was dead when they found her—stone cold. Later, the coroner said that perhaps she'd had a stroke and fell and hit her head, and then rolled down the mountainside. Or perhaps she had climbed down to help the young ewe and slipped herself. They would never know. The whole village was bereft, since she was a gracious woman and had been like a mother to Jean-Paul ever since his own mother had died when he was young.

It was almost a week after her death before Jean-Paul thought back to the night of the incident and wondered. That same night, before the accident, he put Lena to bed early. She had a cold and a slight fever and had been cranky all day. At seven-thirty, however, she awoke screaming. At first Jean-Paul thought perhaps her fever had risen or that she was in pain, but when he ran to her room, Lena was sitting up in bed crying. He scooped her up and checked her forehead (which was cool) and then her diaper (which was clean). Lena kept crying and tried to twist out of Jean-Paul's arms, reaching toward the window.

"*Mon amour*, it's cold by the window," Pére told her, gently rocking her, but Lena wouldn't be consoled and kept kicking her feet, crying and opening and closing her fist toward the window.

When he finally took her closer, she peered toward the hills and kept reaching out her hand. "*Mouton,*" she said finally, whimpering. It was the first time she had said the word, and at the time, Jean-Paul didn't know what to make of it, or why the thought of sheep would make her cry. Later, when the church bells started ringing and he went out with the other men to look for Christian's mother while a village woman stayed with Lena, he forgot what Lena had said.

But now as he stood up from the small table in front of the fire, both he and Vivi, who knew of the story from Jean-Paul, looked at each other.

"Yes, you should check," she said, when their eyes met.

"I'm sure Christian is okay," he said. "But it is strange that he is bringing the sheep in so late. Usually, he has them in by nightfall."

"That was hours ago."

"I'm on my way," Jean-Paul said, slipping on his wool coat, but pausing at the door to look back at Vivi and his daughter.

"It's okay," he heard Lena say, patting Vivi's cheek as though she were comforting the older woman, instead of being the child who needed to be comforted herself. Again, Jean-Paul was struck by how beyond her years Lena seemed and by his own reaction to her. Somehow, Lena's words had comforted him too—as though she knew somehow that this time, everything was fine. Perhaps Vivi was right—sometimes Lena did seem to know things before others did. Jean-Paul frowns. But why always bad things?

He puzzled over this as he crossed the place to Christian's house. Two years ago, the weather had been exceptionally bad. This year, they were having an unusually warm December, with very little rain, all of which seemed to make an even bigger mockery of the white-flocked Christmas trees the major's office had posted around the village. Jean-Paul looked up at the night sky, which was bright with stars. The animals were getting closer—he knew from years of hearing the metal bells, hand-painted by Christian's mother, that they'd round the corner and head toward the grange just about—he looked into the void of the hillside—now.

Just then, the first of the sheep and goats came running toward him. A bulge of animals, seemingly unaware of his presence, came streaming toward him and then parted around him, as though he were some immobile, inanimate object. It never ceased to amaze him how dumb goats and sheep could be, mistaking him for something other than who he was. He knew if he moved or waded through them they would split apart, startled by his presence, and perhaps head off in directions other than the grange. And yet, he felt silly just standing there. Suddenly it occurred to him, isn't that what he was doing with Rita? Standing frozen, afraid of what direction she might veer off too? It wasn't a matter of attachment—there was never any attachment on her part, and little on his, even though in the very beginning when she told him she was pregnant, he had secretly hoped that they might fall in love.

He moved his hand as though pushing away the thought, startling the ewe next to him and making her turn from her path. He was just about to make his move to head off the splitting flock when Christian came around the corner with one of his border collies. Seeing the straying animals, the old dog ran along side the flock and leaned into them to turn them back.

"He's good," Jean-Paul said, nodding at the dog.

Christian chuckled. "*Oui.* The young ones can't compete." He nodded toward a young dog, who was trying to guide the flock by nipping and biting their legs and who got nipped himself in warning by the older dog. "He tries to teach them, but some of them are too stubborn to learn. Kind of like women sometimes, eh?"

Jean-Paul just smiled. Despite her good French, Rita had not made any friends in the village with her arrogant attitude.

"*Tout va bien?*" Christian asked. He nodded at Vivi's car. "I see your lovely friend has arrived."

Jean-Paul pursed his lips and nodded, still thinking of Rita. "*Oui,*" is all he said.

"A good woman. And a good mother for Lena, even though she is American like the other one." Just then Vivi and Lena appeared at the window—Vivi having lifted her so that Lena could see out. Both waved to Christian, Vivi working the latch to open the window.

"Everything okay? Why are the animals out so late?" she called down in French once she got the window open.

Lena was standing up on the meter-thick windowsill, having been lifted there by Vivi. "Yes, why?" Lena said, standing in the tall window with her hand on her hip, looking every bit like a nagging, scolding old woman. The adults couldn't help but laugh. And then Lena laughed too.

"A man is entitled to his privacy," is all Christian would divulge, winking at Jean-Paul.

"I'll be right in," Jean-Paul said, waving the woman and child back inside.

"She's precious, that little one," Christian said, once the window was shut.

Jean-Paul nodded.

"Cut from a different cloth than her mother, eh?"

"Rita's not always so bad."

Christian raised an eyebrow at the younger man, but didn't say anything.

"I'm hoping that eventually she'll get her big part in the movies and leave us alone."

Christian shook his head. "Don't make the same mistake your father and I did. Playing nice with a conqueror will get you conquered."

Jean-Paul looked down at his shoes before glancing up at the other man. "I'm afraid of Rita's tactics. Lena is my life."

Christian watched the goats as they disappeared into the grange and then nodded at the old dog. "Pay attention. He could teach you something."

He tipped his hat toward Jean-Paul. "*Bonsoir,*" he said, as he limped toward his door.

Twenty-three

An airplane, its belly full of passengers, breaks through the clouds, a glint of silver in a vast blue sky, and then it is gone. In her mind, Lena is riding a comet past the plane into darkness that cuts color so sharply it feels like pain. Nick is riding the comet with her, but with effort she squeezes him out, pushes herself back and through that tiny speck of light where the glint of the plane can be seen.

She is strapped into her seat next to Daniel on a plane bound for Los Angeles. Stay here, she commands herself. Don't let your mind wander. She wonders how she let Isaiah talk her into staying on a few days after her meetings and Tommy's shower, while Daniel is heading out almost immediately to San Francisco to shoot footage for a documentary film. He owes me, she decides.

Daniel reaches for her hand. His lips move to kiss her palm, but his movement is diverted by the flight attendant who stops to ask if they'd like a drink. Daniel orders a scotch and soda. Lena glances out the window at the water far below. But no—they are flying over land to San Francisco. She had momentarily lost her place in the geography of space. Lifelong partners—Nick's words to her at the airport echo inside her making her shaky, like she's balancing on a tightrope.

"Lena," Daniel says. "The baby will be good for us." He smiles. "But she needs to know her mother will be there for her. There'll be lots of times when you'll want your freedom—no baby, no responsibilities." His smile slips. "You won't be able to tell her: You wait, I'll be back." A red blotch streaks his cheeks.

She looks down at her hands folded in her lap. "I love you, Daniel, you know that."

"All I know is that if you ask twelve of our friends, all

twelve will tell you you're wrong. I know that doesn't matter to you—you think you know best—but it should."

"Daniel, please."

"It's fine for you to do, but not fine for me to be upset about? Bugger that."

She was surprised by the bitterness in his tone. "It's not easy on me either."

"What the hell kind of thing is that to say?"

"You know it's hard for me to come to L.A.—don't make it harder," she pleads.

"This ennui you have about L.A., your family, particularly your Gran, is what is making you behave in this crazy way! Your Gran is a perfectly lovely, proper woman. Why do you hate going to see her?"

She looks at her husband as though he's gone mad. Usually, he is the one who complains about her crazy family—or rather, her crazy mother (whom he never met) and her unusual family. Now he's blaming her family, or her attitude toward her family for her situation with Nick? "I love my grandmother. It's just difficult to come home."

"Home. Isn't that the word Isaiah uses?" he says derisively. "As though where we live isn't your home?"

"What is wrong with you? You are twisting everything. I thought you liked Isaiah."

"What's wrong with me?" He raises an eyebrow. "I think that's a question you should ask yourself. I did like Isaiah before he started this follow-your-heart stuff with you."

She lowers her gaze. (How did he know this without reading her journal again?) "I followed my heart when I married you," she says softly.

"That's different and you know it. You weren't married to someone else."

"No. But you were."

His head snaps back; her words have surprised him. "That was different. Our marriage had been over for a long time."

"You hadn't left her."

Although this is true, he doesn't miss a beat, nor does

he tell Lena the whole truth, which is that he left his first wife for her. "No, I hadn't. But I don't want to go into my past—it's right now that I'm concerned about. If we're going to adopt a baby, I need you to snap out of it."

"Are you threatening me, Daniel?"

"No." He gulps down his drink.

"Then why bring up the baby?"

They stay in an old-fashioned hotel on the cliffs of Santa Monica, though of course, Gran had suggested they stay with her in Pasadena. Their room is pleasant though not modern, the furniture comfortable though not new. As soon as they dump their bags in their room, they rush out to have dinner with two of Lena's colleagues. Both have become good friends; having dinner at the nearby Italian restaurant is a tradition of sorts.

"How is the adoption going?" one colleague asks, after the waiter has brought their entreés.

Lena tells him excitedly that they've finally located a baby—actually a fetus. Some friends of hers in India had connected them with an unmarried Muslim girl who is pregnant. "My friends found a home for her to stay in and a good doctor, too. We want to make sure mom and baby stay really healthy."

The waiter brings a second bottle of wine.

"Did Lena tell you," Daniel says when the waiter finishes pouring, "that she's having an affair?"

Lena gasps. Two sets of eyes swivel to look at her and then back at Daniel. There is an uncomfortable pause in the conversation.

"We're adopting a baby, but that's not good enough for her—she needs attention from another man as well."

Lena holds her breath, looking down at her plate, hoping—no praying—that Daniel will stop.

"Lena, is this true?" one of the men asks.

"It's true, and she knows it," Daniel interjects. "She's breaking my heart."

Lena places her hand gently on Daniel's arm. "Please stop."

"What? It's okay for you to do, but not for me to talk about? They," he says, nodding his head at the others, "are my friends, too."

"I'm sorry," Lena says, looking at their friends. "You shouldn't be in the middle of this."

"Brilliant! Blame me. Lena, you, by your actions, are putting everyone—all of our friends—in the middle of this. You need to snap out of it now."

A tear rolls down her cheek and onto the white table cloth.

"Ah, now, finally a tear. What about all the tears I've shed?"

"Daniel, I'm so sorry. I don't know what else to say." She folds her napkin on the table and pushes back her chair. "I will see you guys in the morning."

"Sometimes sorry isn't good enough," she hears Daniel tell the others, behind her retreating back.

The next morning, Lena is sitting in an old brown tweed armchair in their hotel room with Daniel's laptop balanced on her lap. (Hers is in the shop due to a nasty virus.) Daniel has gone out to photograph the morning light as it shimmers across the bay. Lena is hunkered down in that place where her mind races with facts and figures while she shuts out the world. She is so absorbed in he work, that the signal announcing a new email startles her. She looks, forgetting that she's using Daniel's computer. Dear Daniel, Sorry things are no longer good between you and your wife, but bring your new friend and come visit me soon. Lena rereads the broken English, looks at the email address (a woman with a Nordic sounding name)—then shoves the computer off her lap just as Daniel's key jiggles in the lock.

He has his hands full of camera gear so he kicks the door shut with his foot. "I didn't realize you'd still be here."

She stares at him.

"Are you hungry?" He dumps his gear on the ground and slips his arms around her waist, kissing her neck. "Do you want to go get breakfast?"

She pushes him away. "How could you tell that woman our marriage is over? Is that how you feel?"

"No," he says automatically. Red splotches appeared on his neck. Then, as though an afterthought, he asks, "What woman?"

"This woman," she says, pointing at the computer screen.

He glances down at the screen. "Lena, I—"

"Yes?"

"It's not what you think," he says, frowning. He moves to the pink and brown plaid chair by the window. "Ursula's English isn't good and she must have misunderstood the e-mail I sent her."

Lena is like a mannequin silhouetted in a store window. "Who's the friend she mentions?" she asks finally.

He shrugs.

Outside the window, cottony white clouds roll over the hills of buildings, stopping only when they meet the resistance of a steel-gray sea. "Don't lie."

He paces the room. "It's all a mix-up. There isn't anyone. Just a friend I met in Georgia at Christmas. I told Ursula about her." He sits down on the taupe bedspread. "You're not like you used to be. You never leave a trail of clothes from the door to the bed. You're always tired or busy." He reaches out to yank on the bottom of her black blazer.

"Get away from me," she hisses. "Is that what you were doing after Christmas in Georgia? Fucking some woman you just met?"

"No."

"You let me berate myself, tell all our friends how evil I am while . . . while you've been off fucking some woman! I haven't even slept with him! How could you?" She retreats to the blue-tiled bathroom.

Red-rimmed eyes stare back at her from the mirror, a look of confusion stamped across her brow. She splashes cold water on her face, takes a few deep breaths and emerges from the bathroom acting more composed than she feels.

She grabs her coat, pulls her hat nearly down over her eyes as she shoves it on her head. "I have to go to work," she says mutedly, slamming the door behind her.

In the taxi she stares dejectedly out the window, feeling nauseated as the taxi glides along the coastal highway. She wipes salty drops from her lips. She can't stand Daniel's deceit, but she knows too, it is no more than she deserves. In her heart, she has betrayed her marriage, though that is not what she ever meant to do.

For the last few days Nick has sent her emails to which she hasn't responded because she's been trying, really trying, to rebuild her bond with Daniel.

From:	Nicolas Block
Date:	January 16
To:	Lena Holloman

L

I'm sitting here, trying to focus on work (after a productive morning, so I don't feel bad about it) but thinking about you. Somehow it seems things have become even more serious between us in the past few days; maybe it's just that my feelings for you have become stronger, or maybe because we've let the toothpaste out of the tube and now it won't go back in. (I mean openly discussing the idea that we might want to be together.)

Anyway, this note is just my way of coming as close as I can to reaching across the table to take your hand in mine and smile into your eyes. I hope everything works out for the best—and I wish I had your belief that it will.
Yours aye, N

From: Nicolas Block
Date: January 17
To: Lena Holloman

L

As I was falling asleep last night, I was overcome by a sense of how nice it would be to fall asleep with you. It's funny, because I don't remember ever having had that particular fantasy about you before. I've thought about waking up next to you (although that's not likely to happen given how early you wake up), but not about the warmth and security of feeling your presence in bed with me, falling asleep.

At the time it was not particularly reassuring, because it created a great longing in me, but looking back now it makes me feel happy. Yours aye, N

From: Nicolas Block
Date: January 18
To: Lena Holloman

L

I leave for Argentina in two days and had hoped to speak to you before I left. Your unusual silence makes me fear something has happened to you. But perhaps it's only that Daniel has again recaptured your complete attention. Such fear—yet his capturing your attention would not be so wrong (at least from your perspective) would it?

Despite these twinges of doubt, something inside me says I can wait, for I know there is something long-lasting between us.

I know you would say that I have not made a move to clear myself from my obligations to Hildy, but I have. After all, it's the mental attachment that keeps us most firmly rooted in place. I hope to talk to her soon.

And you? What is it that binds you to Daniel? You're never spoken of your "connection" to him—certainly it's not the same connection we share—is it? Ah, that old doubt—

but I am shoving it away. For I am,
Yours aye, N

She huddles against the bank of phones, her body compressed in on itself, her fingers tapping out Nick's phone number. The din and clatter behind her hunched back (her colleagues on a break) pelt her already tensed nerves. Now, there is no reason to restrain herself; Daniel, not she, has finally broken their vows, crossing a sacred barrier from which he could no longer turn back. Now, she knows why sickness had come upon her so suddenly Christmas week when she had vomited all day. (She had thought it was simply the flu.) Now, the implication was clear: her body knew the thread binding her to her husband had been broken, ripped apart in the frenzy of a stranger's womb. How dare he! But then again, isn't it what I deserved?

Nick answers on the second ring. "Lena, what's wrong?" Nick asks when her voice sounds a ragged octave lower than normal.

"He's seeing someone else."

"Daniel?"

"I've never lied to him. He always knew when I saw you—each time he always knew. He kept tabs on me like a guard; and told all our friends how wicked I've been. And all this time, he's been fucking some other woman."

"Lena, are you sure? Daniel doesn't seem the type."

"What's the type? And yes, I'm sure. He met her in Georgia."

"At Christmas?"

"Yes."

"Maybe that's all it was."

"Maybe, but I don't think so; he's hiding something—I can feel it."

He tells her that certainly she should have known that this could happen. He reminds her that Daniel asked her to not speak with him and that he can't like that she still does. "It would make most men mad."

"Mad enough to fuck some other woman?"

"Lena—"

She watches the last of her colleagues disappear into the conference room. "Look, I can't talk about this now—my meeting is starting again. But I wanted to give you my Gran's phone number, in case you wanted to call. I will be busy with family things on Saturday, but I'd love to hear from you on Sunday."

"Hildy's coming with me."

"To Argentina?"

He tells her not to get upset. Hildy is only coming for the weekend. "She insisted on coming because it is a sunny place to get away. Besides," Nick says, "I need to talk to her."

Lena wants Nick to tell Hildy the truth about how he feels—but why Argentina? Why can't they talk at home? "Are you sure you want to talk to her? She said she would leave you."

"Don't be silly," he says. "I need the security of neutral territory—that's all."

"Nick, it'll be warm and sunny—you'll be having fun and won't want to disturb the peace with an awkward discussion."

Silence echoes across the line. "Nick?" she says finally. "I need to know that what we have is special."

"Hildy and I don't share anything remotely similar to you and I," he says, sounding annoyed now.

She is silent.

"Lena?"

"Yes?

"I will call you from Argentina, but just not on Sunday."

Later that afternoon, Nick sends her an email.

From:	Nicolas Block
Date:	January 17
To:	Lena Holloman

L

I'm taking a short break from work just thinking of you. I confess my thoughts keep circling around to your anger toward Daniel. You were upset for lots of reasons, but one of them was that he had lied to you. Of course, I am effectively lying to Hildy now. I haven't lied explicitly, but she did ask me not to see you again. I agreed, but I didn't keep that promise for long. Lena I want to be devoted to you, but if we become partners and I promise not to lie to you, will you believe me? Or will you not expect the promise? Or will you just detect when I'm lying in that mysterious way you have?

Obviously, thinking of you, N

Early that evening, Lena goes alone to her grandmother's house in Pasadena. Daniel stays at the hotel in Santa Monica so that in the morning he can make his way—a day early—to San Francisco. When she arrived at Gran's arts-and-crafts-style house, she is struck—as she usually is when visiting California, by how meticulous the house and gardens are. The white two-story house where Lena grew up has a wide wraparound porch with a fieldstone foundation. Two antique wicker rockers stand on the porch, positioned to view the amazing array of roses in the garden. Lena's eyes take in the agapanthus, canna lilies and other tropical flowers not typically found in the East. Funny how her eye had changed, so that this is now the unfamiliar.

As she approaches the porch, Isaiah comes out of the house, letting the screen door bang. "Wasn't me!" Lena shouts automatically, and then laughs at herself for this childhood habit.

"Gran isn't here, she's at the florist," Isaiah says. "You okay?"

Lena nods.

"What, cat got your tongue?" He walks down the steps and grabs Lena's suitcase, then puts it down on the ground and gives her a hug. "He's a bastard," he says as he holds her tight. "I'm devoted to you, even if he isn't."

She pulls away and wipes a tear. "I suppose I deserve it."

"Come on, let's go in and have some wine. Or better yet, some bubbly. I confess, I opened a bottle."

"Isaiah!" She gives him a stern look.

He takes her hand and they walk up the stairs. "She's expecting an army. She bought two cases. And told me, as usual, to make myself at home. So I did." He opens the screen door and she steps in to a large living room full of antiques and beautiful built-in cabinets. From the living room, she can see Gran has placed a magnificent bouquet of flowers on the dining room table. "She's outdone herself," Lena says, throwing her purse on a chair.

Isaiah holds up her suitcase. "Get comfortable. Let me take this up and I'll come back down and pour us a drink," he says as he starts up the stairs.

"Isaiah, I'm not a stranger in this house, " she snaps, but then immediately apologizes when she sees the hurt look on his face. "It's just that. . . you always seemed more welcome here than I did."

He trots back down the stairs. "You are being silly," he says, putting his hands on her shoulders. 'This is your home and Gran loves you more than she's ever loved my . . . handsome mug." He laughs. "You thought I was going to say ugly, didn't you? I am, if nothing else, truthful."

She smiles. "Take my bag up and come back and pour me a drink and I'll wallow for you."

Later that night, after Gran goes to sleep, Lena and Isaiah, who is staying for a sleep over, as Gran calls it, creep up to the attic with their glasses of wine in hand. Lena's grandfather was governor Nixon's speechwriter, and Isaiah—

his screenplay still in the works—is hopeful that they will discover some unknown tidbits in gramps' papers. Lena, in particular, is more than slightly inebriated, and Isaiah has to help her up the ladderlike stairs. When she gets to the top, she crashes into an old sewing mannequin, which topples over with a clatter. Shhh, they both say at once. It's not that they aren't supposed to be in the attic, it is more that they suspect Gran wouldn't want them prying into old papers belonging to Lena's grandfather. After his death, he was a topic that Gran clammed up about.

"Do you think Gran would be upset if she knew what we were doing?" Isaiah asks, as he pulls open a box.

"To tell the truth, I've never been good at predicting what my older clan would get mad about," Lena says as she bends down to look in the box. "They are all so prickly and secretive."

"Funny that we are looking for some of the old speeches your gramps wrote when he worked for Nixon."

"Funny how?"

"You know, Nixon secretive, your family secretive—birds of the feather flocking together, that kind of thing. "

"Perhaps I was adopted," Lena says, moving boxes out of the way to reach a trunk she spies way back in the corner under the eaves. "Help me," she says. "I don't want to drag it, might wake up Gran."

They lift the old army trunk over the boxes and set it under the naked bulb that hangs from the ceiling. A small padlock keeps the trunk tightly shut.

"Should I pick it?" Isaiah asks.

"Can you?"

He gives her a look like, come on, this is child's play. In a minute or two he has the lock undone. "I never noticed this trunk when we were kids."

"Me neither. But then how often did we play in the attic?" She is bent over the open trunk. In it, folded neatly, is his old uniform and other WWII paraphernalia. When she carefully lifts his uniform out of the trunk, an envelope falls out of a pocket.

Isaiah picks it up and takes out the sheaths of old paper. He reads it under the light, his mouth agape.

"What? Give it to me."

He moves beside her so they can read it together. "Holy shit, gramps had a second family. What the hell?" She looks at the postmark. London, 1952. Wow, mom would have been fourteen. Aunt Clarissa a lot younger.

For a moment Lena feels dizzy; her world wobbles as she adjusts to the idea of a family secret so big it was locked away. She'd loved her gramps, how could he be such a cad?

"Two kids," Isaiah says. "Twins. They must run in his side of the family."

"Why did we never know them?"

"From the sound of it, they were secret. Look here," he says, pointing to a passage. *I know it was a risk for you to come see William, but it was the child's dream finally to meet his father. I'm glad he did before he died.* How tragic. I wonder if Gran ever found out?

"I don't know, but let's not tell her. Help me put this trunk back where it was." She pockets the letter in her jeans. "Tomorrow is her big day and I don't want her upset. It's the past. The old past."

Isaiah plucks the letter from her rear jean pocket when she bends over to close the trunk.

She whips around. "What are you doing?"

Isaiah slips the letter into his inner jacket pocket. "I might need it."

"Look, you," she says, grabbing his shirt. "I don't give a damn about the past, but don't you dare write anything that might upset, or even worse, shock Gran. She shakes him a little, as if to say she really means it.

He pries her hands from his shirt, and smooths out the wrinkles caused by her grip. "Don't be an ass," he says. "I love Gran, too."

From below, they can hear Gran moving around in her bedroom. Afraid they've woken her up, they quietly finish moving the boxes back where they were and tiptoe down the stairs.

"We will talk about this more later," Lena says, before shutting her bedroom door.

Twenty-four

It is not yet noon when Nick crosses the expanse of Avenida 9 de Julio and heads for the city center. His face is flushed from the heat. He kicks a Coca-Cola can, watching the letters loop round and round. Now that his mind is freed of business, he must plan how he is going to tell Hildy that he is leaving her, and tell her about Lena, too. Lena was right, the Playa Del Sol resort is not the right kind of place to talk. Tonight, once Hildy leaves, he will move to a quieter, less ostentatious hotel.

Nick pauses before a butcher shop. Rows of dead feathered chickens hang by their feet. A half-cow swings from a hook on the ceiling.

He looks away, shaken by a memory from his youth: his mother on the days when her body seemed to move in slow motion, cave in on itself until she retreated to bed and lay death-still. Nick always suspected that his father left for another woman, but his mother would never say. As a child, he promised himself he would never do to any woman what his father did to his mother.

Nick pushes these thoughts from his mind and pulls open the oak door to a Parrilla. It is early yet for lunch, the streets quiet still, not yet time for the tip tap of women's shoes, those spiky stilettos still the fashion in this country.

In the back corner of the steak house, he finds a seat facing the door. Out on the boulevard, he had felt the pull of pen and ink, words to a page, something he'd mostly avoided since college. He once envisioned himself a poet, but instead, he steered toward a path of charts and figures, the black and white shapes of an economist's pen. He wanted a way out of the poverty in which his father had left them.

He grabs two packets of sugar and tears them in half,

making a small pile of sugar on the table. He wishes Lena were here with him—Lena whose passion was not unlike that of this city: lively, an undertone of something hidden.

Nick orders coffee wondering why his thoughts had roamed so wildly from his earlier meeting with the Ministry of Finance. What freedom does he now feel? He is still obligated to Hildy. Nothing has changed.

Or has it?

He looks toward the plateglass window, which frames the front of the restaurant. The awning deflects the sun. He stands and walks toward the front, suddenly wanting to see the sky—the urge is like thirst. The buildings around the bistro, shoulder to shoulder, dispel the heat. There has been too much damn construction, too much planning of this perfect small arcade. He is annoyed that even at the window he can barely see the sun.

He pulls open the door and steps outside. Heat shimmies off the cement plaza but disappears into the shadow of buildings.

He steps further out until he sees the orb of sun as it soars high above the boulevard—and then, in the distance, Hildy moving purposefully down the cobbled path toward him.

When she gets closer, she says, "Here, Nick, take my bags."

He grabs four or five from her hand. "Whoa there, how are you going to get all this back?"

"I bought another suitcase, a Louis Vitton. La Recoleta is fabulous—you should have come with me. I had coffee on the patio of the La Biela café, which is just steps away from the crypt where Eva Perón is buried."

He eyes the labels on her bags: Hermès, Pérez Sanz, Christian Lacroix, Valentino, Max Mara. (Must be her cheap purchase, he thought.) He wonders what she'll do if she ever actually has to pay a mortgage herself. But he supposes that her father would never let that happen.

"Are you hungry?" he asks, holding open the oak door.

"I don't have much time before I have to be at the

airport—and I still have to pack." She steps into the dim restaurant. "It's much cooler in here."

"I have a table in the back—we'll tell them we're in a hurry."

Even after they have ordered and the waitress has brought their food, Nick lets Hildy guide their conversation to her shopping and the sights she's seen, rather than steering the conversation himself.

"This is really good," she says, pointing to her vacío—her grass-fed steak. "How's yours?"

"Good. Do you want to taste? " He cuts a piece of meat and pushes it to the side of his plate for her.

"Yum, what is it?"

"Chinchulines. Grilled intestines."

She laughs. "Sounds better in Spanish."

"Hildy, are you happy?" he asks abruptly.

She looks at him a little surprised, and then laughs. "Of course, how could I not be happy? Look at all the shopping I did."

Suddenly he realizes this discussion is going to be harder than he thought. He launches into a discussion of whether she is happy with him, satisfied with their interactions, content with the organization of their life and how it is unfolding.

"Of course, Nick. We just bought a house. I would be happier, however, if we hired a decorator instead of trying to do it ourselves." She tells him about her sister's house, looking wistful as she describes the phalanx of professionals her sister used to get the house just right. "Her husband entertains more than we do, but I am the eldest, so it is a bit shameful for me."

Nick looks perplexed. "Shameful?"

"In my culture, when a younger sister marries—and particularly when she marries well—before an older sister, it is shameful. For me and my family. If we were living in my country, people would wonder if I perhaps was defective in some way."

Nick's face drains of blood. "That's absurd. Your family aren't peasants."

She cuts a piece of steak. "The stigma is worse among the upper classes. I love my sister, but sometimes I feel bad." She tells him that her sister is always asking, when are you going to get married?, why hasn't he hired a designer for your home?, why are you still working at a job that requires so many hours?, and so on. "It's not appropriate, for me to be living like this."

"We live well," he says, defensive now. "And in answer to my original question, it sounds to me like you aren't happy."

She eyes him with a blank stare. "I am happy. I just think we need to move on with these other things. You asked and I told you." She asks him why he is getting angry. And then she launches into a discussion of how in relationships, one person is always a little oppressed. "And that person just has to make the best of things," she says, as though she's that person.

She thinks I oppress her? He is shaken by that thought, but presses on. "But if a person isn't happy, why would they stay in a relationship, particularly if it oppresses them?"

When she picks up her wine glass, her hand shakes slightly. "Is it the sex? Are you unhappy with the sex?"

He sighs. "No, of course not. I'm just trying to understand whether we are on the right track with this relationship—whether you and I are both happy."

"We just bought a house."

"Damn it!" he explodes. "That's not what I'm talking about."

The waitress comes to clear their plates and bring them coffee. Nick waves her away when she approaches with a dessert tray. He knows Hildy is careful to watch her weight.

"Nick," she says, looking down at the table, "Men and women are fundamentally unequal and hence incompatible in the true sense of that word." She looks up at him. When he doesn't respond, she tells him that it's best if women seek happiness—as he would put it—with other women, and men with men. As long as both sexes understand their roles, their lives and household will run smoothly. "Love isn't a fairy tale as you Westerners like to imagine. It's about hard work, avoiding conflict, and creating a stable structure. That's why most happy marriages are arranged. Two families join for strength in the community."

He thinks of Lena and wonders for a moment how compatible they really are. Is she right? Do I believe love is a fairy tale?

"I'm going to miss my plane if I don't get back to pack," Hildy says. Are you coming with me to the hotel?"

He flags the waitress for the check. "Of course; I'm moving to a hotel downtown, so I need to pack and check out as well."

When they stand, Hildy looks at him as though disappointed he hasn't pulled out her chair. Damn her, what does she want from me? As they exit the restaurant Nick's shoulders hunch just the tiniest bit as he wills his thoughts to recede. He wants only the surge of warm freedom he felt crossing the boulevard this morning with Lena on his mind.

In his hotel room in São Paulo (a one day trip on his way home from Argentina), Nick stands by the window. It wasn't so long ago, maybe four or five years, that Nick left his first wife (suddenly, his wife had thought, though the possibility had been in his mind for a while). When had his feeling of claustrophobia, the dissonance between his inner thoughts and his outside world, his ever-persistent feeling that this is not enough? Was it this feeling that opened the gap into which his mistress fell? He smiles ruefully. The fiber-optic speed at which Sophia sniffed out his pheromones could hardly be classified as a passive encounter. With a darting tongue she captured him . . . or at least his penis. But how could he help it? Her tight ass had targeted him that day in the hall when she'd rubbed against him, supposedly because of the crowd; but he knew better and so did she. Pressed against him, she turned to say excuse me in her Latin tongue, but managed somehow in the process to rub her hardened nipples across his arm. Her mouth, fully red, pouting slightly, said fuck me. So he did, again and again. Holding her short black hair in his hands while she begged him (always begging) to fuck harder.

It came to the point, those six weeks in Spain (where he was temporarily working) that she need only look at him, a slow lick of her lips with her tongue, and he, like a hypnotized man, would go to her—she loved the violence of her clothes being ripped. They even did it on a plane (during a weekend excursion they took to London) in the small boxlike lavatory, as the other passengers slept.

Why is he thinking about Sophia? Nick searches the night sky for the sequence of stars he remembers as a child, dimmed now by the lights of São Paulo. The apple of his cheek brushes the window. His eyes look upward. His fingers grope for the complicated mechanism installed to keep the hotel window shut. With difficulty, he turns the circular lock: the window creaks, then sticks for a moment as he leans his weight to force it open. Blunt-edged light shines down from high above, obscured by the bright life of the city.

Nick turns from the window. Sophia's escalating requests for violence created in him a subtle self-loathing and a slight perception of stench around her musky smell. Was his craving for Lena also a compulsion of the penis that would eventually leave him undone? Self-loathing has not shadowed him since he met Hildy. Their encounters are pleasant, the sex not bad; she does not draw from him that strange craving.

The boxlike shape of the room suddenly seems comforting. He turns to pack. With effort, he re-creates his earlier meetings and the financial analysis that he obtained from the Brazilian Ministry.

He reaches for his briefcase and rummages inside until he finds an earlier report he once wrote on the future of the Brazilian economy. He sits back to read, his feet propped on a small table. A sheet of paper falls from the report's pages—it's the poem he wrote for Lena yesterday when he woke up.

His fingers tremble as he unfolds the small square and reads the poem again.

Carefully, he folds the sheet and tucks it behind a small pocket in his briefcase. He sits back, the Brazilian report in his hand, determined to push all other thoughts from his mind.

But there it is again—her voice: And I shall dream you into existence.

Twenty-five

There are moments in every life that are caught—stilled like a snapshot to look back on— moments when the inner becomes the outer and the outer moves in, converging to a singular understanding, like the perfect scene rendered on a lit stage while everything else falls into shadow.

Twenty-six

"Do you plan to take your girlfriend to Norway?" Lena asks sarcastically, banging the orange enamel skillet on the stove.

Daniel turns away and goes to the window. In their back yard, their terrier paws frantically at the cedar fence trying to reach with his too-short legs a black squirrel spitting down bits of bark on his head.

"What a devil." Daniel's laugh is hollow.

Lena stands in their blue-tiled kitchen. Her hands are on her hips. She knows he is afraid to see the hurt in her eyes, and she knows he takes pleasure in it as well.

He turns back, steps toward the stainless steel fridge.

She stares at him, her wooden spoon raised above the skillet. He hadn't called her after she left him in San Francisco, when he made his way to Los Angeles to shoot a short sequence for another director. Five days and not one word. She didn't know where or how to contact him. Now, he's been home three days and has hardly spoken to her, refused to tell her where he was or what he's thinking.

He opens the fridge door.

"Daniel?"

He doesn't answer.

She grabs his arm and spins him toward her. "Why won't you speak to me?" she asks, confronting him face to face.

"I'm leaving you," he says finally, looking away.

Lena stares at him. Daniel's voice sounds far away, as though she is standing down a long dark tunnel.

A man's arm.

A blue shirt, starched but crumpled, is pushed up to the elbow.

Long slender fingers—ink stains at their tips.

She is concentrating on this blip of scene trying to make sense of it all.

I love you, Lena, she hears Daniel say back in that other world where she lives. Her attention snaps back to the kitchen. She grips the counter to stop the room from spinning. "Then why are you leaving?" she asks.

Daniel stands with his arms at his side, his legs in a wide stance. "Because you're going to leave me."

"I'll never leave you. I told Nick that. Call him. Call him now. Ask him."

Daniel crosses his arms. "I can see it in your face."

"I'm your wife. We can make it work." Her words falter. She wants to say more, but something makes her mute.

He takes the blue glass salad bowl from her shaking hands. "It's too late. I've made up my mind and now I'm committed elsewhere."

Her head jerks as though he's slapped her. "How could you be committed to a woman with whom you've spent less than a week?"

"She's not in love with someone else, and she's loyal."

Lena is silent. In her mind she sees a door, and beyond it, the bright sun. Then the arm and crumpled shirt reach through mottled light, and then, there is darkness.

Daniel turns to leave the room. "I can't take this anymore," he shouts. "It's obvious you are always thinking about him."

"Daniel? Don't turn away! I'm not thinking about Nick, for God's sake!"

But he has gone, slammed the back door, left the glass shaking.

She runs to the door, but he's already at the back gate. "Daniel, wait! I want to tell you something."

The door of the car is open and he is sitting in the driver's seat, his hands on the steering wheel. For a moment, he closes his eyes. "I've heard enough," he says, his voice shaking like he's about to cry. "I don't want to hear any more of your explanations or stories. We're done. It's over," he says as he slams the door. He starts the car and drives away.

In their backyard, Lena sinks down to the ground with her back against the gate—she curls in on herself while an image of a wine bottle spinning round and round on an ancient stone floor floats through her mind.

A week later, Lena sits in her bedroom, the disappearing sun shading the room in a blue-tinged gray, a backdrop of color with blobs of form (the furniture)—indistinct, like the memory that won't distill itself in Lena's mind. Next to the bed, a tiny blob of yellow light haloes her head. Her stomach is punched in, her shoulders hunched over. She is on the phone with Isaiah.

White noise from the street enters the room, connects with the crackle and sphish from a bad long-distance connection.

"I'm so sorry," Isaiah says. "Daniel loves you, but he's not strong."

Lena wipes a tear from the corner of her eye. "What do you mean?"

"Do you remember before you married, when I asked you why Daniel, what you said?"

In her mind's eye Isaiah floats before her, separated by a pane of glass, like a dolphin in an aquarium. She imagines the blip blip of bubbles escaping from Isaiah's lips while she rests her ear against the glass to hear.

"You said, I'm marrying him because he needs me to love him. He made you feel safe—safer than you've ever felt."

She expels her breath. She tells Isaiah that she thought he'd never leave.

"Exactly. But that's not really a great reason to marry a man, if you ask me, which you didn't at the time."

Lena picks lint from her black pant leg. Her ears ring, pounding a little inside her head, as though she'd ascended too quickly from beneath the sea. Abruptly, she stands and flips on the overhead light, surveying the room like it was a canvas—a painting of another place. "He doesn't even want the farm," she whispers.

Lena sinks back down on the bed.

"I'm no expert on Daniel, but it seems to me if he's made up his mind, there's nothing you can do."

"But Isaiah, he's my husband. I love him. And I thought he loved me. How can he have made up his mind?"

Lena sits slumped on a black barstool in Anita's kitchen. Behind her, narrow wooden stairs stacked like small shoe boxes disappear into the dusk of the second floor. The room is stuffed and small, no more than a galley attached to the back of the house with yellow retro appliances, once perhaps a summer kitchen. Brown plaid shades, a Ralph Lauren logo clearly visible, hang at the window above the sink.

Anita roves the cramped space, setting up a battlefield of cookie sheets and cooling racks. "Lena, I was afraid this would happen," she says. "But you can't let that low-class, sleazy woman steal him from you—from what I understand, she's barely even a receptionist. You've made a big investment in Daniel and that's what matters." Anita slides three cookies off a hot baking sheet onto a plate she's set before Lena. "Milk?" she asks, pouring her a cup before Lena answers. She wields the spatula like a baton, shoving cookies off their sheet, knocking the wooden spoon against the bowl after each blop of new dough. She tells Lena that at their age, all the good men are taken. Lena needs to fight for what she has.

Lena stares down at her hands, briefly wondering about Anita's keen interest—is it just that Daniel's actions don't fit with Anita's idea of the choices people should make?

"We all make mistakes—I almost made the same one—but you don't deserve this."

"Did you know?" Lena looks up holding her breath.

Anita steps back from the counter, her back pressed against the hot stove. "About his girlfriend?"

Lena nods.

She shakes her head and turns back to her cookie

battalion. "You have to turn the other cheek to his infidelities. And you need a battle plan to get him back. What will you do without Daniel?"

Lena's living room is a blaze of light, oblong color in the center of the room, a framed canvas. Even with every light turned on, the corners aren't exposed—angled shadows shade the threadbare spot on the Persian carpet, the wine spilt on the couch, the African mask with its saffron face and pink tongue half split off, the wilted orange Gerber daisies. It is a life—a circumference of sorts that can't be seen from the center. There is no perspective. It takes darkness to see fully a lit room and the detritus of a marriage.

Lena again asks Daniel not to leave, but he insists he has no other choice.

"I don't understand."

"You love him. I can see that."

"Daniel, please?"

"He's what you really want. I see it in your face . . . in fact, sometimes it seems like I see him in your face when I glance at you. And I can't stand that."

When she can't convince him otherwise, she tells Daniel he should keep their Vermont house—it was bought for him, according to his tastes. He asks if his girlfriend can buy Lena out of her half.

She steps back as if struck.

He looks away.

"What about the baby?" she whispers.

"What about the Vermont house?" he asks again, pressing her back into the shadows of the room.

Her eyes narrow; she is seeing him as though for the first time. His face is impassive like a mannequin in a window. She sees that he never wanted a child; the child was for her, so she could be happy and make him happy in return.

The clock ticks loudly.

"And if you change your mind?"

"I won't."

"Do you love her?"

"I loved you."

She takes a step toward him.

"Lena, can my girlfriend buy you out of the house?"

Her hand falls away. His lips move but she can't hear the words.

She is a lone boat, bobbing in the waters of her mind.

Unmoored. Again.

Twenty-seven

The windows are upside down now, the doors too. Pieces of flooring hang from the roof. The phone wires have electrocuted the cat. In her dream Lena is showing two nuns the crater where the bomb fell. It killed the baby. Lena too. She's a ghost now, rushing from side to side, trying to make it all better. They took over the Capitol and the geese flew away. She is running and running trying to find the place where the park once was, where she once lay her ear on the sharp silvery grass to feel the earth turn and turn. But everywhere is only nowhere. And now she is falling, falling into the depth of the murky gray water of the Potomac, her arms and legs outstretched; she is turning like a four-pointed star. Where do people go when they die? her five-year-old self shrieks. But God doesn't answer.

From somewhere deep in her sleep, Lena hears someone calling her name. She opens her eyes. The house is quiet. The world is blanketed in sleep. Beyond her bedroom window, the morning sun is just rising on the horizon, a straight line of white, like the strip of light under a closed theater curtain.

"Lena? You cried out." Isaiah says, sticking his head through the doorway.

Lena turns to look at him.

Isaiah stands framed by the door jam. He's dressed in black and red plaid flannel pajamas. "Scoot over," he says, moving toward the bed.

Lena scooches over and Isaiah lifts the down comforter and slips under. He gropes for Lena's hand and holds it tight, like he used to when they were children.

Lena stares out the window. The horizon is now pinky-gold and breaking apart in billows. "How could he leave me?"

she asks, groggy, but awake now.

Isaiah strokes her hair. "He didn't deserve someone as vibrant and alive as you."

"But how could he? I thought he would never leave me. I would have bet my life on that. I don't understand."

"If it wasn't this, it would have been something else."

Lena turns to her friend. "Why do you say that? I thought you liked Daniel. Now I'm finding out he doesn't like you, you don't like him. Why?" She bursts out crying.

"Lena, shhh," Isaiah says soothingly, rolling over onto his side. "He wanted you all to himself. He never wanted to share you. Your friends saw that, but you were happy, so we never complained."

"I thought no one had ever loved me as much as him," Lena says, staring up at the ceiling.

"I love you," Isaiah declares fiercely.

"You don't count."

"How can you say that?" he says, sounding injured.

"You've known me forever. You're my best friend, so you're not a good judge."

Isaiah frowns. "A good judge? Of what?"

Lena shrugs. "Character maybe. You're biased."

"Lena, stop! I know it hurts to lose him. . . and yes, you did cheat on him."

"I did not cheat!"

"Okay, whatever."

Lena sits up angrily and smacks Isaiah hard with a pillow. "Don't whatever me!"

"Ouch!" Isaiah rolls over, his arm shielding himself from another pillow attack. "Don't take it out on me. I'm still here, remember?"

Lena bursts out crying again. "I'm so sorry. You're right, it is my fault."

Isaiah wraps his arms around Lena. "Stop. You're going to make me cry, too. You've got to believe it's not your fault, or it will drive you insane."

Lena pushes him away and climbs off the bed. "I can't

stand this," she says, pausing in front of her oak dresser. She fingers a bright turquoise-blue enamel humming bird Daniel brought her back last year from Mexico. "I think I am going insane," she says, her back to Isaiah.

"Or maybe," she says, turning around, "I'm having panic attacks of some sort. Weird things keep popping into my head."

Isaiah rolls his eyes. "You've always known things. Remember the time you aced the IQ exam?" Isaiah laughs. I thought the principal's eyes were going to bug out of his head. What was his name?"

Lena rearranges the decorative boxes on her dresser. Ebony with conch inlay, silver and gold, shellacked red paper—the ones that weren't antiques from her mother or her Gran were presents from Daniel. "I don't know." She turns toward Isaiah. "I became a scientist because I like my world ordered and rational. And besides, I always felt guilty about that test."

Isaiah looks puzzled. "Why?"

"Because I didn't know the answers, they just popped into my head. So it was cheating."

Isaiah reaches out for Lena's hand and pulls her back to the bed. "How can it be cheating? Did someone tell you the answers?"

Lena stares at him without answering.

"Of course not. You just knew them. That's not cheating, by any definition of the word." Isaiah sighs. Lena stands and starts dressing. "Look, let's not talk about stupid things. There is a new Egyptian exhibit at the Smithsonian. Or if you want, we could go see the Hope Diamond—I've heard it's fantastic. Or we could go see sculptures at the Kreeger, or if you felt like something Asian we could go to the Sackler.

"Whoa!" Isaiah says, putting down the book of poetry he grabbed from Lena's nightstand. "Too many choices. Too much stimulation."

Outside the window, a giant gust of wind blows the trees. For a moment, Lena is distracted by how the trees bend and sway with their bulky grace and solid presence. She turns back to Isaiah. "Certainly, at one of those places we'll see something far more interesting to talk about than the things I know."

Isaiah groans. When they travel together, Lena always likes to be on the go, while Isaiah prefers to relax—it's always been a tension between them.

"You choose," Lena says. Nearly dressed, she suggests a place they can stop for coffee and a bite to eat on the way. "I'm going to walk the dogs—be ready when I get back," she says.

Isaiah salutes her.

"Don't be mean," she says, disappearing through the door before Isaiah can object.

Later, the two of them are sitting on a wooden bench in the Sackler museum. It is late in the afternoon, almost dark. They have visited the Hope Diamond and the special Egyptian exhibit at the Smithsonian. Lena has been particularly disinclined to talk and has kept them moving from gallery to gallery. They are sitting only because Isaiah declared he was worn out and had developed a hole in his shoe. "My head is spinning with too much stimuli," he said grumpily. He threw himself down on a bench in the Peacock room and refused to move. Other than the two of them, the room is empty.

"What is it that you aren't telling me?" Isaiah says finally.

Lena demurs and tries to change the subject back to the art of the day, but Isaiah intervenes. "Not art," he says taking Lena's hand. "What's making you so cranky?"

"Besides the fact that my husband left for another woman?

Isaiah winces. "Yes, besides that one detail."

A tear trickles down Lena's check. "I try so hard, but in the end, nothing I do turns out right. I destroy everything."

Isaiah looks shocked by this statement. "Do you know how many people envy you?"

Lena's eyes rest on the picture of two peacocks

squabbling over a sack of coins. "Good, they can have my life. And my divorce too."

"Did he ask you for a divorce? You didn't tell me that."

Lena shakes her head. "But he will soon. His new girlfriend won't let him stay married." Lena tells Isaiah that all he wanted was money and his freedom.

"Nothing else?"

Of course Lena's exaggerating—he wanted half of their art collection, the grandfather clock, the dining room table, bikes, and the car. The list goes on. Only things, she says, but not the baby they're adopting. And not her. Lena is pondering how she could have so miscalculated Daniel's personality.

"What else?"

Lena frowns. Can she tell Isaiah about the strange visions she's been having? Maybe even he will think she's losing her mind.

"You're feeling guilty, I can tell." Isaiah again launches into the story about the principal who was shocked when Lena finished a two-hour IQ exam in twenty minutes and passed with flying colors. "I know you always felt guilty that everyone thought you were so smart. You are smart."

"Lot of good it's done me."

"I don't get why you blame yourself for everything all the time."

Lena is anxious now, wobbily in her stomach. It's not just that Isaiah won't let up, it's that well. . . she can't explain, even to herself, what's needling her. It's as if someone is knocking on the door of her brain and wants to stretch it wide open and step inside. She hangs her head, rubs her temples. Her elbows are balanced on her knees. "Remember how easy French was for me in high school?"

"Yeah, Rita freaked and wouldn't let you take any more French after the teacher said you were a natural."

"I think it was my telling her that I was dreaming in French that sent her over the edge."

"Yeah, that was weird."

Lena shrugs. "She didn't want me repeating her life, I

suppose." She turns to Isaiah. "After all these years, I'm dreaming in French again."

"How cool. Any idea why?"

Lena tells him about the song that keeps running through her head, about remembering the conversations in French when she wakens. The weirdest part of the whole experience is that she thinks somehow it's connected to Nick. She tells Isaiah of the vision she had the first time she met Nick—the little boy running through the field of flowers toward her, their brief game of chase.

"Do you think it was Nick?"

Lena shrugs. "I don't even know why I think the French dreams are connected to him. It's just a feeling I have."

They sit quietly for a while, both lost in thought.

Finally Isaiah says, "There's something else."

Lena sighs. "What do you mean?"

"You're holding back. I can feel it."

"You're as bad as me," Lena mumbles.

"They aren't dreams, are they?"

"What?"

"The French episodes."

Lena confesses that they are visual memories—visions?—she doesn't know, but she's been having them ever since she met Nick. They speculate for a while whether Lena could have spent time in Paris with Rita, her mother. But they rule that out because Rita never went back to Paris after Lena was born. "But assuming she did," Isaiah surmises, "maybe she took you with her. Maybe your father wanted to see you just once to verify that you were his."

Lena shakes her head. Isaiah is on the wrong track. Why would her father even care? Especially if he didn't want her to begin with. Isaiah interjects in her thoughts. "Maybe it was all a lie—the part about your father not wanting you. You know how theatrical Rita could be." Lena stares at him. But if it was all a lie, where was her father? Why didn't he ever contact her? She stands.

"Let's get going, I'm hungry. And Isaiah?"

"Yes?"

"Thanks for being here for me and coming to stay." She reaches over to hug him. "I know I'm not the best company at the moment," she says, muffled in her friend's arms. I don't know what I'd do without you."

Isaiah hugs her tight and then releases her. "I love you," he says, looping her arm through Lena's. "And if I married you, I'd never leave you."

With their arms entwined, they exit the exhibit.

Three weeks later, Lena is standing on tiptoe dusting the top of the three-hundred-year-old mahogany clock, waiting for Nick to arrive. The clock was a wedding present from Daniel's father, and keeps remarkable time for an old clock, although if she forgets to wind it each week, it does make time stand still. She sighs, wishing Daniel wasn't taking the clock and wondering again (as she has several times in the past few weeks) if she should move to California to be with Isaiah.

Lena misses Nick but she's been avoiding him ever since Daniel left, for reasons she can't clearly articulate, even to herself.

The clock strikes the hour. Lena looks up expectantly and sees a shadow pause at the edge of her yard. Before she can even put her dusting cloth down, Nick is on her porch and at her front door. For the past month, he has called her nearly every day, both at home and work—he even called Isaiah, when Lena wouldn't take his calls. Mostly, she's worked and stayed hunkered down in her house, not answering the phone or speaking to anyone. Without admitting it to herself, she's been waiting to see if Daniel will change his mind and come back. Isaiah convinced her that it was time to quit moping and call Nick, so finally, she did.

Nick opens the door, and when she steps up to him, he wraps his arms around her waist and presses close. "Hello, you."

She blushes and pulls back, but he keeps her circled in his arms. They stare into each other's face, searching for something readable—a look perhaps, or an indentation around the mouth, a line above the brow. She is reading the topography of Nick's features, hoping that she will find clues of the path she has taken to get here. For a moment, she sees a big brown dog, but she shakes the image loose. "Dinner is ready," she says, pulling out of his arms and pointing to the kitchen. The pungent smell of tomatoes, olives, and garlic fills the air.

"Can it wait?" he asks, pulling her back into the warmth of his arms. "I've missed you."

She nods, her cheek brushing the wool of his coat.

He walks her carefully backwards, his arms around her in a strange kind of tango. Past the kitchen and up the stairs. At the top of the landing he hesitates. She lets him lead her to the guest bedroom where he lays her carefully on the bed, not letting go. Gently he entangles his hands in her hair.

The bed becomes an amber arc of moon, where they swing like children for hours. He's a nova, a crescendo, a symphony of pitched sounds, the horn, the mad pianist; he calls and she responds, ever tighter and deeper and singular until finally, somewhere in the dark of the night, they reach one sustained sound. She tilts her face skyward. A tiny slip of smile creases the corners of her lips.

Afterwards, he kisses her eyelids. "I'm glad we waited," he says softly.

She traces the contours of his cheek, feeling rooted yet expanded. "Me too."

"It's funny," he says.

"What?"

"I saw a blue light around you—around us, the whole time."

"Like an aura?"

He cradles her tight. "Something like that," he whispers against her hair.

They close their eyes and drift off to sleep.

The next morning, Nick cuts diagonally across the road, his coat billowing behind him as he hurries to work. The press of the cold against the warmth of his skin causes his body to scissor back to last night: his fingers are etched with her smell, the press of his body against her warm skin and then (at last!) penetration. His legs skip a beat. With Lena he feels as if he extends beyond his body.

But then, thoughts of Hildy protrude against these happy images. He found her message on their answering machine when he returned home this morning. She'd be returning from Manila in two days. Two days! For a brief moment, he stops to wonder what ever attracted him to the containment he feels with Hildy.

He presses these thoughts from his mind, chiding himself for his wandering thoughts of women and cock. This morning he has meetings ahead. He smiles to himself. But his is a happy cock. No, not just some dismembered thing; it is he who is happy. (The thought shocks him.)

The gray granite stone of his office building looms before him. He strides forward to the elevator bank. When did he lose the concept of happiness? During his marriage, or long before? He glances at his watch. The Brazilians always like to linger over long complicated meals (not to mention the caipirinhas), but today he'll beg out, ask his boss to go alone, claim that other things must be done. He must find a way to prolong these two days, to give Lena and himself more time. Surely now he should tell Hildy he's leaving.

He hangs his coat and hat on a peg. When he turns around, his assistant is in the doorway with her arms crossed. She looks pointedly at her watch.

"I'm not that late, am I?" Nick asks sheepishly.

"The Brazilians were supposed to be here, forty-five minutes ago," she says with her Latin accent. "They rescheduled for Friday."

Yes! Freedom. Nick raises his fist in the air.

His assistant looks quizzically at his raised arm.

He lowers his hand, tells her Friday is fine—it'll give him two more days to prepare.

He begins to sort through his mail. Without looking up, he asks his assistant to shut the door on the way out.

When he hears the click of the lock, he smiles and reaches for the phone.

The taxi crosses two lanes (amid the honking of several horns) and skitters to a stop. Lena opens the back door and climbs in. She leans forward to give the driver directions, placing her arms on the back of the brown Naugahyde seat. The man's cologne prompts Nick to mind. She blushes.

"You getting a late start this morning?" the taxi driver asks, his voice thick with accent.

She turns her head to watch the city slide by. "Not so late."

The taxi bounds down 16th Street, then turns left on Florida Avenue and heads toward Capitol Hill. At this hour, there isn't much traffic.

The taxi draws to a stop in front of her office building, knocking the curb with its wheels.

The driver twists in his seat to look at her. "The path looks slippery," he says, "Be careful."

She pulls her coat more closely around her to climb a bank of snow that hinders her way. It's so icy she skids, but then rights herself.

Inside her office, at the reception area, she asks if her meeting has started. Her assistant comes around the corner with a cup of coffee for Lena and tells her the meeting was cancelled. Lena takes the hot mug, relieved. She wasn't prepared for this meeting and was feeling a little anxious because she only knows how to be her best—erudite and articulate—it's the high price she pays for praise.

In her office, sunlight blazes so sharply against her skin she closes her eyes. For a moment, she is with Nick again. A small smile plays on her lips. Nick's smell had been tinged with bourbon and the sharpness of spice. Bourbon and spice is a scent she's been attracted to ever since she was a small child, though she can never remember why. An image of a man hovers just beyond her grasp. He is splayed on the floor next to the big brown dog. Only the dog is clear in her mind. Lena sits pensive for a long while trying to sort out who the man is and what the image is of.

The bells in the tower of the old church across from her office ring, signaling noon. Lena looks down at her phone. She is not surprised Nick is calling her. "I ache," she says when the phone rings and she picks it up.

He laughs. "Why don't you come over?"

"Where? Your office?"

He clears his throat. "Why not? My assistant is . . . gone, and the rest of my team is out traveling. No one's likely to barge in."

"Nick. We can't."

"Why not?" he teases.

"Are you serious?" she asks.

"Never been more."

"Okay. Warning: I'm going to take you up on your dare. See you soon." With a smile, she hangs up and swivels her chair to look out at the Capitol dome. Her shoulders are shaking with laughter.

Nick lays the phone on its cradle. The corners of his mouth turn up in a Cheshire grin. Then the chart on his computer screen pinpoints his attention, pulling him momentarily into his economist's world. When he was younger and with a woman he really liked, he'd often find that an icy chill ran up his spine and a racy hotness bumped against his heart, and in between the two he stood paralyzed. Now he's learned that pushing down helps him stay safely detached.

He frowns in concentration at the chart. But after a short while the numbers on the screen no longer hold their spell. Lena has crept in; she lies naked across his grid. He laughs out loud at the thought of her arms stretched across his computer screen, her bare bottom on his desk.

He swivels his chair to face the window. A small bank of snow collects on the sill. His eyes shift to take in an office devoid of personal things—not a single picture.

For a moment, he feels an icy chill, but then pushes away the feeling and any negative thoughts.

On the street below, a taxi makes a U-turn on Pennsylvania Avenue and skids to a stop in front of his office building. A woman steps out. She's wrapped in verdigris. For a moment she's Liberty, her arm raised to a robins-egg sky. When she turns, she's Lena.

Two men stare at her as she walks by.

Nick smiles. With her he feels happy.

He meets her in the lobby, kisses her cheek and whispers that he hasn't gotten much done.

Her face reddens. "Me neither."

They both laugh as they enter the elevator.

In his office Lena stands at the window, her head bowed to look down on Pennsylvania Avenue. The rubber plant sways. The snow seems to melt against the window.

He steps up behind her. She turns. Her smile is an arc of light so bright he steps back.

Gently he lifts her onto the edge of his desk. He unbuttons her dress—ten buttons down the front. He counts them slowly until the dress drops open.

Her thighs are milky white like the moon, her dress the dark blue of the sea, her smooth belly the hot sand on shore.

Slowly, slowly.

And then he is running in the waves, the sun on his back as he bores down, so far down her salty sweetness is on his tongue. "You're mine," he shudders. She quivers in his arms, a shy smile crosses her face. He bends and gently rests his lips on hers. He can hear their hearts beating in rhythm. "It's love," he says.

She nods.

He holds her for a long time, feeling her heart beat against his. He knows she understands.

28. France, 1965

The February air was unseasonably warm for the South of France. Tiny white and ultramarine flowers were beginning to dot the meadows, creep over stonewalls, and sprout in unlikely crevices. All around the village, gullies were filling with water from the snowmelt coursing down from Mt. Aigoual. The stones on the hillsides, normally bone dry, were slick. Despite the warm air, clouds hung low forming a face, a flower, a funnel and scoop, and a long corridor of violet gray. They drifted like a canopy over the blue mountains and small village. Lena, Jean-Paul, and Vivi all lay on their backs in the green meadow above the village naming the shapes they saw in the sky. Though they were only a ten-minute walk from the house, they brought a picnic basket full of food—*sanglier* (the wild boar common in the area, and caught in January by Christian's son), olives *pistou and tapanade, Abbaye de Belloc,* and a *chèvre* made by the neighbor, as well as wine, bread, fruit, cold *haricots verts*, and a cream-filled *gâteau.*

Vivi tore off a chunk of baguette and sliced a hunk of cheese. "Ooh, this is fabulous—what did you say it was called?"

"*Abbaye de Belloc*. It's from *brebis*—sheep."

"Is it local, too, like the chèvre?"

Jean-Paul pursed his lips and clicked his tongue—a regional habit of those in the South when they wanted to say, no never, not at all, absolutely not, impossible. "It is from an abbey, as in the name, that is in the Pyrenees. It's made by the monks. The monastery, and the region, is very beautiful. I want to take Lena there to ski when she is a little older. I have my original set of skis downstairs in the cave—I was four when my father first took me. Have you been? Do you know how to ski?"

"To the Pyrenees? No, but my family used to go skiing in Vail every year."

"Ah, I've heard of Vail from Rita. A place to meet great skiers and the rich and famous. You must be a good skier, no?"

She shrugged. "I'm fairly good. My brothers were better. My uncle—my father's brother lived in Denver and had a house in Vail where our families met every Christmas. Mother couldn't bear the heat of Georgia at Christmas time. She always said, it's not a proper Christmas without snow."

Jean-Paul grinned. "The mayor of St. Bresson would agree."

She laughed. "Ah, yes, I remember the hideous flocked trees."

Lena, who was a bit drowsy from all the *gâteau* she had eaten, laughed too.

Vivi turned to tickle her. "What are you laughing about, silly girl?" Vivi took her white scarf off her head and wrapped it around Lena.

Lena shrieked and rolled away, and then a game of chase ensued, the dogs—their own and several from the village who had followed them to the meadow—joining in by barking and jumping and nipping gently at the humans.

"Mon dieu," Jean-Paul said. "Where did all these dogs come from?" Four from the village and Silence were now running in circles, joining fully in the spirit of the game.

Lena and Vivi ran around the meadow. "They love us, they love us," they chanted together as the dogs chased them, barking.

"They think we're sheep!" Vivi gasped, stopping next to Jean-Paul, slightly bent over and heaving from all the exertion. Lena made another turn around the meadow on her own with the dogs trailing behind. Then, she ran straight at her father screaming with excitement. Just before she crashed into his legs, he grabbed her and tossed her high in the air, taking hold of her legs as she rose up. She laughed so hard she started to choke, and Pére brought her down and cradled her to his chest. Her face was red, tears were streaming down her eyes, and she was gasping for air, but she begged for more.

"Shhh. *Tranquille, tranquille*. Let's rest a while, my dove," he said, laying her down on the blanket and stretching alongside her.

She squirmed and squealed and didn't want to sit still until Vivi sat down on the blanket too.

"Vivi, here," she said pointing to her other side, as she scooted closer to her father. Though she was excited, she was also tired, and it was obvious that soon she would be asleep.

"The pied piper," Lena murmured, lying on her back with her legs bent and one leg crossed over the other.

"Yes, I will tell you again the story of the pied piper." Vivi glanced up at Jean-Paul with a sheepish look on her face. "I know it's about rats, but she loves that story. She thinks I'm the pied piper of the dogs."

Jean-Paul smiled. "I've noticed, too, how Silence and the other chiens from the village follow you. When you are around, they seem to be everywhere."

Three of the dogs lay in the meadow close to the blanket, panting. Silence and a young border collie had wandered over to a gully to drink water.

Vivi plucked a large leather-bound book of fairy tales from her bag. On the front of the book was a faded-looking picture of a princess on a horse climbing up into mountains. She turned to Lena with the book in her hand. "A story, or a book?" she asked.

"Book," Lena said, patting the red leather binding. "Ohhh," she said, when she looked more closely at the front cover. "Très jolie."

"Oui. This was my favorite book when I was your age."

Jean-Paul held out his hand. "It's in English?"

Vivi passed him the book. "I've been reading to her in English—I figure it's better if she learns early, and she seems to understand." She blushed. "My parents want to come visit and they don't speak French."

Jean-Paul handed the book back carefully. "It's a beautiful book and looks very old. Did you buy it around here?"

"It is very old—turn of the century and hand-painted on the front." Vivi turned a deeper shade of pink. "My mother has been sending me some of my old things," she said in English, hesitating. "For Lena."

Sitting up, Lena tapped her father's arm. "*Oui, Papa. J'aime*." She pointed to herself and then to the book, as though translating for her father.

Jean-Paul, startled that Lena seemed to understand a bit of English, raised an eyebrow. "Do you think she understands?" he asked in English.

Vivi and Lena both nodded at the same time.

"*Mon dieu*."

Vivi and Lena glanced at each other but said nothing. Then Vivi started giggling and so did Lena.

"Shall we read?" Vivi asked, when they stopped their full-blown laughter.

Lena nodded, then lay back on the blanket. Again, she bent her knees and crossed one leg over the other.

"She looks like a princess when she lies like that." Vivi brushed the bangs out of Lena's face.

Jean-Paul picked a blade of grass and stuck it between his teeth. He looked rueful. "She gets that from her mother, who unfortunately acts like she was born to be a princess."

Vivi looked surprised. "She's mimicking her posture?"

Jean-Paul shrugged. "Not mimic. She did this when she was a baby, but it's a posture Rita favors. I never lie like that."

"Never?" Vivi smiled.

Jean-Paul shook his head. "Jamais!"

"Maybe it's a girl thing or an American thing. I have a baby picture of myself lying like this."

"Really?" Now Jean-Paul looked surprised. "I thought it was from Rita."

"Try it." Vivi turned onto her back next to Lena and bent her knees and crossed one leg over. "It's *très confortable.*"

"*Oui*, papa, try it!" she said in a perfect English imitation of Vivi.

"*Non*," Jean-Paul said stubbornly, lying on his side.

Vivi burst out laughing. Lena too, though undoubtedly she wasn't quite sure what Vivi was laughing about, but Vivi sounded happy so she joined in. Jean-Paul just frowned, being the butt of the mirth.

"Jean-Paul," Vivi finally gasped, still laughing, "Rita doesn't own this pose."

Lena shook her head. "Papa," she said, as though he had said something preposterous.

Jean-Paul just pursed his lips in a frown.

Vivi sat up. "Shall we get him?" she asked, turning to Lena.

"*Oui!*" Lena yelled. The woman and the child jumped on Jean-Paul and started tickling him until he laughed, and then laughed so hard he couldn't stop while Vivi made him say over and over, people everywhere lie like this.

Finally spent, they all flopped on their backs and stared up at the sky.

"I see an umbrella," Vivi said after a while, pointing at the sky.

"*Brebis,*" Lena said. "*Deux,*" she said, pointing.

"*Non, c'est un mouton,*" Jean-Paul said.

"*Brebis,*" Lena firmly insisted.

"What do you think?" Jean-Paul asked, turning his head toward Vivi. "Sheep or goat?"

Vivi smiled. The sun had started to arc toward the horizon, turning the now-dead leaves on the trees on the hillside a sienna color. The light was diffused but bright, more like the intense, focused light of autumn than the budding of spring.

When Jean-Paul looked into her eyes he could see Vivi was happy. "Well?" he asked.

Vivi looked first at Lena and then at Jean-Paul. She pursed her lips, as though trying to make a serious decision.

"Yes?" Jean-Paul asked.

"Yes?" Lena chimed in.

Vivi made a face at them both. "I see," she said slowly, turning to Jean-Paul, "an old goat—"

"*Oui*!" he said.

"—and a precious little lamb," she said, turning to Lena. "And I love you both."

Lena clapped her hands.

For a moment, Jean-Paul and Vivi just stared at one another. Then he took her hand and held it to his lips. Lena, for once, sat still without squirming, as if she, too, knew this was an important moment. The three of them hung like that in the stilled air.

Then a cloud obscured the sun, casting a shadow on Vivi's face. Even in shadow, Jean-Paul could see the shine of Vivi's eyes and read upon her face the love she held for him and his daughter. Words weren't necessary—he knew, and knew she knew, how right—no perfect—Vivi was for them both. If only . . . he thought, but didn't allow his mind to head in that direction. The sun came out from behind the cloud, lifting his burgeoning depressed thoughts, until he felt that perhaps he, too, was the stuff clouds were made of.

Suddenly, the winds of Mt Aigoual, fifty kilometers northwest of them, swept down cold air and pushed rain clouds directly over them. In a flash, the sun was gone and it was raining.

"Oh my," Vivi said, jumping up to shove food in their basket. Vivi pointed to a bottle of water that had rolled away in their antics. Lena scurried to get the bottle.

Jean-Paul picked up the blanket just as it really began to pour. Suddenly, they saw lightening crack and heard the sound of thunder crash against the stone village.

"The lightening is still a ways away," Vivi said, looking worried.

"Here, give me the basket and take the other end," Jean-Paul said, handing her an edge of the blanket. "Let's huddle under it and run together."

Lena took her father's hand on one side and Vivi's on the other. Jean-Paul held the picnic basket and the edge of the blanket over their heads with his other hand.

"This is fun, isn't it, Vivi?" he said, seeing the worried look on his daughter's face. He nodded at Lena.

"Oui," Vivi said. "Let's pretend we are goats running back to our grange from our tasty outing to Mt. Aigoual."

"Brebis," Lena said firmly, stealing a glance at her father, as they began to run.

Vivi laughed. "Touché, Lena." Over the child's head she smiled at Jean-Paul as they continued moving. She's smart, she mouthed.

Suddenly, Jean-Paul stopped the trio, and turned around with the blanket edge still in his hand, so that he could look more directly at Vivi. She looked radiant, with her pale cream skin and rich auburn hair. Her eyes blazed. Her lips parted.

"Vivi, I know—" He stopped. Unable to find the right words, he just stared at her.

After a moment, a smile broke across her lips. "Yes, yes, yes," she almost shouted, as thunder rolled over their heads. "My answer is yes, but can we talk about it when we get inside? Look, the dogs have already run back." She pointed to the village, where the last of the village dogs turned the corner. Silence pushed his head between her leg and Lena's. "We are awfully exposed out here, and I think he's afraid of the thunder and lightening. And I don't know about you, but I'm a little afraid myself."

"Your answer is yes?" Jean-Paul asked, searching her face. "It's settled, then?"

She looked into his eyes and nodded. *"Oui."*

"Oui, Papa," Lena said in a tone that sounded as though it was meant to reassure him.

"Ready?" Vivi said, looking down at Lena. "One, two, three."

"Run!" they both yelled, as they all sprinted toward the village.

29. Siesta

The happiest hour of the day is when the shades are drawn, the covers pulled back, the hour of siesta when the sun is hot and high with dinner still to come, but for this moment a little sleep, a little peace, a silvery-gray room with white fluffy curtains billowing at the window, the slow droning of the fan, the wasp settling into its corner, everything moving down to a place below the surface.

Thirty

Lena is cocooned in her bed, the phone cradled in the crook of her neck. She plumps several goose-down pillows behind her. "I want to read you something," she says to Nick, lying back and pulling her down comforter up to her waist.

Through the phone lines she can hear noise from the streets of Caracas, where Nick has traveled for business. He's been gone five days and has called her every night. "It's from a book I'm reading by Jack Kornfield called *A Path With Heart.* He quotes Carlos Castañeda." A dragonfly stares at Lena with cobalt blue intensity from the rim of the Tiffany-style shade. Narcissi are perched in a vase on her bedside table and perfume the air.

"I'm taking liberties in what I read," she says. "Look at every path closely and deliberately . . . Then ask yourself and only yourself one question. This question is one that only a very old man asks . . . Does this path have a heart? If it does, the path is good. If it doesn't, it is of no use."

"I tried to read Castañeda in Spanish but I couldn't." Nick says.

She tells him that she will read to him and lull him to sleep. Perhaps Castañeda will appear in his dreams.

"I'm not sure I'd understand Castañeda even in my dreams."

Since Castañeda doesn't seem his cup of tea as a nighttime dram, she offers instead to read him *Corelli's Mandolin* by Louis Bernier.

"My head is on the pillow."

As she reads dramatically, she's so immersed in Corelli's problems, the war, and the separation of the lovers that she's almost forgotten herself, Nick, the very room she's in. But then suddenly, she becomes aware of Nick's silence. Usually he chimes in when she's reading, sometimes taking the book from her and reading aloud himself for a while, but tonight he hasn't said a word. "What's wrong?"

Nick sighs. "It's nothing."

"It's not nothing. Tell me."

Nick sighs. "It's stupid. Really, it's not worth talking about."

"Nick, please."

He is silent for a moment. "My ex-wife used to read to me," he says slowly, as though trying out the words. When she doesn't say anything, he continues. "It was a tradition of ours."

"Tell me more." She has a need to understand why he turned suddenly silent during this new ritual of theirs.

He tells her about the time when he and his ex-wife, both graduate students at Tufts, were on a date when his old Fiat broke down on a country road with a nor'easter coming their way. They couldn't get a tow and an old woman in a dilapidated farmhouse in New Hampshire let them stay. Though they were strangers, she was old and trusting and gave them a lantern and showed them to a room at the back of her house. It was early, only six thirty or so, and his ex-wife especially was restless. To calm herself she selected a book from a dusty shelf to read. The bed was creaky and old and uncomfortable, and to distract them, his ex-wife began to read aloud. They took turns reading to each other until late in the night. "That became our ritual through our dating years and even later when we were married. Somehow it drew us closer," Nick says.

"I'm sorry," Lena whispers, not sure what else to say.

"I love when you read to me," Nick says softly. "It's just that . . . it brings back old memories, nostalgia, and, I guess, pain."

They are silent for a long while. Finally Lena asks, "Do you miss her?"

"My ex-wife?"

Lena fingers her bookmark.

"I'm just tired, that's all. I had a breakfast meeting this

morning and I have another one tomorrow. You have nothing to worry about, mi amor."

She glances at an old black and white photograph of her grandfather on the bookshelf. Next to him, her mother sits perched in a silver frame. Somewhere in the very back of Lena's mind a picture grows clearer: A little white book. On the cover is a drawing of a field of flowers and a little boy and girl sitting under an apple tree reading. *Ail. Euil eil eille*. A young girl is repeating sounds, her finger moving along the page. *Peur. Soir. Cour. Fleur. Voir. Four*. And then, a deeper voice—a man's bass voice is reading. *La petite poule rouge grattait dans la cour, quand elle trouva un grain de blé*. Lena hears the words but can't see the face. Who are they? Someone I once knew? At first, she doesn't realize they are speaking French.

"Lena?" Nick asks, breaking the momentary silence.

"Hmm?"

"You okay?"

She struggles to hold onto the picture, even while she speaks to Nick. "I'm not sure. I . . . I keep having visions . . . of a sort."

"Visions?" he asks, sounding intrigued.

"I'm not sure they are visions. More like blips of scene. I'd say they're memories, but I can't recall who the people are or whether I've ever known them."

"What people?"

Lena sighs. "A man and a little girl. But Nick, I also had a similar experience the day I met you. I saw a little boy running through a field of flowers with a little girl who was clearly me."

Nick laughs. "I've been wondering if we could possibly be twins."

She laughs. "That would mean our mother was in labor for five years, unless you are younger than you think. I know I'm not older. Isaiah can verify that we were in 6th grade together. "

"Wow, you've been friends that long?"

Lena stares at the picture of Isaiah mixed in with the

photos of her family. "We're more like siblings than friends." Lena pauses. "Nick, do you think things will be okay between us?"

"Why do you ask? I hope so."

"It just seems so . . . difficult for you sometimes."

"Not difficult. I just don't feel comfortable with strong emotions."

"But things are strong between us."

"Yes, they are, mi amor, aren't they?"

She thinks again of the man and the little girl. Suddenly she wonders if the prospect of adopting a child—having the responsibility of a child so soon into the relationship—will be too much for Nick. "Nick, I want to adopt the baby—I mean I plan to continue, even though Daniel has left."

"I assumed you would."

"But what does that mean for us?"

"Lena, that wouldn't come between us—at least from my perspective. Does Daniel still want the child?"

"No." Lena hesitates. "Would you adopt her—I mean, after I do, if we end up together?"

"Of course. As long as—"

"What?"

"I'd want us to have a child as well, and I'm getting old."

"What are you saying?"

"I'd want you to get pregnant right away."

Relieved now, Lena tells him that of course she'd try to get pregnant—that's what she and Daniel had planned: two children close together in age. But that of course, he has to leave Hildy first. They talk a little more about the kind of family traditions they'd want. After Lena hangs up, she leans back against her pillows drinking her now-cold tea, happy that she and Nick have had this talk about the baby. Qui est-ce qui va semer le blé? Dit-elle. That voice again! Suddenly she realizes that the man and child were speaking French. Hmm. More French. I wonder what Isaiah will say about this? Maybe Rita did lie about never taking me back to Paris. Lena reaches for the phone to call her friend, not letting go of the picture that still lingers in her mind.

Thirty-one

Three days later, Nick is in his office on Pennsylvania Avenue, having just finished a meeting with several colleagues. After they leave, one colleague—the one who encouraged Nick to take a Spanish course in Costa Rica—lingers behind. Nick has been busy lately and the two men haven't had time to meet for their weekly beer, and the colleague tries to find out why. But Nick won't divulge any secrets about his life—he doesn't say a word about Lena, even though he considers his colleague a good friend.

"Can you close the door on your way out?" Nick asks his colleague.

The man, about Nick's age, stops and looks back at Nick, an eyebrow raised.

Nick avoids his eyes, begins to shuffle papers on his desk. The man doesn't move. Nick looks up. "Out of my office," he says, suppressing a smile. "And shut the door behind you." Nick shakes his head. The colleague must know something's up. Hell, maybe he can even read it in my face.

When the door clicks shut, Nick dials Lena's number. Outside his window, two pigeons press together on the ledge. He hears them coo. When Lena answers, Nick wants to say, Yesterday was downright wonderful, but his throat constricts and instead he croaks, "I miss you."

She laughs.

He wants to confess that he'd actually skipped his last day of meetings in Caracas to fly home to be with her (Hildy would never suspect he was not in Venezuela), but somehow all he can manage is, "I had fun yesterday."

She laughs again.

He watches the pigeons nuzzle each other, and for some reason with Lena on the phone and the damn birds nuzzling, he gets aroused. The cooing echoes in his ears.

He turns from the window. "I love being with you. The other night, lying next to you, relaxing, and then waking up next to you in the morning meant a lot to me." He picks up a pen and doodles her name on the edge of a notepad. "I wish I had more of you every day." Nick knows without a doubt he wants to be with this woman—to be good to her, devoted, to make her laugh, make her happy. But he's also fears that he will leave her in shambles. He knows this is probably an unreasonable fear, but it's one he can't shake.

"I suppose these last few weeks should give us courage," Lena says, sounding happy. When he is silent, she continues. "These last few weeks have really helped me envision us together." She laughs. "Who could reject something so good?"

Her words strike a strange cord of fear in him. Does he believe in happiness? Does he believe he can have happiness? Nick remembers his dream from last night—how he'd bolted out of sleep in a cold sweat. Should he tell her about the dream? But what's to tell? He remembers the feeling of dread more than the details. "I'm not sure I can make you happy. I'm not sure I believe in happiness."

"What are you implying?"

Perhaps it's his imagination, but Lena's tone to him sounds tinged with fear. Already I am at fault for her unhappiness. Nick looks down at his pad; Lena's name is written everywhere. He crumples the paper and tosses it in an arc toward the trashcan. Why do I keep writing her name, like a stupid kid? He clenches his jaw. "I don't know." He pauses. "I couldn't make my ex-wife happy and I can't go back to that kind of relationship." He paces in short circles next to his desk, but then pauses when a flash of memory from his dream passes through his mind. The knife pressed into his throat. Red beaded out. He slumps down in his chair, suddenly tired. "I haven't figured out how to resolve my situation with Hildy. She is from a Muslim country. And in her mind if I leave her now, after we have lived together, I will have ruined her life, at least from the perspective of her culture. What may seem an impossibly long period of time to you may be only three twinklings of an eye for me. Maybe until I do resolve my situation, it would be safer for us to be apart."

Even as he says these words, Nick knows it's not safety he wants. He wants to be big, do a jig, stand on his head, to leap and play, to feel that joy in his body he feels when he's with Lena—he wants to abandon the inarticulate sense of oppression that shapes him into some smaller, more sequestered version of Nick.

"Are you saying you don't want to see me?"

The fear in her voice makes him grow cold. "I didn't say that."

"Then what are you saying?"

"Nick?"

He is silent.

Suddenly, Nick feels deflated. "Forgive me, Lena. I'm tired, that's all." He glances at a notation on his calendar. He and Hildy have dinner plans this evening with friends. "And I'm under pressure at work, and . . . otherwise." He looks out the window to find the two pigeons that were cooing on the ledge, but they're gone. "Can you meet me for lunch? That's why I called. I want to see you."

Their table is in the back of the restaurant, pressed next to an orange-colored wall. A purple paper lantern serves as their light. Just above their heads, the Indian god Ganesh beams down on them from a gilded frame where he perches his blissfully round, elephant-headed body on a tiny stool. "Lena." He takes her hand. "I'd really like you to go on my trip to Latin America with me," Nick says.

The mélange of color, the hum of diners' voices, the clatter of dishes, the hurried tempo of the waiters' feet, all contribute to Lena's feeling of being pressured and under stress. She jumps at the sound of a crash behind the thin partitioned wall. "I'm not sure I can." She peeks around the corner. The busboy has dropped his tray.

"Why not?"

She pushes aside her menu. She tells him she's been invited on another trip that same week.

"A work trip?"

"No."

He presses her to come with him. He has meetings in Chile and Argentina. He's added Uruguay to give them a whole week. Nick raises his hand for the waiter. "Uruguay would be an hour meeting," he says, turning back to her. "We could take the hydro-jet from Montevideo to Buenos Aires. It'll be fun," he pleads. He takes her hand. "It will help me leave her."

She raises an eyebrow.

Nick nods. "It will. I promise."

She turns her head to look out the window. The air and the currents and the swoosh of trees on Pennsylvania Avenue draws her out, takes her back to the Great River, to the pink dolphin she filmed with Daniel. One befriended her and nipped and squealed and pushed her down farther in the water than she thought it was possible to go.

"Lena?"

Her eyes meet Nick's but she is silent—she's listening for the bass of another man's voice. "I've been invited to go on a sailing trip along the Baja peninsula the same week," she says finally. She shrugs her shoulders. "It's a boondoggle—a seven-day public relations event to raise awareness. The Japanese want to build a salt plant in a protected lagoon. It's where gray whales birth their calves. They come all the way down from the Aleutians."

He takes her hand and pleads with her.

Her eyes search his face.

"I've concocted this trip for us."

"The Baja cruise is a trip of a lifetime."

Nick sets down his water glass. His face has grown pale.

Her eyes shift to the water as it sways from side to side in his glass. "If it means that much to you," she says finally.

"Is it a plan?" Nick asks, pressing his momentary advantage.

Her head tilts forward in a half-nod. For a moment, in her mind, she and Nick are walking hand in hand through an old Latin city, heading for a café, openly in love, no longer clandestine—but there's something else in the picture. Something she can sense but can't see. "When we get back maybe we should stop seeing each other until you leave Hildy," she says.

He frowns. "I hope this trip will help me leave her."

Lena looks beyond Nick. In her mind's eye, she sees the heart-shaped face of a woman laughing as she flings tiny white daisies in the air and they come showering down on a foot, a leg, a torso, a body of a man whose face she can't see.

"Lena?"

"Hmm?" she says, not looking at Nick, not willing to give up the picture in her mind. From the corner of the picture she sees two tiny hands, a small head, then a child's body summersaults and lands on the man's stomach. And then the woman reaches down to lift the child up, to swing her toward sun and sky until she is flying higher and higher, so high she almost touches the clouds. Church bells ring. Through the din, far below, she hears the man say I will leave her. And then the child flaps her wings and flies off into an ever-blackening sky.

"Lena, I will leave her," Nick says, taking her hand. "Will you come?"

She nods and turns away from him, not wanting him to see her tears, not able to explain how she feels.

From:	Nicolas Block
Date:	February 15
To:	Lena Holloman

L

I shouldn't really be writing now from the office because I feel extremely irritated with the constant interruptions to my work from the idiots I work with, and bad karma is hanging over my head. I wish I could snap out of my mood, but the whole issue of whether we ought not to see each other for a while at some point adds to my feelings of unhappiness. You're right, I do derive enormous emotional sustenance from my relationship with you, and the dynamic that is being set up is unhealthy and unsustainable. It's another reason why I don't want this to go on the way it has. (I've been saying this for quite some time now, haven't I? And yet I know the months go by . . .)

It's so hard to imagine life without you now, even on a temporary basis. I think that's why I haven't wanted to stop seeing you while I extricate myself from Hildy. I want to say more, but at the moment I feel my wheels are spinning and that I'd better stop this note and return to the subject when I feel a little calmer.

Thinking of you . . . (I was sitting in a wretched meeting this afternoon, worrying about getting everything done so Chile will happen with few distractions, and I found myself, like a teenager in class, doodling your name on the sheet of paper in front of me. This was probably when you were calling me.) Yours aye, N

Thirty-two

Lena orders a decaf latte and sits down at a small café table by the window to work. She thumbs through her notes preparing for her meeting at the United Nations—the numbers and facts, the key points she will make to the Oceans Committee members later in the day (they're discussing driftnet fishing again). From this coffee shop across the street from her hotel (a popular hotel with UN types), she can watch who is coming and going.

A smile creeps across her lips. The prospect of seeing Nick tonight makes this last-minute trip to New York almost worthwhile. She reaches for her phone before it rings.

"What time are you coming?" she asks, clearly happy.

He coughs. "I'm not."

"Oh. What about your meeting?"

"Umm, it was canceled."

"And you don't want to come to New York anyway?"

"I can't, Lena. I have too much to do for the Chile trip so we can have free time while we're there."

Even while she listens to Nick give his excuses, some part of her can't shake the feeling that Nick is coming to New York today.

She watches a cab pull up in front of her hotel and a porter point a gloved finger at the cab's trunk. It's really a mediocre hotel, so the pomp seems out of place, if not pretentious, but then again perhaps the porter doesn't like smudges on his newly polished brass door. She glances at her watch. "Oops, I've got to go. I'll call you later."

She's a little late by the time she slips into her chair at the United Nations. Long-winded ambassadors are already marking their countries' positions like dogs peeing on a tree, their sonorous accents almost melodious as their words meld together. This goes on for more than two hours. It's easy in this context for Lena to lose the meaning of what's said, writing down words one after another like little soldiers marching off the page to a battle whose purpose they don't know. But when she's not focused and thinking, her mind tends to float, even while she scratches out words on the page.

Suddenly she freezes. The plane is descending from a great height and hits the runway with a jarring thud. Her eyes narrow. She feels the doors open. Nick stands to exit. Tightness creeps into her belly. Then suddenly, she slams down her pen.

A colleague seated next to her jumps.

She pushes back her chair, stumbles from the room, and runs toward the area where she knows her cell phone will work.

She dials Nick's office number, but gets his voicemail.

She hangs up.

But then a minute later, she's dialing again. "You're not going to believe this," she says, leaving him a message, "I was sitting in a meeting at the United Nations, when suddenly I knew you were on a plane that had just landed in New York. Funny, huh? Nick, what are you up to? You're a slimeball! Call me when you get my message . . . later at my hotel. I'm turning off my cell now." She snaps the lid shut. And returns to her meeting. Later, she walks slowly back to her hotel. All day strange images floated through her mind—a clip, a fragment of a sentence, a blip of scene. Lena seems to remember seeing her mother talking to her father—but how could that be? She can't possibly remember her father's face—she never met him. She knows what he looks like only because she's seen a photograph of him. Her mother once told her he was a con man and a liar and should he ever contact Lena, she was never to believe anything he said.

From the hall outside her hotel room, she can hear the phone ring. She pushes open the door to catch the phone on the fifth ring.

"It's the world's biggest slimeball here," Nick says,

when Lena answers.

She sets her briefcase on the floor. "Were you in New York today?"

"Yes," he says sheepishly.

"Why did you lie?"

"I'm sorry. I came into the office early this morning and panicked that I wouldn't get everything done before our trip. I did bring a bag with me and figured I'd surprise you if I decided I could stay. I'm back in my office now."

"Staying late?" she asks snidely.

"Yes. I swear I'm not lying. I'll be here for another few hours. Look, I shouldn't have lied. I am sorry."

"Nick, it's just that—"

"I'm beginning to realize—"

"What?" Lena asks.

"It's weird that you know me so well. It makes me feel . . . strange."

She tenses. "Strange good or strange bad?"

"A little of both. Sometimes I feel like you are my double. Not me exactly, but—"

"I know what you mean," she says quietly. "And the bad? I mean—I assume that's the good."

Nick laughs. "Yes, that's the good, I suppose. The bad? Well, it's a little of the same. It scares me to think that you could know me so well that you can know, or guess, what I'm doing."

"I just pick up on your moods."

"Yes, but how did you know I was on that airplane today? That had nothing to do with my mood."

"You were lying and I picked that up when we talked on the phone. After that, it didn't take much to surmise you were on a plane."

"Yes, but you felt it."

"That's just my vocabulary. I could have said, I believed you were on the plane."

"But you didn't, you said 'felt.' That's the natural word that popped out of your mouth. And remember a few nights ago when I was thinking of you and masturbating?" Nick says, pensive now. “You knew even the exact time and length I was doing it.”

She laughs. “That’s different. You were thinking of me, fantasizing, sending me strong vibes. That’s why I felt it. It’s nothing more than that.”

“I’m not sure that’s true. There is something . . . well, innate between us.” Nick pauses. “But it’s more than that,” he rushes on. “Lena, you’re gifted in a way, that’s . . . well, unusual.”

“It happens mostly with you.”

“It doesn’t, Lena. What about the other day—the story you told me about Isaiah?”

“You mean him running into his ex-love-of-his-life at that club? That was just a coincidence. I don’t know why I was thinking of him—I haven’t seen him in years.”

“Exactly. But you knew he’d run into him.”

“I just thought he would.”

“But Lena, the last you knew he lived in Baltimore. Isaiah lives in L.A. Why would you think they’d run into each other?”

“I don’t know, Nick. It was just a coincidence.”

“And what about when you knew John wouldn’t pass his foreign service exam?”

“That’s because he’s a dumbshit—it was a lucky guess.”

“He studied hard for that test. He really wanted to work for the European Commission. We all thought he’d pass with flying colors, but you knew he wouldn’t.”

“For God’s sake, Nick. It’s a coincidence.”

“And what about when Daniel fell into that ice hole in the Arctic?”

Her cheeks grow warm. “Nick, cut it out. I don’t want to talk about it. It’s stupid. Just please don’t lie. Okay?”

He exhales slowly. “Lena, I love you—it’s just that, sometimes you scare me.”

Nick lays down his pen, his forefingers steepled, the rest interlaced like in a child’s prayer. The blackened sky seems to have inhaled the stars, or perhaps the fluorescent lights that line Pennsylvania Avenue have simply dimmed their glow. But at least he has finished his project; Chile will be clear sailing. His eyes follow the red taillight of a retreating car. The streets are empty now.

How is it that Lena knew of his trip to New York? He ponders the thought, but there is simply no rational explanation for their "connection," as she would call it. Even as he tells himself this, a simple thought enters his mind: We are somehow the same. It is not the first time he's had this thought. Tonight he pushes it away, tries to banish it from his mind; but it rises again at a distance, so buoyant—he knows it will return.

Nick pushes back from his desk. His eyes catch the shine of his black polished shoes. He wiggles his toes, but his shoes seem an odd thing. He stoops to grab his briefcase. The darkness under his desk catches him for a moment but he pulls back, slaps off the strange sensation. Why is his need for Lena to accompany him on his Latin trip so strong? Will it really make a difference?

He crumples his empty coffee cup. His eyes shift to the window. He is startled by how bright the stars suddenly seem. He longs to be out in the night air.

In the hall, the thick carpet muffles his footsteps. The office is empty. He feels like an interloper, as though he's someplace he shouldn't be. The elevator announces its approach with a shrill ring. He steps up to the brass door, then rears back. For a moment, in the shine of its coppery front, he has seen his reflection and behind him the outline of her head, the long flow of her hair.

He steps firmly into the elevator and turns to face the office, almost expecting to see Lena behind him. And then the crest—I shall dream you into existence—is upon him again as the elevator doors gently close.

33. France 1965

They stood next to the grange and watched the sheep and goats pour out toward the fields. Père took her hand when the animals trampled too close. The sun was already high in the sky; perhaps because it was Easter, Christian had turned the animals loose at a later hour.

"*Brebis*," Lena said, watching a black ewe hesitate at the bend at the end of the cobbled road. Her calf, born just yesterday, had been left in the grange and was crying.

"*Bébé*," Lena said, pointing toward the grange.

"*Oui,*" *Père* said.

The ewe ran back to the grange but the door was closed, so she turned and took a few nervous steps toward the bend and her herd, then back to the grange again—back and forth, back and forth—torn between the cries of her calf and her herd instincts.

Père looked around for Christian, but he'd left with the herd. "Let's put her in the crib with her baby," Père said. But just as he was leaning to catch her by the collar she panicked and started in the wrong direction—up toward the house where Père and Lena lived. *Qeeqeeeqee!* Père shouted, and the ewe turned. He slapped her rump and she ran the direction her herd went, ignoring now her calf's cries.

In the grange it was dark and smelled of sweet hay and mother's milk. The calves, six in all—hobbled up to a standing position next to the bars of the crib. Père held out his hand for the calves to smell. They licked his fingers, looking for milk. Lena held her hand out too and giggled when one of the calves bit softly at her fingertips.

"Shall we go see what Vivi and her friends are doing?" Père asked. Vivi had come for the two-week Easter break and brought two Spanish friends from Barcelona, both divers like herself, although she was the only trained botanist in the group. They were all working on a film project for Jacques Cousteau.

When Lena and Père entered the house, Vivi and her friends—Josep and Sonia— were huddled around the kitchen table. "Lena, come see," Vivi said.

Lena ran up to the table and held on to the edge while standing on tiptoe. The adults were sheltering something with their bodies.

When the trio parted, a basket full of hay and a giant chocolate fish emerged. Lena's eyes got large and a smile broke upon her face. The fish, almost black, had brightly colored details on its fins, and all around it, nestled in the hay, were hand-painted eggs.

"Look, Lena." Vivi picked up the fish and shook it. It made a sound.

Lena took the fish in her hands and stared, almost afraid of what was hidden inside.

"Sweet girl, you need to break it open to see."

Lena looked up at Vivi, uncertain. Her Père had told her repeatedly to be careful and never to break things.

"Here," Vivi said. "Let's cut it open like a fish and see what treasures we find inside." She took a sharp knife and carefully slit the belly along its seam. Inside were a dozen brightly colored foiled chocolate eggs and other hard candies. All the adults clapped. Lena laughed and clapped too.

"*Mon cœur*," her father said, hugging her tight. "What a lovely gift from Vivi. *Aux petits oignons. Oui*?"

Lena nodded.

"It's from Josep and Sonia too," Vivi said. "We bought it yesterday while she was sleeping and you were writing."

"Ah, I wondered where you all had gone. I thought for a walk in the hills."

"Such a lovely area," Sonia said.

"We noticed quite a few *cerisiers*. Is this an area where they are grown?" Josep asked.

"No, the cherries are mostly grown further south, though we have quite a few here. This area is known for its *chataignier.* We cook them in the fireplace."

"Roasted over an open fire, as the Americans say."

"*Chataignier?*" Sonia asked.

Vivi broke the fin of the fish and gave a piece to Lena. "I don't know the Spanish word. In English it's chestnut tree."

"Will you go back to the US after the work with Cousteau is finished? Josep asked.

Vivi shook her head. "My studies in Florida are finished. France is my home." She smiled at Jean-Paul.

"But it's hard to find work here as a botanist with a marine background, no?"

Vivi shrugged. "It's hard to find work anywhere doing the kind of botany I want to do. No one has money to catalogue the sea, unless of course, there is a commercial interest. France is no different than anywhere else."

"But the US seems more focused on fisheries at least."

"Josep," Sonia said sternly. "Leave her alone. It's hard enough without you reminding her how tough it is to find a job in her field." She turned to Vivi. "Don't listen to him, he's such a pessimist."

"*Moi?*" Josep smiled.

"Vivi and I are getting married," Jean-Paul said. He puts his arms around Vivi and Lena. "My girls want to be together."

"But I thought—" Josep began. Sonia slapped him rather hard on the back.

"That Jean-Paul is already married?" Vivi finished for him. "He is." She looked at Jean-Paul. "New subject." She nodded at Lena.

"*Maman vient?*" Lena asked.

Vivi raised an eyebrow at Jean-Paul. He picked Lena up. "*Non, ma petite puce*. Later you will see Maman."

"*Maman aime le poisson*," she said, pointing to her chocolate fish.

"Wow. She comprehends a lot doesn't she?" Joseph said.

Jean-Paul nodded. "Yes, and has a big vocabulary for her age. I have to be careful what I say."

"Yes, you do," Vivi said. "You never know what she'll repeat." She bends down next to Lena.

"It doesn't matter, the other is never here," Jean-Paul said. "And besides, she still thinks of her as a baby and never really talks to her."

"I'm a big girl," Lena said.

Vivi laughed. "Yes, you are a very big girl with big ears too. Shall we save a piece of your chocolate *poisson for Maman?*"

"Vivi. Don't encourage her."

"Oui," Lena said. "*Maman l'aime.*"

"It's not encouraging her. She knows her heart." She looked up at Jean-Paul. "I hope one day she'll feel the same about me."

"*Je t'aime Vivi,*" Lena said, giving her a hug.

She hugged Lena back. "I love you too, my big girl."

Thirty-four

Sometimes being in a body is just too much to bear. The way muscles, tissue, synapses tighten and swell until they are stretched beyond limit, screaming with pain, while the heart quickens, the hand shakes, the legs won't move without effort, and in the belly someone prods with a hot poker, while the excrement of the mind is already hardening; soon they'll need a chisel and a blowtorch, a forklift and a crane to lift the body up, to plop it down in Medusa's domain.

Thirty-five

Lena and Isaiah are talking on the phone late one night in early spring in a bickering kind of way. It is dark and stormy, and Lena, for reasons she can't explain to herself, is in the mood to argue. Through her bedroom window, she watches the clouds cross the moon like thieves sulking through the night.

"I can't believe you would pry like that."

Isaiah is trying to convince her to come to Los Angeles for the weekend to hunt through the attic for more information about her grandfather's other children.

"What's past is past."

"Give me a break. I know you are as curious as me about those kids. You have English relatives. Don't you want to know more about them?"

Lena glances at a photograph of Nick that she has placed on her bedside table.

"Maybe there is a reason you are always attracted to English men."

Lena rolls her eyes. "Two hardly constitutes always. Are you making a point here? "

"Moi? Point? What could the point be? We don't yet know the facts, though I confe. . . oh never mind."

Lena knows Isaiah well enough to know that he's already snooped more than he's letting on. She says that Gran mentioned he came by a few weeks ago for a visit. She is lying, but she figures there is a good chance it's true, and one way to smoke out what he already knows.

"Well, " Isaiah says, sounding sheepish. "I thought she might need help."

"Cleaning out the attic?"

"Don't be a bitch." He complains that she never comes to visit and Gran is getting old and needs help. "Though we aren't— "

"I know I know—blood kin, you are kin. Where was Tommy?"

"He and Mark are super busy with their family. What's up with you? Why are you acting like you begrudge my time with your family?"

Lena climbs out of bed to open the curtains more, ashamed now that she has been taking out her bad mood on Isaiah. It's not his fault that lately she has felt so disconnected from everyone and everything—or perhaps preoccupied is more like it. But then, as she looks at the moon, she remembers that Daniel has left her. For a moment, she had forgotten that aspect of her life. I have more than enough reason to be miserable.

"Alright, I confess. I did go back up into the attic and search more thoroughly through that chest. There is much more to your family's past than anyone has ever let on."

Lena turns from the window and surveys her bedroom. For a moment, it feels like it is someone else's room. "Yes?" she says to Isaiah.

"My lips are sealed. You need to come home to help me look more thoroughly." He tells her there is more to be found and that Gran is going to stay with Isabella so that Tommy and Mark can get away for a weekend alone before the new baby comes. "It's the perfect time for you to come. "

"She won't want me to come if she is staying with Tommy and Mark."

"We won't tell her, then."

Lena walks down the stairs to the kitchen to get a glass of wine. "That doesn't seem right."

Isaiah sighs. "Look, you keep having weird visions of people you don't know. Your family has a big secret they've kept secret. Don't you think the two could be connected?"

Lena misses the last step of the stairs and almost falls. The thought hadn't occurred to her that perhaps she was picking up on someone else's life. "I'm dreaming in French. That other woman is English. The two can't be related."

"You aren't dreaming."

Lena opens the fridge and talks out a bottle of French white. She pops open the freezer and takes out a piece of chocolate from a box she bought last time she was in Belgium. When was that? She can't remember, but it seems odd to have had chocolate last so long. Usually, when she buys chocolate, she buys a box for Daniel, who eats his immediately, and a box for herself, which she consumes slowly—until eventually, Daniel can't resist and eats hers as well. I guess I don't have to be annoyed about that anymore.

Suddenly, Lena realizes that Isaiah has been talking about Nick. "It wouldn't be that implausible," he is saying.

"Implausible?"

"Did you listen to anything I just said? There were two twins, William and Elizabeth."

"How do you know the second one was a girl?"

"I will divulge my sources once you are here. Two children. One died. The other one lived and could have—"

"How do you know? Isaiah, what have you been up to? Honestly, you are as sneaky and secretive as Rita was."

He laughs. "Come visit. I need your help. That attic has fifty years worth of crap in it."

The next weekend Lena is sitting in the kitchen of her Gran's house with Isaiah. Isaiah has opened the French doors and placed fresh-cut flowers on the kitchen table. He's laid out Gran's English teapot and linens and put out store-bought scones, double Devonshire cream, and jam on the table. He is pouring her tea. "Cream?"

It feels weird to be in her Gran's house without Gran knowing it. "Does she know you are here?"

He nods. "I told her I needed a quiet place to write."

"Do you feel guilty about lying?"

"Lying? Lena, there is a story here."

Lena gets up and walks out onto the deck. She knows Isaiah would never hurt her family, and especially not her Gran, but his interest in this so-called story unnerves her. If it were up to her, she'd let the past stay the past. For a moment, awareness of her tendency to hide things even from herself creeps into her mind. Why am I like that? She ponders the thought while she walks down into the garden. The roses are in bloom—in Lena's mind, they seem to be in perpetual bloom. For a moment she holds on to an image of a stone house with pink roses creeping up its side, but the image fades almost as soon as it came. She turns back toward the house. Isaiah has come out onto the deck. She smiles weakly at him.

He holds out his hand.

She walks up the five stairs and he puts his arm around her waist. She leans her head against his shoulder.

"What's bugging you?" he asks.

She shrugs. "Honestly, I really can't say."

"You want to rest some before tackling the attic?"

She shakes her head. "I slept some on the plane. I've been sleeping a lot lately."

"Depression."

"Maybe. Though I'm happy with Nick." She tells him Nick's working this weekend. "I know you were about to ask." She smiles at him. "Let's eat our English scones," she says with a bad fake English accent. "And then get to work."

"Atta girl."

Later, after they've had their tea (getting into the proper frame of mind, as Isaiah calls it) they make their way to the attic. Isaiah has opened the old trunk to show Lena what else he found there: a second letter mentioning the second twin, Elizabeth.

"I wonder if Gran knew about the twins," Lena says.

"How could she not have? Letters from England coming to the house."

Lena picks up an envelope and scrutinizes it. It was sent to her grandfather's office address."

"And you don't think his secretary told your Gran about the letters? Weren't they good friends?"

"Yes, but she was also Gramps' secretary for more than thirty years so perhaps felt loyal to him about this. Is this all you found so far? These two letters?" She holds up the two envelopes.

Isaiah nods. "But clearly there are more because those letters reference an ongoing correspondence."

Lena closes the trunk and sits down on it. "True, but we don't know they still exist, or if they do exist, that they are here."

Isaiah walks over to the attic window. He rambles about war and love and how people are split up, and lives changed. When Lena gives him the raised-eyebrow look, he finally says, "Don't get mad, but it does sound like they might have had an ongoing love affair."

She scoffs at the idea.

"I don't mean physical. What I'm saying is, that there is affection expressed between the lines, so to speak, in those letters. Sure it could have been one-sided, but if your Gramps jilted her, which he clearly did in some fashion, why would she be so kind, if he wasn't in some way affectionate toward her?"

Lena ponders this silently. The deception unnerves her, almost as much as Daniel's deception unnerved her—and make her feel as if her reality has shifted, as if she isn't quite sure who she is any more. She wonders for a moment if that's the nature of secrets—that they create alternate realities that sometimes end up being more real than what people are living.

She looks up at Isaiah, who has come back to stand next to her. He touches the top of her head.

"What's the strategy?" she asks.

"We have to start going through the boxes."

While the attic was relatively neat, there were dozens of boxes stacked around the room. "All of them?"

He nods. "We can assess relevance once we open them."

Lena stands with a sigh. "Let's get to work."

Hours later, they've come up empty-handed. Lots of old memorabilia, some of it new (to them), some of it interesting, but none of it about William and Elizabeth. Lena looks at her watch. They had long ago turned on the attic light, and at some point, Isaiah even went downstairs to bring up a lamp.

"I think we've struck out, and I'm starving, " Lena says.

Isaiah nods. "A lot of work for nothing. I was so sure we'd find more."

"To be honest, so was I. We haven't gone through everything—we can continue tomorrow. I'm here at your disposal until Monday." She smiles at him.

She's about to push a box she's just gone through back into the corner when she spies an old red tool box. Funny that it was here rather than in the garage.

Isaiah comes up behind her. "I don't recognize it, do you?"

She shakes her head, saying that her Gran is not likely to use tools, so maybe she put it up here to keep things tidy in the garage. They drag the box out into the middle of the floor and open it. They talk for a few minutes about whose tools they could have been. Everything is clearly old-fashioned, yet looks hardly used. They speculate that it could have belonged to Gramps when he was young, before he became a partner in his law firm—a job that would require clean fingernails.

"Do you remember ever seeing your gramps fix things around the house?"

Lena shakes her head. She remembers that Old Tony always did the work on the house. "Remember when he made that swing for us in the weeping oak tree? Isabella still uses it." They talk a little longer about whether they could have been Old Tony's tools, and then wonder why they always called him Old Tony, rather than just Tony.

"It is strange," Isaiah says, picking up the box to put it back in the corner. "Hey, what's this?" He puts the box down on the ground and turns it over on its side, holding the lid shut with his other hand. "Latch it for me, will you?"

Lena latches the lock while Isaiah turns the box all the way over. "Lookie here. A compartment on the bottom." He slides the lever and the bottom springs open. Dozens of letters fall out.

"Oh my God."

"Bingo. Gramp's secret stash."

Lena looks aghast at all the letters strewn about the wooden attic floor. While she thought there might be more letters, secretly she hoped there weren't. The thought of her grandfather's deception was almost too much for her to bear at this moment when her own marriage had fallen apart. Was this just how men were? Or was it a genetic defect in her family?

Isaiah is bent over the letters, gathering them up.

Lena kneels down. "Are they all from her?"

They flip the letters over so they can see the return addresses. "Seems so, doesn't it?"

Lena nods.

"Hand me that box, will you?" Isaiah throws the letters into the box and suggests they take them downstairs to read. Lena agrees, but then hesitates on the threshold of the attic. "Can we just read them later?" She is tired and hungry and can't bring herself to read the letters just yet, but doesn't want Isaiah reading them without her. She suggests they call out for Chinese food and watch a movie. "We have plenty of time to read the letters tomorrow," she says, sounding suddenly exhausted.

Isaiah looks at the depleted look on Lena's face and sets down the box to put his arm around her. "Hey, this isn't about you. It's the past we are exploring. Try to remember that."

Lena nods, but can't help but feel it is about her in some way. These are her family dynamics they are digging into. They framed the way her grandparents and perhaps even her mother and Aunt Clarissa, functioned. And in that way, this secret is about her as well. Though she tries to act different from her family, as a biologist, she knows she was acclimated from birth to respond in a certain way to specific stimuli—and that both the stimuli and her reactions have become part of what seems normal to her in the world. Reality is a matter of perception.

"Do you think my divorce from Daniel was inevitable?"

Isaiah rubs her back and then hugs her tight. "Just because your grandfather had an affair, doesn't mean you or the man you are with are destined to have an affair too. Some men are loyal," he says, pointing to himself. "Moi."

She bends down to pick up the box. "You don't know that you will be loyal—you aren't the marrying type."

"Ouch. That was mean."

She turns to go down the stairs. He takes the box from her. "You mean because I can't marry I can't be disloyal? What kind of faggot-hating statement is that? You don't think Mark and Tommy are loyal?"

Halfway down the stairs, she turns back to him. "Now you are the one who is being sensitive. Of course I know Tommy and Mark are loyal to each other. I just meant, you haven't found anyone yet that tests your loyalty. Anyone of a long-enough duration."

Isaiah turns toward his room with the box.

"Hey, where are you going with that?"

"You said you were too tired to read the letters tonight, so I'm going to stash the box in my room."

She shakes her head. "I want us to read them together."

Isaiah nods. "I heard you." He tells her he has to put the box somewhere, unless she suggests he holds it all night, and so he is going to put it down in his room. She reminds him that he abhors secrets and surely will be tempted to read them in the night. "You won't be able to sleep—your fingers will itch too much."

"Yesum, yesum," he says, mimicking a bad movie version of a black southern slave. "Where would you like them?"

Something about his attitude, maybe his peevish derisiveness, combined with her own tender state, makes her start to cry. She knows she is being silly, but she can't help it.

Isaiah sets down the box and goes over to her. He pulls her over to a comfy chair tucked into an alcove in the hall. "It's okay," he says, pulling her onto his lap. "I know this is hard for you. I'm sorry I'm not making it any easier."

She cries harder, burying her head against his chest. He soothes her hair and rocks them both slightly. When she is calm, he says, "I hope my shirt doesn't shrink. It's very wet, and very linen and my new favorite."

She looks up at him. "I'm sorry," she mumbles.

He cradles her again and tells her not to worry, that it was a joke to make her laugh. "Lena, I love you," he says. "And I always will. I promise I'll never stop."

The next morning, Isaiah is already down in the kitchen making pancakes when Lena gets up. She can smell the distinctive aroma of batter on the griddle and sweetness of real maple syrup being heated as she walks down the stairs. And then, the smell of coffee. Suddenly, she is very hungry. Outside, she can see that the sky is the perfect blue so typical of Los Angeles (when it isn't smoggy). The world seems brighter, easier, not so full of heaviness. Suddenly she wonders why sometimes life feels so hard, dragging her down heavy, while other times, like now, she's able to put everything into perspective and realize that sorrows and mishaps are just part of the cycle of life.

In the kitchen, she snags a pancake from the plate where Isaiah has been keeping them warm.

"Um, missy, put the lid back on the plate so the pancakes stay warm for everyone."

Lena looks around the empty kitchen. "Everyone?

"Tu, moi—I like my pancakes warm, thank you."

She reaches over to the oven and turns it on low. "Silly, put the plate in the oven, yes with the lid. "

"Good?" Isaiah asks, as Lena licks her fingers.

She kisses him on the cheek. "They are perfect, scrumptious."

Isaiah comments on her more chipper mood this morning and asks her to set the table on the deck, and to cut some roses while she's at it. He brings out a bottle of champagne and adds it with fresh orange juice to two flutes.

"What's the occasion?" Lena asks, nodding at the champagne.

Isaiah lifts his glass. To us, to a life of adventure."

"You mean," Lena says, laughing, "to another day of uncovering secrets."

Isaiah demurs that that is his motivation and then laughs, asserting that secrets give spice to life, particularly when they are about to be uncovered, and even more particularly, when they aren't about something you don't want to know about.

Lena frowns, but then decides what the hell? At least she can say she has an interesting family, if not particularly trustworthy or stable. "Do you think stability is something to strive for?" she asks.

Isaiah ponders her question. "Too much of anything, is well, too much," he says. "Too much stability is limiting, too much movement is destabilizing. I think the key to happiness is finding balance."

"Funny, I was talking about happiness the other day, and one of my colleagues thought that was strange. "Who thinks in terms of happiness?" he asked. I thought it was strange that he thought it was strange. Can you imagine not thinking about your life in terms of happiness? He said happiness is a Western cultural bias. Do you think so?"

"Pancakes are ready," Isaiah says, carrying the plate to the deck. "And I know I'm happy about that, cultural bias or not. Perhaps if other cultures ate pancakes, they'd understand happiness more." He puts the plate of hotcakes on the table and pulls out Lena's chair.

"Why, thank you, sir," she says, laughing.

Isaiah touches her cheek. "I love it when you laugh."

She grabs his hand. "Enough! I'm going to read the letters with you as soon as we are done eating. I promise."

Isaiah feigns a hurt look.

Lena rolls her eyes. "Don't even go there. I know you love me, and I know you are also dying to read the letters and want to make sure I'm not feeling too mopey to do so. I'm not. So let's eat. "

When they finish, Isaiah brings the box of letters out to the deck. "Let's more over to the loungers," he says, "and read in comfort. More mimosa?"

Lena nods. Might as well be a little drunk if she is going to unearth her family's dirty underwear.

It takes them awhile to decide how to read the letters. Lena thinks they should take the shotgun approach, but Isaiah says they should be more methodical—that they should read the letters in the order they were written. Lena protests that they are only reading one side of the conversation anyway and so what difference does it make what order they read in? They'll still be missing half of the context. It's not like that, Isaiah protests.

"Think about all the letters throughout history that people have found and pieced together stories. They are always one-sided. It wouldn't be correspondence if you found both sides."

Sure it would, Lena insists. "They just can't be star-crossed." She reasons that there must be plenty of men who went off to war, wrote their sweethearts and then came home and married them. And the two sets of letters could be bundled together in attics all over America.

"You miss the point of a story. Where is the story there? Hi honey I'm home."

"Does it always have to be dramatic to be a story?"

"Of course it does, silly. Are you going to pay to see a play about an ordinary day of getting up and eating cheerios before heading to the office? There's got to be drama."

Lena frowns but agrees they can first date-order the letters. They decide they will read each letter together. But Lena reads faster than Isaiah, and in exasperation at her attempt to turn the page before he is ready, he suggests that he reads them out loud. She protests, saying she should be the one to read them out loud. When they realize they've come to an impasse, Lena says, "Oh, never mind, I don't care what order I read them in. You read in order and I'll read whichever ones I want. "

When she sees the deep look of hurt on Isaiah's face, she relents. "Okay. You read first and then I'll read second. This is your project."

"You sure?" he says.

"Of course I'm sure. Let's just stop arguing."

He smiles at her. "It makes us like an old married couple."

She frowns. "I never argued with Daniel. And my grandparents never argued either.

He looks at her pointedly. She grimaces at him. And then they settle down to read silently for a while, until Isaiah whistles. "Wow, she was a woman of great forbearance. She really seems to have loved your grandfather. I can't say I would have been as kind under these circumstances."

Lena grabs the letter he passes her.

Dear Jack,

I just received your letter about your daughter and felt very sad not to have been there to help you. Whooping cough is quite serious. I can only imagine that Bernice is out of her mind with worry about contagion and her just having had another child. I feel sad that you had such a reaction to her having this child, her having wanted a third, but can only hope that you have gotten over it now.

I suppose the best I can do from here is pray for you and your children. I have also enclosed a recipe for an herbal compress my mother always used with great success for us children when we were little. I wish I could have made the packs myself and sent them to you, but the recipe (enclosed separately) tells you how. Perhaps you could tell Bernice your source was a client?

The children are growing fast and were so looking forward to your visit. I have told them that you love them very much but are away doing a very great deed in America. Little William, in particular, wants to know when he will finally get to lay eyes on his daddy again. I think so much of you and feel you are very close to me these thousands of miles away. It is still sad and terrible in London, but not as dreadful as it was on the front. I wish I could be more help at the hospital, so many of the men are so dreadfully sad. But as you've said, I must devote my energies to the children. Perhaps once they are in school full time, I will return. The money you have sent has helped us a great deal. Once tricycles are available again in London, I promise I will use the money to buy one for William and Elizabeth as you've instructed.

Be well. I love you. Ann

Lena hands the letter back to Isaiah feeling a little sick to her stomach. From the letters, it does seem that there was more than just a war-time fling. Or perhaps her grandfather was simply being his normal responsible chivalrous self—taking care of two children he accidentally fathered in trying times. But no matter how much she tries to make excuses for him, the news of his other family has shocked her and made her wonder what other secrets her family has kept under wraps.

"Maybe she was just trying to pretend to herself that she was close to your grandfather."

Lena looks at Isaiah, not quite sure what he's getting at.

"People do that, you know. They want to be close to someone, so they pretend they are. She mentions three children, but your grandparents only had two—your mother and Aunt Clarissa.

Lena nods, still lost in a foggy haze of thought about her family and her own past. The thought that perhaps she is someone different has crossed her mind more than once these past several months. "What if—?"

"What if, what?" Isaiah asks.

"What if I'm not who I think I am?"

Isaiah sighs, putting down the letter in his hand. "Come here, darling." He puts his arms around her shoulders and tells her that he knows this news is upsetting to her, but it shouldn't be. She is still who she is, no matter what her grandfather did or didn't do. He reminds her that they don't know the whole story—as she said, they are only reading one side of the correspondence. For all they knew, Ann was insane, writing letters to a man who didn't love her. When she starts to protest, he holds up his hand to stop her. "True," he says, "she did possibly know some details of your familys life." But then he points out that her grandfather could have written and said, please leave me alone, my family is sick—or something like that. "Do you want to stop reading?"

Lena looks down at her own ringless finger. "I'm okay," she says, giving him a fake smile. "Let's keep reading. As you say, these lies are not about my life."

Thirty-six

There's a gaggle of blackbirds in Lena's backyard. They've come en masse today, like a throng of penitents going to chapel on a holy day in Rome. She steps closer to her bedroom window to get a better look. She's never seen so many birds in her backyard before—there are hundreds, if not thousands. Where have they've all come from? They waddle and creep along her garden, tightrope the fence and the deck railing, and squat on the bare branches of her big oak tree. Their movements seem synchronized and somehow, preordained.

Suddenly the flock rises in unison, blackening her view with their mass. And then, as suddenly as they appeared, they are gone, leaving Lena with the momentary feeling that she is caught in a dream.

She turns back to her packing. Something about how the birds seemed to instinctually arrive and retreat glides Lena over the rocky promontory of her doubt. When she awoke this morning she immediately wondered whether she ought to get on the plane today for Chile, whether this trip with Nick was the right thing to do. But now, with the birds still in her mind, she simply knows. For a moment, she wonders if Daniel felt the same surety when he made his decision to leave her and start his new life—but then she pushes this thought away. How could that be instinctual? Annoyed at herself for thinking of Daniel, she snaps closed her bag. She must concentrate on getting herself and her luggage to the door so the taxi is not left waiting.

Once on the way, she relaxes a little. The cab glides down Rock Creek Parkway, past bikers and joggers and skaters who whiz by on the adjacent footpath into a bright blue sky drawn all the way down to the shocking yellow petals of the narcissi that line the road. Lena rolls down her window and breathes in the spring air. The colors—the reds and blues and greens and oranges—that people are wearing combined with the yellow flowers and bright blue sky look almost overwhelming, like a photograph sharply rendered. Lena wonders whether everything here, now framed in the taxi window, fits into some pattern in her life that is inevitable, that brings her to this very moment, this very place, and exposes her to these feelings, this anguish, anticipation, giddiness—for yes, all three are mixed in her, emphasized and de-emphasized as her thoughts bring certain elements to the fore, pushing others to the background, until the mix seems like an entire concerto, with the first movement only tangentially related to the last. Is that how it works? One thing ends, another begins? Or does the bird see no difference between it and the worm—are they each part of one long continuum? Her thoughts continue like this all the way to the airport.

In the terminal Nick is sitting among a throng of people, his slender fingers flipping the pages of a magazine. He looks crisp, wearing his dark blue blazer and tan pants, more neatly groomed than Lena expected. At his feet is a tiny satchel. "Hello," he says when she enters the lounge.

She blushes when he raises an eyebrow to her bag. She points inquiringly to the duffle by his feet.

"I'm a minimalist," he says.

"I guess so."

The terminal is packed with bodies, children darting among the dense crowd, babies crying. Nick suggests that they get on first to make sure there is room for Lena's bag.

"Are you excited?" she asks as they board.

Nick stares at her for a long moment. "I'm glad you decided to come."

She makes a face. "Were you worried?"

He leans over to kiss her gently on the lips. "I hoped you'd come. This is important to us both."

She pulls back. "I hate being the other woman, Nick."

He squeezes her fingers, "You're not the other woman."

In Santiago, their plane is one of the first to arrive in the early morning hours. They exit to a nearly deserted airport, eerily empty of color and sound. The sparsely populated plane (they changed planes in Miami) and lack of people in the terminal create for Lena a sense of something gone wrong, as though the world beyond this unremitting expanse of beige linoleum floor and steel-gray walls has suddenly disappeared. She expected something more vibrant and lush like the airport in Leticia, Colombia, where she and Daniel first met.

Nick is silent. Neither slept much on the plane, and both are a little groggy. As they quickly exit customs, Nick holds his blue bag in the air. “Aren’t you glad we only brought carry-ons?” Without waiting for her answer, he strides ahead toward the exit marked “taxi.”

She watches Nick talk in Spanish to some man he doesn’t even know, heedless that he’s left her like a packhorse to carry her own gargantuan bag even though she’s bone-tired, even though she lags behind, too burdened to fend off thieves. Part of her thinks, what people? what thieves?—but she pushes that thought away and clings to the question of whether she’s made a terrible mistake by coming to Chile with Nick. The thought—has she done something wrong?—hits her like a fist in her stomach. She wants to run back to the plane, to return to a place she knows—her garden where the birds hover and the flowers grow. She’s tired and at some level she knows her erratic thoughts are unfair, but she can’t help it. Her body has stopped—the muscles, the tissue, the very synapses have tightened, her legs won’t move without effort, and in her belly . . .

Nick stops and looks back.

She lays down her bag. He retraces his steps. “Lena, what’s wrong? The taxi’s this way.” He nods toward the exit.

“I want to change money.”

“I have enough for us both—from my last trip.” Nick picks up his bag and starts walking toward the exit. He stops again. Lena hasn’t moved, she’s still looking around.

"I want my own money," she says as he approaches. "Nick, I just don't feel . . . safe without my own money."

She looks toward the information desk. "I want to ask if there is an ATM." She takes a step toward the information desk, then glances back at Nick.

He is frowning. "Are you mad?" he asks.

She shakes her head, thinking of the differences between Nick and Daniel and then the betrayal of her grandfather. And then, for some reason, she's thinking of her mother, and then the man, the child, and the dog. In her tired state, various images are suddenly rolling and churning, flipping right over in her mind—she can't get her bearings, can't move until she submerges all the conflicting pictures in her head.

Only then can she pick up her bag and trudge ahead.

They stay on Avenida Ricardo Lyon in the heart of the city in a small luxury hotel (the Santiago Park Plaza), where the sheets are white, the linen crisp, and the service excellent. The hotel's old-European charm is a chimera in the midst of a country of rampant poverty and new industrialization.

The hour is early, not yet seven o'clock in the morning on Monday (it was an overnight flight from Miami) when they nestle in bed. Nick pulls her close against the warmth of his skin. Lena is fidgety. She complains that the air-conditioning makes the room too cold.

Nick rolls over and out of bed, hoping she's not regretting the trip. It's hot outside, but he shuts down the air conditioner. As he climbs back into bed, his lips graze her nipples. He longs for her in a way he can't understand, and the longing makes him feel weightless, like he's lofted into space, she a nimbus around him, while he's bound to her by some invisible thread. He kisses her eyelashes. Coming home, he thinks, as he pushes inside her.

Her green eyes are awash in tiny yellow specks that circle the black center, a hole in the universe. He's a nova, and she too; brighter and brighter and brighter they grow until there is nothing but brightness but also its opposite: only night, a ceaseless night that never ends.

"What do you want to do today?" Nick asks three days later—three days that have passed like a clock that doesn't move: it is seven o'clock in the morning on Thursday. They leave for Montevideo later that afternoon.

Lena's thoughts are languid; she's been tempered and molded, shaped into a new shape that is shapeless, a form that is formless, she is he and she is her, and she is the continuum, the energetic force that appears in the gap between their bodies. It's not difficult to see the gap, but she has seen the secret: the lines and the lay of the gap's grid are so bright they can't normally be detected; they mix with the air, the ethers. But they are in fact so strong, so subject, they cradle and illuminate all form: the table, the chairs, their two bodies on the bed. Lena has seen this; with her own eyes, she has seen it. A voice said, wake up, wake up, and she did, but while she was awaking her mind forgot its distance, the separation, the stampede that normally declares, I am. Lena saw it in the moment, in the wisp of time before she became anything old or new, anything remembered or made up; she saw the lines, the lay of the grid and how Nick and she were one.

Now she runs her finger down the dampness that still clings to her stomach. She smells like him, like the two of them mixed together. She watches him watching her.

"Lena, we've been here three days and we haven't done any sightseeing."

"We've meant to."

He laughs and asks if there is anything she wants to see before they leave.

"The fort. I haven't been there."

She straddles him, riding deeply, slowly, while his contours melt; he's fire, he's the sun, he's calling her name, he's scorched into the lay of her skin; she's incandescent; and the continuum casts and re-casts, creates and re-creates until all is one.

♠♠♠

The old fort, in the middle of the town, is perched on a pinnacle, its own little hill of soil, shrubbery, and trees. From the top, Santiago looks different. Crumbling buildings, skyscrapers, and hazy pollution cap the skyline, and in the forefront a wake of scaffolding and flashes of silver ascend and descend as the sun rolls over the sky. The dirt and grime and industrialization shock Lena into silence. Man has dug and dug with his various machines until there's no earth left, until the earth's beckoning call has been sliced from the earth's mouth.

"You're being hard on the Chileans," Nick says, when Lena finally voices her thoughts.

She stares down at the city. "They could've done better than follow the American model."

"Lena, they needed to industrialize."

"They could've done it without ruining cities, cutting down forests, killing off their wildlife."

"What are you talking about? They still have millions of acres of primary forests left."

"Yes, but it's diminishing every day—mostly due to trade and industrialization."

He sighs. He doesn't want to battle over environmental issues; she's too good at her profession and always has a way of gaining the upper hand.

She glances over her shoulder at an ancient stone building they passed on the way up that had a small sign out front that said toilet. "I'll be right back," she says.

Once inside the building, Lena frowns at the waist-high stalls, the woman collecting money in her too-high seat (she can look right over the toilet partitions), the way the woman doles out paper two and three squares at a time, the dank, rancid smell of the walls. Something about the stone and the rank smell (so like an animal's den) pulls Lena down. So far down she's fallen out of her shoes, she's upside down. It's dark and she's navigating by echolocation.

The rain was tapping the roof, like tiny fingers on a window pane. Something was trying to get in. She climbed out of her bed and went to the window, pushed back the latch. Something hovered just beyond her window in the dim gold cast by the village lanterns. Then it dove into her room, staggered, and fell. In the darkness of her room she could hear the bat mewing like a newborn baby. Downstairs she heard a crash, a man's shouts, and then crying. Long sobs that sounded like the wind tearing the house apart. She approached the stairs. And then, she was falling, falling . . .

Lena pushes away the chaotic images in her mind, her distorted sense of the toilet stall, the room, the woman doling out bits of toilet paper. She pushes herself up and back out into bright sunshine.

When she gets outside, Nick is gone.

Alone, the sun can't hold her, can't stop what's begun. Lena, Lena, Lena, she's gone. The young Lena steps gingerly over the spilled red wine, the broken glass. She reaches her hand out. . . but it falls through space. She looks down. Santiago is so different above than below. Below it appears vibrant, alive with laughter, vendors sing-songing their wares, lovers kissing in the park; but here, now, this high up, the steel girders and scaffolding are prison bars pressing down, boxing the city in. Soon there will be nothing left of life.

Nick creeps up behind her. "I love watching you," he whispers.

She swings around. "It's you," she says.

He laughs. "Who else did you expect?"

She shrugs.

A perplexed look crosses his face.

She turns back to the city.

He turns her around, takes her forearms in his hands. "Lena?" She doesn't answer, instead, she looks away.

"Shall we go?" he asks, smoothing her hair.

When she nods, he takes her hand and leads her to the back of the fortress, where they descend the modern stairs that reach down to the street.

"My father left when I was one," Nick says, staring into space.

They have stopped halfway down to rest on a bench shaded by the long branches of a big oak. Nick holds Lena's hand—he has not let go. Like a thin string, she tethers him. "He told my mum he was going on a business trip. Two weeks later, she hadn't heard from him. When she called his boss, he said my dad had quit two weeks before."

"Jesus. Nick, I'm sorry."

"Almost a year later he called Mum from Detroit. He wanted us to come."

"It's a funny place for him to go."

"Not really. He wanted to work on cars. But after a few months in Detroit, he wanted to move to New York City. According to my mum, he was always restless. So she packed our bags and took us home to England." He glances over his shoulder at the street below. An old woman in tattered clothing stumbles down the road, a homemade-looking wagon trailing behind her. Ramshackled houses lean precariously toward her. And in the background, new skyscrapers. It won't be long before all the houses in the city center are torn down. "Our house didn't even have a toilet inside until I was thirteen."

"No toilet?"

"Just an outhouse out back. The government eventually paid for the conversion to indoor plumbing."

"One benefit of a socialist government, I suppose," she says.

He stretches. "Social democracy. Swept away by Thatcher," he says, sweeping his arm dismissively. "But the system had stopped working long before she came into power."

"Maybe so. But if she had been prime minister when you were young, you probably would not have had an indoor toilet." She laughs. "England would still be substantially toiletless."

He grins at her. "Maybe you're right," he says, holding out a twig for a squirrel.

"And you never heard from your dad again?"

Nick tells her that, coincidentally, a few weeks ago he got a letter—junk mail—about the genealogy of his name.

Among other names, the letter mentioned an Arthur Thomas Block, originally from Coventry. Nick knew it had to be his dad. So he called him and left a message. "When I told Mum she was pretty upset."

Lena frowns.

"Mum's had a hard life—it wasn't easy raising my sister and me."

"It's not your fault," she says quietly.

They sit silently for a while.

"Do you think you'll ever move back?" she asks, curling up against him.

He ponders her question, wondering if he can ever live in England again. He was too ambitious for Coventry, and at Oxford his lack of social status stood out. In the US he's been able to avoid emotional entanglement by the way he's structured his life with Hildy, something he couldn't accomplish at home.

She touches his arm.

He stands and pulls her to her feet. "Let's keep going."

The plane banks sharply to the left as it descends into Montevideo—too fast, it seems, to stop safely on the tiny white strip of land between the Cerro de Montevideo and the sea. Lena braces her arms against the seat. The engines reverse but the belly is coming down too fast. Too fast!

Then suddenly they are safe.

The aircraft taxis to a stop.

An old Mercedes-Benz with soft leather seats takes them into a city that's never lost its fifties-era feel—that benign and temperate period when the city felt peace, a time that held and held until it solidified into a pastoral stratification where the haves and have-nots were not mirrored so strongly in the structure (except down at the harbor where the cruise liners anchor and the tourists come to shore—there, thieves prey on the rich).

"It's nearly impossible to make an overseas call from a

hotel in Montevideo, but it's purposeful on their part—this lack of modernization. They wanted to maintain their agrarian roots," Nick tells Lena.

The hotel lobby is filled with the smell of exotic flowers, and cut crystal hangs down from vaulted ceilings lined in stone. Antique tables, scattered among deep-seated maroon velvet sofas, hold tiny beaded lamps of beaten silver. A gilt elevator carries them up to the seventh floor. A thick dove-colored wool carpet muffles their steps down the hall.

Their room is airy and dressed in white. A small bottle of champagne has been left on ice; Lena fingers its foil.

Nick pulls her toward the door. He's late for his meeting, and Lena has said she prefers the warm cobbled streets as a place to wait for his return.

He leaves her in a shaded place not too far from the hotel. She sits on a bench under a canopy of branches that sweep down, nearly touching the ground. She has her book, but mostly her eyes follow the people who pass by her stone bench: pregnant women pushing old-fashioned carriages, small children skipping, mothers so serene they seem unharassed by the need to be anything more than a family. Occasionally a husband strolls by, too, hand in hand with his wife or ruffling a child's hair.

A little girl in a frilly lavender dress stops by Lena's bench. She's eating an ice cream cone, and the dog by her side is watching her with rapt gaze. The dog wags his tail as the little girl stoops to give him a lick . . . oops! It's gone in one bite. The little girl looks back at her mother who calls to her rapidly in Spanish. When the child shrugs her shoulders, the mother shakes her head, clicking her tongue.

Lena watches the crowd, entranced by the peacefulness of the city.

Nearly two hours later, Nick appears weaving in and out of the strollers. His blue dress shirt is opened at the throat, and his tie is tucked into his pocket. His navy blazer flaps in the wind. He seems in that moment like an eagle come to land at her feet.

"You look like a bonny lass sitting there," he calls out

when he is but a step away.

He pulls her to her feet; for a moment it seems he is going to lift her into the air, but instead he pulls her close and kisses her forehead.

Hand in hand they stroll down the tree-lined path back to their hotel.

"I'm done with my meetings in Montevideo," he says, his mouth compressing a smile. "I have an hour meeting in Argentina and that's it. The rest of the time I'm yours."

She pauses at the threshold of the hotel. "All mine?" she says.

He looks at her with half-closed eyes.

At the seventh floor they exit without a glance back. They move slowly. Three full minutes it takes them to get to the door. The key in his hand presses into the lock. It opens.

Her shirt is blue, the color of the ocean. Underneath, her skin is the pale white of sand. Light from the window tints the room, encircles her shoulders as he lays her on the bed.

They are like the moon, a concave slip of light with shadow overhead. And then an eclipse: they are inside and outside groping through the dark sky, two bellies of light pulling them down and in, to the blue of the sheets. They both rise up and look around.

"Where are we?" she asks.

"You are magnificent," he says.

And the moon glides its way across the sky.

37. France 1965

Père unwrapped the diamond ring and laid it on the table for Lena to see. "It belonged to my *mère*, your *grand-mère,* Briget."

Lena looked up at her Père.

He nodded.

She fingered the stone carefully, as though it were a baby bird.

"*Bijou*," her Père said. "Like you, my *Bijou*."

"*Bijou*."

"It's for Vivianne. Do you think she'll like it?"

"*Oui,*" she said. Her small fingers held on to the edge of the table.

"Père is going to put it in a glass of champagne and give it to Vivi when she comes tonight. And afterwards, we'll have a party. You and me and Vivi. Would you like that?"

Lena laughed and did a little jig.

"Yes, we will dance and be happy, ma puce. But for now, we must dress and go to town to buy a cake."

She clapped her hands.

The *pâtisserie* had a display case that was low enough for Lena to look in. She pressed her nose against the glass and stared. The chocolate curlicues so perfectly aligned and balanced on the top of a gâteau. The *éclairs* bursting with cream. The large macarons so white and fluffy looking. But most of all, she loved the *gâteau* avec des fraises, the fresh strawberry torte filled with cream and chocolate ganache. "That looks perfect for Vivi, what do you think?" Père asked, pointing to the strawberry cake. "There's one left. It must have been made especially for Vivi."

"*Oui,*" Lena nodded.

"And for now, ma petite? While Père has his coffee and reads the paper?"

Lena pointed to a cream horn with rock sugar on top and chocolate sprinkles on the ends. "*Deux*," she said holding up two fingers. "*Maman aime.*"

"I know Maman likes them, but Maman is not here."

She nods. "*Maman venir.*"

"Not today, Lena. Vivi is coming to visit, not Maman."

"*Oui, Maman.*"

"She's a little obstinate," Père said to the woman behind the counter.

"They all are at that age," the woman said, smiling at Lena.

Père paid for the pastries. Outside, under the lapis sky, the plantain trees were budding. Next door at the Tabac, Père bought a Midi Libre and ordered coffee. They took their paper, coffee, and pastries to an outside table. While Père read his paper, Lena sat kicking her feet, intent on licking the cream off the ends of her pastry.

A quarter of an hour passed. Lena had finished her pastry, but Père was still reading his paper. Lena climbed down out of her chair.

"Where are you going?" Père asked, looking up.

Lena started skipping across the street.

Père stood up. "Lena, come back here."

In that moment, Rita turned the corner and walked toward them, a small overnight bag swinging in her hand. "Baby!" She dropped the bag and scooped Lena up in her arms. "What's this? Chocolate all over your shirt?"

Lena pointed to her shirt and then Maman's mouth and laughed.

"Did you eat it all yourself, bad girl? None for mommy?"

Lena's laughter peeled across the quiet street as she wriggled from her mother's arms. She ran back to Père. "*Maman s'aime*," Lena said, stamping her foot.

"What are you doing here?" Jean-Paul asked when Rita approached.

"I've missed you too," she said, smiling.

"This isn't funny Rita. I have friends coming for the weekend."

Lena shyly took her mother's hand.

"Good," Rita said. "I love a party. You can be so dull."

"Sorry, the beds are all taken."

"I am your wife. Surely no one will notice if we sleep together."

"Why are you here?"

She bent down to wipe cream from Lena's mouth. "To see my daughter, of course."

"You should have called. That was our agreement."

"Jean-Paul, what difference does it make? Do you not want me to meet your friends? Are you afraid I'll find them more attractive than you?" She handed him her bag.

"Why did you marry me?"

She shrugged. "I didn't want a bastard child." She put her hand on Lena's head. "She deserved better than that."

"You can spend the day with Lena, but then you have to go."

Her eyes narrowed. "Don't dictate to me, Jean-Paul. I'll come and go as I please. We've had this discussion already."

He crossed his arms. "Not this weekend."

She smiled. "Ah, special friends?"

"If you want to take her for the day, I'll pick her up here at five."

"Don't be silly. Where would we go? I have no car."

"You can take mine."

"Jean-Paul, you know I don't drive."

"You drove once."

"Well yes, but I've forgotten how." She shrugged. "Being a starlet does that to you—always chauffeured everywhere."

"Look, I'll make a deal with you. Come back next weekend, or anytime you choose, and I'll leave the house so you can spend some alone time with Lena."

She raised an eyebrow.

Or if that's too dull for you, I'll be your chauffeur and take you wherever you want to go."

"She sounds like a good lay."

Jean-Paul clenched his fist. "Don't make me use this," he said.

"You've turned to wife beating?" she said boldly, looking him in the eyes.

"Think of how it will play in the papers. Famous American actress beaten by her French husband."

She picked Lena up. "Ooof, you're getting too big for Maman to hold." She moved a strand of hair out of Lena's face. "Would my baby like to come with Maman back to Paris?"

Lena clapped her hands and laughed.

"Give me a hug, sweet girl. You and I living together in the city. It would be so much fun. You'd like that wouldn't you?"

Lena nodded.

"Rita."

She turned her back to him. "Père is a bad Père, baby girl. You tell him bad Père for Maman."

Lena looked from her mother to her father. The smile sunk from her face.

"You're hurting her. Just look at her face," Jean-Paul said.

"You're the bastard," her mother said.

"What do you want? Just tell me." He tried to take Lena from her mother, but Rita stepped back.

"First, don't ever imagine you will take my child from me. I don't care how many women you fuck, she's my child, and I and only I will always be her mother." She hands Lena to him, gives her daughter a kiss on the cheek. "Next time I come back, you'd better be nicer, Jean-Paul, or you will pay dearly. Got that?" she said, cocking her head.

"When will you be back?" he asked, holding Lena tight.

She shrugged. "You aren't my keeper. I don't need to let you know my every move. When you write a play that amounts to something, we can talk about living together as a family. I wouldn't mind having you and Lena closer in Paris or

L.A. or wherever I happen to be, but I'm not going to support you. Until then, I don't answer to losers."

Jean-Paul pursed his lips.

"And watch that," she said pointing to Lena's thumb in her mouth. "I don't want her teeth ruined. "

"She understands what you're saying."

"You have such an imagination. Use it in your writing, not on me. She's just a baby. Here, give her to me and run along home and get your car. The next train doesn't arrive for several hours and I don't feel like hanging around in this dumpy town. You can drive me to Montpellier." She patted her lap. "Come here, baby girl."

Lena wriggled from her father's arms and climbed onto her mother's lap. Rita fanned herself with her hat. "I didn't think it would be this hot already. Jean-Paul, before you go, get me some coffee please, and water." She turned to Lena. "Would you like some juice?"

Lena nodded.

"Juice too."

Jean-Paul stared at her.

She waved him away. "Go on. Get your girls some drinks before we swoon, and then you can get the car." While he went into the Tabac, Rita turned to the pastry box on the table. "What's this?" she asked Lena.

"*Frais!*"

Rita opened the box. "My favorite! She took Jean-Paul's coffee spoon and cut a chunk of cake. "Want some?" she asked, holding a piece out to Lena.

Lena's face grew solemn. She shook her head. "Vivi's gâteau," she said.

"Vivi?"

"Oui."

"Oh, well, I'm sure Vivi won't mind if Maman and baby Lena have a bite of her cake."

"I'm a big girl," Lena said.

Maman laughed. "You certainly are." She moved Lena off her lap and brushed crumbs from her silk skirt. "And messy. Now you sit over here in this other chair. Let me see your hands."

Lena held up two grubby palms.

"Jesus, doesn't your father ever wash you?"

"*Oui. J'aime me bain.*"

Rita laughed. "Your language skills are quite good."

Jean-Paul approached with the drinks. "Damn you, Rita, that cake was for my guests."

"Watch your language," she said sharply. "That's not language for a child's ears. And I'm sure Vivi won't mind if we eat a little of her cake."

"Vivi?"

She gave him a sarcastic smile. "Lena and I have been having a little chat."

Lena looked up at her Père, a little afraid that perhaps she'd done something wrong.

"It's okay, ma puce," Père said, caressing her head.

"Why do you call her that stupid name? "Bug" is not appropriate for a little girl. Not for one as pretty as Lena," she said, taking her hand. "Come here, my sweet girl. Let's you and I chat more while Père goes to get the car."

Jean-Paul pulled Lena back toward him, but Rita moved quickly and tugged Lena back into her lap.

"Hello, Madame Belcher," Rita called, waving to the proprietress of the pâtisserie.

"You're making a scene," Jean-Paul said.

"Don't be absurd, she loves me. I always take her pastries home with me to Paris." She turned to Madame Belcher. "Great cake," she said, holding up the box. She motioned toward Jean-Paul. "He knows it's my favorite."

Madame Belcher nodded.

"Do you have another?" Rita asked. "To take with me back to Paris? My director will love it! I came just for a brief visit to surprise Lena and Jean-Paul," Rita said, smiling adoringly at them both.

"That was the only one," Madame Belcher said. "But are you going to stay until tomorrow?" She looked at Jean-Paul. "I can make another for you."

"Oh, I wish," Rita said. "I miss them so much. Jean-Paul and I were just talking about how he and Lena are going to move to Paris to be with me once he finishes his play. We'll miss your cakes, but it will be nice to be a family." She kissed the top of Lena's head.

"Stop. You're making a fool of yourself," Jean-Paul grimaced in English.

She turned to Jean-Paul. For an instant, her eyes narrowed. "Why would I be making a fool of myself by saying how much I miss my husband and child?"

"The village is small."

"So?"

"Everyone knows everyone's business."

"That I am a hardworking mother, distraught that my husband must stay at his parents' home in the South while he finishes his play? Is there something else they know?" She smiled at Madame Belcher, took Jean-Paul's hand.

"Rita, stop."

"If there is something they know about this Vivi, Jean-Paul, it is you who had better stop. Think Paris. Think of your daughter." She stood and took Lena's hand. "Let's go have a chat with Madame Belcher and pick out some pastries for Maman to take back to Paris, shall we?"

Thirty-Eight

Nick enters his house like a thief, the tip tap of his shoes quieted by his careful walk. The light of the moon through the tall mullioned windows in the living room carpets his path.

In his office, he dumps his bag and briefcase on the floor. A soft circle of light pitches over him as he mulls through the mail on his desk. The mail is stacked neatly to the side, no doubt pushed there by the cleaning lady. Hildy likes to leave his bills centered in the middle, in two neat stacks (like eyes that stare up at him), though he's told her this habit annoys him. It seems an aggressive act, a reminder that he is responsible for the house and their maintenance.

In the corner of the room, a red light blinks (Hildy on the upstairs phone). His week with Lena had been calmer than he had imagined. He feels too good to be back, too good to hunker down to bills and responsibilities.

He unpacks his briefcase. He's condensed so much inside that the contents seem endless.

"You're home."

He looks up, startled. Hildy is framed in the doorway.

"Yes, I just got in."

"Good. I made arrangements for us to have dinner with Anita and John. Can you shower quickly? You know how Anita can be about social etiquette."

He hesitates. "Yes, of course." He picks up his bag and heads toward the door.

She steps aside to let him pass. Her perfume lies upon her like a second skin. He's never noticed before how it fails to blend with her own natural scent.

"By the way," she says as he steps past her, "I've made a booking for Spain. Shall I use your upgrades?"

He drops his bag. "Spain?"

She arches her brow at his dropped bag. "Yes, Spain. You've a trip planned next week, don't you?"

"Yes, of course, the conference. Did you want to go?"

"I just said I made a booking—I called your assistant to find out the dates and which flights you were on. Maybe we can go skiing in the Azores afterwards."

"It's going to be a quick trip," he says, studying her face. Her eyes are widened by a dark rim of liner, her round cheeks shadowed with rouge, her lips reddened to the color of blood.

"Can you get ready . . . unless you're too tired?" She turns away. "Would you like a glass of wine?"

"Hmm? Oh, get ready. Yes, wine."

"I've ordered a Weimaraner puppy. It'll be ready when we get back from Spain."

"A dog?"

"I know you wanted one."

"I said that?"

"You want a family. It's a beginning at least. Here, take this up with you." She hands him his bag.

He climbs the stairs wondering how he will explain this to Lena.

Lena calls Isaiah from the phone in her kitchen, smiling as she tells him about the trip to South America. "It was fabulous," Lena says, looking out her kitchen window at the Buddleja bush in bloom. "I haven't recovered yet."

The lid of Lena's orange enamel pot hisses and fizzes, the water for the spaghetti she's cooking having reached the boiling point. She remembers a scientific tidbit she'd picked up somewhere: evaporation doesn't have any sharp beginning or ending point; it just gets slower and slower as the temperature goes down. "He's coming for dinner and he's been here every night this week."

"Is Hildy out of town?"

"Nope, she's at home."

Isaiah whistles.

There is a moment of silence and then Isaiah asks Lena how the adoption is progressing.

Lena pauses her chopping. She flips the pages of a small Anne Geddes calendar—photos of babies dressed like ducks and tea roses—and stops at a page of babies with bunny ears. She tells Isaiah that the birth mother had her last checkup four weeks ago and she's due in another six weeks.

"What does Nick say?"

Lena pours herself a glass of wine. "About the adoption? He doesn't mind adopting a baby girl, as long as I promise to get pregnant right away with his child. I told him he has to leave Hildy first."

"Well, I'm glad you told him he had to leave Hildy. Speaking as a man, it seems to me he wants to have his cake and eat it, too."

"Oh Isaiah, don't ruin my good mood. And don't compare him to my grandfather—that depresses me to think about." She asks him if he finished reading through the letters yet. She didn't have the heart to finish them herself when she was in Los Angles, so she asked Isaiah to read them after she was gone. They weighted her down and at the same time made her feel like a ghost, like a thin sheath of self that has no grounding point. When she tried to explain to Isaiah how the letters made her feel, he said she was being silly, so she just shut up about it. "I think he's going to leave her soon," she says to Isaiah, not wanting to think of her grandfather or whether Ann had once had the same hope.

She pauses. "Do you think most American men have been with hookers?"

"What a question!"

"Nick told me that most British men have had at least one experience with a hooker and that he thinks this is true of American men too."

"When did he tell you that?"

"On the plane home."

"True confessions."

"Sort of. That's what makes me think he's ready to leave

her. He's told me every sordid detail of his past. As though he wants to make sure I'm okay with who he is."

"It seems a little inappropriate."

"Inappropriate? Why?"

"You two had just spent a fabulous, intimate week together. Why did he need to tell you about his hooker experience just then? He hasn't seen one recently, has he?"

"No, of course, not." Lena stares out the kitchen window at dozens of black butterflies that hover over the *Buddleia*. In that moment, the setting sun captures two of them caught in a complicated dance, and then one breaks away. Lena turns to the pot on her stove, the black butterflies etched in her mind as she continues to tell Isaiah about her trip.

"It seems funny I'll be flying east and you'll be flying west," Lena says, "when just a week ago we were together."

The logs in Lena's fireplace pop and crackle, an anomaly in the spring season, but Nick's built one anyway for reasons he doesn't articulate to himself. He's going to have to tell Lena that Hildy is coming to Spain.

"By my estimation," she says, smiling, "you'll arrive in Spain about the same time I arrive in Japan."

"It's an odd synchronicity in our schedules," he says finally, peering down at the glass top of the old antique Korean cooker she uses for a coffee table.

"At least be thankful you're not going to Japan."

"I am thankful."

"As you know," they say in unison, "I hate traveling all the way to Japan." They laugh.

"Hildy's going with me," he says, sober now. "She wants to shop."

Lena looks startled. "Well, tell her she can't," she snaps.

"I can't," he says, turning away.

She lays her hand on his arm, but he doesn't respond. "How could you spend a week with me, growing closer . . . so joyful, and then spend a dead week with her? How can you be so cowardly?"

Her face has grown pink, her eyes a supernatural green.

He wants to tell her it will be okay, but he is silent. Somewhere inside himself he is remembering a scene from when he was three. He hears the horn of a tugboat, the slap of water, sees Liberty lifting her torch.

Lena lifts her arm in the air, a balled fist before it drops to her side.

Chills run down his spine.

Her fingers creep over his hand.

The plane is bent sideways, circling in a gray sky, high above Tokyo—moving in tighter and tighter circles (it seems to Lena), even though the pilot has announced they are in a holding pattern. Lena's melancholy is unhappiness remembering happiness, expansion and contraction, two extremes competing for her mind, her emotions, her whole abstract is. Lena says to herself I'm depressed but she means something other than down a dark slope; she means she's feeling lightness and darkness all at once—she's being stretched further and further toward the opposites of space and compression, poles that pull and tug from her memory something she can't name.

When the plane lands, Lena heaves herself up and out of her seat and stumbles into the aisle. She's in Japan to attend a meeting of the International Whaling Commission.

She's so tired and bleary eyed (she couldn't sleep on the plane) she barely remembers moving through the long line at customs. Even now, outside, there seem to be too many people in too small a space. And the air feels stale. She joins a group of schoolchildren who stand quietly waiting for the bus bound for Nagoya, an interior city in the southern part of Japan. From Nagoya, she will have a three-hour ride by rail to the coastal town of Taiji. The children are uniformed; they don't say a word—no smiles, no movement. Their black suitcases (all the same) are lined up in two neat rows. To Lena, the children look more like a picture than something real—the only relief is the children's light blue school shirts and the shininess of their jet black hair.

When the bus arrives, Lena stumbles up the steps after

the children and huddles down on a naugahyde seat. The grayed sky creates a mirrored effect in the bus window where her brooding face stares back at her. For a moment, she imagines Nick and Hildy in Spain—the parties they attend, and at the end of the night . . .

An old man with gold front teeth catches her eye. He stares at her in a way that is not considered polite by the Japanese.

She turns away and huddles further down in her seat.

A scene she can't place haunts her: A man softly sings a song. Locks of black hair fall over his forehead. Across the room, a bottle spins around and around on the stone floor, a liquor label ripped from its side. A rope, tied taunt, hangs down before firelight. Scattered under the man's stocking feet are little blue pills . . .

The sun sets over the green-tiled roofs of Taiji, a town where whalers still live. Though the spa town is filled with five-star hotels (Lena suspects the Japanese government is at fault), somehow she has ended up in a decrepit inn just outside of town. The walls of the building are crumbling in places, and the bare walls of her room are streaked with a yellowish tinge. The cheap linoleum is peeling back from the plywood underneath, and her bed is so tiny it's more a berth than a place to sleep. Lena fingers the beige synthetic blanket; it looks dirty.

She frowns at her black bag, left on the floor. She hasn't unpacked—there's no closet and no space on the floor for storage. She tries again to shove her suitcase under her bed, but her butt hits the wall, knocking her forward.

Red-faced, she unbends and stretches her arms: her fingertips touch the wall. She turns ninety degrees and again, her fingertips touch the walls. Damn them.

She glances at her watch: it's not yet seven o'clock L.A. time, but what the heck, sometimes Isaiah gets up early. She picks up the ancient-looking black phone and dials his number. By the look of the phone, she is surprised it is digital.

Isaiah answers on the third ring. "Where are you?" he asks sounding sleepy.

"I'm in Japan—where else would I be?" Lena says sarcastically.

"Your travel schedule is insane."

"Yes, I know I'm insane."

"I didn't say—"

"I'm so pissed. The Japanese, our hosts for this trip, took everyone on a secret trip today and left me behind."

"The government?"

"Yes, the government. They were going to a traditional whaling village, and as you know, I'm no friend of whalers."

"Do you blame them?"

"For leaving me behind? Of course I do. I'm an official delegate—they had no right!"

"Hey, calm down."

"Don't boss me."

Lena can tell that Isaiah has sat up in bed and is paying attention now—that he's fully awake. "Tell me," he says.

Lena sits down on her bunk. "Hildy and Nick went to Spain."

"On a vacation?" Isaiah sounds surprised.

"No, Nick had a Bank meeting," Lena says, picking at the nap of the dirty blanket. "Hildy wanted to shop."

"Why didn't he tell her no?"

Lena stands up and walks to the window. "That's what I said. Isaiah, am I a fool?"

He sighs. "Lena, come home and marry me, will you?"

Lena blows her nose, trying not to cry. "But he doesn't even love her."

"Thanks Isaiah, I would love to marry you too. Do you want me to get down on my knees?"

She tells him not to be stupid, that marrying him would be like marrying her brother—in every respect. "Remember? You like men."

"A little affair here, a little affair there."

"You are an ass."

He sighs. "What's the problem? I'm no expert on hetero men, but it sounds to me that all you have to do is wait. You know he has issues."

"Ghosts."

"Whatever. Lena, most men don't like to be pressured. Moi, I'm the exception. That's why recently I've been thinking we should just get married. You're intense, Lena, and you're not one to keep an emotional distance. I want children. You want children—"

"Isaiah."

"Okay, but if you are going to jilt me at the altar, so to speak, at least give my competitor time to adjust to your new single status."

She asks him if he is writing a new screenplay about a gay man who tries to turn straight. "Why all the marry-me stuff now? And what about me," she asks, wiping her tears with the back of her hand.

Be realistic, he tells her. "That's what you always tell me." He goes on in a pragmatic way and tells her to do the calculation--will he leave her, will he not? "You can't change him. All you can do is be wise about your actions and wait to see if he can jump. Or if it gets too hard, you can bail. Those are your only choices."

Lena holds her breath, holding back so Isaiah doesn't hear her cry.

"I'm worried about you. You shouldn't be in Japan."

She tells him she had to come for work—it is an important meeting.

"That may be true, but it doesn't seem like it's the best thing for you."

"Working keeps my mind off things."

Isaiah clicks his tongue. "Have you heard from him recently?"

"Nick? He called me from Spain—twice already."

"How long have you been in Japan?"

"Three days."

He sighs. "Lena, he's called you two out of three days. From Spain to Japan. That can't be easy—or cheap. And I can't say any man has ever done that for me."

"I know." She blows her nose again. "He said I was right—he should've told her not to come. And, that he's planning on telling her . . . on this trip."

"So why are you moping? "

"I don't believe him. He says he wants to make a life with me—but then, why is he in Spain with Hildy? And anyway, I think I'm distraught because I keep having that nightmare I first had last December when Daniel and I came back from Singapore. Remember, I told you? I woke up screaming, No! I can't go through that again. I can't remember the dream once I'm awake, but I have this queasy feeling that stays with me all day."

"Is it about Nick?"

Lena shrugs. "I wish I knew."

Nick wakes with a start in Madrid. He dreamed about a judge in black robes with a bulbous nose. He can't remember what was adjudicated, only that the jury box was empty; everybody had gone home.

Hildy is huddled before the mirror: up and down, right and left—he can't see her face, only the movement of her arm. His eyes move to the clock. He jumps up. "Goddamn it, why didn't you wake me?" he says.

Her arm pauses. "I assumed you knew what time you needed to get up."

He marches into the bathroom. In the shower, tepid water trickles down his back. The night before, they'd started with tapas at a local restaurant. He was tense even before Hildy entered the bar. She wanted him to go the bullfight but it was something he couldn't do, so he told her to go alone. Afterward, she met him at Casa Mingo on Paseo de la Florida. His meetings had been over for nearly two hours when she finally appeared and, without a word, swung her bag up onto the bar and ordered a martini. She didn't mention the bulls and he didn't ask. It wasn't that he was queasy about animal blood, it was Lena. With her way of knowing things, a bullfight wasn't something he wanted to explain.

He grabs a Turkish towel. As it was, when he spoke to Lena yesterday by phone, she accused him of having sex with Hildy as a ruse. (He objected—he hadn't had sex . . . at least, not when he talked to her.) He takes a shirt from the closet, his trousers from the pressing rack.

Hildy is still bent over the mirror, up and down, left and right. Why hadn't he told her No, she couldn't come on this trip?

"Nick." Hildy points to her back. She's wearing a cream knit dress and the zipper is undone. On Lena the dress would look provocative; on Hildy it emphasizes the delicate lay of her bones.

He pulls at the clasp with the tips of his fingers, not wanting to touch her skin.

"What time shall I meet you?" she asks, leaning toward the mirror, wiping lipstick from the corners of her mouth.

Wind rattles the windows. It's been an unseasonably cold spring in Madrid, so cold that even the green tips of tulip leaves have turned brown.

He'd been with Hildy last night. But at her request. (So he tells himself.) He'd drunk so much he'd lost count of his drinks. (Objection sustained. The judge's gavel bangs. Now he remembers a tiny snippet of his dream.) Or maybe it was Hildy's icy stare or the way she flopped her bag on the bar without speaking. To Nick, holding out was never worth the tension he felt in his belly when he contemplated saying no. He knew she knew she would lead him this way; she always did. It was her way of making up—perhaps the only form of intimacy she knew. "Are you happy?" he asks suddenly.

Her arm stops its movement. She stares at him in the mirror.

It was mechanical, he tells the absent jury, we were both performing a rite we didn't feel.

Hildy's eyes move back to her face. "We've had this conversation already, Nick."

A man can always perform, it doesn't matter, he wants to say.

"Why bring it up again?" she asks.

Her question stops his line of thought. Why is he bringing it up? he wonders. He knots his tie. "I think happiness matters."

"Grow up, Nick," she snaps, turning to him. "It's not about happiness—some romantic notion of love. It's about compatibility, knowing your roles. Men and women are essentially incompatible except when restrained by their mutual obligations. We've had this discussion before." She bends down to smooth up her nylons, buckle her shoes. There is a straight patch of black hair on the top of her head where the perm didn't take. It parts in a jagged line, leaving a small scrape of skin exposed.

"I'm still seeing Lena," he says.

Hildy's head snaps up. She stares at him for the longest time. When she finally stands, the top of her head barely reaches his shoulders. "Is it the sex?" she asks. Tears spill down her cheeks. "My sister was right."

Nick looks down at his feet. "Right about what?" he mutters.

"You were going to use me and throw me away." She's crying now, sitting on the edge of the bed.

"Hildy, it's not like that."

"What is it like then? What am I suppose to do? Go back home?"

"You weren't a virgin when we met."

"How dare you." She stands and slaps him.

He brings his hand to his cheek. It's hot.

"It is about the sex, isn't it?" she asks, standing close to him, looking up into his face, as though to gauge his reaction.

Her perfume is so strong it almost makes him gag. He takes a step back. "No."

She puts her hands up to cover her face—her whole body is shaking.

"Hildy." He stands next to her, but can't quite put his arms around her. "I'm sorry. I didn't mean—"

She looks up at him, her mascara streaking her face. "To ruin my life?"

He shakes his head. "It's not like that. Come on, pull yourself together. You wanted to shop and we're going to meet later, remember?"

She nods. Her crying subsides. "Will you help me?" she asks, stepping toward him. "Some hair is caught in the zipper." She turns around.

Slowly he tugs on the zipper, careful not to yank at her hair. A patch of skin is exposed, sullen ivory. His finger brushes her back as he pulls on the zipper. What time is it in Japan? he wonders.

Hildy taps his arm. "Nick, what time shall we meet?"

When. Nick? What time will be right? It's Lena's voice that he hears.

Thirty-nine

Birds huddle on the ledge outside Nick's office window. The trees along Pennsylvania Avenue sway from north to south. Trash runs down the street, flies up in curlicues. The sidewalks are empty. From the large picture window in his office, Nick stares down at the empty street while he speaks to Lena on the phone. He has just returned from Spain and he's telling Lena about his discussion with Hildy. "She cried and said she was disappointed in me."

"What did you expect?" Lena asks. "Did you tell her you were leaving?"

Rain pummels the window in rapid staccato. "Only that I was still seeing you."

"Nick, you promised."

He pushes back from his desk. "Jesus, Lena, that was hard enough."

"She'll be happier in the long run—maybe she'll find someone she really loves."

Nick heaves a sigh "She says love is a cultural bias from the West."

"You need to tell her you're leaving her, otherwise you're keeping us both on the hook," Lena says adamantly.

"What I need is to do this without you telling me what to do."

"I'm not telling you what to do."

"You're interfering."

Lena can't believe what she's hearing.

"I have a relationship with Hildy and I have to deal with her in my own way. And I need—" He stares at the phone listening to the dial tone, not understanding for a moment that Lena has hung up. "Fuck!" He throws the phone across the room, ripping the cord from the wall. When he realizes what he's done, he sits at his desk, hunched over with his head in his hands, wondering how he is going to resolve the mess. He loves Lena, but he can't stand to see Hildy cry, and also, her crying brings up his own fears that he's making the wrong choice.

He gets up and walks over to pick up the phone from the floor. The bottom panel of the phone has come off and its guts are exposed. He wonders why it is that Hildy doesn't get to him like Lena does. All Hildy has the power to do is make him feel guilty. But is that how he wants to live?—with a woman to whom he has so little attachment, except for guilt? Nick's thoughts circle round and round like this until finally he sits down and writes Lena an email.

From: Nicolas Block
Date: April 24
To: Lena Holloman

Dear L

I wish you hadn't hung up. I find it difficult to speak of these things and yes, I am conflicted.

I feel I owe Hildy some loyalty for all she has done for me (however little you may perceive that to be). If nothing else, she's given my life a certain sense of peacefulness I've never had. And yes, I admit that might be because of our lack of connection, but nonetheless it seems a positive result in my life. As you know, I'm British and have a hard time with strong emotions.

On the other hand, I love you, Lena, I have no doubt of that. But for me it's not just a question of how much I love you but also, how much I owe her, and whether on the whole the benefits I derive from my relationship with you outweigh what I receive from her. My experience with love relationships has not been good, while in contrast I've derived from Hildy the benefits I sought.

I feel hesitant to say more as this does not seem to be a topic we should be discussing via email. I can leave the office shortly. Let me know if you can meet. N

Three days later, Nick stands in front of Lena's house. For a long time, he just leans into her front gate not wanting to push it open. Through the light of her window, he can see her crouched on her couch reading a book, her head bent down.

The minutes tick by slowly, like a film at half speed as he walks the dozen or so steps to her porch and then mounts the stairs. Only when he stands directly in her doorway does she unfurl herself and rise—though he suspects, knowing Lena, she knew he was outside.

He sees from her face that he looks like he feels: starkly vulnerable—or like a hand-painted egg, too fragile to touch.

She steps back from the door.

He enters her house.

She gestures vaguely toward the living room area. "Have a seat. Do you want some tea?"

"No thanks." He sits stiffly on the edge of the couch. A litany of words without beginning loop in his mind. He searches her face hoping she'll know what to say.

She sits down in the middle of the couch and reaches out to him, but her arm falls, empty-handed, to her lap. He understands in the moment that her fingers fail to reach him that she can't turn back the clock to a time when he wasn't falling head first into his own solitary abyss. He wonders how she stays so strong.

She moves closer to him and draws him to her, so close he imagines her breath is the flapping of a butterfly's wings. "Nick?" she asks, pushing the hair from his forehead.

Words tumble from her mouth in a thin stream and encircle him like a tether. But he slips away. He has withdrawn into himself, like a pill bug curling inward when you poke it in the spine. A long moment passes, but when he finally looks up at her, he sees that her eyes have turned the green of the sea. Her wheat-colored hair lies across her breast, shielding her heart. She has grown so slender she's almost invisible.

Suddenly, he wants to shake her to make her respond. It's her calm repose that disturbs him. She seems both immune to him and at the same time, able to absorb his pain. This frightens him.

The Tiffany lamps cast light in the corners of the room where shadows should be. "Nick?" she says softly.

He stands, disentangling himself from her, and walks to the window where he tries to find some pattern, any pattern, of stars in the now night sky.

She creeps up behind him, but he remains soldered to the window, unwilling to turn around. "I don't care," he whispers to the windowpane. A tear trickles from the corner of his eye. He wipes it with his sleeve.

She touches his shoulder. "I love you and you love me . . ."

He turns to face her. "Damn you—I want to be like Samuel Beckett!"

Startled, she steps back.

Like a champagne cork that's popped, he can't stop spewing. "He once knifed himself in the hand as he sat in a café—just because he could. I want that same freedom to choose."

Her eyes are like saucers.

"I'm reading his autobiography," Nick says coldly, though inside he is cursing himself for his own unruly behavior. He wonders suddenly if it's the Beckett book that has partly caused him to be so depressed since he returned from Spain. He's felt wobbily—like he can't get a firm footing on his own decisions, no matter how hard he tries.

He looks down at the floor, ashamed at how he's behaving to this woman he loves, but at the same time, not able to access the firmness he felt when he and Lena were in South America. He loves her, so what is it?

He glances up at Lena, but she has turned her face away.

Shocked at what she has just heard, she is looking into the distance, to a place where she abandons the world of words and rational thought and enters a space where she can read beneath the skin. Lena doesn't realize she loses herself when she shadows people like this, enters a world of ether, where bone and gristle have no bearing on the things she sees. Jumbled images occupy her mind: Nick and people she recognizes, but doesn't know. She becomes dizzy with her effort to access the answer to a riddle that plays in her mind in a language she doesn't yet understand.

For a long time, they are both quiet.

The clock ticks.

The dogs whimper in their sleep.

That's enough, she tells herself firmly. She stands and walks over to Nick. She hesitates, but then she bends and pulls him up. Holding him firmly, she wills him to return to the man she knows.

At first, he stays skeletal in her arms. Then slowly, slowly, he fills himself until she feels his heart beat, then the pulse of his body. He clings to her—like a child, he gives in to her warmth.

Tenderly, their lips meet.

It's only later, after Nick leaves, that Lena reacts strongly to his strange behavior. When she bends to pet her dogs whining at her feet, the room spins before her eyes and then, for the tiniest moment, she blacks out.

When her vision returns, she is squatting and holding onto the back of the couch. With effort, she heaves herself up to standing.

In the kitchen, she cracks two eggs in a pan and watches the whites spread to form a solid texture. She wonders why the whites and yolks don't intermingle, why something creates a barrier to keep them apart. She lays her head on the counter. She hasn't eaten much in the last month. The pop and crackle of hot butter sound loud to her ears.

When the eggs are done, she carries a tray upstairs to her bed. But even there, in a nest of pillows, she can't eat. She is falling

out of her bed
out of her body
she's a speck
her mind can't hold her

she's a lovely blip of color
engulfed by a radiant white light.

The child laughs and claps her hand. There are white daisy petals strewn on the green grass around her feet. Someone picks her up and swings her high until she is squealing with glee. In the background she can hear the tinkle of bells and the bleating of goats, but she can't see them. Say you'll marry us, a man dressed in crumpled pants and a sweater says. Of course, I'll marry you both. I love you, a woman outside of the picture says. . .

Lena opens her eyes to the soft green of her walls and the painting of a lone woman on horseback. Her dogs sit next to the bed, heads cocked. Quietly, she tells them to lie down as she floats, not wanting to let go of the light and sweet sensations that fill her, not wanting to think of Nick.

Forty

Later that week, Lena and Anita meet at a shop in Old Town, Alexandria, to buy baby things.

"You wanted a sleigh style, what about this one?" Anita asks, pointing to a hand-painted crib.

Lena fingers the blue-and-white-striped wood. "The zebras are lovely, but look at the price!" She steps back from the crib. "And it doesn't even look convertible into a child's bed."

"It's a Clark & Lee design—heirloom quality. I'd say nothing but the best for my child." Anita wanders across the room to another crib. "Here is one for four hundred dollars but it looks cheap."

Lena glances over to where Anita is standing. The crib is square and boxy and made of blond wood. "No I definitely want a sleigh style—I just don't want to spend over a thousand dollars for a baby's bed. That's crazy."

"My sister says if you acclimate them early to have good taste, they'll marry well."

Lena laughs. "Your sister should know. She certainly married well."

Anita looks up from a hand-painted rocker covered in teddy bears. "Did I ever tell you the story of how she met her husband?" She tells Lena how after college her sister decided she wanted to marry a millionaire. So she researched the richest, most eligible young bachelors in the United States and found that many of them were tech geeks who lived in Seattle. So she moved there, determined which one she wanted, and then targeted him until he capitulated. "It worked for her—before he could marry her, his company insisted on a prenup. She held out for fifty million—now even if he turns out to be a creep, she still wins."

"I'm not sure I'd call that winning. What do you think of this one?" The sleigh bed had a solid headboard and footboard and was pickled white.

"Lovely, but not as nice as the hand-painted one. You should think about the future."

"I am thinking about the future. I think it is irresponsible to spend a thousand dollars on a baby bed, when I have nothing. Anita, I have to buy everything."

"All today?"

"I was hoping to get most of my purchases out of the way. The baby is due in a few weeks, and the adoption, hopefully, will occur soon after that."

Anita sits down in the rocker. "Do you really think you should be adopting this baby? Daniel left you."

Lena stares at her friend, puzzled. "Why would you say something like that now?"

"I'm concerned."

Lena turns back to the beds. "About what?"

"How are you going to raise a child on your own? Daniel told me he wants nothing to do with the baby and he wished you wouldn't go through with it."

"He's not going to adopt her."

"I know. He said that he promised you he wouldn't tell the agency that you are getting divorced."

"I can trust him."

"It's not a matter of trust. Why do you want a baby on your own? Do you know how hard that is going to be?"

"What do you think of this changing table? It's not the same brand as the pickled-white crib, but—"

"You don't have any family nearby."

Distracted, Lena turns to Anita. "What's up? Nick and I will manage."

Anita stares at her, perplexed. "Nick hasn't left Hildy."

"And your point?"

"Don't you think a baby ahead of marriage is a little premature?"

"Oh my god, look at this." Lena points to a layette set. "I love baby things."

"Apparently. But have you thought about what you're doing?"

Lena turns to Anita looking hurt. "I thought you wanted to shop with me. To help. Don't you like babies?"

Anita shrugs. "I'm worried about you—you aren't being realistic."

Lena sits on the edge of a blanket chest. It's hand-painted with yellow and white stripes and ducklings all along the edge. "Daniel and I started the process of looking for a child almost two years ago. I asked Nick and he's okay with adopting the baby. It's just that—"

"What?"

"He wants me to promise I'll get preggers right away."

"Is that what you want? To have a horde of squalling babies in diapers?"

"We agreed we'd have a total of two children."

"He might want two of his own. Besides, he hasn't left Hildy yet so he can't or shouldn't be making these kinds of plans with you. Men do change their mind."

"But he's told everyone he will—even his mother. Hildy is the only one who doesn't know." At that moment, Anita's cell phone rings. While she talks, Lena wanders over to the baby clothes. She picks up a pink bunting, holds it up to her nose. It smells like clean cotton. Startled, she wonders what she expected to smell. The smell in her mind is distinct, like a memory she can't place. And then she's wandering down a green grassy hill. The sun a bright yellow ball in a lapis sky. "Mommy," she shouts as she runs down a rocky path filled with tiny pink, lavender, and white flowers. At the bottom, she falls, tumbles right over, but her mother isn't there to help her. Where was she? Lena wonders. Had she perhaps taken Lena to the park that day? Or perhaps Lena had been with her grandmother and is confusing the memory with her mother. She searches her mind trying to find a memory to fit the picture, but none will come. She begins to hum to herself. Alouette, gentille alouette, alouette je te plumerais . . .

"Sorry, that was my office, then John. Have you decided?"

Lena smiles at Anita.

"What?"

Lena shakes her head.

"Are you okay?"

"Of course, I'm okay. I'm happy, that's all. I feel like smiling."

Anita sighs.

"What?"

"I'm worried about you."

"Worried? Why?"

Anita shakes her head. "You have nothing to be happy about."

41. France 1965

"I spoke to Madame Belcher today," Vivi said. "She said Rita was here again this week." She took off the ring Jean-Paul had given her and set it on the scarred table.

Jean-Paul was cooking dinner at the stove. He turned to Vivi. "Does Lena want me to read her a story?"

Vivi shook her head. "She's asleep now."

Actually, Lena was lying in bed watching the stars through her tiny window, half-listening to the adults in the other room.

Jean-Paul picked up the ring and tried to take Vivi's hand, but she pulled away.

"I don't want to wear it until you've resolved your situation."

"It's resolved. I want a divorce."

"Wanting a divorce and getting a divorce are two different things."

"The only reason it hasn't happened yet is because of Lena."

"I understand that and I would never want you to lose her—I love her, too, but Rita's been telling people in town you both are moving to Paris shortly."

Jean-Paul turned back to the stove, flipped the lamb chops on the grill. "It's just her stupid talk."

Vivi poured herself a glass of wine. "And the baby?"

Jean-Paul looked over his shoulder. "Lena?"

Vivi set down her glass of wine. "Don't play games with me."

"Vivi?" He tried to embrace her, but she pushed him away, then slapped his face. He turned from her, stunned.

She grabbed her coat from the back of the chair and walked off.

Jean-Paul caught up with her on the terrace. "What is wrong?"

"You said it was over between you—that you were tied by a mere formality."

He nodded. "Oui. And for that I deserve a slap?"

She looked away. "People talk."

"Rita plants seeds on purpose so people will talk."

"Yes, well, she's not the only one who's been planting seeds."

He took her by the forearms. "Talk to me," he said. "What stupid things have you been hearing in the village?"

She stared at him.

"Vivi?"

"Madame Belcher said Rita's pregnant."

Jean-Paul laughed. "For Rita, the bigger the story the better."

"She wouldn't make up something like that."

"She'll say she lost it, or make up some other wild story about a misdiagnosis and how terribly sad she is. That's Rita."

"Madame Belcher said she looked pregnant."

"What do you mean? She certainly hasn't put on weight."

Vivi looked at him pensively. "You noticed her figure?"

"Damn it, Vivi. Why are you doing this?" He sat down in one of the terrace chairs. "These are stories Rita has made up on purpose. She knows about you."

Vivi sat down. "What do you mean she knows about me?"

"She found out from Lena the day I gave you the ring. She came unexpectedly. I told her she had to leave. Apparently, Lena said something about you and she put two and two together."

He got down on one knee. Placed his arms on her thighs. "Look, I love you, okay? Rita has been threatening me a little more than usual lately. She asked Lena if she wanted to move to Paris to live with her. She'll use Lena to hurt me if she has to."

Vivi shook her head. "What motive does she have to

hurt you? Only that she loves you. There's no other reason, Jean-Paul."

He shrugged. "I can't pretend to understand Rita." He sighed. "Maybe she thought I'd turn out to be a fabulous writer or something, and when I disappointed her—"

"You are a fabulous playwright."

"Yes, well—"

"So you haven't slept with her?"

He shuddered. "I'd rather have sex with a wine bottle."

"Jean-Paul."

He stood. "If Rita is pregnant, I'm not the father." He opened the door and turned to her. "Coming inside?"

"But—"

"What?"

"Madame Belcher said the child would be yours in any event. The same thing happened to a cousin of hers. By law, the child would be yours."

"That's assuming she's pregnant. I don't think Rita would be that stupid."

"It happened once."

"Père?" Lena stood at the door. "Je voudrais de l'eau."

Vivi turned to Jean-Paul. "I thought she was asleep. I hope she hasn't heard."

Jean-Paul shook his head.

"Hey, sweet girl, let's let Vivi get you some water and put you back to bed, so père can finish cooking dinner, okay?"

Lena nodded, her thumb in her mouth. When Vivi picked her up she laid her head on Vivi's shoulder and let herself be led back to bed.

The next day, when Père and Lena walked Vivi to her car, Vivi looked pensive. She put her bag in the backseat and turned to Jean-Paul. "I've been offered a job with Florida State University that I'm going to take. One of my professors recommended me. It's not permanent, just six months."

Jean-Paul took her hand in his. "Because of Rita?"

She shook her head. "I'll be going on an expedition to

the Indian Ocean for six weeks, and then afterwards, I'll be cataloguing plant life in the Eastern Gulf of Mexico."

"You haven't mentioned this before."

She shrugged. "I wasn't sure I was interested."

"But now you are?"

She placed her hand on Lena's head. Lena hugged her legs. Vivi bent down to pick her up. "It will give you time to resolve things," she said, looking back at Jean-Paul.

He leaned against the side of the car. "I'm resolved. I know what I want."

"What you want isn't necessarily what you have." She handed him Lena.

"Don't do this."

"Don't make a scene." She squeezed Lena's thigh. "Baby girl, be good for Vivi, okay?"

Lena nodded.

Vivi got into the car.

"Will you be back before you leave?"

She looked up at Jean-Paul. "Probably not."

"But you'll come home? For a visit?"

"Home?"

"Here."

She stared at him. "We'll have to see what happens."

"I love you."

"I know you do. But I want what's best for Lena, and myself, and you, too. If there is any chance—"

He shook his head. "There was never any chance. She's just playing games, that's all. Soon something else will attract her attention and she'll be gone, leaving her," he nodded at Lena, "behind."

She closed the car door. "Au revoir Jean-Paul."

Jean-Paul leaned over so that Lena could give her a kiss. He kissed Vivi too. "We'll wait for you to come home."

Forty-two

The night air hums with the sound of mosquitoes. A colony of yellow jackets has made a paper nest under a low-hanging eave of Nick's house. One straggler, ignoring the setting sun, hovers over a bloody piece of meat sitting next to the grill. Distractedly, Nick watches the wasp take interest in the meat, but ignore the piece of salmon he bought for Hildy, and the red and yellow peppers and slices of purple onion on the plate. Music drifts through the French doors and the open, oversized windows of Nick's living room. He turns up the grill and steps over to the hot tub to take off its protective covering. Last fall, he and Hildy hired contractors to install the cedar deck and hot tub, but so far they haven't used it except for the one night it was finished. Perhaps tonight he'll have a soak.

From the deck, he can hear Hildy enter the house. Though he has asked her many times to leave her shoes at the door, she often wears her stilettos in the house, making divots in the maple floor with her sharp heels. He takes it as an affront, but says nothing because she considers the house her domain. Not that she will do any of the labor of decorating or caring for the house—manual labor is not her thing.

"What's for dinner?" Hildy asks, standing at the French doors. She steps to the grill and opens the lid. "Salmon again? I had salmon for lunch."

"You should have emailed me and let me know if you wanted something specific."

"Don't be boorish—you should have called me before you went shopping. Or were you too busy?" she asks, arching her brow.

Nick glances at her. "Would you rather go out?" He reaches over to turn off the grill.

"Nick," she says, grabbing his forearm and digging her nails in, "did you see Lena today?"

He wrenches his arm away. "You drew blood," he says, looking down at the red half moon marks that mar his skin. "Damn you."

She slaps him across the face. "Don't you ever speak to me like that while you are whoring around."

Stunned, he says nothing.

Hildy crumples into a deck chair and begins to cry. She tells him that she's told her sister that he was having an affair and that her sister said all men have affairs, but usually wait until after they are married. "I felt so ashamed when she said that. Is it the sex?" she asks for the umpteenth time, and then bursts into tears again.

Nick sits down next to her and puts his arm around her shoulder, but she flinches away. "You don't understand—you're a man. It doesn't matter for you. For me—an Indonesian woman, my life is ruined. My sister told me I should never move in with you until we were married. I thought she was being old-fashioned. But clearly, I'm the fool."

"Have you been happy?" he asks, trying to be gentle.

"Happiness!" she shrieks, standing up. "What does happiness have to do with it, Nick? How many times do we have to have this conversation about your silly sentimentality?"

"I think love matters," he says, standing up too.

Hildy covers her face with her hands. "You think I don't love you?" she says finally, raising a makeup-caked face to his. She tells him a story about her mother and father—married now for forty years. "They struggled together for our family. They don't sleep in the same bed anymore, but they still love each other."

Nick's eyes narrow. Hildy has told him numerous times that her mother hates her father—that's why she lives most of the year in Indonesia even though her husband is in D.C. "I thought your mother—"

"Don't say it—my mother loves my father in her own way. Nick, marriage isn't about some fairy tale love story, or soul mates, as you Americans like to say." She starts to cry again. She tells him that marriage is about knowing one's role, caring for one's family, and keeping a good face in the community. "I've done all that for you." She gives a litany of all the things she's done for Nick—appearing at his side for work functions, decorating a home he can entertain in, being kind to his passive-aggressive mother when she comes to visit from England. "If it is children that you want, I will have one, even though I think kids are brats."

"My mother isn't passive-aggressive."

Hildy snorts. "The point is, you've ruined my life, do you understand that?"

Suddenly, Nick remembers being three and standing dockside, hearing waves crash against the hull of a giant ocean liner. The boat was in port, but its weight caused small waves to lap between hull and dock. He was wearing gray tweed shorts and a blue dress coat with a black velvet collar. He stamped his foot in a small puddle of muddy water, but even this his mother hadn't noticed. She was crying, hanging on the arm of his father. Nick remembers hearing the loud honk of a tugboat. And how in the distance, across the water, a large green-tinged woman held her arm up to the sky. He didn't know then the word torch back then, but Liberty touched him in a funny way—kindled a yearning that his three-year-old heart couldn't decipher. His young eyes traversed the man's big shoes and then his long black coat until he was looking up into the face of his father. They had crossed the ocean in a big ship to join him. While his mother cried, his father patted her shoulder. Nick remembers how his father's hand was almost as large as his mother's face. He remembers his mother pleading with his father, but his father claimed he wouldn't go back to England, that his home was in New York. "But there's no point in you staying. Better bringing the kids up back home in Coventry. The parents can help." Nick remembers how his mother's face hardened, and how this frightened him. "Mummy," he said, tugging at her gray trench coat. When she finally took his hand, her palm felt calloused. It scratched his skin. His father tried to kiss Nick and his sister goodbye, but his mother jerked them backwards. "They're not yours anymore," she said, picking up their suitcase. She needed both hands to carry the bag, so young Nick clung to her raincoat—was pulled along. Behind him he could hear the clip clop of his father's big shoes, and he watched how his father's shadow followed them. When Nick tried to slow down to look back at his father, his mother jerked his arm. "Don't look back," she said.

Shaking his reverie, Nick glances at Hildy's tear-stained face. "I'm so sorry," he says, looking down at his feet.

"Are you going to marry me?" she demands. "Or should I just commit suicide now?"

He closes his eyes, squeezes them shut. He thinks of his father and the hard life his mother had.

"Well, are you?" she asks, in a small weepy voice, drawing closer to him.

He thinks of Lena and the life they have planned together. The long shadow of his father hovers over him.

"Nick, please don't do this to me," she whispers. "Don't go back on your word. Please tell me you will marry me."

Ever so slightly, he nods his head.

The next night, Nick meets John at a bar. It is packed with people watching basketball, and smoke permeates the air. The wood-paneled walls look dull in the haze and the red leather seats are blackened. Nick flicks ash away from his olive-green jacket.

"You've been living in the States too long," John says when Nick complains about the smoking and the ash. John blows smoke rings in the air. His shorn head is tilted toward the television, and his white, tailored dress shirt has come slightly untucked from his trousers.

Nick stirs the remaining ice from his scotch with his finger.

John pounds his fist on the bar, shouting at the television screen. The bartender has asked if they want another drink, but John hasn't answered. His mouth hangs slightly open as he watches the game. Nick whacks him on the elbow.

John turns to the bartender. "I'll have another one." He gulps the last of his beer. "And?" He raises an eyebrow at Nick.

"Jesus," Nick says, when John immediately turns back to the basketball game.

John pulls his barstool closer to the bar. "Sorry, man. You were saying about Lena?"

Nick shakes his head.

John stubs out his cigarette butt. "We met you and Hildy as a couple—I can't quite imagine you apart."

Nick looks away. "I love her, Lena I mean, but—"

"I don't envy you."

"I can't suppress the thought that maybe she's used me to get rid of Daniel."

"That's crazy. Women don't do that shit."

When Nick studies his thoughts they strike him as wrong, yet he can't suppress the feeling, nor the opposite—that without Daniel, Lena will somehow become dependent upon him.

John lights another cigarette. "You and Hildy have been together a long time." He takes a long drag. "What did she say?" he asks, expelling the smoke.

Nick signals the bartender. "I haven't told her I was leaving, only that I was still seeing Lena."

"And?"

"I assumed she'd chase me around the house with a carving knife, but instead she cried."

"Is she related to Lorena Bobbitt?"

Nick laughs. "I could have dealt with her anger."

"Maybe you should put things on hold with Lena until you figure things out with Hildy."

Nick gulps down his drink and asks for the check. "This situation is driving us both crazy, but I'm just not sure of the right thing to do."

John shakes his head. "Man, I don't understand you. If I had a chance at a woman like Lena, I'd jump."

Nick picks up his jacket from the empty barstool. "The problem is, I'm not sure I still know how to jump."

"We still on for the weekend?"

Nick nods.

That weekend, Nick goes with Anita and John on a biking trip to the Shenandoah Mountains, a few hours outside of Washington D.C. Hildy doesn't go. She doesn't like to bike, and besides, she says, her sister is coming from Maryland to visit. Nick is relieved to be out of the house and away from the city.

"Isn't it gorgeous?" Anita says as they drive along Skyline Drive. Cool air rushes in through the windows from the lush canopy of trees. They are heading toward Lewis Mountain, where they have booked a cabin—"Rustic Charm in Tune with Nature," the ad said, according to Anita. They plan on two days of biking.

Nick half-listens to John pontificate about the best trails to ride and why. Though he has left the city, he can never quite leave Lena behind, and he wonders what she is doing in this moment. She told him she had to work all weekend and that two days in mountain air would be good for him. He wonders, as he has before, how she stays so calm. Compared to Hildy, Lena hasn't put much pressure on Nick, and though he appreciates the respect she shows, it also bothers him a little. Does she really love him as much as he loves her? Is there a quantitative way to measure love? He grows queasy at the thought—mostly because in his mind, his bar chart exceeds hers. And for the opposite reason—that over time, his own measure becomes grossly deflated.

"Nick, what do you think of doing the Hawksbill Mountain trail tomorrow?" Anita asks, shaking him from his thoughts.

He shrugs. "Sounds good," he says, not knowing what his other choices were. Anita planned this trip and he'd left the details to her, thankful to be away from the heat of the city and the pressures of Hildy. When Anita turns back to John, Nick sinks back into his own quiet thoughts. Why am I more animated with Lena around? he wonders vaguely. But then he lets this thought, too, slide by like the passing trees.

After dinner, they sit outside the cabin watching the night sky. Nick talks to Anita about his predicament with Hildy. John has fallen asleep inside in a chair. "I've never felt as close to anyone in my life as I do Lena. I know this sounds crazy, but sometimes I wonder if she's my twin."

"Do you think you really love her?" Anita asks. "She's my dear friend, but sometimes lust and love can be misconstrued."

He tries to explain the quality of his reaction to Lena, but Anita cuts him off. "Lena makes everyone feel that way. She doesn't try to charm people—she just does. I've been her friend for a while; everyone reacts to her that way."

Nick frowns. "She is gifted and unusual—"

"And to be honest, sometimes a little weird. Daniel had his hands full."

Nick is puzzled by her comment. "They seemed to have had a good marriage."

Anita purses her lips. "Then why did he leave her so fast? To me, it looked like he flew out the door the first opportunity he had."

"Lena was shocked."

"Maybe she shouldn't have been. It's not always easy living with someone of. . .umm, unusual talents."

Nick is surprised that Anita is expressing such dissonance about Lena. He had the impression that Anita adored Lena—not quite like Isaiah, but that Anita was very fond of her at the very least.

"Do you like Hildy?" Nick asks, watching Anita's face closely.

She shrugs, not giving anything away. "I don't dislike her. Besides, it's not me that matters—it's how you feel about her."

The next day the three of them head out just after sunrise on a long bike ride. Even at this early hour, the dew has dried from the grass. They bike through the woods and past spectacular vistas of rock and trees and intricate winding canyons. They've biked nearly thirty miles.

Just past noon, John says he's tired and wants to turn back. Though Nick is tired too, he decides to press on alone a bit farther. The summer sun beats down on his head as he pedals along an open path. Already it's blisteringly hot and it's only the first week of May. With his head bent against the sun, he peddles harder as he climbs a steep incline. Sweat drips down his brow. He's focused on the position of his body and the speed of his bike, but then a thought breaks through his concentration: I'm causing them so much pain. His hand jerks; he almost falls.

Nick skids to a stop before a stand of old oaks and leans his bike against a tree. At least his water bottle still feels cold in his hand. He squats down to rest.

Nearby, two crows take a few steps toward him. Odd-looking creatures. He wonders how close they'll come.

He told Lena he would talk to Hildy again—tell her he was leaving. But so far he hasn't. Why is it so hard? Hildy never asks anything of him—at least, not much. But is that the way to live? He brushes off the seat of his pants. He's made his decision—but for some reason he can't seem to carry it through.

The crows take a few more steps toward him and then spread their wings and are airborne. They land on a branch just above his head, where they look down.

He rolls his bike forward.

The crows eyes follow him.

I'm going to leave her.

The birds wobble their heads.

I am!

They cackle.

He mounts his bike, his foot poised on a pedal.

The crows flap their wings.

He peddles away, afraid to look back, wondering if—no, frightened that—they'll peck at him. Faster and faster he rides; the birds' cawing close to his ears. They are riding his back, their talons so close to his skin. He gathers his courage to come to a stop and face them, yell be gone!, flap his arms, shoo them away, but when he looks back, he sees that the birds haven't actually followed.

Forty-three

Nick parks his car a block away from Lena's house. From her perch on her front porch, she looks like grass bending in the wind. He's never noticed before how willowy she is, almost ethereal. As he gets closer, he can see from the expression on her face that she is pondering something deep. In fact, she is wondering whether the universe expands, stands still, and contracts all at once. Conjecture and theory always lead to something less, so why not three at once: explosion, implosion, stasis? Even stasis doesn't stand still; it deepens.

Though Nick has parked Hildy's silver Jeep at the end of the block, he thinks that Lena sees the car, though surely it's too far away for her to have noticed. Her breach of the physical barriers that keep him in place frightens him more than anything else. But even as this thought creeps into his mind, he knows it's untrue: it's his own stasis that repels him.

His foot falters on her front path. He stumbles as he mounts her stairs.

Close up, her face is unreadable, her voice an octave lower than he remembers. He kisses her briefly, brushing past her, his body barely touching hers.

She doesn't move from her seat on the rail. "Dinner's cooking," she says. She bends to pat her dogs while he takes off his shoes and leaves them by her door. The blades in her back poke against her shirt.

He wants to move toward her, to smooth out the frail bones that were hidden before, but he's lassoed to the spot. When she stands, he follows her to the kitchen at a pace that seems too slow.

"How was the bike trip?" she asks.

Nick straddles a wooden bar stool at the counter. "It

was nice. It rained a little. John isn't the most vigorous biker."

"How was Anita?"

"She was fine. It's just that John complains a lot."

Lena laughs. "That's John. When I spoke to Anita this morning, she mentioned that you two had a long talk."

"Yes."

"She didn't tell me what you talked about."

"Six years is a big investment," he blurts. "Too big to casually throw away in the hope that I'll find something better."

Lena's fingers curl around the handle of the oven door. "That's Anita's parents speaking," she says finally. "Last spring, when Anita was having doubts about marrying John, her parents said those exact words to her."

Nick wiggles his toes; there's a hole in his sock.

"I felt bad because I knew she didn't love John, not really," Lena says, turning back to the stove. "But Anita is obedient when it comes to her parents."

"You're being unfair to John."

She looks over her shoulder. "Am I? You think it's good to calculate security and rationalize love—or the lack of it—as simply one equal factor among many?"

Nick turns to look out the kitchen window. The flowers in Lena's garden are in full bloom.

Lena raps her wooden spoon on the edge of her orange enamel pot. "She told me her parents said he'd be a good provider and that in the long run that's what was important."

"What do you think is important?" he asks.

She faces him. "To you?"

He nods.

"Samuel Beckett. The freedom he offers is important to you. If it's not your free choice I will always fear losing you, so make your own decision," she says, turning her back to him and her attention to the stove.

There is a long moment of silence. The clock on the wall ticks loudly. So quiet he can hear the squeak and gurgle of the hose outside watering Lena's garden. "I've decided to stay with Hildy," he says finally.

Slowly she turns. "Do you mind telling me why?"

"I can't leave her, it's not right. She's counted on a life with me. I led her to believe that would happen." He pauses, considering briefly that he'd also made the same promises to Lena. "I keep trying to cross the abyss to reach you"—his tone sounds defeated—"but I keep falling into a chasm."

She lays down her wooden spoon, wipes her hands on a green plaid dishtowel. "I love you," she says, standing before him.

He nods.

She lays her head upon his chest. His arms encircle her. She takes his hand and leads him to the living room, while he walks woodenly behind.

To Nick, the room looks suddenly too vibrant and too red. The blood red in her Tiffany-style lamp casts shadows on the ceiling; red stains the flowers on her couch and the beaks of birds that perch on the flowers, red wings spanned. He touches a red mottled bird. There seems to be too much noise in the room, too, though Lena is silent. He watches her hands in her lap. Her lips are pressed shut. He wants to hear her theory but she won't tell him, she's moved too far away from him now. He knows this; he knows that he knows and that she does not. She imagines them in the same jet stream, moving outward, ever outward, to discover—what? the world? his heart? He can't see her intent, how far she's trying to take them, and that terrifies him. Suddenly he realizes it's his own voice he hears, a baritone that's lost its bass. He's telling her a story about a college buddy in England.

"I saw him last fall. We were driving to the nursery to buy some bedding plants. He was telling me something about his three kids, when suddenly he was crying." Nick furtively brushes his cheek. "I don't think I've ever seem him cry." Nick chokes on these last words. He wipes his sleeve across his face. "I'm sorry," he says.

"Let me wipe them," she says. "Nick . . . please try."

"I'm not sure I can." He presses against her chest like a child curled into the nest of its mother.

They stay that way for a very long time.

♠♠♠

Nick is careful to slam the front door when he enters his house: he's an hour late and he wonders if Hildy will care. In his library, he turns the stereo a notch louder than he usually would—a sultry Latin voice fills the air. But even before one full song has finished, the CD player skips to Diana Krall's "Popsicle Toes," her voice whispery and nostalgic. The song makes him think of Lena.

Sighing, Nick bends down on one knee to examine the machine—it was a present from Hildy, a cheaper model than he'd wanted, but regrettably, he'd said nothing at the time.

Nick is so intent on trying to decipher the problem he doesn't hear Hildy enter the room. Only when she looms over him does he see first her feet, then her nylons, her short skirt, and finally, her face.

"You're late," she says, looking at her gold watch. "I was hoping you'd walk the dog."

"I got caught up," he mumbles. He's bent down at her feet, his head cocked to the side so he can see inside the CD player.

"Can you please shower and change or we'll be late."

He looks up surprised. "Late for what?"

"I've made arrangements to have dinner with my sister and her husband at Ruth's Chris. Her husband is here for a business meeting."

"The steak house? At this hour?"

Her red lips are a straight thin line. "Yes."

He gets to his feet. "You know I'm allergic to beef."

"You'll have to make do. I've made these plans."

A chill runs up his spine. He wonders why he can deal with Hildy, even now when she's being such a bitch and so cold, when with Lena—

"Nick."

His head snaps in her direction.

"Will you get ready? Or shall I leave without you?"

Leave without him? Or did she say, leave him?

He hears the click-clack of her shoes in the hall as she heads toward the kitchen. Come Daisy, he hears her say. He follows the sound, making sure she's gone before he approaches the door.

Above him, through the darkened stairwell, he can barely see the two flights to their bedroom. Beside him, wind blows against the front door, knocking the long windows that flank each side. Through the sheer blue curtains, the light from the wrought-iron lantern on the edge of his walk softly glows. He installed the lantern himself last fall, proud that he'd been able to accomplish such a complicated electrical feat.

The light in the lantern flickers, then steadies. He looks up the stairwell, then back at the light. He doesn't want to come home to a dark path. He's always been afraid of the dark—the inability to discern what he can't see.

"Will you please get ready." Hildy is poised at the bottom of the stairs, the dog's leash in her hand.

He jumps, then glances at the lantern (it's still shining), and heads up the stairs.

Later, Nick stumbles across the road, his head bent down and his body huddled against the storm that's blowing sheets of rain and hail all around him. They stayed too long at the Ruth Chris' bar, and now the cab has dropped him off at the wrong street. He'd said 21st, but when he looks at the sign, he sees he's crossing 25th.

He can't remember now whether Hildy was mad; he'd had too many drinks at the bar. Or perhaps it was the meat. It had been swimming in blood and he couldn't eat it.

Had she harassed him on purpose? Taunted him to eat the meat as a sign of his decision? He wonders whether she even knows.

Don't flatter yourself or be a fool. He stumbles on the sidewalk, his foot not rising high enough to manage the curb. Hildy would never consider that he would leave her now. His nod was enough for her. To her, a bargain struck is a bargain made. She'd think he's too much of a gentleman to back out now—or perhaps, too much of a coward.

He approaches his house from the opposite corner—

jaywalks diagonally. The house is dark. Had Hildy gone dancing with her sister? He can't remember what she said.

Something about the house makes him stop and stare: the house seems oddly proportioned. Something is different.

A gust of wind blows open Nick's khaki-colored trench coat. He pulls the belt tighter around his waist. But, touching his belly is like touching a switch. Suddenly, he's bending and heaving at the side of the road. When he's finished, he wipes his mouth on the back of his hand and glances up.

His house rises like a tower against the gloomy midnight sky. Its straight lines make it hard to tell which way to enter, which way to go; but now, staring at it, he knows what's different.

The lighted lantern leading to his front door has gone out. The stone path is dark.

Forty-four

Now that I have reached this crucial point, I will not fear the peaceful and wrathful deities that arise from the nature of my own very mind.

—The Tibetan Book of the Dead

Forth-five

Maybe the astronomers and some theorists have it wrong, Lena writes in her journal. She is on a plane bound for San José and an international fisheries meeting. What if the physical universe, the very tables and chairs, the windows and doors are nothing but illusion, what if it's all only a dream? Maybe what seems static is actually moving inward—to become the clay, the paint, the note from which a whole new universe unfolds. She'd like to create a new life—one that won't slip through her fingers.

Two days ago, Lena learned that her soon-to-be-adopted baby died. The unmarried Indian Muslim mother was killed in a car accident in Hyderabad and the baby suffocated in the mother's womb before an ambulance could arrive. Lena had been practicing her Urdu when she heard the news. Though stunned, she couldn't make herself cry. She never even called Isaiah. Instead, she hunkered down in her bedroom and wrote in her journal. All night, until the wee hours of the morning, she speculated about the meaning of life and death. The next day, she searched the Internet and found a reference to the Tibetan Book of the Dead. She went right out to a bookstore and bought it, hoping it would give her answers.

Sighing, she sets aside her journal and picks up the big book. A flight attendant stops at her aisle and asks what she'd like to drink. She glances at her watch. Two more hours and she'll be in San José. Work keeps her focused with its charts and graphs, the things she needs to say to the commissioners at the Inter-Tropical Tuna Commission. But this solid world of ecosystem interaction, over-fishing, algorithms, and statistics also collides with the boundaries of her inner world—

threatening to combust her inner, her outer, everything at once. She's being stretched wide open.

The plane descends.

Outside the plane window, squat buildings, various shades of brown stucco, are strewn like junk around barren dirt. She expected lush topography, not this sleepy hacienda town that greets her.

She closes her eyes. Nick's voice, his laughter, the sound of rain, his trip to Costa Rica not even a year ago all reverberate inside her. She realizes that for everything she knows about Nick, there is something she doesn't know. That's how it always is: each of us private and alone even while connected.

The drive through San José reveals a scattering of two-story buildings, signs declaring ¡Salida!, fast food joints in pink buildings leaning close together. In no time at all Lena's taxi barrels out of the city and down a barren two-lane highway. Even though she's never been to San José before, something about the place feels oddly familiar. Giant billboards pepper the desert horizon—the terrain so like that of Lena's first four years.

At the hotel, Lena walks up bright white steps and approaches the front desk with a weary smile. After checking in, she enters a nearly full meeting room and takes a seat near the back. The act of staying present has become very difficult for her.

An hour passes.

And then another.

The distance between her thoughts and the official meetings grows so vast it takes her a minute to realize she's sitting with her flag raised high in the air.

When the chairman looks at her over the top of his glasses, she blushes. She has nothing in particular to say, and wonders briefly what to do in the few minutes before the Señor from Mexico finishes his speech.

When the chairman calls her name, she stands, shifting her weight forward, hoping maybe she'll keel over and faint. She's about to say it's a mistake, I have no comments to make, when, like a ventriloquist's doll, words tumble out of her mouth.

She talks for more than fifteen minutes. When she's done, a colleague leans toward her. "Nice speech," he whispers. "When did you prepare that statement?"

She looks down at her empty notepad. She's so lost in space that she doesn't know what she's said. The Mexicans wanted to maximize the tuna fishery, dolphins be damned—perhaps she'd told them to stuff it.

That night Lena dreams a dream so lucid it seems like she's awake, so lucid that later there's no difference between the dream and writing the dream down in her journal.

Nick and I were standing before a priest to say our vows. N looked into my eyes and suddenly, I realized he was a Frenchman. My mother was there crying. Then suddenly I was a child sitting on a blanket next to my father. My father disappeared and reappeared like a magic trick. First he was father, then he was Nick, then both were gone. I fell into the water and sank. I couldn't breathe and I was thrashing around trying to resurface. Father reached out his hand for me, but then let go. Spread eagle, like a four-pointed star, I lay on the riverbed staring up at Nick. Mother came running down the hill, screaming, "Don't ever, ever tell!"

Two days later, Lena arrives home to a hellacious summer storm—and a vestibule filled with mail. As she bends down to scoop up the pile, a small cream-colored envelope falls from the heap. It's a letter from Nick.

Dear L

There is so much to say and yet, so little. I'm not sure whether to continue this letter. I am writing in the notebook I took to Costa Rica with me, building a little bridge for myself to a past when things were, for the most part, simpler. I keep thinking of my time in Costa Rica and our many conversations by phone and email. I'm not sure why this particular memory haunts me. Perhaps it's the rain.

I've been thinking about how much has passed between our computers. I have all your e-mails in a special file and I suppose if I leave here I'll print them and keep them with the faxes and letters of yours that are also filed away, even my drafts of the poems I wrote for you.

I don't know what to write. My hands feel heavy. I suppose that, most of all, I'm sorry I wasn't able to walk across the gap between us. As you said, while there is much we know about each other, there is as much, perhaps more, about which we are ignorant.

This is all too difficult. N

Lena fingers the letter, feeling strange. As far as she knows, Nick didn't know she was in Costa Rica on business. And she knows she never said anything resembling the last line of his letter—it was a thought she herself just had the other day. She wonders, as she has before, if Nick can somehow read her mind, too.

Just then, the phone rings. She pushes her bag further inside the house with her foot, and tosses the mail, including Nick's letter, on a small table that's by the front door, dumping her computer bag and her purse on top of the mail. She's not sure she wants to answer the phone, but when she hears her Gran's voice on the answering machine, she races to pick it up.

"Where have you been?" Gran asks, when Lena picks up.

Lena looks down at the phone. "Did you call? The message light isn't on."

Her Gran tells her that in her day, people talked in person, not to a machine. They catch each other up on their news and are chitchatting when, out of nowhere, her grandmother asks, "Do you remember living in France as a young child?" She tells Lena a few facts about her past.

"I lived with my father? I thought Mom came back as soon as I was born."

"You and your mom lived in France until you were nearly four."

Lena grips the edge of the counter. "Why didn't anyone ever tell me this before?"

"Your mother thought it was best if the past was the past. Your grandfather and I honored her wishes." She pauses, than clears her throat before launching into a story about Lena's great-grandmother. "Mother told me once, when I was young and newly married, that she was captured by a presence—not a real man, one she knew only inside herself, but a passion that held her all the same. She loved my father, but somehow it wasn't the same."

"Gran?"

"Yes?"

"Why did you just tell me that story?"

"I don't know. I've been thinking a lot of the past lately, and I suppose in some way you remind me of my mother. You have her brilliant green eyes and I've always wondered if that secret friend you had as a child was like the presence that had captured my mother."

"You knew I had a made-up friend?"

"You used to talk to him before you went to sleep. I could hear you behind your closed door. As a child you were—well, different."

"Did Mom know? Is that why she was never . . .?" Lena feels suddenly exposed. She changes the subject. A small black clay raven peers at her from the shelf where her cookbooks are stored. Daniel bought it for her when they were in Ireland last year. She presses the clay bird against her cheek; it cools her face.

She stands like that for a long time while her Gran continues to talk.

The dogs lie sleeping on the floor.

The cat is curled up on a chair.

The room slowly darkens.

The street lights illuminate the window, but still she does not move.

Gran finally gets around to telling Lena that her father

died while she was in Costa Rica. Lena's father who was never a father because he was never there. Lena now knows that a few weeks before her fourth birthday, her mother took her from her father's house in France. As her Gran continues to talk and to describe her father, Lena remembers that she saw her father at her mother's funeral. (How could she have forgotten?) She remembers how he entered the church, a stranger to her twelve-year-old eyes, and slipped into the back pew. How her Gran gripped Lena's hand tighter when she saw him. Her father took one look at her Gran's face and turned and left. It was only later Lena learned the man was her dad. She overheard her Gran and Aunt Clarissa talking.

Secretly, Lena always dreamed she'd meet her dad one day. In the back of her mind, she thought she had time to reverse the tape on that non-existent father-daughter relationship. But her dad didn't wait. She hadn't seen him in twenty-three years, since her mother's funeral, and now she never would. Mother and father, like DNA, make up the strands of who we are. Some internal warning tries to stop her at the mid-point of her reflection but she falls over the side. Maybe it was her dad's dying, or maybe the baby's death—or the combination of the two that push her over the edge. Suddenly, she can't stop crying. She is hiccupping and crying and blowing her nose all at once.

Gran offers to come visit, but Lena tells her No. The only thought that keeps looping through her head is why did they (whoever they are) call Gran?

After hearing from Isaiah, Nick comes to Lena's house. He slips in through her back door wondering why the dogs haven't barked. He knows Lena's home—her car is in the driveway—but she hasn't answered her phone.

She is slumped on the living room couch, a red mohair blanket drawn over her, though the house is not cold. "Lena?" He approaches the couch. Her dogs lay sprawled around her, their tails thumping at the sight of him.

She looks up.

He is startled by eyes that seem too large. They look dark emerald, black almost; and then when she begins to cry again, her eyes become the green of the sea, a watery blue-green that penetrates his brain like a fossilized shell. She is the Mediterranean, an alabaster stone polished smooth with skin so translucent it pulls to the edge of bone; she is now that thin.

He picks her up and carries her to her bed, though she refuses to sleep. There is no smooth course now—only a jumble of uncertain memories. Her words tumble out without meaning.

It is only when he lies down next to her, belly to belly (he imagined his belly an engine regulating her pulse), that she becomes calm. He knows she wanted a father she never had. Father, father, father—the word echoes inside him and reverberates off her too. He hears the echo when he lays his head against her chest.

And then he too is on a wave of his own, so long the night never moves.

In the darkened morning he still lies against her, stamped to her skin. The shadows jut and move outside her window. Her finger curls around his. Dawn is still far away; she has miles of sleep before she'll reach him, before she wakes up.

Early the next morning after a sleepless night of uneasy dreams, Lena's Gran wrote Lena a letter sitting at her ebony writing table in her house in Los Angeles. The paper she used was stock white, the ink indigo blue.

She wrote the letter because she felt guilty about all the things she never said.

She wrote the letter to right a past wrong.

She wrote the letter hoping it would make a difference.

She wrote the letter offering to open a door that had been closed.

When she finished, Gran licked the envelope shut and chose a purple iris with a yellow center from a book of stamps called "spring flowers." Her freckled hand trembled as she placed the letter in the blue mailbox on the corner of Grant and Main.

It was Sunday. The letter sat on a small pile of solicitations placed in the mailbox for the neighbor-to-neighbor United Way campaign. Only Gran knew that her letter was in that box.

Only Gran knew.

Forty-six

The yellow taxi pulls up in front of Nick's house. When he steps out of the cab, he is greeted by pink, orange, and red zinnias lying limp on their sides. He stares at the dead flowers, furious that Hildy failed to water the annuals he so carefully planted and asked her to tend while he was away on a business trip to Russia. He places his bag and briefcase on the ground. Bent over, he touches the dead flowers, and then grabs a pinch of soil. The ground is bone dry.

Angry, he storms up the brick path and opens the front door. He is greeted by the sound of laughter and the low hum of music.

The front door bangs shut behind him, causing him to jump. The firecrackers in Moscow made him edgy too. Perhaps he's been traveling too much.

Slowly he walks toward the voices he hears. Empty glasses are strewn on the glass-top coffee table. As he approaches the French doors, he hears Anita, John, and others out on the deck.

Nick steps out into mottled sun. The tall oak in the neighbor's yard casts a shadow on the deck. For a moment all he sees is that shadow, then faces appear more distinctly as his vision adjusts. More than a dozen pairs of eyes are watching him expectantly. He steps back.

"They've come to help us celebrate our engagement," Hildy says, stepping out of the shade.

Nick knows these faces, but it seems odd to see them here, now.

"You must be tired," Hildy says, standing before him. Her eyes hold a warning—they tell him to pull himself together, don't act so surprised.

He glances behind him.

"Why don't you change and come back for a drink," she says, pushing him toward the door. "No point in a celebration without the groom-to-be."

Nick looks up into John's narrowed eyes. He realizes that everyone here but Hildy's sister knows he intended to leave Hildy and marry Lena. The heat seems suddenly oppressive.

"Yes, I'm a little tired," he says, looking down at his feet

"Plenty of time to rest later," Hildy says. "Go change so the party can begin."

Nick trips as he backs over the threshold. Hildy catches him by the arm. Her nails dig into the soft skin of his underarm. He jerks himself away.

"I'm going to help him unpack," she says to the crowd as she follows him. "We'll be back in a minute."

"You could have called to say you'd be late," she says to his back once they're inside.

He doesn't break stride. "And you could've asked if I wanted a party."

"It's an engagement party, Nick."

He pauses, his foot on the stairs leading up to their bedroom. "We've only just talked about it. And it would have been nice if you'd asked."

"You weren't around."

"You could have called my assistant to find out where I was."

She looks toward the French doors. "I didn't think it mattered."

He stares at her, then turns and walks up the stairs. He hears Hildy crossing the hall, the living room, heading back toward the French doors.

At the top of the first landing he pauses and looks down at his hand resting on the balustrade. He discovers that it's shaking. His legs feel weightless.

He climbs the rest of the stairs and enters their bedroom, then his bathroom. He pauses on the threshold and looks back at the expanse of the bedroom: A bed with a brown coverlet, two blond side tables, two identical blond dressers, two metal lamps, nothing more.

He unbuttons his shirt, drops his pants to the floor; his chinos blend in with the tile.

His eyes sweep the bathroom wanting to see something bright: a yellow towel, blue soup, some small detail in red, anything but the bland tan that greets him. Even the tile in his shower is a light shade of sand. He cranks the faucet, his hand lingering to gauge the temperature.

Then, he steps into the spray. It pelts his skin, turns him red. Relieves him of all thought but one.

Several weeks later, the summer heat beats down on Nick's head, reddening his pale skin. Across from him, Anita sits hunched over, her elbows on the white plastic table, her head shadowed by a red and white umbrella. Her pink lips (poppy pink) rest on her balled fists as he tells her about his new job in Boston. A waiter drops two beers at the table and scurries off in the noon lunch rush.

Nick swigs his beer and glances across the table at Anita. His belly is humming like a hundred little drummer boys beating at his gut.

"Nick," Anita says, moving her hands to the table. For a moment he's afraid she'll try to take his hand in hers, so he pushes his chair back from the table. "You can't call her."

He'd hoped Anita would be his conduit back to Lena.

"It's not fair."

Why do women always say that to him?

"She's not a ping pong ball . . . and you've hurt her enough."

Nick gazes at her.

"I know you're afraid of getting married. I was too. At the last moment I panicked that John wasn't the right one. That's normal." She shrugs. "But life is about compromises."

Nick stares harder at Anita. Lena was right—Anita isn't happy with John. Her marriage was a calculated risk on her part, just like he's taken with Hildy.

"Nick, Lena doesn't want to talk to you. She told me that herself." She reaches across the table for the salt. "I don't want to be unkind, but you've ruined her life. Her husband has left her."

"Did she actually say she didn't want to speak with me?"

For a moment, the lunch crowd blurs before his eyes. He hopes he's not going to cry.

"You're playing with Hildy's life as well. She expects to marry you. You've committed to her."

Nick's water glass trembles in his hand. He looks up to see Anita eyeing him. Light spills across her face. Her blue eyes look almost luminous: so caring, the same color as his mother's.

"What else did she say?" he asks, his teeth crunching ice.

"Mum's the word. Lena's my friend and I don't want to betray her confidence. But you've got to leave her alone, let her get on with her life. You can understand that, can't you?"

Nick nods.

"Hildy said you start your new job on Monday."

He nods again.

"Have you found a place for you and Hildy to live?"

Suddenly he can't stand this conversation anymore. He pushes back his chair, mumbling that he's late for a meeting he's just remembered.

He holds the check in the air for the waiter and waves away Anita's movement toward her purse.

When the waiter comes, Nick turns to go, but something in Anita's posture makes him hesitate.

She is sitting with her elbows on the table, her chin resting on her fists. A smile spread across her face.

A week later, Anita steps out of her house dressed in white shorts, a white shirt, a straw hat, and red huarache shoes. From her front steps she waves to Lena, who has stopped on the sidewalk across from Anita's house. "Where have you been?" Anita asks as she crosses the narrow street to the other side. Her black and white Dalmatian wags his tail at Lena's dogs.

Lena bends down to pat Anita's dog. From her crouched position she smiles up at Anita and tells her she's just been working hard, that's all.

"Do you want to come over for coffee?" Anita asks.

Lena gazes at a point beyond Anita's face. "I can't. I'm expecting a call."

"Have you heard from—?"

Lena's eyes move to Anita's face. "No, I haven't."

"Oh, I thought— "

"I thought, or hoped he'd call . . . I really felt he knew he made a mistake, but now— " She bends down again to pat Anita's dog. "He's getting married in August."

Anita gasps. "Did he tell you?"

"No." Somehow just by standing near Anita, Lena could pick up that vibe.

"Well, I wasn't going to tell you, but we were at their house in June a few days after. Hildy had arranged an engagement party, although Nick had just gotten back from a trip. He didn't look very happy to see us all there. In fact," she says, pausing, "he looked quite mad and uncomfortable."

Lena looks down at her dogs; they are pulling on their leashes, wanting to go.

"Hildy, on the other hand, looked like a fat satisfied cat. Apparently she wouldn't agree to go to Boston with him unless he married her. "

"He's moving to Boston?"

"He moved already. Hildy's moving up later. She's probably holding off because he made her promise they'd have kids. Hildy hates kids." She pauses. "How did you know they were getting married?"

Lena shrugs.

"We're giving them an engagement party at our house next weekend."

Lena frowns. "But you practically live next door! Can't you have it somewhere else?"

"It wouldn't be appropriate."

"You don't even like her."

"But I like him, and he gave John and me a party at his house when we got married. It's only appropriate I reciprocate."

Suddenly it seems to Lena that she doesn't know Anita at all.

"Look, Monday after the party is your birthday. Why don't you come over for dinner?"

"I can't."

"I won't take no for an answer."

Lena is silent.

Anita touches her arm. "Lena?"

She looks into Anita's blue eyes. Until that moment, Lena had always believed that Anita looked out for her and was concerned for her welfare. Now she realizes that Anita is twisted in some odd bitter way. It's as if she wants the whole world to make the same choices as she does so she doesn't have to face her own stupidity.

Anita's face hovers close to hers, a puzzled expression crosses her brow.

Lena turns to walk away.

Anita grabs Lena's arm. "We'll see you Monday, then?"

Lena flinches. "Maybe," she mumbles, as she lets the dogs pull her home.

Forty-seven

Lena loops the hose around a brass dragonfly reel on her back deck while she talks to Isaiah on the phone. "I'm tired is all," she says, when Isaiah asks why she is so quiet. The late August sun makes Lena's world sharp with color: a true blue sky reaches down to kiss the moss green paint of her brick home and the sleek duck-colored cedar of her deck. Below her, on ground level, yellow water lilies erupt from a small man-made pond they installed when she and Daniel first bought the house. She sits down on the edge of her metal chaise-lounge. "Today in the woods, I felt a particular feeling that comes over me lately. I feel things in a different way than I'm used to. I become them, they becomes me. I can't explain it any better than that." She had risen early to walk the dogs and the rising sun had shimmied through the leaves, while some thin, delicate branches gently touched her cheek, as if to say, we are One.

"Sounds nice."

"Last week when I was flying back from New York, I was looking out the window watching the clouds when a funny thought popped into my head: I wondered why I became a marine biologist, and for a moment, imagined myself as someone else, doing something different."

"That's not so strange."

"I mean I literally felt like maybe I'm in the wrong life. Or maybe like I've lived this life for someone else—

"That's odd."

"Ever since Gran told me that my mother and I lived in France during my infancy, I've felt . . . different."

"Lena, sweetheart." He tells her that she takes these things too much to heart. First her grandfather's affair, and now this. "You are who you are, no matter what your past was."

Lena shrugs. It's difficult for her to explain how she feels almost like an entirely different person. "I'm not sure I'd agree. We are a product of our environment."

"So what's the problem?"

"I thought I was the product of one environment and now I'm finding out I'm the product of another." She tells him it's probably similar to finding out you are adopted. "Suddenly, life feels different. And I feel a little betrayed."

"I'm not sure I follow you."

"Gran should have told me, at some point, don't you think? It almost feels like she punished me for gramp's affair."

"Whoa! You're making leaps here that I can't follow." He tells her to slow down and explain what she is thinking.

She reminds him that the letters he read and told her about make it clear that Gran knew about the affair and the children, but chose to forbid gramps from mentioning it. "All that history went into deep freeze."

"I am a little surprised about that. She's such a sweet kindly old lady now."

"By punishing Gramps, his mistress, his other children, she punished me too, because she did the same thing about my past. What the fuck? I had a right to know."

Isaiah sighs and reminds her that life is complicated. He tells her he is serious when he asks her to marry him, yet he is a gay man. "What the fuck's wrong with me?"

"Oh, Isaiah, please don't start."

"See, you don't even believe me."

"Yes, I believe you. I believe you are confused. You want kids, you see how happy Mark and Tommy are"—he starts to interrupt but she talks over him—"yes, you love me, and you feel like you're getting old and there is no one good out there. As you said, life is complicated."

Isaiah is silent.

"I love you," she says, "It's just that—oh, never mind, can we just not talk about it?"

"No, we can't just do that. Sorry. I'm concerned about you."

"I'm okay, really. I feel remarkably calm given

everything that has happened."

"You don't seem that calm. And I'm concerned that you are avoiding things, just like your grandmother."

"I am not my grandmother, and you're not here—"

"You haven't said a word about your father since he died, or about the baby dying. Or even for that matter, about Daniel. How are you feeling? Do you cry at night? Why won't you talk to me?"

Lena closes her eyes. What's there to say?

"Hey—"

"I just don't like talking about death."

"Daniel didn't die."

"For me he sort of did. He's not the man I thought he was. I thought he'd never leave me."

"Lena, you had a hard childhood."

"Don't tell me it's because my mother died when I was young."

"You did know it was going to happen."

"Maybe I should have warned her." Lena pushes herself out of the lounger and wanders down to the pond. "Isaiah, why am I so weird? Why not you? You're the one who reads weird books about strange occurrences. Remember how after you read Communion you imagined you'd been abducted by aliens as a child?"

"Don't be so derisive. What are you so afraid of?"

Lena's turtle pokes its head out of the water. She sprinkles dried food into his mouth then wiggles her fingers in the water. A fish swims up to nibble the tips, bringing her back to her moment of oneness with the trees. She closes her eyes.

It was raining outside. Fire was lapping at the curtains of the room, and the small table with its delicate flower-rimmed china was in flames. Just beyond the fire, a man was laughing and crying all at once. A child sat on the floor, thumb in mouth, curling tiny toes back and forth, back and forth on the neck of a discarded liquor bottle. Smoke billowed in the air. The man started swatting the fire with a towel. He was screaming her name. A brown dog howled. He barked and clawed at the door, finally opening it. He ran back to the child, tugged her by the shirt, dragged her to the door. . .

"Maybe he tried to kill me," she says finally.

"Who?"

"My father."

"Why would you think that?"

"Isaiah, I don't know."

Isaiah is quiet.

"I keep trying to put together the pictures in my mind—but it's like a puzzle missing pieces."

"Why don't you ask your Gran?"

"I don't think she knows anymore than she's said. And besides, clearly she has things she wants to hide. So what's the point? "

"Why would she want to hide something about you?"

"My father probably wasn't very nice to my mother. You know how protective my grandparents always were."

"Your mother was their world. I mean— "

"I know, I never quite filled her shoes."

"I don't think that's true."

"Sometimes I wonder why she married my dad. He seemed like such a loser."

"You probably have a biased picture."

"How so?"

"Your mother's version."

Lena laughs. "She did exaggerate a bit."

"It's funny what we remember."

Lena shrugs. "Or not." And then she remembers something else. There was a photograph in a silver frame on that table. She struggles to remember the picture. But instead she sees a woman with brown hair and a heart-shaped face. She's standing in a meadow of purple and yellow wild flowers, with blue mountains in the background, holding a white scarf in her outstretched hands. Below her sits a child clapping her hands.

48. France 1965

Imagine this, Père wrote. (He was writing a letter to Vivi in his notebook.) Lena and I are sitting on top of a small bluff looking down. Below us is a sea of green fields. Blue gentian and Spanish broom in brilliant yellow splash against the terrain. A small windy road runs through the canvas up into the sharp expanse of hills. The hills look almost rainbow-colored in the setting sun. Can you imagine where we are? Below us are goats and sheep with their bells and baying; we are close to their grange so we can hear the babies' waa, and from the field, the mamas' baa. Do you see us? We are waving, Lena and I, Silence and our new dog, Lilly. She is seven years old and an Australian cattle dog who has never herded in her life—yet her biology and instinct kick in. She crouches on her belly to look down at the goats and sheep; then quickly moves to a better locale for a closer view. She quivers with excitement. Back and forth she creeps hoping for—? I'm not sure what. She's smart—in no time she's learned if she lies still the goats and sheep will come close as they voraciously eat their way home. She could watch goats and sheep all day if I let her. But now it's time to go back to the house so I can copy these thoughts from my notebook onto clean paper—to capture our lives in a thumbnail for you to share. We miss you. Rita is coming tonight. She says she has a business proposition for me that will result in our divorce and my getting custody of Lena. I don't trust her, but I will wait and see. . .

Jean-Paul closed his notebook. Lena had been picking wildflowers. She handed Père the bunch. Père called to the dogs, who had nosed closer to the sheep. Hand in hand, Lena and Père strolled up the stone path toward their house.

"Hungry, ma petite?" Père asked.

"*Oui.*" Lena nodded.

"Shall I make Vivi *crêpes?*"

Lena clapped her hands and skipped ahead.

"Vivi has spoiled us with her fancy cooking. Now a chop and potatoes doesn't satisfy us, does it?"

Lena turned. "Vivi vient?"

"Not tonight. Vivi is on a boat in the ocean. Remember I showed you that photo? But tonight Maman is coming from Paris."

Lena scrunched up her face, made a happy snorting sound through her nose. "For Maman." She took her flowers from Père's hand and stuck her nose in the bouquet.

Père kept walking, but when he realized Lena wasn't with him, he looked back. "What's wrong, Ma petite?"

The flowers were on the ground. She was stamping on them. "No *parfum*," Lena said. Tears rolled down her cheeks.

"Maman, Maman, Maman," Lena said, her hand on her mother's red and white skirt. With her finger, she'd been tracing the roses printed on the toile.

"Lena, Lena, Lena," Maman snapped back.

Surprised, Lena looked up.

"Rita, she's only a child."

"She doesn't need to say Maman a million times. It's a bad habit."

"Come here, ma puce." But Lena pulled away from her father.

"You indulge her too much."

"She's still a baby, and perhaps she missed you."

"Of course she missed me. I'm her mother." She turned to Lena. "Let me see your hands."

Lena held up her hands, pensive. "I a big girl," she said. "I go with Maman to Paris."

"Dirty, dirty hands." Her mother led her by the wrists to the sink. "Little girls with dirty hands don't get to go to Paris. You must learn to stay cleaner if you want to go to Paris with Maman."

"Rita."

She glanced at Jean-Paul.

"Maman will teach you how to be a proper young lady, not a heathen like your Père is raising you." Rita turned to Jean-Paul. "Why do you let her touch those filthy sheep?"

"She loves the sheep."

"I don't want my daughter raised this way. Come here, Lena, let me brush your hair." Rita sat down in a chair at the table. "Bring me a brush, Jean-Paul. And some scissors."

"No!" Lena put her hands to her head and wriggled out between her mother's knees. She ran to the kitchen door.

"Lena, get back here."

"Rita, stop."

"Don't you tell me how to talk to my daughter," Rita hissed.

"Just stop. You've been on her ever since you arrived."

"You make it impossible for me to be around her, Jean-Paul. You've turned my daughter against me."

"You're being irrational."

"Am I? Look at her." Lena was stooped down in a corner by the door. "Come here, baby, let Maman brush your hair."

Lena shook her head.

"She's like a wild animal, Jean-Paul."

He bent down before Lena. "Ma petite," he said, stroking her head. "Maman has a headache, that's all. She had a long trip from Paris."

"Don't you act like it's me who is crazy," Rita shrieked.

"Where are your pills?"

By now Rita was crying. She shook her head. Jean-Paul went to the bathroom and brought out an orange plastic vile. "Here," he said, twisting open the cap. He tilted two blue pills into her hand.

"One more," she said. "My nerves are a wreck."

Later that night, when she awoke from her nap, Rita told Jean-Paul of her plan. How she auditioned for the film Yesterday,

Today and Tomorrow. "It's a part that will make my career."

"I'm happy for you."

She lighted a cigarette. "Don't be snide. Jealousy doesn't become you."

"I am happy that you are happy with your career. Now what's the plan you propose?"

"I've heard Sophia Loren wants the part."

"Rita, are we going to talk business or not?"

"She's too old. The part is for a pregnant woman."

Jean-Paul strummed his fingers.

"She's in her thirties," Rita said, blowing smoke rings. "I want the part. And I'm going to get pregnant to get it."

Jean-Paul pushed back his chair, stacked dishes in a pile. "Not with me," he said, shaking his head.

"Don't be stupid. You're my husband. You have no choice."

He looked at her. "I have a choice. And that choice is No."

"It's the perfect solution. You'll get Lena, I'll keep the baby—we'll get divorced and each have a kid once the movie has been declared a hit."

"No."

"Jean-Paul. If I get pregnant, under both American and French law you're the father. Wouldn't you rather have it be your child?"

Jean-Paul shook his head.

"It's the only way you'll get to keep Lena." She stood and walked to the phone. "Shall I call my parents and tell them to come pick her up?"

In two strides he had her by the neck. To him, her face, the air around her head, the whole room was suddenly red. "There is another way," he said, squeezing ever so slightly as his hands shook.

"If you bruise me, you're a dead man. I have a shoot on Monday."

"I wouldn't worry about bruising if I were you."

"Papa?" Lena said, standing sleepily in the doorway.

"Baby!" Rita ran to her. "You woke her up," she said,

looking over her shoulder at Jean-Paul. "Come with Maman, sweetheart, let me put you back to bed."

"Papa." Lena wriggled out of her mother's arms.

"Jesus, Jean-Paul, she's wet." She turned to Lena. "Did you wet the bed, bad girl?"

Lena stood crying.

"Rita, leave her alone."

She arched her brow. "Or what? You'll finish what you started?"

"Ma puce." Père picked Lena up. "It's okay sweet girl. I bet Mr. Bear helped you wet the bed, didn't he? You two think you're so funny, making papa work so hard."

"You're disgusting," Rita says. "Stop warping her—she's never going to be normal."

"She's just a baby," Père said. Lena leaned her head against her father's shoulder and sucked her thumb.

Rita stepped back to the phone. "I'll be on the phone with my parents while you're changing the bedding, papa. I know how much you like baby smells. Let me see, by my calculation my parents could be here by, hmm, Tuesday." She stepped toward Lena. "Would you like to see grandma and grandpa, Kitten?" Lena turned her head away.

"Just wait," Jean-Paul said, carrying Lena up the stairs. "We'll talk more when I come down."

Forty-nine

Lena is standing on her head in a room of her house that is empty of all but her yoga props. The room was her office, but after Daniel left, she moved her desk and filing cabinets down to his old office in the basement. Nowadays, Lena stands on her head often—*sirsansana,* a yoga pose, calms her mind and keeps it clear.

She thinks frequently of the blue pills, the fire, the rope, the dog—but she can't make sense of any of the pictures that form in her mind. It's been three months since she's seen Nick and he moved to Boston for a new job, and during this time she's tried to banish him from her thoughts; but the more she pushes down, the more frequently these other pictures pop up. Somehow, Nick seems connected to these memories—if they are memories.

Slowly she lowers her legs and then comes into a sitting position. Today is Nick's birthday. She woke up this morning wondering if she should send him a belated birthday card. Later, as she was dressing, a picture of a strawberry torte came to mind. The torte was sitting on a plaid blanket next to a basket, glasses and plates. It was her birthday. The memory is clear—almost like a photograph—but she can't place it physically in her past.

Slowly she pushes herself up from the floor, though she has not finished her yoga practice. Nick's presence is amplified inside her—she feels the press of a crowd around him, the hum of other voices. She tries to banish the feel of Nick from her body, but as with other times, it's as if she's more there with him than here—as if she, Lena, has ceased to exist.

Before she knows it, and without realizing what she's doing, she is in her bedroom dialing Nick's office number. Her hand trembles when his assistant answers. "Is he in?" she asks.

Several minutes pass before the assistant comes back to say he's unavailable.

"Tell him happy birthday. He knows the number," she says, and without another word lays the phone on its cradle, carefully, like an egg balanced on a pedestal. She sits stock-still with Nick inside her.

Time passes.
The clock chimes
eleven times like a church bell,
like a cuckoo bird,
a dog baying at the church bells.

I'm here, I exist, time suddenly seems to say. The phone joins in the symphony. At first Lena doesn't hear the phone—only the church bells ring in her memory—but the ringing won't stop. Won't let up.

"Hello?" she says, cradling the receiver on her shoulder, wondering why her machine didn't pick up.

"It's me," Nick says. "I'm sorry I couldn't talk, I was on the stock floor with colleagues. As soon as I could, I came back to my office to call you."

Her mouth opens, but her vocal cords clamp shut.

"Lena?"

She wants to ask him why he's inside her when he's chosen to stay with Hildy but all she says is: "Do you like Boston?"

Lena believes she hears Nick inside her because he wants her to hear him; she doesn't realize she also hears him because she doesn't want to let go. Something won't let her let go.

"Boston is okay, but it's not D.C." Nick tells her of his efforts to find a place to live and of the everyday things he has done to make Boston home.

As they talk, Lena's voice loosens. The old warmth between them creeps in like the sun rising after a moonless night, spreading pink across the horizon as dawn stretches skyward. She wakes up inside herself during their talk and finds the place of joy inside herself, carved there by Nick. She tells him stories that make him laugh, embellishing her more innocuous adventures, deleting the details that might frighten him, enlarging those that won't. She wants to touch him with her words, to wrap him full-bodied around this moment, so that later she'll have more substance to hold in her memory.

"I have such deep regrets," Nick says slowly. "I've made a big mistake marrying Hildy." His voice has become a whisper. "When you and I made love it was . . . well . . . making love. I've wanted to speak with you all summer, but Anita told me not to call. She said to leave you alone."

"She what?"

"I dreamed about you all summer."

"Nick, I . . . I wanted you to call. I told Anita that." She pauses. For a moment, Lena is lost in a forgotten fragment from her childhood . . . An open door through which she can see bright white light. Just beyond the door, a Plantain tree casts its shade. The smell of plant and soil and something else she cannot name. Just as she draws near the door, an arm reaches out from an unseen body and slams it shut. She is bathed in shadow.

With effort, Lena pulls her attention back to the present, back to Nick. "You asked me to wait and I did," she says finally.

"How did you know?"

She hears his surprise.

"Lena, on my drive to Boston shortly after our last talk I did pray you would wait. I prayed harder than I've ever prayed in my life. And, I prayed that you'd hear my prayer."

For a moment she is angry that he would utter such a prayer and then leave her to marry Hildy.

"I'm sorry, Lena."

She knows he's trying to remember how his bargain with Hildy was struck. And why he had agreed. But suddenly, it seems wrong that she should know this. "Nick, do you ever know what I am thinking?"

He is quiet. He can't deny that Lena pulls him into a world that is fuller and more buoyant, a place where he too can sometimes feel something beyond the range of his normal senses.

And yet.

He swallows hard.

Just this morning Hildy called with news that she kept her part of the bargain; she'd gotten pregnant.

"Lena." Nick hesitates. His mother looms large in his mind. The way she'd retreat to bed for days on end after his father left. "I can't have you in my life." He kicks the desk. "I've made a commitment. When you're in my life I can't focus on Hildy." His voice trails off.

She is silent.

He begins talking, telling her stories from his childhood, from college, from yesterday, anything, it seems, to keep her on the phone. For three hours he talks, engages her so she won't hang up. He knows it will end soon, but he doesn't want it to end yet.

Her voice is soft. Tears drip down his face. Somehow he knows they are dripping down her face too. "I'm surprised you've never cried in front of me," he says softly.

"I was afraid that it would make it worse for you if I cried."

"I have to try to make a life with Hildy. For better or worse I can't leave her."

"If you loved her you'd know it. You knew right away you loved me."

He is quiet. In his mind, Nick sees Lena floating away, changing shape; she's a porpoise swimming toward an underwater mount. "I'm sorry," he whispers.

"These are my clues," Lena says to Isaiah, crooking the phone in her neck. "Blue pills, fire, rope, a brown dog, and also a really earthy smell."

"Aren't there some other things as well that keep repeating themselves in your memory?"

Lena slices a tomato and sprinkles salt on top. "How can a father know his daughter for four years and then—poof!—disappear and never see her again? It makes no sense to me, but somehow at the same time, it makes me understand Nick better."

"I'm not sure I get the connection—Nick doesn't have kids. And you don't know your dad didn't try to see you."

"No, but his father left his mother when he was one, and never came back. I wonder why I have no early memories of my mother, only dad and that other woman. Do you think they were having an affair?"

Isaiah sighs. "You're driving yourself crazy. And I'm worried about you."

Lena pours herself a glass of wine. "Okay, I admit—I'm a mess. Does that make you feel better?"

"I'd feel better if you cried."

"I hardly ever cry, you know that."

"Maybe you never had anything to cry about before."

"And now I do?"

"Jesus, Lena."

"I know—I need therapy."

"Something, girlfriend. You're just not behaving like—"

"A normal person would. Maybe I'm not normal. Maybe something happened that warped me as a child. If my dad was having an affair, don't you think my mother would have known? They lived in a small village—how could my father possibly have sneaked a woman past my mother? Godzilla that she was?"

"Maybe when she wasn't around."

"What do you mean? I was only three. She wouldn't have gone anywhere and left me with Dad and his girlfriend."

"What are you eating?"

"Mâche and salted tomatoes tossed in olive oil."

"At least now we know where you got your exotic taste in food. What makes you think your mother didn't travel? She traveled a lot when you were young."

"That was always for work. There weren't a lot of movie studios in that small village in France, that I can recall."

"Smart ass."

"Maybe my dad tried to kill his girlfriend when mom found out about her."

"Why are you stuck on this theme of your dad killing someone?"

"The blue pills, the fire, the rope. Come on, Isaiah, you're a screenwriter, what does that equal?"

"It could mean a lot of things other than that your father was a murderer."

"I didn't say he murdered her. I said maybe he tried and mom found out and because she was concerned for our safety, she left. Maybe that's why dad laid low until mom was dead. He didn't want anyone to know."

"It seems a little far-fetched—like something your mother would make up."

"God forbid."

"Lena?"

Lena places her plate in the sink.

"You've done a good job of changing the subject from Nick and why you haven't cried, but ah, girlfriend—?"

If all of life is a dream, colored and contoured by consciousness, then perhaps death is a dream too, where flowers still bloom. Perhaps dying is not so different from falling asleep. In a dream state, dogs speak, faces change, things appear and disappear, escalators go up and up and get nowhere. Yet in a dream it all makes sense. These are Lena's jumbled thoughts as she packs her suitcase. Her Gran has had a stroke. The neighbor just called with the news. While Lena listened, she felt like she was dreaming, or watching herself move in slow motion while the room hung upside down. She thought she saw her mother in the corner but it was only the cat. The red flowers in the painting on her wall wobbled. Nothing, nothing would stand still. While talking to the neighbor, Lena tried to unbind her mind so that her world wouldn't move, but a shift in perception took her to the hospital room where Gran was. Then, Lena was twelve again watching Gran's face while Lena's mother lay immobile (dead) in the background. Gran peered questioningly at her, searching her face. At age twelve, Lena had thought Gran blamed her for what happened; now she knows Gran wanted to know what Lena knew, how much she knew. Too much for a child, that's for sure.

She reaches for the phone. She wants to call Nick, to crawl into his arms and be cradled, but she can't do that now. Only Isaiah is left to help her through the trip, the hospital, dealing with the self-absorbed Aunt Clarissa. Lena's mom died before Christmas, and after Lena got older and moved away, she always avoided going home for the holidays, using work as an excuse.

"I'm so sorry," Isaiah says. "How are you holding up?"

When Lena can't seem to string her sentences together, mixing up words as though dyslexic, Isaiah takes charge. "You go get into the bath. I'm going to make your plane reservations. And when you get here, we'll go to the hospital."

"Thanks, but you don't need to."

"Don't say it. Afterward, I'm going to cook us the best home-cooked meal this side of the Mississippi. It's Thanksgiving and what your Gran would have wanted."

"She's not dead. And I don't want a meal."

"Don't you fuss with me. I'll get one of those fake turkeys—they sound repulsive, but the picture on the box looks good—and cooking one will prove to you how much I love you. And I'll pop over to Canter's and get one of their world-famous chocolate pecan pies, and get a nice bottle of wine."

"You're being me, now."

Isaiah starts crying. "I'm sorry."

A silence grows between them.

"Why Gran?" Lena asks finally. "I'm not sure I can stand another loss."

"Oh Lordy, I don't know. I'm stabbed with grief myself. I loved her almost as much as I love you."

Lena half-laughs. "Remember how we used to make fun of your mama's southern accent?"

"You can cry now. I know you've been holding back, but it's me, Isaiah, remember? I like it when you cry. That way I don't worry that you're getting cancer from holding back your emotions."

Tears pool in Lena's eyes. She tells Isaiah she'll want to go straight from the airport to the hospital to see Gran. And warns him that Aunt Clarissa may be there too.

Isaiah sighs. "The last time I saw your Aunt Clarissa, she was hopping mad. I knew I'd have to pay penance someday."

"You were lucky that she didn't show for Mark and Tommy's baby shower. You know how she holds grudges. And you did just cut her favorite dress into a miniskirt for our show."

"How was I to know that old rag in the tub was your Aunt C's favorite dress? Who puts their favorite dress in an old washtub?"

Lena wipes her tears with the back of her hand. "I thought she'd lop your head off with that broom the way she was swinging it."

"How old were we then?"

"I don't know . . . thirteen, fourteen something like that."

"Old enough to know better."

"Yep, that's what Aunt Clarissa thought. I heard her telling Gran we both needed to go to a detention home."

"Lena, I want you to come home."

"I'll be home soon."

"No, I mean I want you to come home for good."

At the airport, Isaiah pulls up in an old red convertible coupe, a tan-colored baseball hat on his head, and an old Dodgers long-sleeve shirt. "What the hell, Lena, you are far too thin."

Lena throws her bag into the back of her car. "Well, at least I've been eating gobs of olives every day. When I was little Gran used to try to hide them from me. The olives and the dog biscuits." She turns to face Isaiah. "What kind of family lets their kid eat dog biscuits?"

Isaiah leans over the gearshift to give her a hug and a wet sloppy kiss.

When they arrive at the hospital, Isaiah hops out of the car and runs over to open her door before Lena can get out.

"Stop it," Lena says.

"Let me be. Let me grieve in my own way."

To Lena the hospital looks like a Lego-construction: squat and square with an alternating pattern of beige and red brick. Glass doors swing open when Lena and Isaiah approach.

A stern-looking receptionist with a blue-tinged bouffant tells them Gran is on the fourth floor.

Isaiah grabs Lena's hand and squeezes.

On the fourth floor, they peek through the open door of Gran's room. The walls of the hospital are patina blue. The light from the window is too bright. Gran is held in the bed by a silver railing, much like a baby's crib. Lena approaches. Gran's toes are purple, the nails long and overgrown. Her body twitches, though clearly her mind is not present. Dank gray hair soiled with sweat grazes her temples, falls over her forehead. Lena slides the rails down so she can lie next to her Gran on the bed. "I remember the endless stories she used to tell," Lena whispers. She smiles as she remembers her grandmother as she was in Lena's youth.

Gran coughs, bringing Lena back to the hospital room. She sits up and shifts Gran's body into a more comfortable-looking position. She smooths her grandmother's cheek with the back of her hand.

Her thoughts wander to darker memories. She remembers how her grandmother broke down after her grandfather died. It seemed at the time that she withdrew from Lena and the world, not wanting to take part any longer. Day after day Gran sat dreaming of—what?—Lena didn't know. Her grandfather or perhaps of her great-grandmother—Gran said they were close. Lena remembers hating Gran's new world, how Gran kept her at bay, kept her out, seemed to forget that Lena was alive and still loved her.

Lena gently touches the papery dry skin of Gran's hand, brings it close to her face. The skin is warm; it smells of sweet almond lotion. Lena moves her hand to Gran's mouth, sunken now without her false teeth, and cups it there. There is no discernible breath. She lays her ear on Gran's chest. There is silence at first and then some deeper rumble as though Gran has begun to speak in a different voice, from some other place. Lena brushes hair off Gran's forehead. She holds back her tears as she smooths her Gran's brow, silently communicating.

Isaiah is openly crying. "Hon, let's go home. You've had a long trip and need to rest."

Three days later Lena's grandmother dies. Black clouds descend, dense immobile air presses Lena down, further down than she ever believed it is possible to go. So far down she reaches nowhere. She is nothing. She lives in an empty spot, a ledge on which she rests before letting go and falling deeper, further still beyond the blank spot, beyond oblivion, so dark, so small, so void she is not even a blip of energy, not a molecule, not a wisp of thought. She implodes when she enters Hades' domain and is lost.

But it is a recombinant death. And it changes her.

Fifty

How do you describe what happens after death? The body decomposes: mind and matter and emotions. And what's left? Maybe dying is like dreaming and dreaming is like becoming with the mind's eye free—no longer hampered by bone or tissue, muscles that tighten and swell; maybe the mind is clairvoyant, highly mobile, existential.

If dying is all that, then perhaps Lena is dead too. After Gran's death, Lena's mind shifted into a state of endless endlessness; her childhood fear of becoming unmoored came true. She sat dreaming and dreaming and dreaming—of what? Only bits and pieces of memory of that time remain. Time stopped, then eked forward, Isaiah came to stay, prodded and pushed Lena to wake up, but she refused. It was only after the U.S. Postal Service in Washington, D.C. was audited by the U.S. General Accounting Office that Lena began to revive. The GAO-authorized inspectors found over three million pieces of undelivered mail dumped in trucks in a back lot owned by the U.S. Postal Service. One of the letters was from her Gran. Isaiah placed the letter in Lena's hand. When Lena made no move to open or read the letter, Isaiah plucked it from Lena's fingers and began to read it out loud.

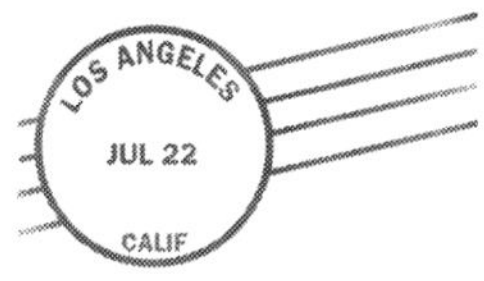

Dear Lena:

After our talk, I realized there is much about our family and your past you don't know. I wanted to broach the subject of your father (not just his death), but when I brought him up you seemed disinclined. I suppose I should have told you some things many years ago, but I was protecting your mother. She once said, Don't ever, ever tell, and I suppose I felt I never could. You were there in the room with us the day she made this plea, though at four, I don't suppose you remember.

My own instinct has been what is past, is past, and what you don't remember can never hurt you. But I'm not sure anymore.

As I told you, you lived in France until you were four. Your father and mother were married, but your mother was gone most of those years on location. She was very focused on her acting career and your dad and I were surprised that she had a child. Your father, as you know, wrote plays. I think we'd call them off-Broadway—they were never a huge success.

After you were born, your mother seemed happy to leave you in your father's care. You were only a month old when she left. We offered to care for you while she was away, but your father refused. He seemed to dote on you.

I'm not sure how often your mother came to visit: but I think often. One day she came home suddenly, as a surprise. Usually she'd let your father know, but that day she missed you and decided it would be a treat to surprise you both. Lena has stopped listening. Her mind is topsy-turvy. She can smell the burned coat of the big brown dog. She remembers how she looked up to see fire lapping at the curtains of the front room where Père worked and slept. The small table with its delicate flower-rimmed china was in flames. The fire from the curtains was threatening to leap across the void to the bed and duvet too. Père was standing before the fire, like a god in the light. He was singing a lullaby, laughing and crying all at once.

She sat on the floor, thumb in mouth, curling tiny toes back and forth, back and forth on the neck of a discarded liquor bottle.

The brown dog howled. He barked and clawed at the door, finally opening it. He ran back to Lena, tugged her by her pajamas, dragged her to the door. That's when Père snapped out of it. "Merde!" He poured wine and water on the fire, slapped it with a towel until it was extinguished. Then he picked up Lena. "Ma petite," he crooned drunkenly. Her pajamas were in tatters from the dog. He undressed her and placed her on his day bed. "Père will get you some clean pajamas, my puce." As he turned to leave the room, a photograph on his desk made him pause. He began to moan. Lena's mind turns back to Isaiah. He is still reading Gran's letter out loud. . . *You were naked on your father's day bed. You had soaked the sheets. From the smell, your mother knew you'd been that way for a while. Your mother says you didn't cry or make a sound when she came in. You only sat there with your thumb in your mouth rolling an empty wine bottle with your toes. Your mother packed your things and left the country with you that very night. She came straight here. Your father called a few days later frantic, but your mother wouldn't speak to him. Your granddad told him to stay away or risk trouble. Your mother was afraid she'd be blamed for leaving you with your father if anyone knew. We were never sure if anything ever happened other than benign neglect, and I believe your mother hoped that's all it was. Perhaps it was wrong not to ever tell you, but she was so desperate to make a go of the acting, and after she died, it never seemed to matter. The only effect that I could see was that as a child you rarely cried. But some kids are like that. After your mother died, I worried that you'd blame yourself for your mother's death and your father's disappearance—children are like that. But your granddad told me not to worry so much. Your father came to your mother's funeral, but your granddad told him that after all the time that had passed, it was best to leave you alone. Your granddad wanted what was best for you.*

I thought I'd tell you this in a letter because I thought you might want to digest it some before we speak. If you have questions, I'll try my best to answer them, although there is not much more that I know. Both your mother and your father loved you very much. Of that I'm sure. I know you are pained that you lost the baby you wanted to adopt. Sometimes we carry a sense of loss without realizing we carry it, and that sense of loss can affect our relationships. Your mother always was a little distant with you and now I fear perhaps that was because of the loss of her twin sister when she was young—I know, you never knew. It was too painful for your mother so we never talked about it. They were identical and so close that even I sometimes couldn't tell them apart. The death broke your mother's heart and I don't think she ever got over it. I don't want that for you.

Perhaps you could come home for a visit? We could talk more in person then.

I love you,
Gran.

Lena sat listening with tears running down her face. It wasn't that the letter contained any answers for Lena, it was that it contained old buried memories and new facts. These facts, almost against her will, engaged her mind. She'd lived her first four years alone with her father in the south of France! Had he loved her after all?

"How weird," Isaiah says. "Another set of twins."

"And one dies," Lena says softly.

"Perhaps sometimes silence is the best policy. I'm not sure Mark and Matthew need to know about the tragic twin syndrome in your family. How weird that your grandfather sired two sets of twins and one each died. It's a little eerie. But what a great story."

Lena takes the letter from Isaiah's hand and clutches it in her own. She doesn't want to think about her grandfather or the dead twins—she only wants to hold onto the knowledge that her father loved her. "I'm so tired," she says. "Can we talk about this later?"

An image of bright white light comes to Lena more often now. Even though it makes her tremble and brings a sense of heaviness to her limbs, she returns to that light to decipher its meaning. Her mind circles round and round, touching forgotten moments of her past, intermixing these moments with memories of Nick. Day after day under Isaiah's care she gets stronger. When finally one day her mind rests on the fact that Nick has moved north to Boston, Lena decides she too will move. She craves nature, so with Isaiah, she visits six northern states and for a second time, chooses Vermont.

Isaiah helps her pack.

Together they move her to a new state.

Closer to the bright white light.

Lena catches her breath at the sight of the verdant waves of grass, the pond that sparkles in the sun, the reeds that sway, the wild ducks that preen. A meadow—purple, pink, and white—mottled in color like an impressionist painting, lies at the edge of an expanse of maple, oak, and birch.

Isaiah places his hand against the window of the living room. “It’s lovely.” He interlocks his arm with Lena’s. “It’s even nicer than your previous farmhouse.”

“It’s funny how quickly it sold.” Lena turns to a man who has entered the house with a big box. “If it’s marked fragile put it there,” she says, pointing to a big empty space near the kitchen. The space seems so large Lena’s afraid she’ll hear the rattling of her bones. Tears roll down her cheeks when Isaiah takes her hand. “Am I making the right choice? I’ll be so far from you. Maybe I should have moved to Gran’s place in Big Bear Lake.”

Isaiah cries too. “You’re going to be just fine here.” He wipes a tear from Lena’s cheek. “You needed to get away. You’d stopped living.”

Lena stares out at the pond. “Not stopped, just frozen.”

Isaiah wraps his arm around Lena’s waist. Their two heads touch.

“I hope I like it here.”

“If not, one day you’ll let me carry you away.”

Later that night, Isaiah and Lena sit listening to the air whistle like a flute. Gray clouds play with the moon, hiding its sliver; only a few stars peer down. To Lena, the universe feels vast, and she a mere speck in its transcendence. It's so black it doesn't matter whether her eyes are open or shut—it's the same color. She holds back a yawn, not yet wanting to go bed.

A strange melody transforms the darkness. Amphibian lovers call out to each other and permeate the silence with a chorus that penetrates her mind and makes her smile. The tenor and texture of each call seems unique, yet so harmonious only a god could have created such a sound. The frog god, she smiles.

As she looks up at the night sky, she remembers as a child peering out a tiny window at the stars. They seemed so close then—like she could touch them. A warm feeling invades her body, makes her smile. She doesn't know why she feels suddenly happy. She searches her mind, but there is no reason for the anticipation she feels.

She turns to Isaiah.

Isaiah's eyes are closed, his face titled skyward.

Lena stands. "Going to bed soon?"

Isaiah's eyes remain shut. "Hmm. Bliss."

Lena laughs.

"Heaven today, reality tomorrow."

"You could stay longer."

"Some of us have to earn our keep."

Lena flinches. "I told you, I'd share. I don't know why Gran left me so much more than the others."

Isaiah sits up. "Don't be absurd. She left me money too, remember? I'm just saying, no I can't stay. If I did that, neither of us would be getting on with it."

Lena frowns "I know it's probably because Gran died, but I feel like everyone is always leaving me."

Isaiah takes Lena's hand.

She sits down next to him. "It's not my fault."

Isaiah frowns. "Who said anything about fault?

"I mean, the same drama keeps playing out in my life and I keep landing the same part. I sound like my mother."

"Your life is different than your mother's. And frankly, you have more heart. There was something a little warped about your grandparent's and mother's generation."

"Are you picking on Aunt Clarissa?"

"She's the perfect example of warped. What kind of mother doesn't really want to have anything to do with her son? Or her granddaughter?"

"I've asked myself that question—about me I mean—so many times. I guess it's complicated. My dad in fact, did love me. Maybe Aunt C in her own crazy way loves Mark too. And also mom did lose someone she loved at a very young age. Perhaps this made her afraid to draw close to me." She turns to Isaiah. "This thought just came to me: maybe, to identify with her, to please her, to say Mama, mama, mama, I'm here, I'm like you, love me, I played out her drama of loss."

Isaiah looks surprised, "Wow! That just came to you?" He pauses, looking up at the stars. "Why don't I ever get big insights about my life and why men are always leaving me?"

Lena sighs. She doesn't know why Isaiah hasn't had a successful relationship yet. He's certainly a sweetheart. Lena is silent for a long time. She thinks about all the people she's carried on her back. "It's not my fault that Mom died, or gramps or gran, or that Daniel left." she says finally.

Isaiah sits up and takes Lena's hands. "Sweetie, of course not! Your family is biologically strange—look at all the twins, that alone is statistically odd. "

Lena is crying now.

Isaiah hugs her. "Oh Lena."

"I'm sorry. It's just that—I've always felt it was my fault."

"Shh." He cradles her.

She pulls back, still encircled in Isaiah's arm. "You won't leave me, will you?"

Isaiah starts crying now, too. He sits down on the chaise and pulls Lena down too. "Heavens girl. Remember that program we saw on the Discovery Channel last week? How the three cheetah cubs narrowly escaped a pursuing lion by changing course and climbing a tree? And when the lion departed, the three cubs came down and began to play? And how it seemed to us they each took turns playing the part of the aggressor—the lion while the other two practiced different escapes?"

Lena nods.

"Well, that's no different than what you just said about repeating the patterns of your mother. Maybe, we keep re-enacting like those cubs did and eventually it becomes so dull, or a just a game, and that helps us release the fear, fright or whatever."

"I don't know—it seems a little far-fetched. Maybe you are trying too hard for the insight thing."

Isaiah shrugs. "You're a biologist—look at the animal world. Shit happens to them and they don't get all fucked up like we humans do. Those cubs are a great metaphor for us, Lena." He pauses. "Hmm, I wonder if I could work that metaphor into the screenplay I'm writing." He laughs. "Talking about my screenplay, here's a thought: Remember the Magellan story we once read? How when he first landed at Tierra Del Fuego the villagers couldn't see his ships?"

"I never got that. How could they not see those ships? And what does that have to do with your screenplay? I thought it was about Capitol Hill, an East Wing kind of thing."

"I finished that screenplay a long time ago—you really have been out of it haven't you? Now, I'm working on a play about loss of identity, or rather, it's about not wanting to lose identity, and thus resisting change. When everything we know stays static and habitual, we feel contained and safe—like being in a mother's arms."

Lena arches her eyebrow.

"Okay, not your mother or my mother—but safe, nonetheless."

"Or maybe," Lena says, "those villagers never developed individual identities, and they couldn't see what the herd couldn't see, so to speak."

Isaiah nods. "Good point. Got to remember that when I rework this draft."

Lena looks up at the night sky. "Sometimes I feel I have no identity."

Isaiah laughs. "You?"

Lena steps to the railing. "I was always trying to please my mother, and in doing that, I tried to be what she wanted me to be."

"A marine biologist?"

She turns to Isaiah. "Not that—but personality-wise, trying to please, not be too clingy—to see the world as she saw it."

"But you don't and never did."

"Maybe it's the trying that matters. And in trying, I lost myself, and could feel that, and so at the same time, I was always fighting for my own identity."

"A conflict of self."

"Maybe."

Isaiah stretches his arms over his head. "Going to bed?"

Lena nods. "I hope I don't have that nightmare again."

"You still having the same one? From Malaysia?"

"Not from Malaysia, just after. But yes."

"Gotta crack that nut."

"Umm. If only I had a giant nutcracker."

The next day, after Isaiah leaves, Lena again tries to piece together clues—the little blips of scene she's slowly recovering. With Gran gone and no one left in her family to ask but Aunt Clarissa, Lena has to piece together these clues herself. She could ask Aunt Clarissa, but somehow she feels it would be a betrayal of her dead mother to ask, and in any event, Aunt Clarissa probably doesn't know. Rita loved secrets; it was her way of creating intimacy, of keeping some in and others out. Or maybe keeping secrets made her feel more like a movie star.

All morning Lena struggles with an uncomfortable feeling in her body: a sense of her skin being stretched wide open. The feeling scares her: it seems to pull her out farther than she wants to go. But pushing down makes her feel the tiniest bit crazy; and the more she pushes down the more something eludes her.

Beyond the deck where she sits, weeds grow waist-high, thick as a hedge. Lena imagines taproots spread out in an underground web, and the snakes and other critters that might live in that hodgepodge of tangled greenery.

She hops off the deck and enters the gardening shed that's underneath. Inside, it's damp and earthy. Cobwebs crisscross the walls, and a snake slithers across the floor. She breathes in deeply. A sense of the familiar stirs in her memory—she wonders if her father liked to garden. For a moment, she thinks of the woman with the heart-shaped face. She grabs her blue gardening gloves, pitchfork, and trowel and walks out of the shed and into the center of the weeds, not knowing what she'll find.

For hours she yanks and digs, bent over, bent into herself, lost in a world of weeds and memories. She remembers how light dappled through leaves onto the cool stone floor. A big hairy dog towered over her. She watched a green gecko race up and over the terrace wall. Puce. A big wooden door (almost like a castle door) swung open and there was light and an arm—and then it was gone, the light, the arm, everything. These fragments stir her mind.

When the sun carves its way toward earth again, she sits back and surveys the ten-by-ten plot of soil she's uncovered. The soil is a dusty brown, dead looking and devoid of worms and other signs of nutrients. She lets it flow through her fingers, back to the ground. From where she stands, she can see, hidden just behind the red barn, a rusted green wheelbarrow. She remembers the big pile of manure by the barn that she saw when she pulled her car out of the way of the moving van. Will she have time to double dig before the sun goes down?

Later that night, as she plumps her pillow and turns on her side, she wonders again about the nightmare she's had several times in the past year—the first time just after her trip to Malaysia with Daniel. She doesn't remember the content of the dream, only a feeling of pain and terror. The dream always ends the same way, with Lena propelled upright shouting No!

But tonight she's too tired to dream, or so she thinks, as she drifts off to sleep.

But in her sleep, she dreams that Nick and Hildy are on a movie screen. I'm pregnant, Hildy says to Nick. The scene changes and Lena is a child lying on a bed with her father, nose to nose. He tickles her belly. Then Nick is crying. Her father's face is red, his eyes large and wet as he presses his lips against her head. The woman with the heart-shaped face appears. Vivi, her father says, reaching out his hand. And then a car is spinning and spinning—it leaps up and over the edge. Vivi is spinning and spinning, her arms outstretched, a white scarf flapping in the wind. Goodbye Lena, Nick says. At these words, she bolts upright. "No!" she screams, still asleep and bathed in sweat.

She's screaming and crying—somehow awake, remembering the dream, and asleep in the dream all at once (though this seems impossible). The sensation of being awake and in the dream at the same time overwhelms her. Still groggy, she forces her legs out from under the covers and out of bed, but as she places her feet on the cold floor and shifts her weight to them, her knees buckle and she falls. Crying, with her face now on the cold floor, she pinches herself to wake up more—or to figure out if she is asleep and still dreaming. The pinching hurts, so she hauls herself back into the bed.

She first had this dream more than a year before Nick left her—how could she know before it happened that he would leave? And her father . . .

The dawn sky gathers tinges of oranges and pinks. Lena lies back in her bed. Vivi—maybe that's her name. She sees an image of the woman with the heart-shaped face—Vivi, sitting in her car, the window rolled down. Lena feels herself drawing closer and closer. Vivi reaches out—for what? And then, suddenly, a chill runs through her body. The word No! rings through her mind, shakes her dry until she is paper-doll thin, pressed flat from the sound.

Much later, in the bright light of day, Lena takes a pen and her journal and wanders out to the deck. Beyond her, in the meadow, the dogs bark and wag their tails at something she can't see. Yesterday she came upon them barking at a snake as it was swallowing a frog. The scene so surprised Lena she touched the snake with a small stick, causing it to eject the frog from its hinged jaws. Her terrier moved quickly to sit down between the frog and the snake, a peacekeeper between warring factions.

Lena shakes her head as she remembers this scene. She opens her journal. For a while words flow, but then her hand pauses. Suddenly she remembers being ten. She begins writing again: I was in my fifth-grade classroom, my eyes on the speckled linoleum floor, when a blip of dream from the night before streaked through my mind. She closes her eyes. The dream was about her and Nick. One of many she had as a child. Over the years my memory of these dreams became dimmer until finally, as I got older, I forgot them altogether. Even after I met Nick, I simply couldn't remember what in fact, some deep part of me knew: that I'd been dreaming about Nick since I was a child. But then, who governs her life by childhood stories?

Suddenly, Lena lays down her journal and pen and jumps up. She grabs her helmet hanging from a peg by the door. And takes her bike from the red barn.

She rides up and down,
up and down,
ascending and descending
green roller-coaster hills,
passing red barns,
overgrown meadows,
and small brooks.

Lena rides and rides. The crisp air whips her face, billows her shirt. Finally she stops at a very small bridge and lays her bike against the guardrail. She climbs down the bank through a profusion of wild white daisies to reach a creek full of cool, clear water. Small fish play in the golden light reflected by the sun. Chipmunks scamper, ignoring her presence. A small black-and-yellow snake slithers into the water. Lena surrenders to this world as she sits on the bank, her feet dipping into the water as she watches a woodpecker boring into a tree. A squirrel jumps from log to log as though it has somewhere to go.

Lena bends down to touch the water with her fingertips. She feels a freedom inside that wasn't there before. More like herself than she's ever felt. It's not something she can name, it's not something she ever knew she wanted.

But she's glad it's there.

Fifty-one

Nick paces the floor of the pink waiting room watching the clock on the wall. Hildy wanted to see the doctor alone; she said she wanted privacy, as though he wasn't intimately involved in the life that grew inside her belly. But she'd been like this from the beginning, telling him that the examination room wasn't a place for men to be. Nick pauses in his pacing, trying to remember for a moment the bargain they'd struck. She carries his child and that's what mattered, or so he thought last November when she first told him the news. At first he wasn't as happy as he thought he'd be, but perhaps that was because of Lena. Events had passed so quickly—finding a house, Hildy's move, the baby's progress—that only now has he allowed himself to wonder about his choice. Was it a choice at all? He looks at the clock, wondering where Lena is, but he pushes the thought from his mind; he can't think of her now.

He approaches the nurse. "How much longer?" he asks.

She tells him the doctor is coming down the hall and his wife is getting dressed. "Would you like to join your wife?" she asks.

Nick shakes his head, turning away. The room is full of women with oversized bellies and men, too. He's the odd one out; the only man alone.

Finally Hildy emerges, dressed in black slacks and a tan knit shirt pulled taut over her belly. "Is everything all right?"

"Of course, it's routine," she says. She walks to the door, waiting for him to open it.

He fumbles with the knob. Hildy's formality bothers him the most. He watches other pregnant women in the doctor's office and on the street, and they don't seem as distant and reserved. She's not that way with other women—or even other men for that matter. Only him.

Hildy enters the elevator and turns to face Nick. Her face is swollen and puffy. Her lipstick is too red; her pregnancy has changed the tone of her skin. Around her neck is the gold necklace he bought her in Malaysia when they got married. It was custom, she said. She had picked out several items she wanted from the jewelers her family used and told Nick to pay the bill. At the moment, the bracelets didn't fit her wrists (perhaps that's why she was mad—he'd made her fat.) He steps aside to let another couple enter. The wife takes her husband's hand and smiles at him as he removes a piece of hair from her face. Nick glances at Hildy. She is staring straight ahead. The perm in her hair didn't curl all her hair; there are straight patches lining her face. (Hadn't he read in one of those doctor's office magazines that pregnant woman shouldn't have perms?)

The elevator bell rings, signaling the lobby. Nick steps to the side to let the other couple pass. Hildy marches out without waiting for Nick, without looking back, leaving him to follow in her wake.

The room is dark; the night is quiet. From their bed, Nick watches a red taillight weave down the road in the distance. He can't sleep. On her side of the bed, Hildy lies motionless. Her pregnancy hasn't bothered her at night; if anything, she sleeps better.

He creeps out of bed, bends his knees to look straight up through the window, searching for the Big Dipper. He knows he's at the wrong angle, but he searches anyway. From this room the stars seem dim and far away. The building next-door blocks his view, but their brownstone was in a fashionable neighborhood and it was the house Hildy wanted. He grabs his jeans and a t-shirt from the corner chair and slips them on, then tiptoes from the room with his tennis shoes in his hand.

He pauses at the kitchen door but doesn't stop. He's gained a little weight during Hildy's pregnancy; it seems he is always hungry. From the living room, he tries to see the stars, but even there their light is obscured. He steps out onto the front stoop—but even that's not enough. He wants something that has no name.

He jumps down the steps and begins to run. Slowly at first, then faster—so fast he works up a sweat. The streetlights are a blur.

The light ahead turns red. He stops, perches on the curb, and looks both ways. He steps out into the street, ready to sprint.

From nowhere, a black Porsche heads straight at him. A man (looking quite a bit like Nick) is driving the car. The woman in the passenger seat is laughing at first, but when she sees Nick, she points, a look of panic on her face. "Watch out, Nick!" she yells as he jumps back. The car swerves but doesn't stop. The woman's long brown hair streams out the window.

Lena? Nick watches the red taillights recede, his heart pounding. He wonders for a moment whether he's asleep, caught up in a dream.

The Porsche has disappeared into the city streets.

Nick cradles his daughter, looking down at her head of brown hair, her pink wrinkled skin; she looks a lot like him. From the hospital window he watches dawn rise, lets the morning sun kiss his daughter's cheeks.

Hildy had been heavily sedated at the end, her voice rancid as she screamed "Get this child out of me." She expelled her into the doctor's arms, who then passed her to Nick; from that moment she was his. Minute by minute she crept into his heart, like the sun creeping along the horizon. For him it was a revelation that his heart could soar so freely. For a moment, he holds her away from him to see her better.

She cries from being held in the air, from losing the close proximity and warmth of her father. He cradles her against his chest. She's his child.

He wonders what Hildy felt in the moment of delivery. Was it freedom, too? He rocks the child, smiling down as her milky-blue eyes seem to focus for a second on his face. She knows he is her father.

The nurse comes bustling in, checks Hildy's pulse, and puts her hand to Hildy's forehead before approaching Nick's side.

He pushes the blanket a little further back from his child's face. She's so beautiful.

The nurse smiles down at the child, tells Nick she'll have to wake his wife soon so the baby can feed.

Nick steps back, startled. He'd forgotten his child needed her mother's milk.

"The little tyke will be hungry soon," the nurse says.

He takes another step away. "I'm not sure she will nurse." Nick nods toward the bed and tells the nurse Hildy hopes to return to work soon.

The nurse smiles. "Wait till she wakes up. Her instincts will kick in. Even the most reluctant mothers want to nurse initially."

Nick's eyes narrow. He glances at Hildy, surprised at the distance he feels. Last night he had felt so close and protective of her body as she pushed and pushed and then finally screamed that she couldn't do it anymore. In that moment he had felt closer to her than he ever had before, wanting to release this child from her womb.

He looks down at his daughter.

She is watching him, her eyes unfocused.

The nurse touches his arm. "It'll be okay," she says. Then she turns and walks from the room.

Nick looks down at his daughter. He can see his own features in her face. He wonders what trajectory her life will take and hopes it will be different than his own. "I'll always be here for you—I'll never leave you," he tells her. He imagines that she smiles.

And then a dark thought crosses his mind. What if Hildy decides she wants to raise their daughter in Indonesia? Hadn't she once said if she had kids she'd want to raise them in Indonesia so she could get the proper kind of help? She had been raised by servants from the sounds of it. No, but her father is here. And surely she wouldn't leave Nick now that they've had a child? Besides, divorce isn't common in Muslim countries.

Nick turns to look at Hildy. She gained a lot of weight in her face, and her belly is still bulbous. He wonders how he ever thought she was attractive. And wonders if they'll ever again have sex. From what she was screaming last night, he guesses no—but then realizes, he doesn't really mind. He almost can't imagine touching her again. For a moment, in his mind he reaches out to Lena, but then he clamps down his thoughts. The comparison is too painful.

He turns back to his daughter. Her eyes are open. She is staring at him. Suddenly, he realizes that if he lets this moment fill him—he is happy. Nothing else matters. He takes his daughter to the window to show her the sun.

Fifty-two

Untimed
Be cheerful, sir;
Our revels now are ended. These our actors,
As I foretold you were all spirits, and
Are melted into air, into thin air;
And, like the baseless fabric of this vision,
The cloud-capp'd towers, the gorgeous palaces,
The solemn temples, the great globe itself,
Yea, all which it inherit, shall dissolve
And, like this insubstantial pageant faded,
Leave not a rack behind. We are such stuff
As dreams are made on, and our little life
Is rounded with a sleep.

—The Tempest

Fifty-three

The sun is low on the horizon, an orange half-lobe in a lavender sky. Lena hunkers down in her bed, pulls the blankets over her shoulders. Her body curls in on itself, twitches with memory of another strange dream, until finally she pulls one arm out from under the covers and grabs her journal from the bedside table.

I flew in a tiny plane with a faceless pilot over snowy mountains

intricately carved into a female face with snakes curled around her head. It was Medusa! The plane landed on the crest of the mountain, the top of her head, among the snakes—or perhaps it was her hair wound up in braids. I got out and stood on the topmost curve of the mountain. The plane disappeared. A voice rumbled up from deep within the mountain. "It is very cold," the voice said. A chill wind blew me off the mountain. I floated in space, slowly falling, my mind active, my thoughts simple: I didn't know I would die like this, I said to myself. I thought I would have time to put things in order, to tell people I was leaving. I wonder if they'll find my body in the snow below? My body tensed. No, I said, willing my body to relax. It's okay to die. As I died, I woke up.

It wasn't a normal falling dream; her limbs didn't twitch or flail. Dying felt peaceful—she felt no fear. But why Medusa? A God that could turn her to stone?

The next night she dreams of Nick. A pink sky sweeps over the peak of a mountain. In the twilight, Nick's black Porsche climbs a steep incline. A cool wind shrieks against the car windshield. Nick's hands shake against the steering wheel. His mouth is grimly set. His skin looks gray, pulled taunt over the square bones of his face. Ahead, the headlights of his Porsche illuminate a sign: ROAD CLOSED. He accelerates past the barrier. Nick? Lena says in her dream. She is bodiless—just a voice. For an instant, his foot depresses the pedal. And then he re-accelerates, banking his Porsche sharply around a steep bend in the road. A gust of wind slams into the car. His tires screech, then skitter across pavement until metal hits metal; then he's airborne. NO! Don't go! she shouts, before he goes over the edge.

On the third night, she's awakened from sleep by a dream of a bodiless voice that says: Awaken! Awaken! You've been awakened by Persephone, the Goddess of Fertility. Lena. Awaken!

She sits up in bed, wide awake. It's dark in the room; no moon. She turns to look at the green iridescent face of her clock: it's only four o'clock in the morning. She lies back down wondering if she can fall back to sleep. But then suddenly, something propels her. "Damn, it's too early to get up," she grumbles aloud, as she climbs out of bed and gropes for her slippers, not wanting to rouse the dogs with lights. She grabs her robe from a hook in the closet and tiptoes out of the room, shutting the door behind her. In the hall, she turns on the lights and makes her way down the stairs.

In the kitchen she lights the wood stove and fills the kettle, then goes to search for her old dictionary with its faded red cover. She finds the entry: Persephone, daughter of Demeter, wife of Pluto, God of the Underworld. The wife of Hades. She grimaces as she reads the definition a second time. Great! I've been awakened by the devil's wife. The dictionary says nothing about Persephone being the goddess of fertility.

The kettle whistles, so she shuffles back to the kitchen, her slippers slapping the floor. As the hot water splashes into her cup, she reflects upon her dream. Not much to grab onto, but somehow, it seems important.

She climbs the stairs back to her bedroom, wondering if she still had her old book Classical Mythology. Padding quietly past the dogs, she switches on the light to the small solarium attached to her bedroom. Tucked back in a corner is a floor-to-ceiling shelf lined with books. A forty-watt bulb hangs from the ceiling. She peers at the bindings, barely able to read in the dim light. Ah! Here it is. The book is in a corner on the top shelf. A thick, diaphanous web covers the top edge of book—a bottom anchor, it seems, for a spider's complex home.

Gingerly, she sweeps off the web, attaching it to the edge of the wall. She dusts off the cover of the book and returns to bed.

Her finger scrolls down the index looking for the word "Persephone." The myth of Demeter and Persephone represents another variation of a fundamental and recurring theme—the death and rebirth of vegetation as a metaphor or allegory for spiritual resurrection . . . In this Greek hymn, the allegory is rendered in terms of mother and daughter; more often the symbols and metaphors involve the relationship between a fertility Goddess and her male partner . . . Lena's heart pounds as she reads the story of Demeter and Persephone and the author's commentary. According to the translation by Morford and Lenardon, Persephone is the seed of life—the fertility goddess who brings her lover back to life after she is taken to the underworld by Hades.

Sitting back on pillows, Lena ponders the authors' words. The Earth, in response to Persephone's being taken to Hades, turns cold—crops freeze, humans suffer. The cold theme! She knows she is close to resolving the mystery.

Lena looks down at her hands, at the dent in her middle finger and the ink stains from writing in her journal. Slowly she turns and looks out the window. The early morning sky is turning lavender blue—the same sky from her childhood in France. Slowly the picture forms in her mind, it's the same memory that came to her when Isaiah was reading Gran's letter, only more complete.

Scattered under her Père's feet were little blue pills. He softly sang as he wound a rope twice over the beam in the front room and pulled it taunt—knotting the end in a loop. He hung on the rope to see if it would hold his weight. The ancient chestnut beam creaked but held. The big brown dog barked, bared his teeth, pulled at Père's pants as he held onto the rope. Père just smiled, then let go of the rope and went to get a small wooden stool. Slowly, he placed the stool under the rope and then came to kneel before Lena. She was still naked. When he turned from her after the dog had tattered her pajamas he intended to get her clean clothes, but his eyes caught the picture on his desk. Instead of her pajamas, he retrieved a rope from the cave. "Ma petite puce," he said, gathering her in his arms and rocking her. "I love you."

"Vivi?" Lena asked.

He sobbed. "I have killed her as surely as with my own hands." He hugged Lena so tight she almost couldn't breathe. And then he stepped up onto the stool and placed the noose around his thin neck. She remembers how his dark hair fell over his forehead as he kicked the stool out from under his feet, while the dog barked and the fire roared . . .

She closes her eyes, wondering how she could have forgotten. Opening her eyes, she stands and walks to the window. "Père," she says aloud. Outside, a tiny red squirrel follows a larger squirrel with big bulging cheeks. Why? Tears creep down her checks. A small sob escapes from her throat. She realizes she's always loved her father—she tamped down her memory of him so she wouldn't re-play his attempted suicide over and over. Without him, her life had been rather cold. No matter what he did—he still loved her.

She wonders why he had not died. Then she remembers: the rope had frayed and broke under her father's weight. He fell to the ground unconscious. Her mother had found him like that. And Lena still without her pajamas.

Lena turns back to Classical Mythology. The book feels heavy in her hands. It reminds her of the big book of fairy tales she'd loved as a child.

And what if life is only a dream?
I will dream you into existence, he said. . . .
It was foretold that we were spirits.
Yes, that's right. We are such stuff
As dreams are made on, and our little life
Is rounded with a sleep.

Lena remembers now that this was Nick's favorite poem and that he first recited it to her when she was ten.

Lena remembers.

She knows she's loved Nick since she was a child, in the same hidden way she's always loved her father. Maybe that's what we do to cope with the things we can't explain, she thinks. We hide them.

Fifty-five

The phone rings, jarring the silence and startling Lena. She glances toward the kitchen where the phone hangs on the wall—then back at the meadow, now a brown field, where she's been watching two deer play out by the old stone fence. The deer are the only sign of life, but after almost two years, Lena is used to how the seasons pass, how the earth turns to a drab brown before snow. She had signed her divorce papers only a year ago, but to Lena it felt like forever.

She pushes the soft red mohair blanket from her lap and rises from the couch.

The woman on the phone is pressing so many words into such a small space of time that it takes Lena a minute to realize the caller is Anita. "I knew you two would end like Romeo and Juliet, or something like that," Anita says.

"What? Anita—"

"Nick's sister called me at my office—I'm not sure how she got my number. Nick's assistant was on the phone as well. Apparently, his sister and his assistant have been looking for you for quite some time."

Upon hearing this, Lena stands very still. She closes her eyes and reaches out to Nick. . . Then suddenly, she remembers her dream of him on the mountain. Opening her eyes, she steps to the sink to fill the silver kettle and turn up the burner on the old black stove. Anita's voice sounds tinny in her ear. She bends down to grab a tea bag from the cupboard.

"Nick's sister sounded nervous." Anita says. "I told them I hadn't spoken to you in eons, ever since you moved to Vermont, but that I'd try to get your number. His assistant said he's out of the office indefinitely, no one knows when or whether he'll return. Lena, are you there?"

"Yes, I'm here," she says, rising from her bent position.

"When she was cleaning out his desk, Nick's assistant found old letters you had written to him, and apparently a slew of letters he'd written to you, but were never sent. The envelopes with his letters were addressed but unsealed.

Lena is silent. Anita's voice echoes strangely in her ears. The clock ticks loudly. There's no other sound in the room.

"How did you know?" Anita asks.

"Know what?"

"He's in the hospital. He's had an accident. Like the one you predicted. In one of his letters, one that he never sent, he said that he's been thinking a lot about what you said—How tragedy will bring him closer to understanding himself. I haven't read the letter, his assistant told me all this when I called her back to say I found your phone number. How did you know he'd have a car accident?"

Lena floats out beyond the room to a faraway place. She knew she had never told Nick any such thing—not in linear time at least. She didn't want to interfere with his choices, so she kept her letters light and newsy—telling him she'd begun to dive again and had spent some time in the Indian Ocean on an expedition. He had never replied—not to any of her letters. "What happened?" she asks finally, her voice sounding distant to her ears.

"It was a car accident."

"Is he all right?"

"He's in a coma. He hasn't regained consciousness. The doctors aren't sure he'll live—or if he lives, that he'll ever come out of his coma." She pauses. "Are you there?"

"Yes." Lena grips the phone, staring at its white base, the illuminated numbers, the iridescent green plastic triangular on/off button.

"His sister wants to speak to you," Anita says. "She's staying in his apartment."

"What about Hildy?"

"His assistant didn't say. Only that his sister was adamant about speaking with you. Do you want her number?"

Lena slowly lets out her breath. "Yes, of course. And Anita—"

"Yes?"

"Thank you for calling with the news. But please don't ever call me again. I'll never forgive you for telling Nick not to call me that summer he moved to Boston."

Lena walks back to the couch and pulls the red blanket around her shoulders. Somewhere Nick lies silently, waiting for her, looking for himself—in the shadow, the underworld, the unconscious. His journey is much like the one they've shared—difficult, different, hard to explain or put into words—but he is neither alone nor dead. Far from it. She feels him as he walks along, seeking his way home to a different time when he can be a different Nick, and at peace.

She wonders if she should explain this to Nick's sister. Or will his sister instinctively understand the bond between Lena and Nick?

Slowly Lena dials the number, unsure what she'll do if Hildy answers. When she hears a British accent, she says hello and repeats what Anita has told her.

"Yes," his sister says, almost whispering. Lena can hear her choking back tears. She tells Lena that he was at the top of the mountain when his car jumped the barrier and rolled down, landing on its top. It was late, but workers from the Mt. Washington Observatory who were hiking up to work saw it happen and called for help. "He was in a coma by the time they got to him. He's never fully awakened."

Lena knew all this, but said nothing. "And Hildy?" she finally asked.

"He received his divorce decree the day of his accident. She got custody of their child. Apparently she planned to take their dog and their child back to Indonesia. I think he thought he'd get custody of his daughter."

"Nick's child?"

"The child's almost two. My mother and I, we never understood why they married. They were so unhappy, even after the baby was born. I used to think that Nick sometimes hoped for something better. Somehow the way he described you—Mother felt he would end up with you. But then he surprised us both and married Hildy. And then the baby came. I'm sorry, Lena."

"Is there anything I can do?"

The sister's voice chokes. "My brother was unhappy, but he wouldn't talk about it. That's how it is in my family. He'd been drinking when he crashed. But the reason I wanted to speak with you," she says quickly, "is because of my mother. She died several months ago—before Nick's accident."

"I'm sorry."

"Before she died she had a strange dream. She was obsessed by this dream—sure it contained a message about my brother. Nick came to visit and she described the dream to him. That night after he went to bed my mother took my hand and said to me, The dream is about Lena. Please help him find her—when he's ready." Her voice breaks. "My mother died that night."

Lena is quiet.

"I suppose it's too late for him. Too late to hope he'll find happiness . . . or simply peace. But then maybe he's peaceful now. He's called out for you once or twice, though he's never fully awakened. Can you come?"

Lena wanders back to the couch. What is it that keeps us loving—beyond separation, beyond death, even beyond memory? In all great literature, lovers die or are somehow separated—and yet, the strong feelings remain. Is it archetypal to fear what love demands—the continuity and ever-present connection? Is that why we replay these dramas? She looks for the two deer in the meadow, but they have gone—moved on to a new destination together. And when one of them dies ? Lena remembers reading somewhere that elephants mourn for several days over their dead and that once, when a car hit and killed an elephant walking down the road, the rest of the herd stayed by the side of the highway for several days, rampaging other cars that tried to pass, and otherwise blocking the road.

Perhaps there is something biological about the desire to stay connected even beyond absence and death.

She fingers the mohair blanket remembering

something Nick said to her long ago. He said that he prayed she'd wait.

Fifty-six

Lena walks into Nick's hospital room. A pool of florescent light captures his bed, her chair, various gray-green monitors, a J tube, an IV, and a vase of seasonal flowers—lavender roses, pink peonies, Rembrandt tulips. In the middle of this still life, Nick is lying in his bed nearly dead. For a moment, she wonders if perhaps she is dead too; perhaps life and death (and everything in between) are only a matter of perspective.

A nurse enters the room, distracting Lena from her thoughts of Nick and the accident.

"Has he moved today?" the nurse asks.

Lena shakes her head. From her chair, she watches the nurse move mechanically, efficiently as she adjusts Nick's life-support system, checks the central venous line, applies salve to the bed sores on his back.

When the nurse leaves the room, Lena bends forward to touch Nick's powdery-pale cheek, to check if the hospital smells that cling to the nurse's skin have changed his smell. Tiny particles of his skin imprint her fingers. She closes her eyes, rubs her finger across her lip, just under her nose, to marry that tiny part of him to her.

She holds at bay the machines that blip and beep next to Nick's bed. The chair she sits on is hard. It keeps her here, next to him—it won't let her float away.

"There you are," Isaiah says, entering the room. "I just put Nick's sister in a taxi to the airport. Are you okay?"

Lena touches Nick's arm. She imagines the sinews that once made him run, leap, wave wildly, hold her in a strong embrace while they made love. She turns to Isaiah. A tear trickles down her face. She wants to straddle the worlds of then and now, to bring them together in a future through the strength of her thighs—she knows this can happen all at once, since time unfolds only in the mind.

Isaiah holds her for a long moment.

Lena turns, leans forward against the rails of Nick's bed, picks up a stack of dog-eared letters she's put on his bed. He is far away. Her breath touches his face but he does not move. She fingers the sleekness of the bedrail; its coolness soothes her.

Isaiah tries to take her hand, but she withdraws to the window of the hospital room. She is mesmerized by the milky brilliance of planets far away. She turns. Nick and his bed are highlighted in relief against the beige hospital walls.

From the window she can smell the roses next to Nick's bed. She'd gathered them yesterday morning, just before Gran's lawyer called. The lawyer had long finished the probate of her Gran's estate, and she was surprised to hear his voice. They chatted a few minutes and then he told her he'd been contacted by a French lawyer about the settlement of Lena's father's estate. Apparently, these things take longer in France. The only address the French lawyer had was her grandmother's.

Isaiah comes to stand next to her. "The whole thing about my father's estate seems unbelievable."

"Why? You were his daughter."

"I know, but— "

"Lena, we've talked about this before—there is no reason for you to be afraid."

"I'm not afraid. It's just that— "

"Do you want me to come with you?"

"This is something I have to do myself."

"And Nick?"

Lena moves to the bed to cover him with a blanket. "His sister said she'd come stay."

"How long will you be gone?"

"I'm not sure. There are papers to sign and I have to go through my father's things. Decide what to keep and what to sell."

"And the trust?"

"From Vivi?"

"It is incredible."

Lena shrugs. "She was my father's girlfriend. She left her trust fund to him during his lifetime, and then to me."

"So she died, as you thought. But I thought a trust fund couldn't be passed on except to an heir."

Lena fingers the rail of Nick's bed. "I spoke briefly to the French lawyer, but he said he would tell me more when I get there."

"The south of France in April."

"I think when I was a child, it was my favorite time of the year."

Lena is standing on a grassy knoll full of yellow wildflowers above the crossroads to the village. The sky is golden with tinges of pink from the rising sun, making the village look all copper and sienna. All around her, the blue hills are dappled in a faint mist. Yesterday she drove here from the airport, on a flat but windy road under a bright sun and heat, passing fields exploding with red poppies and greening grape vines, craggy mountains as a backdrop. As she drove, she felt like she was going home.

To get to the village, she had to drive seven kilometers up a hill on a road that was all bends and angles, sharp curves. The road seemed like one in an old Ingrid Bergman movie—the movie where she parts her lips just enough to let her gapped smile show while her scarf, tucked over her head and wound around her neck, blows in the wind (was it a pink scarf?) as she rides in a green Aston Martin driven by Mel Ferrer or Yves Montand, or someone like that. Lena can't remember the name of the movie. It's a vague memory, but then, she has lots of movie memories from her mother—that's how they spent their mother/daughter time: watching movies. There were no edges to the road, no barriers. Only cliffs. And white marks—little stepped rectangles—embellished the center of the road. Someone in the village told her that the rectangles were the universal sign for no passing. She chuckled to herself.

The French think everything French is universal—but in front of the villager she had only smiled.

From the grassy knoll, Lena watches the old sheepherder with his shaggy dog pushing his sheep and goats farther out to pasture. She wonders if the dog is related to the one from her childhood. Or perhaps the dog is a common breed.

Yesterday she had not done much; mostly she walked through the house touching things, letting her memory come back. Her father had pictures of her as a baby hung throughout the house. In all the pictures, she looked happy.

Lena tries to remember the little girl she was, but only blips of scene remained. Last night she'd slept in her old room—she pulled the mattress from her father's bed and placed it on the floor by the tiny window, pushing the small child's bed out of the way. From the window, she could see the stars. She'd forgotten how the bats hung about the window and flew back and forth attracted by the street light just beyond her room.

Lena turns and walks back toward the village. Today she must go through her father's books and papers.

As she walks down the tiny hill and into the village, people smile and greet her shyly. There are no secrets in this village, and everyone knows who she is—if not actually, then by word of mouth.

Lena pauses in front of her father's stone house. It is the house from her childhood memories. The outside is covered with a gigantic purple wisteria, now in bloom. The flowers hang down over the lower terrace making her think of a scene from Romeo and Juliet. It appears like a house made for love—and therefore, tragedy.

She pushes against the large wooden door leading into the garden. Inside the garden, pink and red roses climb up and tumble over the old walls. Lena had forgotten about the roses—and the peonies, just budding, and the lilac and the dozens of other flowers now in bloom or just peeping up in her father's garden. Slowly, she mounts the stone stairs leading to the lower terrace. From there, in the distance, blue hills are framed by a yellow sun and lapis sky. Jutting at an angle from the terrace are five more old stone stairs that lead to the dining room, the salon de manger, as the French call it. Lena enters the room, ducking under a low ceiling beam. She had forgotten the beam was blue.

She pauses before the fireplace and remembers her father, then turns and looks out one of five tiny ancient windows. On the cobbled lane below, an old man with a cane is squinting up at her. He lifts his cane in the air and then continues walking.

Lena enters the front room where her father's desk is. Against the wall is the daybed, where he sometimes slept. She runs her hand over the thick plaster wall. White dust comes off on her palm and fingertips. Against one wall are handmade bookshelves stuffed with books and her father's journals. He'd kept a journal for nearly forty years. Lena goes to the case, randomly chooses one. "1957," it says on the inside cover. The book is filled with notes, stories, the beginnings of plays, letters; it seems her father wrote everything in his journals. She searches for one dated 1965.

The journal is black. There are grid lines on the cream-colored pages. Her father's writing (black ink) is tiny, though neat. Two sheaths of paper fall from the pages. A letter from her father to Vivi copied out of his journal. She compares the two; they look the same.

She takes the letter in her hand and sits down at her father's desk to read.

Dear Vivi:

It has been wetter here than usual. The Mairie flooded today and water has come in through the roof of my house, turning one wall in the dining room brown and leaking down through the beam. I hope this doesn't mean the beam is rotted and needs replacing. I can't remember the last time we had a series of storms this bad. The lightening has frightened Lena; two nights this week she has come down to sleep on my daybed while I am working.

I think the peaked roof in her room catches and holds the sound of thunder.

Last week I saw a tiny announcement in Le Monde that Sophia Loren got the lead part in Yesterday, Today and Tomorrow. I called Rita right away, but she didn't call me back until yesterday. She said the producer is sleeping with Sophia (she assumes everyone sleeps with their producers) and that they offered her a minor part, which she declined. She said she's decided to go home to America. I was surprised, but apparently her father knows someone at Warner who has promised to help promote her career. I asked her about the baby . . .

Lena stops reading. Baby? She never knew her mother had been pregnant with another child. Every time Lena mentioned wanting a brother or sister when she was a little girl, her mother had said one was all she ever wanted.

I asked her about the baby and she was vague at first, but then said she lost the child. I hope you believe that the child wasn't mine (if there ever was a child); although I did agree to give it my name and say it was mine. Vivi, you do believe me, don't you? Rita didn't say anything about Lena and I didn't ask, but truthfully, I am a little nervous that she'll want to take Lena home with her. I'm hoping she's too bitterly disappointed about not getting the part she wanted to think of Lena—but you know Rita, always full of surprises.

I've been thinking a lot about life lately—maybe it's because I will be forty soon. Vivi, I realize I'm a coward. I hope my saying this doesn't make you love me less, because I do intend to change. I never should have let you leave. You were right—I should have stood up to Rita, hired a lawyer and all that, but I was afraid. And more than that—I realize that I've been like a character in a Beckett book. I haven't been willing to direct my own life, but rather, have let others, including Rita, script how I should live. I've been thinking a lot about the things you said before you left, and you're right, my father's dying in the war when I was young has affected me. It's not Freudian bullshit as I said. My mother wasn't overly fond of my father, particularly after he died (I heard a rumor in the village when I was a boy that my father had another woman throughout my parents' marriage), and I realize now she tried to mold me into the man she wanted me to be. She always told me she didn't want me to be the loser my father was. And I think I let Rita do a little of the same. I should have stood up to her in the beginning after I realized she was going to leave Lena with me and didn't really want to be a mother or a wife. But in my defense, I've always been a little afraid of Rita's father, who is an American lawyer, and as Rita tells it, sharp, aggressive, and with lots of money and resources at his disposal to do with as he pleases. Rita is obviously her parents' darling.

I thought about bringing Lena to you—she and I running away; the three of us living in South America or some place like that together, but I want you to respect me, to not think of me as a coward. I'm going to do as you suggest, and contact my lawyer friend—the one I told you about before. He grew up in my village, so I know him well. I think he will help, or if not, he will know someone who can. I want to marry you Vivi, and for the three of us to soon live as a family. Please come home so we can talk in person.

I am faithfully yours,

The letter is unsigned. Lena looks at the date: November 17—a week after Vivi died. Apparently her father didn't know. The lawyer had told her Vivi was a botanist and she died in a diving accident in the Indian Ocean. Carbon monoxide poisoning from her tank while on an expedition in the Indian Ocean—not too far from where Lena's own expedition had been.

She picks up a silver picture frame from the desk. A woman with a heart-shaped face smiles back at her. The photo is black and white and the woman has what looks like a white scarf in her hand. There is a plaid blanket on the ground and a basket and food. Lena looks closer. In the corner of the photo, on the blanket, a little foot is visible.

Lena closes her eyes trying to remember Vivi as she was that day. Without knowing it, she had always tried to emulate

Vivi—the woman who had been like an early mother to her—perhaps more than her own mother had ever been. She had loved Vivi.

And so had her father. She thinks of the rope. Perhaps so much that he . . .

The church bells ring: it is midday. Lena walks to the window. An old woman crosses the place and enters the church.

Lena turns and faces the room. She can almost, but not quite remember herself here as a child. In the distance she hears the sound of the goats' bells; they are roaming the hills right outside the village. She touches her father's chair. Pulls it before the blackened fireplace and tries to imagine how it was when she was young. Her père's little girl. He had loved her! She smiles to herself. Then thinks of what her father had said in his letter to Vivi.

She fingers the letter, thinking of Nick. Had he too, always let someone else direct his life? Create a picture for him? Is that why he stayed with Hildy? Because she helped him define himself in a way Lena never did?

Why didn't she, she wonders? But even as she asks herself this, she knows she always feared she would lose Nick if he didn't make his own decisions; if he wasn't his own person.

She picks up her father's journal and puts it back on the shelf. Maybe she was afraid that she'd be the one to leave him—that she didn't want the responsibility of creating a life for anyone else. Perhaps she is a little like her mother in that respect. Or maybe it is simply that she'd always worked too hard to please others and as it was, she never felt she had anything left for herself.

She pauses next to a picture of herself as a child on the wall. Her mother was never here; that's why she's never appeared in any of the blips Lena remembers. Lena thinks of her mother as she was before she died, and wonders how her father ever thought Rita could have lived in this village or this house for longer than a holiday. For a moment, Lena hardens toward her mother, but then a thought occurs to her: Maybe after her mother's twin died, she also tried too hard to please others; maybe that's what we do for those left behind—we try to make it better. Lena is startled by this thought; it makes her soften a little toward her mother.

She walks to the kitchen and opens the frigo, but it is empty. This afternoon she will buy food. Behind the kitchen door she finds a broom. She searches for a mop and a dusting cloth. The lawyer had asked her if she intended to sell. He said he knew a couple who were looking for a house in the village and would likely buy the house and its furnishings if she was willing.

Is she willing?

She thinks of Nick in his hospital bed. She thinks of her father and her mother, her Gran and her grandfather. She is the only one left now.

In the field beyond the house, the apple and cherry trees are in bloom. A winding road leads down to where? She walks to the kitchen door to see if she can see the end of the road. But she can't. All she sees are yellow wildflowers and a riotous green.

She steps out the door.

The road seems closer. She doesn't know where it leads.

But she intends to find out.

Acknowledgments

I traveled many roads to write this story and along the way I learned a lot about myself, and human nature. The people who helped me with craft, storyline, editing, technical matters or as readers are forever embedded in this story, even if not named here. I give my heartfelt thanks to the Spalding University Low Residency MFA program for nurturing me while I learned craft—Sena Jeter Naslund, Julie Brickman, Neela Vaswani, Mary Waters, Ellie Bryant among many others. I thank Jonathan Weinert for his belief in my story, his technical assistance, and his unflagging support in those early days when I would have bailed. Thanks also to Nicole Legnani and her colleagues at DARTH Harvard for producing all of the e-versions of this book, and for their editing skills. The small village of St Bresson was my inspiration and muse. And lastly, I am thankful for all the creatures who populate my life, and get me out walking so I can observe the beauty that surrounds me—wherever I am.

Made in the USA
Charleston, SC
18 October 2013